The Silver Buckle

ANN ROBERTSON

ISBN 978-0-9956290-2-8

Set in Book Antiqua 10pt

Cover design by Alison Renno
Typeset for print by YouByYou Books
Printed by Scan-Tech, Hastings

YouByYou Books,
Swallow Court,
High Halden Road,
Biddenden,
Kent,
TN27 8BD.

www.youbyyou.co.uk

Contents

To all members of the nursing profession who have worn
their buckles with pride over the years

Part One
Kate Oliphant

Chapter One

The Beginning of it All

Why, oh why, hadn't she been born a boy?

So mused Kate as she wandered disconsolately round the gardens of St. Martha's Hospital for the Poor situated on the outskirts of an unattractive provincial English city. She had seized the opportunity presented by a brief break from her nursing duties to breathe in some fresh air to relieve her nostrils. The ever-present odour of sickness seemed to pervade the grim-looking building behind her until it permeated into the very fabric of her clothes. Even her hair, severely restrained beneath an unbecoming starched bonnet, wasn't immune from those nauseous vapours. In fact, they had become so much part and parcel of existence in this place as to be unremarkable, even to someone whose entire life had previously been spent in the country surrounded by nothing more offensive than the reek of manure. The unmistakable noxious smell of gangrene, emanating from an ulcerated leg which was beyond all hope of saving, was a very different matter, however.

The reluctant sun cast its intermittent rays over the forlorn figure, rendered even more pathetic as a result of the drab, ill-fitting grey dress which covered her slightly ample form from neck to ankle. The rough texture irritated her skin and the black buttoned boots did nothing to ease her aching feet. How she longed to cast them off for a few minutes and feel the fresh blades of grass underfoot. Prudence forbade such an indulgence, and not merely because time was short and the Lady Superintendent would chastise her for such decadence should she happen that way. Kate was by no means certain that, once released from the restricting footwear, her feet would ever be persuaded back into those leather confines. Not for the first time she asked herself what she was doing here, but was all too aware of the answer.

Her father, George Oliphant, was a gentleman farmer and landowner who had been imprudent enough to marry his wife for her looks and her money rather than her child-bearing capacity. Kate made her appearance, loudly protesting, on a dreary, wet day in 1829. On being appraised of her gender he managed to hide his disappointment at the lack of a male heir to follow in his footsteps, confident that there would be ample time and opportunity in which to correct the matter. However, he had not allowed for the lack of cooperation on the part of his beautiful but stubborn spouse. Early in their marriage Emily had discovered a growing distaste for the bedroom activities such an alliance occasioned. A long and tedious pregnancy, followed by an equally protracted and difficult delivery, made her quite determined that there would be no repeat performances.

After gentle persuasion failed and the ensuing arguments only led to tears, feminine fits of the vapours requiring wafts of smelling salts, and episodes of outright mutiny, George finally gave up. Virtually ignoring his wife unless in polite company, he threw himself into the business of supervising his modest but profitable estate, seeking solace in the willing arms of more tractable women across the county. Emily found this behavior somewhat tiresome but decidedly less repugnant than submitting herself to the demands of his healthy sexual appetite. Meanwhile, they continued to entertain and be entertained, which allowed her to perfect the subtle art of flirtatious dalliance, promising much yet having to deliver nothing, all the while satisfying her own selfish vanity.

Not surprisingly, the real person to suffer as a result of this state of affairs was the only offspring of such a union. George largely ignored his daughter and appeased any conscience he might have by providing lavishly for her needs. Her nursery was delightful and only the best clothes filled the drawers and cupboards. He didn't quibble at any financial demands made on her behalf but actual physical contact and emotional rapport between them was quite minimal.

This would have been bad enough in any event but was compounded by the aversion Emily had shown toward the baby. From the moment Kate was first placed in her arms she never ceased to wonder how she could possibly have given birth to such a plain, uninspiring child. A resident nursemaid solved the initial problem, thereafter supplemented by a succession of nursery helpers, until the time came to appoint a governess. Contact with other children was virtually non-existent, therefore, Kate's greatest friends and allies proved to be the domestic staff, farm employees and their families plus, of course, the animals. That was always providing she could escape from the clutches of her zealous tutor for long enough to enjoy their company.

It was extremely fortunate, therefore, that she had inherited two parental traits which would prove to be a great asset. From the outset she had shown a tendency towards stubbornness and considerable determination, which often sorely tried the patience of those forced to deal with her. She could little envisage to what good purpose her tenacity, and inability to admit defeat, would later stand her. Similarly, both George and Emily had been well educated and they spared no effort to make sure that their daughter was afforded every opportunity to acquire the same accomplishments. What the young Kate may have lacked in physical allure, she more than made up for with brightness and intelligence. Book learning was not only enjoyable but came easily to her and this, coupled with a natural aptitude for the piano and a love of music and reading, ensured that she was never bored or lonely.

One attribute which was innately her own was an early evidence of caring and compassion towards all living things. Her concerns were divided equally between humans and the animals and creatures of field and hedgerow. Despite the lack of affection in her own life she had a natural knack of conveying care and sensitivity towards others.

It was not surprising, therefore, that when matters at home finally came to a head and she decided to seek some meaningful employment, the possibility of nursing was the first thing that came to mind.

St. Martha's Hospital, built some 80 years previously by a local philanthropic clergyman, was administered by a board of governors drawn from the great and the good in the county of Morfordshire. Just over 80 inpatients could be accommodated in a far from luxurious environment and the outpatient area was considered insufficient and objectionable. Wards which had seemed adequate in the 1770s were no longer viable and the installation of gas-lighting in 1849 only served to illuminate the dark corners and reveal the deficiencies. There were complaints about rats and bugs from the Lady Superintendent, and continuous disputes between the medical staff and the Board indicated to those worthy gentlemen that it could only be a matter of time before they would be forced to act. Action, however, would prove costly and something to be deferred for as long as possible.

The Chairman, Sir William Kirk, who happened to be a friend and neighbour of George Oliphant's, had known Kate from her childhood. Being rather fond of children he had, over the years, developed a liking for the rather isolated girl and was not completely unaware of the general tenor prevailing in the outwardly gracious home at Painters Court. Nevertheless, he was both surprised to receive a visit from her and more than a little dismayed by her request.

At Granby Hall, in the comfort of the panelled study with its book-lined walls, he had seated his unexpected visitor in front of a cheerful log fire, casting around in his mind what her business could possibly be. Neither did he have long to wait. Failing to see the need for time wasting niceties and always a believer in coming straight to the point, she earnestly appealed to him for help to attain her ambition.

"I want to procure a post as a nurse and wondered whether you would use your good auspices and recommend me to the Lady Superintendent at St. Martha's?"

There was an astounded pause as Sir William absorbed this bombshell. All the while gazing at her with a considerable degree of concern, he finally found the words with which to express his discomfiture at such a prospect.

"Upon my word Kate, whatever has put that thought into your head? I really don't think such a position is suitable to your status and upbringing. Does your father know of your plans, for I cannot believe for one moment that he would sanction them?"

"Sir William, I am a woman of twenty-two with few, if any, pretensions to beauty. I am not anxious to enter into a marriage, even should the opportunity arise, which is extremely unlikely. I have no close friends with whom I care to idly pass the time and I cannot bear to just sit at home sewing fine seams, reading and playing the piano."

"Your parents surely aren't making demands upon you to find employment or urging you to flee the nest?"

"No, of course not, nor do they know that I am here today or what is in my mind. Furthermore, I have no intention of telling them until it is a fait accompli and would appreciate it if you would respect my confidence on the matter. If you feel that you cannot help me in this, I shall just have to try for myself."

Sir William regarded the firm set of the chin and the determined air of the young lady facing him and breathed an unhappy sigh. He recalled his own three compliant daughters who had mercifully harboured no such outrageous notions. Inwardly smiling with satisfaction he recalled that they had been quite content to while away their youthful days in genteel pursuits until happily embarking upon successful marriages. After which they diligently and willingly settled into their appropriate station in life, applying themselves to household management and the rearing of numerous children.

"You realise that you are placing me in an invidious position, Kate? I cannot think that your father will possibly allow such a situation."

"It matters not what he thinks. As I have already indicated, I am of age and the decision is mine," she said with a defiant tilt of her head.

Unhappy to give up, Sir William persisted in his attempts to dissuade her, and the more he tried the firmer was Kate's resolve.

"Kate, you have led a sheltered life. You are not used to hard physical work. Work, I might add, that is not at all pleasant especially for one brought up as you have been."

"Sir William, I am strong and healthy and have the constitution of a horse. I feel at home with the ordinary folk on my father's estate and I have enjoyed the occasions when I have been able to help them. Added to which I have had all the advantages of a good education, which must count for something."

11

"There can be no disputing that fact," said her challenger. "Miss Upton, the Lady Superintendent, is continually lamenting the poor levels of learning among her staff. Consequently, there is no formal nurse training as such. I'm afraid you are only likely to find that in London. Had you considered the possibility of applying to one of the larger hospitals?" he queried tentatively.

"I really have no desire to live in a large metropolis, added to which it would seem an unnecessary move to make until I am absolutely sure that I can cope," said Kate with just sufficient pathos to convince the august gentleman that her venture would be but a short-lived affair.

"Very well, Kate, I will do as you have asked and bring my not insignificant weight to bear on the matter."

"Thank you, oh, thank you, dear Sir William. I promise you won't regret it," said that relieved young lady. "Indeed, I'll make you proud of me. One day you'll be pleased that you helped me over my first hurdle."

On that occasion, neither of them could possibly have foreseen how prophetic her words would prove to be.

Sir William acted decisively and within a short time Kate found herself face to face with the unbending figure of Miss Upton. It had taken only a few minutes for that lady to realise that in employing Kate she would indeed strike gold. Superior in every respect to the normal run of applicant she was forced to consider, she gave unguarded approval to her request.

"You will find the work neither easy nor congenial. The hours are long and the financial rewards small. St. Martha's isn't acknowledged as a training establishment, but I was fortunate enough to receive just such schooling in London and will be pleased to pass on my skills and experience if you show the necessary promise and commitment."

In a matter of weeks, Kate had left the background of comfort and privilege which had been hers since birth and entered a world of hardship, privation and sickness which surpassed anything she had imagined. There had been occasions when it would have taken very little to persuade her to give up. The one thing that prevented her from doing so, apart from her own cussed obstinacy, was the determination not to give her parents the satisfaction such surrender would undoubtedly afford them. They had been appalled, disbelieving and downright angry when confronted with Kate's plans and employed every possible means to dissuade and prevent her. She had finally left home under a considerable cloud, and the working rigours of the past three years ensured that any contact with them was minimal.

Nevertheless, despite everything, Kate had succeeded and stood high in Miss Upton's esteem. Nurses in infirmaries of this kind, and at this period of time, were widely criticised as possessing little or no learning, refinement or morals and, too often, had minimal enthusiasm for the task. Consequently there was a fairly regular turnover following the frequent discharges made for unsatisfactory behaviour or work. Miss Upton had cause to congratulate herself on her good fortune in employing Kate and, seeing her potential, set about schooling her in just such a way as she herself had been instructed under the auspices of the order of St. John the Evangelist. This had been established by the Bishop of London and provided 'trained nurses' to other hospitals for a fee. The Lady Superintendent regarded her provincial post at St. Martha's as the particular cross she had to bear.

Kate responded eagerly, had been quick to learn, willing to work uncomplainingly and was conscientious with an eye for detail. In little over three years she had mastered most that her superior could teach her and was a competent and trusted member of staff. She had recently been the recipient of a gratuity of two guineas awarded for faithful and attentive service, which went some way toward boosting the twelve pounds a year which constituted her salary. Her uniform was provided, of course, as was her humble room and fairly uninspiring meals, although she did have to supply her own butter, tea and sugar. Her talents and behaviour were often the subject of commendation to the hospital board, which reflected favourably on the superior abilities of the Lady Superintendent in no small way. Indeed, there were times recently when Kate had been called upon to stand in for her mentor during any absences. It was clear that she had gone as far as she could in her present situation.

The hospital clock set into the red brick wall of the chapel building

13

struck the hour as Kate dragged herself back into the present. The last of the daylight was fading and on the ward she would be faced with the same endless ailments, misery and hardship of her hapless charges. The inadequately tutored and generally unprepossessing staff under her supervision only added to her problems, enhancing her general feelings of dissatisfaction and disillusionment.

Preparing to cross the highly polished and imposing entrance hall she noticed a newspaper which had been tossed carelessly onto the circular table, probably jettisoned by one of the consultants whilst attending to carry out a round of his patients. Glancing quickly about and finding the area deserted, Kate retrieved and carefully folded her unexpected windfall. It would be good to have something up-to-date to read before eventually settling down for the night.

Meanwhile she set about supervising the extra women brought in to help, called 'watches'. They were originally appointed to assist with night duties and gave the most basic of patient care on the wards as well as undertaking the cleaning. This allowed the nurse in charge to concentrate on the dressings, administration of medicines and writing of reports.

The highlight of Kate's day took place when she handed over to the night nurse at 9 o'clock and made her way to the nurses' quarters. Here she would make herself a cup of tea and, with her shoes off and feet resting on a stool, which she had brought from home in the early days of her employment, allow herself the luxury of doing nothing more strenuous than complete relaxation. Taking out her acquired newspaper she prepared to gently indulge herself before getting into bed to ensure a decent night's sleep before appearing on the wards at 6am.

Her attention was immediately caught by the headlines staring out at her in large letters: 'Where are the Nurses?'

An outbreak of hostilities between Great Britain and Russia had commenced on March 28th 1854 and was greeted with much cheering and patriotic fervour. A few days later, the English fleet, under the command of the gallant Sir Charles Napier, sailed for the Baltic, speeded on its way by thousands of enthusiastic spectators.

Although Kate was not unaware of events, her life was somewhat cocooned within the walls of St. Martha's, with the result that any news was, perforce, fragmented and stale. Now, the headlines stared her brutally in the face. William Howard Russell, the veteran war correspondent at the front, had sent back a horrifying report:

'There has been gross neglect in the war administration. Food, clothing, and comforts have been stowed in vessels beneath ammunition and cannot be got hold of when required. The commonest accessories of a hospital are wanting. Surgeons are often without even lint and bandages and there is not the least attention paid to decency or cleanliness. The stench is appalling and for all I can observe, the men die without the least effort to save them.'

The staff of army doctors was, in fact, insufficient and only the most basic care was available from untrained male orderlies. There was no woman's hand to soothe the fevered brow, administer nourishment, perform the various little offices for the sick, and console the dying.

'Are there no devoted women in England, able and willing to go forth to minister to the sick and suffering soldiers of the East in the hospitals at Scutari? Are none of the daughters of England, at this extreme hour of need, ready for such a work of mercy?'

Kate let the paper slip from her hands and a shiver ran over her body. Her first inclination was to disbelieve it, but quickly came to the conclusion that the article had to be true or *The Times* would never have printed it.

She picked up the paper and re-read the exposé, her precious cup of tea completely forgotten. Then, carefully folding it and laying it to one side, she went through the motions of her routine preparations for bed in a complete daze.

For once sleep did not come easily. She found it impossible to rid her mind of the images of suffering which had been revealed, anymore than she felt able to ignore the impassioned challenge to action. As she tossed and turned, a plan began to formulate in her mind. Long before the orderly knocked on her door to rouse her for duty, Kate had washed and donned her uniform. Then, making her way along the gloomy, stone-flagged corridor she entered the uninspiring and ill-lit room that did service as a staff dining room.

There was no one else about, for which she was grateful, as it

15

relieved any necessity for the trivial chatter which passed for conversation. Removing the lid from a black steel cauldron, left on the range by the night orderly, she helped herself to half a bowl of the unappetising, glutinous mass which passed as porridge. Seated on a bench at the long wooden table down the centre of the room she proceeded to reread the news article, scarcely noticing the insipid offering which was spooned into her mouth. Automatically reaching for a thick slice of bread and jam Kate chewed away reflectively and washed it down with a mug of evil-looking brewed tea. Three years of such indifferent fare had blunted her taste for the finer nutritional delicacies of life and rendered eating a mere necessity for bodily survival.

The old, long case clock in the far corner of the room had been presented by some well-meaning benefactor of St. Martha's, presumably to ensure that the staff neither idled away their time nor failed to obey the rules of punctuality. It now informed anyone interested that there was still half-an-hour before the time to appear on the ward where the spiritual needs of the staff would first be addressed. The founding father had ordained that the daily observance of morning prayers would better equip everyone to meet the more pressing bodily requirements of the patients. These were led by the person in charge, after which there would be a frantic rush to clean both the ward and its occupants before the Lady Superintendent appeared on the scene to make her rounds.

Anxious to press on with her plan, Kate pondered the wisdom of confronting this exalted lady in her study before going on duty, or should she wait and hope to elicit her attention after she had made her inspection? The answer was clear, for it was common knowledge that interruptions in the morning progress from ward to ward were neither welcome nor encouraged.

Hastily gulping the last mouthful of tea, Kate made for the door in time to encounter others intent on fortifying their hunger against the rigours of the day ahead. Mumbling a vague greeting she pressed past them in the direction of the entrance hall. Opening off from this imposing space two rooms had been furnished for the sole use of the resident custodian, one as an office and the other a modest sitting room. The former acknowledged her status and provided a suitably exalted facility from which to administer her small empire, whilst the latter afforded a comfortable privacy not enjoyed by anyone else.

Seeing a faint line of light from beneath the office door, Kate smoothed down her skirts and, taking a deep breath, braced her shoulders and knocked rather tentatively. A firm voice peremptorily bade her enter at which Kate turned the brass knob, walked into the sanctum and closed the door quietly behind her.

Miss Upton raised her head from reading the report on the desk in front of her and smiled with both pleasure and surprise. Ever since the day Kate had joined the band of helpers at the hospital she had never ceased to be grateful to Sir William for providing her with such a high calibre of worker. Unexpectedly she had found herself presented with a girl of pleasing manners, high intelligence, willingness to work and a readiness to learn. It was small wonder, therefore, that she enthusiastically set about instilling into such a protegé the knowledge and skills which she herself had received from her training at one of the few recognised establishments in the country.

Nevertheless, that good lady was completely unprepared for the bombshell when it came. Thrusting the copy of *The Times* across the desk the somewhat startled recipient was commanded to read it. Kate watched her face intently and saw the horror spreading across it and heard the shocked 'tuts' that resulted from the irritated clicking of her tongue.

"My dear, this is terrible. I had no idea, no idea at all. How easy it is to become so immersed in our own problems, which would appear to be trivial by comparison. Dreadful as it may be, I'm afraid there is nothing we can usefully do to help, far removed as we are."

Unwaveringly, Kate met her eyes and announced: "I want to offer my services. I want to go to the Crimea and do what I can to help. The problem is that I don't know the best way to go about it. Can you help me and will the Board release me?"

If Miss Upton had been unnerved by the news story it was as nothing to her reaction on being faced with such a completely unexpected request. For once in her life this usually eloquent lady was at a loss for words. The heavy silence lengthened as she cast around in her mind for a suitable response. The Lady Superintendent wasn't enthralled at the prospect of losing such a key member of her staff and her initial reaction was to dismiss such a notion as preposterous. Could she, however, refuse to consider such a genuine appeal in all conscience? She only had to look at the determined set of this young nurse's face to know that automatic dismissal of the suggestion would not be countenanced without argument.

"You have presented me with something of a problem Miss Oliphant and one that I cannot possibly answer immediately. I will need time to consider the matter and consult with others, after which we'll talk again," she said. "Meanwhile, I think it is best that you concentrate on your duties here."

And with that Kate had to be content. At least her proposal had not been rejected out of hand.

***

True to her word Miss Upton had immediately discussed the matter with Sir William and, through her sources, visited London and made contact with the relevant authorities. Within a week, Kate found herself summoned to the office.

"Well," said her mentor, "I've had a busy but successful time. I met with several old friends and, through the good offices of some, discovered where to go and who to consult. It has all been most exciting and I know you will be keen to learn the outcome."

Seated on the edge of her chair, Kate listened intently.

"It would appear," said Miss Upton, "that the main stumbling block to progress has been the difficulty to get a lady to take in hand the charge of superintending and directing a body of nurses for the front. However, the Secretary of State for War has accepted the recommendation of Mr. Sidney Herbert, in the government, that the matter should be placed in the hands of a Miss Florence Nightingale, and she has agreed to undertake the task."

"Surely, there must have been some precedent to prepare the powers

18

that be for such an enterprise," said a perplexed Kate.

"The difficulty of the situation is that nurses in military hospitals have been of a coarse, low character devoid of education, training nor sympathy for their work. Added to which the class of women employed have been very much addicted to drinking and were found to be even more callous to the sufferings of the troops than men would have been. In the past the average soldier's nurse was little more than a camp follower. As a result of that impassioned newspaper appeal, applications have been received from women of every status. Apparently, many were merely good, kindly ladies who felt they had a vocation for nursing, but, alas had absolutely no experience and would be quite incapable of organising and controlling subordinates."

Kate could control her patience no longer. "Will I be able to go to the Crimea?" she pressed.

"Patience, patience," counselled Miss Upton, her often severe face now pleasantly relaxed and her eyes twinkling. "Miss Nightingale was officially appointed to the office of Superintendent of Nurses at Scutari just before my arrival in London, since when her energies have been concentrated on procuring the right kind of nurses. She approached the few nursing institutions which exist in the hope that volunteers would be forthcoming, and advertisements were placed in *The Record* and *The Guardian*. However, this first appeal failed to bring in sufficient satisfactory applicants. There is no time to start ambulance classes and train candidates but the authorities realise that they are dealing with a crisis of urgency. It is an imperative necessity that the nurses should start without delay, therefore they must have already trained for the work."

"But I have no officially acknowledged training," wailed Kate in frustration, "yet you know that I am capable of carrying out most tasks."

"Indeed I do Miss Oliphant, indeed I do. I have never failed to be thankful for your abilities and will miss them sorely."

For a moment, the Lady Superintendent's remark appeared to hover in the air before a glimmer of realisation began to dawn on the face of the anxious young woman facing her.

"Will miss…? You mean I'm to be allowed to go?"

"It was my great good fortune to meet a former colleague who is herself helping Miss Nightingale. I put the situation to her and the outcome is that she is prepared to take my word as to your suitability. So, yes Miss Oliphant, you are indeed going."

Kate sat and stared in mute disbelief. She had hardly dared to expect such an outcome and was, momentarily, lost for words.

"Aren't you going to thank me?" said her superior wryly. "After all, I am going to be the loser as a result of your aspirations."

"Of course I am grateful but I just can't take it in. Oh, thank you, thank you, thank you dear Miss Upton."

"Yes, well, there is much to be done and I must inform the Board of the turn events have taken. Always remember, Miss Oliphant, that the future reputation of St. Martha's rests, in no small measure, with you and your performance in this venture."

"You may have complete faith in me, I promise you. I won't let you down," responded a jubilant Kate.

"I'm sure you won't. Now, the first thing you have to do is to inform your family. I know you consider yourself to be your own person but they do have a right to be told, no matter what you may feel. Indeed, I'm sure it will be a requirement of the authorities," she said, regaining her official tone. "I suggest you take time off tomorrow to go and see them."

The Oliphants greeted the news with total disbelief. "Absolutely preposterous," bellowed her crimson-faced father, while her offended mother threw up delicate hands in protest. It had been bad enough that their daughter should wish to demean herself with work of any kind. The very idea of a lady of birth and breeding going out to nurse the common soldier on the battlefield was an utter anathema.

"Whatever will our friends say?" she gasped.

"Probably little more than they have been remarking ever since I first left home," Kate retorted unfeelingly. "May I remind you that I was not obliged to tell you? I have done so out of common courtesy and consideration. However, you are also my next of kin and, in view of the nature of my departure, you need to know."

"Well, if you're expecting any praise for such an ill-considered action, you are much mistaken," said her exasperated Papa.

"Such a thought never crossed my mind," she countered truthfully. "Though doubtless you would have lauded my intentions to the skies, had I been a son enlisting for battle," was her bitter afterthought.

"That is a completely different matter," blustered her irate father. "There can be no possible comparison."

"I have not come home to argue with you both, merely to inform. I had hoped that you would understand and be proud. However, I have received no support in the past so I don't know why I thought things might be different now," she said quietly.

"That is simply not fair," chimed an indignant Emily. "If you really felt you had to work we could have supported a position as a ladies companion or governess. To demean yourself, and us, by pursuing the road you have taken was insupportable."

Irritated by her unrepentant daughter's lack of reply she went on to add wistfully: "I shall never understand why you could not be content with pursuing the course of marriage like other young girls?"

In a reasonable voice which masked her considerable hurt and fury, Kate was hard driven to control herself. "You dare to suggest such a thing when I have frequently overheard you lamenting my physical shortcomings in general, and lack of prospects in securing the interest of any half respectable male in particular. You are, without doubt, the most unnatural mother. You may be assured, therefore, that I have no intention of trying to emulate you either as a spouse or a parent."

The recipient of this tirade lifted a wisp of lace handkerchief to her forehead and, groping in her reticule for the sal volatile, turned her eyes beseechingly in the direction of her husband. George, however, suddenly found himself in secret sympathy with his daughter's feelings regarding her mother. Nevertheless, before either could rejoin in any way, and glancing witheringly at the now shaking Emily, Kate bade her to please spare them a fit of the vapours.

"As my news and my presence are so clearly repugnant to you, Mama, I will save you any further distress and remove myself."

Turning to her father she said: "I expect to be leaving from London in a week or so. Meanwhile I shall be going there immediately to make the necessary preparations and meet my other companions in this venture. In the unlikely event that you require any news of me I suggest you contact your friend Sir William Kirk or Miss Upton."

Recognising, and reluctantly admiring, his daughter's spirit, George Oliphant gruffly bade her not to think too harshly of them. But Kate had delivered her message and was now only interested in getting back to St. Martha's. "Perhaps you will be kind enough to allow one of the men to drive me back to town in the trap, Papa? It took me such an unconscionable time to get here and I still have many things to settle in a very short period."

Anxious to make some small atonement, George was more than ready to comply, even suggesting that the kitchen could surely be prevailed upon to produce a few culinary delicacies to take with her. Thus provided for, Kate left her old home without a backward glance, relieved that such a tiresome duty had been discharged, leaving her completely free to concentrate on the task ahead.

Never was so much accomplished in so short a time. Thanks again to the good offices of Miss Upton and Sir William Kirk, Kate found herself in London where the thirty eight nurses selected as the first contingent to accompany Miss Nightingale were assembled. There were fourteen Church of England Sisters, taken from St. John's House and Miss Sellon's Home; ten Roman Catholic Sisters of Mercy; three nurses selected by Lady Forrester, who had first formed a plan for sending nurses to Scutari; and eleven chosen from among miscellaneous applicants, which included Kate.

On October 21st 1854 under the cover of darkness, in order to meet Miss Nightingale's request for no publicity, this devoted band set forth. Early next morning they landed at Boulogne, where a reception awaited them which was in marked contrast to the quiet and almost secret departure the night before. France was similarly involved in this war and had experienced its own casualties in the recent Battle of Alma. Consequently, brawny Boulogne fishwives fought for the privilege of carrying their luggage to the railway station and waved them off with tearful cries of "Vive les soeurs!"

To Kate, who had never been outside her native county, it was a bewildering but fascinating experience. They proceeded to Paris and stayed for a few days at the mother-house of the Sisters of St. Vincent de Paul, where Miss Nightingale was no stranger. After a short rest the little band set out for the port of Marseilles and embarked for Constantinople on board the *Vectris*. The passage was a terrible one, and for a time the ship was in danger from a hurricane. Kate soon discovered that she was not the best of seafarers and was more than a little relieved when the company reached Malta on October 31st. Following a too brief stay they set sail for Scutari and arrived on November 5th, only four days before the Battle of Balaclava.

They had no means of knowing then, just what the price of success in that fight would be in terms of suffering and wounded. Never did a group of women arriving in an unknown land face such a gigantic task.

Their headquarters was to be at The Barrack Hospital in Scutari which, from a distance, proved to be a fine, spectacular edifice beautifully situated on a hill overlooking the glittering waters of the Bosphorous and commanded a picturesque view of the city of Constantinople on the horizon. Kate had never seen anything so grand and imposing and, with her companions, gazed with high expectations at this immense building. As so often happens, however, outward appearances can be deceptive.

The hospital formed an immense quadrangle, each side of which was almost a quarter of a mile in length, and twelve thousand men could be exercised in the central court. Walking, awestruck, through the entrance gate, the nurses straggled behind Miss Nightingale into the interior. There they were confronted with a scene of utter filth, squalor, pestilence, misery and disorder impossible to describe. Wounded men were lying on either side of the endless corridors, closely packed together without the commonest decencies or necessities of life. Surgical cases rubbed shoulders with those suffering from fever, and even typhoid and cholera, and the fetid stench was appalling. Several days had elapsed since the men had left the battlefield at Inkerman, and the majority had neither had their wounds dressed or their fractured limbs set. The whole place was utterly dilapidated and lacking in sanitation.

There was no evidence in the way of food. There were no vessels for water; no soap, towels or cloths, no changes of clothes. Soldiers lay in their uniforms, stiff with blood and covered with mud and vermin. Evidence of disease was everywhere and the scent of death hung in the air.

Kate lowered her canvas hold-all to the ground and stared about her in dumbfounded disbelief. If she had sometimes regarded St. Martha's as shabby and inadequate, it was a palace compared with this place which defied description. What difference could a mere handful of nurses make? Where on earth did one start? It was a heart-breaking experience for them all and a testing moment for the Lady-in-Chief. Furthermore, the doctors and authorities were not immediately welcoming and sullenly disposed to think that the ladies would prove a greater hindrance than a help. It was small wonder that Miss Nightingale maintained that over the gateway to the barracks should be inscribed Dante's words: 'All hope abandon, ye who enter here'.

Notwithstanding, they were shown to a tower at one corner of the great hospital and there set about establishing their quarters. It was with a sinking heart that Kate created a rough, makeshift bed for herself and emptied out the meagre contents of her valise.

During the weeks ahead time ceased to have any meaning as one day merged with another. Kate considered that she had worked hard at St. Martha's but now found herself toiling without ceasing, using her wits to improvise until hidden supplies were unearthed and channelled in the right direction. In company with others she scrubbed floors until her hands were almost red raw, while the rest strove to establish a kitchen and laundry in the Nurses' Tower, all under the firm, unflappable guidance of Miss Nightingale. As soon as each room was pronounced clean, men were washed as best as possible and moved into it. Parched lips were moistened, comforting words spoken and the basic acts of decency attended to. This was all that could be achieved given the absence of any meaningful resources. Throughout this constant activity a never-ending stream of casualties poured across the Bosphorous from the Battle of Balaclava. They arrived by the shipload until every ward and corridor was crowded to excess, forming several miles of suffering humanity. As the hospital filled, so previously reluctant doctors turned to the nurses for help.

Somehow, within ten days of their arrival, and despite the terrible influx of patients, an impromptu kitchen had been fitted up from which eight hundred men were daily supplied with well cooked foods and other comforts. In just one day thirteen gallons of chicken broth and forty gallons of arrowroot were distributed amongst the sick, nearly all the food coming from supplies which the team had brought with them on the *Vectris*. Kate was, indeed, privileged to see a superior organising brain at work as Miss Nightingale brought order out of chaos, cut through bureaucratic red-tape which hindered delivery of care to those in need and gradually gained the respect of her opponents. She marvelled at the seeming tirelessness of this amazing lady.

When Kate was almost fit to drop, and could only pray for the permission to come which would provide a few blessed hours of relief, Miss Nightingale could still be found ministering to the sick or writing endless letters to influential people in order to improve the lot of all at the hospital.

One evening, as Kate was looking forward to a break, she was amazed to be approached by the Lady Superintendent with a request.

"There are five soldiers that the surgeons have set aside as hopeless cases. I have persuaded them to give the men into my care, for I am convinced that with good nutrition and careful nursing, these lives could be saved."

Throughout the night, they sat beside their charges, feeding them with a spoon until their senses wakened and their strength began to return. They gently washed the wounds and dressed them, and by sunrise had the satisfaction of seeing them deemed fit enough to face surgery.

"Thank you Nurse, for your efforts," said the serene figure, and quietly disappeared to continue her duties. Bursting with satisfaction and pride, Kate discovered that she actually didn't feel tired. For almost the first time since her arrival at Scutari she knew that her decision to come had been a right and worthwhile one.

Relentless hard work coupled with the general privations of life in the hospital was sufficient to cause Kate's comfortable figure to fine down. To her surprise and delight she discovered that she quite liked this new body. She could, by no means, be called 'pretty' but there was a striking quality about her which would have been even further enhanced had the curly auburn hair, which was her main redeeming feature, been allowed to escape from beneath the confines of the white headdress.

The uniform provided by the government for its nurses did nothing to enhance any of them. Grey tweed wrappers, worsted jackets, short woollen cloaks and a frightful scarf of brown holland embroidered in red with the words 'Scutari Hospital' were tasteless enough. The fact that the garments were contract work and all made to the same size rendered the situation ludicrous. Tall ladies appeared to be attired in short dresses and the short ladies in long. Slender creatures struggled to wrap the extra folds around them whilst those of a more generous proportion found themselves literally bursting at the seams. For once, Kate found her shape something of an advantgage. She soon became a well recognised and much appreciated form, darting hither and thither, carrying out the mundane, and often unpleasant, tasks with the same diligence with which she approached more complicated techniques.

Between the nurses there developed a camaraderie and closeness resulting from their shared endeavours and they generally pulled together and supported one another but there was little opportunity for relaxation or indulgence in idle chatter.

By Christmas Kate found, to her delight, that she was given the responsibility for three wards. The supplies of clean clothes and linen had improved thanks to the establishment of a laundry in a nearby house which was set up by Miss Nightingale to provide employment for a previously unused workforce. She had discovered close on five hundred wives and widows of soldiers sent to the front, living in a distressing condition in the holes, corners and dank basement of The Barrack Hospital, totally unsupported. Here, they looked after themselves as best as they could and delivered each other's babies when the occasion arose. Twenty-two alone were born between the arrival of the nurses and the end of the year. With a sympathetic feminine hand to

26

guide them and an authoritative voice to speak for them they willingly set to and worked in the laundry, thereby gaining self-esteem and payment with which to subsist.

In one of her hastily scribbled letters to Miss Upton, Kate revealed much of her feelings: *'It really is amazing how much I have seen achieved in comparatively few weeks. There is no substitute for sheer hard work, but common sense and quiet assertiveness can accomplish wonders too. Miss Nightingale has such a clear head and managing brain. Indeed, I am learning a great deal which, I hope, will stand me in good stead for the future.'*

Besides the hospital at Scutari, there were also seven other units which required to be controlled. With the arrival of fifty more nurses from England in the first weeks of the New Year, Kate found herself, in company with some of the other pioneers, being dispatched to bring about a similar transformation elsewhere until each unit became well established.

A day when the temperature plummeted to the lowest she had ever had to endure, saw her arrival in Kullali where expert help and intervention was sorely needed.

One of the nightmares of that bitter winter only served to compound the injuries of the troops and the nurses found themselves having to cope with incidents of severe frostbite which was quite beyond the experience of any of them. In most cases the flesh and clothes were frozen together and had to be cut off, as did the boots, piece by unyielding piece. It had been a baptism by fire for Kate and her companions and, not for the first time, she fleetingly wondered how she would ever fit back into the humdrum life of St. Martha's.

Throughout the spring of 1855 disease continued its ravages amongst the victims of the Crimean War without abatement, compounded by an increase in cases of a particularly virulent form of typhus fever. Death was an ever-present companion, and the stricken took the places of their departed comrades only to die themselves before another day dawned. It was inevitable that such a dreadful scourge should fail to discriminate between its victims. Kate was devastated, therefore, when three of her companions themselves succumbed to the malignant fever. A gloom descended over her as she attended the funeral of Elizabeth Smythe at the English burying-ground in Smyrna, whilst two more were laid to rest on the rocky heights of Balaclava. They could ill afford to lose such stalwart and beloved nurses and a shiver of coldness enveloped her as she pondered her own fate. It seemed even more poignant that such an occasion should be held in lovely spring weather, under beautiful clear blue skies, the air redolent with perfume and the freshness of wild flowers.

Back once again in the familiar surroundings of The Barrack Hospital, and desperate to get some fresh air and feel the breeze on her face, Kate took the rare opportunity provided by a few hours respite from duty to get away from the hospital.

Situated on a promontory high above the sea, with a fine outlook across the Bosphorous, was the British cemetery at Scutari. Strolling beneath the dense masses of cypress trees, where the bodies of so many brave men lay, she looked back on all that had happened since the unexpected quirk of fate which had brought her to this place. Flowers planted by loving hands decked many of the graves and the grass already waved above the deep pits where soldiers lay in a mass grave.

Footsteps on the gravel path alerted her to the fact that she was not alone. Turning her head she saw an upright military figure in officer's uniform walking at a slow pace between the serried ranks of the fallen, gazing intently at them as though inspecting a parade. Catching sight of her, he quickened his pace to draw alongside. His face was unremarkable but the voice which bade her "Good afternoon, Nurse," had a deep, warm resonance. Giving him a fleeting smile she continued her leisurely stroll and was considerably surprised to hear him say: "I think we met briefly the other day. You probably don't recall the occasion, for you were far too busy with the demands of your work."

"I'm so sorry," said Kate. "I usually have a good memory for faces but see so many in this place, and they are usually here today and gone tomorrow."

"I've just come back from the front for a few days and was doing the rounds, trying to trace the fate of some of my men," he continued. "Allow me to introduce myself." Somewhat ruefully he swept a mock bow saying: "Major Roland Masterson at your service."

Smilingly, Kate accepted the niceties of etiquette. Gestures considered 'de rigeur' in polite society, somehow seemed totally out of place given the present situation.

Feeling that some comment was needed, she inquired: "Which regiment do you serve with, Major?"

"The 39th. We were dispatched from Gibraltar to the trenches before Sebastopol and ill-equipped, I'm afraid, for the task."

"Oh dear, you have taken such a pounding in this campaign, haven't you."

"Unfortunately so. It really has been a devilish war. I am a professional soldier but, to tell the truth, I am beginning to feel mightily sickened of the whole thing."

"Indeed," said Kate. "I was just pondering over the appalling sights I have witnessed since my arrival here. These poor fellows resting here are probably better off than many of their companions still holding onto tenuous lives down there," she responded, her hand indicating the imposing exterior of the vast hospital. "I never believed that life could be so wretched or war so vile, until I came face to face with the reality here."

"You will never know what a difference your coming here has meant to the lot of the ordinary soldier," he said. "It is an incredible undertaking but I can't think what made you do it."

Kate paused for a moment before replying. "I chanced to read in *The Times* an article on the war accompanied by an impassioned appeal for nursing help. It came at a time when I was feeling rather dissatisfied with my existence and seemed to present the answer I was looking for. In some ways, I suppose my response was selfish rather than noble," she reflected apologetically.

"Well, whatever the reason, thank heaven for it," said the Major fervently.

They continued to stroll companionably along the winding paths of the cemetery, sometimes venturing the odd remark, at others enjoying an easy silence.

"Have you given any thought as to what you will do upon your return, when this awfulness is finally over?" he asked.

Kate was amazed at her surprise as she turned abruptly towards him. "Do you know, I haven't given it any proper consideration. I suppose we have all been so occupied, and the task so overwhelming, that the prospect of a tomorrow doesn't feel real, somehow."

She pondered for a moment before saying, "I suppose I shall return to St. Martha's, although how satisfied I shall be after experiencing all that I have remains to be seen."

"Where is St. Martha's?" he asked.

"Oh! It's a small and not particularly prepossessing hospital in Morford which is an expanding city in the Midlands," she responded. "It tries its best to cater for everyone's needs but it is far from adequate, I'm afraid. At least, that's what I thought before I arrived here, but it now seems almost luxurious by comparison."

"Is your home nearby?" the Major pressed.

"A few miles out into the country," Kate offered, momentarily absorbed with her own thoughts.

"Your family must be enormously proud of your efforts?"

"I am an only child, and I can assure you that I have constantly flown in the face of my parent's disapproval from the very outset of my determination to nurse, she responded tartly. "Goodness me, you can't be unaware that such an occupation is hardly considered fitting employment for a lady?"

Roland Masterson looked directly into the face of this outspoken creature, and grinned. "I suppose it must have come as something of a shock to them, for you are a lady aren't you? Despite that drab uniform, there is something which makes you stand apart from the usual camp follower."

Before either could venture any further conversation, a bell in a clock tower in the town began to sound the hour. "Gracious, I must fly," Kate exclaimed. "I must not abuse this privileged opportunity to slip outside the confines, or I might not get another. It has been a pleasure to talk with you and I hope all will go well for you," she said politely, and hastily turned to retrace her steps.

"Allow me to accompany you back," he called after her retreating back.

"No! No!" she echoed. "You stay and take further advantage of the fresh air and scenery."

With that she was gone, leaving the Major to gaze after her with interest.

During the days following their unexpected encounter, Kate found herself unconsciously looking out for her afternoon companion. When it was clear that he was no longer in the area, she took to furtively scrutinising each fresh intake of wounded from the battlefield but, mercifully, to no avail. It didn't take long, however, before more pressing matters intervened to put the incident right out of her mind.

Throughout the entire campaign outbreaks of infection exacerbated the expected traumas of battle. Severe incidents of cholera were a constant and demoralising nightmare, particularly as it appeared to have a predilection for striking down the stronger and healthier soldiers.

'It is so frustrating and an appalling waste to see men, who have survived the horrors of war with injuries that are treatable, succumb to virulent disease,' wrote Kate in one of her communications to her former Superintendent.

The nurses fought this curse with the time-consuming methods of stuping and massage with mustard and turpentine, in an attempt to release the iron grip which racked the sufferer's body, but the proportion saved was small indeed.

The usual span of existence was no more than five or six hours. It was both exhausting and disheartening. Week after week the fearful scourge continued until there seemed to be two constant streams of stretchers; one bringing the wounded in, the other bearing away the bodies of the hapless victims.

At last the autumn of 1855 brought the final act in the great drama of this dreadful war. Before nightfall on September 8th, the British troops had taken the Redan, a fort which had previously repulsed the attacking force, with fearful carnage. As a result the Russians then retreated leaving Sebastapol in flames.

Hostilities may have ended but thousands of victims still remained in hospital wards and scattered camps and refuges across the peninsula. Under Miss Nightingale's direction her band of nurses were instructed to promote schemes for the recreation, education and rehabilitation of the convalescent soldiers awaiting repatriation, and those forming the army of occupation. As they had ministered to the bodily needs of the men while sickness reigned, now they tried to address their mental and emotional problems.

The long awaited Treaty of Peace was signed in Paris on March 30th 1856, and the final evacuation of the Crimea took place the following July. Not until all the hospitals were closed, and the last remnant of the British army under sailing orders for home, was the Superintendent of Nurses prepared to quit the scene of her labours. Her band of nurses, battling against overwhelming odds, had not only nursed literally miles of patients but had reorganised the cooking facilities and the laundry, marshalled repairs, provisioned much of the hospital and undertaken the ongoing welfare of the wounded.

At the Battle of Balaclava alone 97,800 valiant men had been dispatched to the field resulting in the immediate death of 2,700 with 1,800 perishing later of wounds. Far worse, however, was the fact that a staggering 17,600 died as the result of disease. Kate could only take heart from the knowledge that these figures would have been even worse but for their nursing ministrations. Weary as she undoubtedly was, the hectic tempo of life abated somewhat. Unlike some of her colleagues she had no burning desire to return home and volunteered to remain in post until the bitter end.

Returning soldiers recounted endless stories of the work, sacrifice and contribution made by the nurses at the scene of battle and it became a major national talking point. Seeking to escape any possibility of a public demonstration, the final remnant embarked at Scutari on a French vessel bound for Marseilles. Travelling through France by night they eventually left Boulogne for England and arrived in London by noon. Tired, and suffering from the after-effects of dreadful sea-sickness, Kate found refuge at the home of one of her companions who lived in the capital, before setting off next day for Morfordshire and whatever the future held.

Chapter Two

Post-War Challenge

L ong before Miss Nightingale and her valiant band of helpers were ready to leave the Crimea, money began to pour in for 'The Nightingale Hospital Fund' as a tribute to a remarkable woman from a grateful nation. By June 1856 over £40,000 had been raised to enable the Superintendent to establish a training programme for nurses.

Her immediate thoughts, however, were not to reform nursing but the army medical service and, if necessary, the army itself. She regarded the Fund as something of a millstone because she had no time to work out a plan, and no clear idea as to how such training should be carried out, and by whom. The health of the sick in the workhouses throughout the country was appalling. It was in places like this that many unfortunates languished for want of appropriate hospitals and she had long recognised the need for properly trained nurses in Poor Law institutions. Nevertheless, it was not until 1858 that the Fund Council accepted an offer from St. Thomas's Hospital in London to form a school of nursing, and training did not get underway until two years later.

Elsewhere, in a Midland city, more immediate plans were afoot. Sir William Kirk and Miss Upton had convinced the board of St. Martha's that they too could make capital out of a victorious homecoming for their local heroine. Grand balls would be held where people could be encouraged to pay handsomely for the privilege of meeting her. A service of thanksgiving in the cathedral; collections in churches and chapels of all creeds; concerts and sales of work, with Kate appearing as guest of honour - what better way to ensure funding for a new St. Martha's?

George and Emily Oliphant also found themselves to be the centre of admiring attention and began to reap the social advantages which came from basking in Kate's reflected glory. If folk had been aware of the unbending refutation previously shown by them towards their daughter's choice of career, all that was forgotten as they proudly extolled her many attributes which were allegedly noticeable from the cradle! Emily could even be heard frequently to remark on their relief that all had been safely accomplished, for nobody but a mother would understand the constant worry she had lived with and the strain imposed on her nerves.

Blissfully unaware of such subterfuge, the object of their deliberations wearily alighted from the train that had taken her on the final leg of her journey from King's Cross to Morford and, unremarked, walked into the station forecourt and summoned a horse cab from the adjacent rank. Her request to be taken to St. Martha's Hospital evoked no comment from the disgruntled driver forced to ply his trade in the steady rain which had commenced that morning and showed little sign of abating.

Before leaving London Kate had visited the bank, into which most of her salary had been paid during her absence, and withdrew sufficient for her immediate needs. As her transport pulled up in front of the familiar, depressing edifice of her one-time second home, she fumbled in her purse and, having tendered the fee plus a generous tip, walked slowly into the entrance hall.

It was completely unchanged and Simpson, the ageing porter, was still manning the desk she noticed. While she had undergone untold experiences in various alien settings, some things never varied. Instead of being grateful for this comfortable stability, Kate found herself struggling to control her irritation. "What is wrong with me?" she asked herself. Before she could furnish herself with an answer, Simpson had raised his eyes, recognised the figure poised on the threshold, and let out a loud cry. "Bless my soul, if it 'aint Miss Oliphant! Oh, my goodness; well I never. No one told us... Oh, my word!"

As he hurried to escape the confines of his cubby hole, exclaiming all the while, Miss Upton emerged from her office to discover what all the commotion was. She stared in astonished disbelief then hastened forward to throw her arms around her former charge.

To her chagrin, Kate tasted salt from the tears silently trickling down her face and endeavoured to dab at them, somewhat ineffectually, with a smutty handkerchief which had seen regular service on the train and was now hastily retrieved from her pocket.

"My dear, dear girl, we had no idea. Why ever didn't you let us know you were on your way? We have been expecting news of you daily but never dreamed you would simply turn up without warning," said that unusually excited lady.

"I never thought," confessed Kate. "It seemed easier to just come."

"Oh, never mind, never mind; the important thing is that you are here. Simpson, go and see if you can rustle up some tea on a tray from the kitchen, and bring it to my office directly. Then get a message to Sir William Kirk. You should find him in conference with some of the Board members at the Deansgate home of the Archdeacon."

Then, with her arm still round Kate's shoulders, Miss Upton steered her through the once familiar office into the intimate comfort of her inner sanctum.

It was here that Sir William came upon them less than an hour later. Kate, though undeniably weary, had regained her composure and he found the pair engrossed in animated conversation. She rose to greet her former sponsor but was gently pushed back into the homely armchair as he simultaneously embraced her.

"Oh Kate, it's good to see you back safe and sound," he cried. "What a surprise you have given us though. We had prepared such a homecoming for you but... "

"That's just it," she interrupted. "I really don't want any fuss."

Exchanging a somewhat uncomfortable glance with Miss Upton, he contented himself with a mumbled: "Well, we'll talk about that later." Then, in a firmer voice he took charge of the situation. "For the present you need a well earned rest, right away from hospitals, sickness and hardship. You look so very tired and thin and pale. Good, clean country air and nutritious cooking will soon take care of that. I have my carriage outside and shall take it upon myself to convey you home to Painters Court without delay."

"I'd really rather not," Kate intervened quickly. "I thought perhaps I might have my old room here for a few days?"

Once more a surreptitious look passed between her superiors before he quickly commented: "Much as Miss Upton and I would love to have you back at St. Martha's, now is not the right moment and, quite frankly, such an arrangement wouldn't be at all suitable given all that you have been through. Beside which, your parents will be most anxious to see you."

"I very much doubt it," retorted the old, spirited Kate.

Sir William eyed her knowingly and said, "I think you may be rather surprised when you witness the change of heart that has occurred since you last saw them."

"Indeed," interjected the Lady Superintendent, "your Papa has been a regular caller here, most concerned to hear the latest news from your occasional, welcome letters."

"What a difference a little fame and publicity can make," remarked Kate sarcastically.

"Try to find a little Christian charity in your attitude towards them, my dear. It can't have been easy for them," Miss Upton contributed somewhat reprovingly.

Turning her full gaze upon both these eminent people, the former nurse from a poor hospital almost exploded with anger. In withering tones, strong words assailed the ears of her startled audience. "You must forgive me. After all that I have witnessed and been through in the last two years, Christian charity is a commodity I'm rather short of at the moment."

The very next instant, she regretted her outburst. It was unfair to vent her feelings on these two respected friends. "Perhaps you're right," she mused heaving a sigh. "I do need a rest and it would seem odd indeed to ignore the comfortable sanctuary of my old home."

Apologising profusely to the rather disconcerted couple, Kate acknowledged the rightness of Sir William's proposal and graciously accepted his offer of transport. Preparing to take her leave, she readily agreed to meet them both again at a later date and, amidst smiles and further embraces, she set out for Painters Court.

Even Sir William's intimations regarding her parents' change of heart failed to prepare Kate for the reality. As the carriage drew up at the front door she saw, through the window, the familiar figure of old Ben leading her father's hunter towards the stables. George Oliphant had not yet closed the door and turned to meet his unexpected guest. Seeing his old friend alight from the interior, he greeted him warmly then started back in astonishment as his daughter was helped out.

"Kate! Kate, whatever are you doing here like this?" There was no mistaking the improved warmth in the tone of his voice but, it held an almost imperceptible tinge of uncertainty as well.

"Hello Papa. I trust my arrival in this way has not shocked you too much and will not inconvenience you and Mother?" she ventured drily.

"What nonsense. Inconvenience indeed. Why, we've had your room prepared for some considerable time." Her father looked at her a trifle warily as though fearing some tart rebuff but Kate was too weary to engage in verbal warfare.

She cast her eyes appreciatively over the luxurious decor of the spacious hall. Although the evening wasn't cold, a log fire gently flickered in the hearth, more welcoming than anything she had seen in a long time. She had forgotten how homely and pleasant things could be. She could hear lively words being exchanged in the informal sitting room from where her mother emerged in a swirl of silk and heady perfume.

"Oh, my darling child, fancy springing upon us like this. We have been frantic with worry for you. We had planned such a homecoming," cooed her over-effusive mother, in marked contrast to anything Kate had encountered in her life.

"Just look at you! You have lost so much weight, and you have positively no colour," she continued agitatedly, clearly trying to prevent any gaps in the conversation which would give her sharp-tongued daughter the opportunity to reply.

Kate let her twitter on until she eventually paused for breath.

"I'm sorry if my appearance offends you Mama but I haven't exactly been doing the Grand Tour," quipped Kate, regaining some of her old spirit.

Sir William, who had been hovering uncomfortably in the background, announced his intention to leave having no wish to intrude further. "What you need Kate, is a warm bath, fresh clothes, some wholesome food and a good rest. Nothing like it, you know, for restoring a body," he offered.

"And, by Jove, she's going to get it. Don't you worry on that score," responded George Oliphant. Turning to his wife he addressed her in a manner somewhat different to his usual terse communications. "Emily my dear, why don't you go and alert the staff and organise whatever preparations need to be made? Although I'll wager the news has already reached them and they will doubtless be rushing round in readiness."

"Papa, I truly am too exhausted to face more than a relaxing bath and a warm drink," his daughter interposed. "I know you both mean well and I am grateful; but I've had a long and tiring day and would simply welcome the opportunity to go to my room."

"Of course, of course my dear," chorused both parents in turn. If there was a slight inflection of relief in their tone, only the sharpest and most cynical of ears would have detected it. Each had secretly been dreading this moment and was grateful that the presence of a third party had eased the situation considerably.

They all watched as Kate slowly climbed the stairs accompanied by a clearly excited but respectful maid. A range of different thoughts occupied each one, but they could wait. The first step had been surmounted and tomorrow was another day.

The first week passed in a pleasant haze as Kate mostly stayed in her room, reading and sleeping for lengthy periods, surfacing only for long enough to enjoy the dainty and tempting meals which emanated from the kitchen. Battle fatigue completely took over her body and she was taken aback to discover just how weak she felt. To her surprise George and Emily did not press her in any way and seemed quite prepared for her to set the pace. Her mother did suggest, quite wisely, that the local seamstress be allowed to visit in order to alter clothes that no longer fitted and to embark upon the provision of some additional gowns. To her amazement, her daughter meekly acquiesced and virtually gave her a free hand to refurbish her wardrobe. Emily, under strict instructions from George, seemed wisely intent on avoiding eggshells, while Kate had neither the energy nor the inclination to engage in verbal sparring.

She was reluctant to talk about her experiences of the war and gave only the briefest of answers to any questions. Mercifully, the nights afforded her release from her waking thoughts which inevitably ranged over the horrors and chaos of all that she had witnessed. It wasn't long, however, before decisions regarding the future began to occupy her mind. Miss Upton had made it clear that she was prepared for her to return to St. Martha's at some time, but Kate doubted whether she would find the mundane life offered by such an establishment fulfilling enough in the light of all that had happened.

Strolling aimlessly along the footpaths and acres that comprised the not inconsiderable Oliphant estate she admired the peace and order which prevailed. Everything had a place and all those engaged on the farm knew their role in the scheme of things. Fields planted in the spring were burgeoning towards a successful harvest. Livestock grazed contentedly on the lush pastures whilst the wildlife flourished in hedgerow and coppice. "God's in His heaven and all's right with the world," was the thought which flashed through Kate's mind, but she knew it wasn't as simple as that. If she didn't do something soon there was a grave danger that she would lose the impetus.

George stopped what he was doing and observed the figure listlessly trailing her hand through the profusion of cow parsley lining the lanes. Despite the absence of a strong bond between them, he sensed the restless uncertainty and the frustration engendered by a seeming lack of purpose, and knew that they would be unlikely to keep her with them for much longer. Furthermore, he guessed that the present amity between Emily and her daughter would soon wear thin. He was astounded that everything had passed as smoothly as it had. Glancing up, Kate caught his eyes on her and moved slowly across to the farm gate on which he was leaning.

"It's beautiful isn't it," she said. "I realise now just how much I've always taken things for granted. Despite all the privations that were part of my life at St. Martha's, I knew that there was always this to come back too if things got really bad."

"You didn't return much though during those years, did you?" George returned.

"No. I suppose I felt it was better all round if I didn't."

They stood in silence taking in the scenery before he asked: "And now? Have you decided what your next move will be?"

"Are you trying to get rid of me?" she laughed, almost teasingly.

"There will never be any likelihood of that, Kate. However, I am wise enough to know that there is not enough to keep you here. Nevertheless, I'm anxious that you shouldn't rush things. You've been through a lot and I'd still like to see a little more colour in your cheeks and a sparkle back in those eyes. It isn't good for you to be so much on your own, either."

"Don't worry about that Papa. I do miss always having folk round me, even if half of them were too ill to communicate with. I've been quite content with my own company really."

"Be that as it may, Kate; I've been mulling over an idea. Why don't you contact one of your friends - the one you stayed with in London, for instance? See whether she too would enjoy a break, at the sea perhaps. I'm sure your old governess at Cromer would be more than willing for you to visit for a week. You always enjoyed her company and she is an excellent conversationalist. Things may seem that much clearer when you return."

Katy looked at her father with surprise and respect. "That truly is a wonderful notion and I'm sure Edith would accompany me provided that she isn't already occupied. Thank you so much for your thoughtfulness."

Whereupon, she set off in the direction of the manor with a definite spring in her step.

The proposal met with considerable resistance from Emily who would have thoroughly enjoyed an excuse to holiday at one of the superior hotels to be found at such a resort. Moreover, she considered herself to be the right and proper escort on such an occasion. Hasty looks exchanged between George and his daughter confirmed that such an arrangement was destined to be a disaster and, to Emily's considerable chagrin, was swiftly forestalled.

To Kate's relief and delight her former comrade responded eagerly to the invitation and the ensuing days were spent in a whirlwind of activity and preparation. Edith spent a few days at Painters Court prior to their departure and revelled in the beauty of the surroundings and opulence of her hosts which was in marked contrast to her own situation. Her presence also had the benefit of smoothing the relationship between Kate and her mother which, although superficially cordial, required little to cause feelings kept on a tight rein to erupt. Mercifully, the days passed without incident and, on a glorious spring morning, they set out for Cromer in a comfortable carriage from the stables driven by the ever-faithful Ben.

Almost as though by a prearranged signal, no sooner had their conveyance left the environs of the village than Sir William Kirk drew up. Descending slowly from his smart gig he handed the reins to the stable lad then turned to pull on the bell cord.

The time had come for various parties to put their heads together and lay the plans which would hopefully result in a new St. Martha's Hospital.

***

Only a few days after Kate's departure, a stranger arrived at the front entrance of St. Martha's. From his position in the porter's lodge, Simpson viewed the immaculately dressed military gentleman with interest, for such a person was quite out of place in that neighbourhood. After taking in the immediate surroundings, Major Roland Masterson strode across the hall to the desk.

"Good morning sir. How can I help you?" queried the guardian of the portal, in a voice used only when dealing with members of the governing body and other such officials.

"I have shortly returned from active service in the Crimea and am trying to trace a nurse who worked in the hospital at Scutari. I understand that she was previously employed… "

Before he could complete the sentence, a broad smile creased Simpson's face and he interrupted eagerly. "Oh, you mean our Miss Oliphant, sir. Well, I'm afraid as 'ow you's unlucky. She did drop by to see us on her return but then went straight off to 'er 'ome to rest up. Proper worn out she were, poor lass, after all she'd been through. But, you'd know all about that, havin' been there yourself."

"Is her home situated far from here?" pursued Roland. He had no desire to be drawn on the subject of the war and was anxious to obtain as much information as possible before someone in authority arrived to question his motives.

"Be about ten miles out of the city to the west. Village of Shepherdstone. Have you any transport sir, or would you be wanting a carriage?" offered the uncommonly helpful Simpson.

"Thank you, but that won't be necessary," came the reply. "I'm obliged to you for your help," said the Major, passing a handsome tip across the counter. With which he turned smartly on his heel and was out through the door just as Miss Upton emerged from her office.

"Who was that, Simpson," she demanded, "and what did he want?"

"An army gentleman looking for Miss Oliphant, Ma'am, but he didn't say why. Knew her from the war apparently."

"And what did you tell him?" persisted his superior.

"Just told 'im as how she'd been to see us but was resting at her 'ome. And 'e said as 'ow 'ed try there."

Miss Upton looked at him searchingly, expressing her hope that he had not divulged any private information to a stranger, before returning to her sanctum.

"Nosy old so-and-so," the porter muttered under his breath, withdrawing the tip from his pocket and regarding it with considerable satisfaction.

Meanwhile, armed with the information he required the Major set out to complete his quest. Springing his horses to a spanking pace he left the city behind him and eventually found himself bowling along the

42

pleasant, quiet lanes leading to Shepherdstone. The drive provided him with time in which to reflect upon his action. After all, it was really just a whim and he wasn't normally a person given to such behaviour.

The chance invitation from an army colleague to spend some time at his home in order to enjoy a spell of hunting with the Mead had been a heaven-sent opportunity. The administrative duties to which he had been assigned following those ghastly months in the Crimea were dull in the extreme. Nevertheless, he found that he had equally little enthusiasm to take any more active military step. Once, the army had been his life and sole ambition but now lay like a discarded sword, blunted and lacklustre. It would need careful attention if it were ever to be deployed again. He had to acknowledge that he was at a watershed in his life and this respite in the country afforded just the opportunity to reappraise his situation.

It was whilst relishing a cigar with the vintage port, which had followed a superb dinner on the previous evening, that the conversation had turned to various reminiscences of the recent campaign. Amongst the kaleidoscope of mental pictures had come to mind that of a spirited young nurse in a cemetery overlooking the Bosphorous.

"She came from somewhere round about this area," he recalled to his friend.

"What was her name?" asked the languid Tommy by way of conversation.

"Haven't the foggiest, I'm afraid," Roland was forced to admit. "I think she mentioned a hospital called St. Martha's."

"Well, I'm blessed, that's not far from here," remarked his companion with interest. "Why don't you go and look her up; see what's happened to her. Could be a bit of a lark! Take a drive into Morford tomorrow."

"But, I've told you, I haven't the faintest idea who to ask for," he demurred.

"For heaven's sake man, there can't be that many nurses from one hospital who ventured out to the Crimea!"

Funny that just a chance remark should find him in this current situation, he mused. Furthermore, what on earth was he going to say?

Oh, damn and blast Tommy with his harebrained ideas. Still, there was no point in giving up now he'd come this far. Slowing his horse down at the approach to the village, he cast around for someone who could appraise him as to the Oliphant family residence. Seeing the parson emerge from the lych gate leading to the ancient church by the green, he drew up alongside him.

"You'll be looking for Painters Court," advised that white-whiskered gentleman. "Less than half-a-mile down the lane there to the east."

Raising his whip in salute the major continued his journey, coming to rest a few minutes later at the entrance gates to a substantial residence. His eyes quickly took in the well tended gardens, the sweep of gravel drive, the rich farmland surrounding the property, and the nicely proportioned, mellow stone house standing well back from the lane, sheltered by trees in which a number of noisy rooks clamoured.

Setting his shoulders purposefully, Roland brought his conveyance to rest before the Georgian-style front door and descended. Before he could bring himself to mount the four immaculate steps, the door opened and he found himself face-to-face with a man, older than himself but equal in height and bearing.

"Heard the sound of wheels and thought it might be a friend I'm half expecting," said a somewhat surprised George Oliphant as his gaze roamed over the figure in military uniform standing before him.

"I'm sorry to disappoint you, sir. I hope you won't think I'm presuming, but I find myself in this vicinity and decided to try to renew a brief acquaintance I had with a Nurse Oliphant from the hospital in Scutari. I called at St. Martha's and was told that I would find her here."

If George was surprised he gave no indication of the fact, behaving as though it were a common occurrence to receive visitors to his home on such an errand.

"Well now, if that isn't unfortunate! You have indeed come to the right place but I'm afraid my daughter is currently away on a well earned holiday by the sea."

Roland didn't know whether to be relieved or disappointed by this news. However, before he could consider his next move, George extended his hand in a firm handshake and bade him come in. Turning purposefully on his heel he rang a bell to summon a maid from the back stairs and requested her to send a lad to attend to the visitor's horse.

"Come in my dear fellow, come in and meet Mrs Oliphant."

Roland followed the sturdy figure across the hall only to be brought to an abrupt halt as his host suddenly stopped in his tracks.

"I'm so sorry, but I haven't inquired your name?"

Furnished with the necessary information he flung the drawing room door open and announced with enthusiasm: "Emily my dear, we have a surprise guest. This is Major Masterson, a friend of Kate."

Rising from a chair by the surprisingly ornate fireplace, and finding herself face-to-face with a quite presentable man, Emily prepared to simper effusively. "How delightful to meet you. What a shame Kate isn't here but do come and sit down. Perhaps we may offer you some refreshment?" she rushed on.

He wasn't exactly handsome, she assessed, but he did possess a certain stature and an even half personable male was a welcome distraction in a rather unexciting existence.

"I thank you for your hospitality but must own that I cannot exactly claim to be a friend of your daughter. Our meeting was rather fleeting, I'm afraid, but the circumstances were unusual, to say the least. I really wanted to make sure that she had arrived back in England safely."

"How absolutely intriguing," murmured Emily. "We were about to partake of afternoon tea. Please join us, and you can tell us all about it."

So it was that over seed cake and bone china, Roland Masterson became better acquainted with the parents of the young woman who had spoken of them with such a lack of enthusiasm. They, in turn, learned a little more detail of the rigours of the Crimea at first-hand and of the amazing work achieved by the gallant band of nurses.

"I'm sure you must know even more of their exploits than I do by now," apologised the Major after a while.

"Indeed no, we don't," interjected George. "Kate has been very reticent, if not outright reluctant, to talk about the matter. Too painful I suppose and she doubtless preferred to spare our feelings."

Roland recalled Kate's remarks regarding the reaction of her parents to her chosen career and hid a secret smile. Despite Emily's frequent protestations of pride and concern, he was not such a poor judge of men that he could not see beneath the proffered exterior. He had already identified the attempts at artless dalliance and noted the fluttering eyelashes cast in his direction. The father didn't seem too bad, so far as could be gauged from such a short meeting. If the fields he had passed en route with their healthy crops and livestock were anything to go by, he was a more than competent landowner. Not that any of it mattered he mused, for his mission had been unsuccessful and was unlikely to be repeated.

"May we enquire where you are staying Major?" George's voice broke into his thoughts.

"I have an old army friend whose family own a small estate near the village of Rosemount. I was greatly tempted by the offer of some good hunting and I haven't been disappointed."

"That wouldn't be the Pateleys by any chance, would it?"

"Good heavens! What an inspired guess," commented Roland in some surprise.

"Not really. Morfordshire isn't such a large county and, being a hunting man myself I know most of the people involved, if not personally then at least by name."

Feeling that she had been ignored for long enough, Emily ventured to regain the Major's attention.

"I do hope you will still be here for the Hunt Ball," she simpered. "We are fully intending to be present and Kate will have returned from Cromer by then."

"I think it highly unlikely, I'm afraid. I do not have indefinite leave from my army duties and I don't wish to outstay my welcome with Tom's family."

Emily, however, had the light of battle in her eyes and was not going to let a chance like this slip away.

"Kate will be so disappointed to have missed you," she gushed unashamedly, not in the least aware or concerned whether her daughter would confirm such sentiments. "Perhaps we could prevail upon you to extend your time here. After all, the Ball is little over a week away."

46

"I truly can't make any promises but I assure you, if it is at all possible, I shall be there," he responded politely with a slight inclination of his head in her direction.

And with that, Emily had to be content. Such an indefinite response could, in no way, stop her mind from working overtime. What a scoop it would be if Kate and this thoroughly satisfactory man could be brought together. If only wedding bells resulted, it would certainly solve the vexed problem of any further unsuitable career prospects which her strong-minded daughter might already be considering.

Neither George nor his wife had mentioned to Roland their particular interest in the Hunt Ball, plus numerous other forthcoming activities in the social calendar. Hectic planning by Sir William Kirk and his committee had contrived a series of fund-raising events to further their ambitions for the new hospital, all of which would be graced by their local heroine. George and Emily's involvement consisted of ensuring Kate's presence at these functions. This was a matter which would require delicate handling and the advent of Major Roland Masterson could provide just the solution to surmounting the first hurdle, which would be the Ball.

Unknown to Kate, a seamstress had been commissioned to create a suitable gown in anticipation of the occasion. If George was a little apprehensive, Emily was quick to point out their daughter's complete lack of interest in anything she wore. Ensuring that she had the wherewithal to fulfil the engagements was the responsibility which she was prepared to undertake. Her husband's task was to guarantee the compliance of their offspring in the matter. Much as his relationship with his daughter had improved, he could not help feeling that it stood in jeopardy as a result of their machinations.

Blissfully unaware of the turn events had taken at home Kate and Edith revelled in the bracing air and lazy days at Cromer supplemented by the appetising meals and homely accommodation provided by Miss Fenton. The three of them enjoyed informal picnics taken among the sand dunes and leisurely walks in the countryside or strolls around the old town. It all seemed light years from the horrors of the Crimea, reminiscences of which they shared together occasionally. Gradually, however, these gave way to more animated discussions regarding the future.

Edith was keen to continue nursing in London in the hope of becoming involved with any plans Miss Nightingale may be considering and constantly encouraged her friend to join her. Kate was tempted but there was a part of her that felt a loyalty to St. Martha's and a desire to employ all that she had learned of organisation and management and put it into effect in order to raise further the standards of nursing in the provinces.

"Everyone will be flocking to sit at the feet of the master in London but skilled nursing is needed across the entire country," Kate protested.

By the end of the holiday, she had more or less convinced herself that her future lay in Morford. There was one problem, however, for she knew that she would find little satisfaction or happiness in a subordinate role. Miss Upton was unlikely to move elsewhere and, in any event, the existing structure of St. Martha's would need a complete overhaul if it was to foster the brave new world of nursing which Kate sensed was about to blossom. Unfortunately, that was all in the future and didn't solve her present dilemma.

So the holiday drew to a close. Ben arrived to transport them westwards and they bade a fond farewell to Miss Fenton who had been kindness itself and done so much to aid the process of restoration to their mental and physical well-being. On the journey home Edith continued to try to persuade Kate to change her mind and share in her London aspirations but to no avail. That stubborn streak, which she had witnessed so often in her friend, persisted. Finally, with warm embraces and promises to keep in touch, they parted at Morford station and Kate waved until the train bearing Edith back to the capital was out of sight. Then, if not exactly with a spring in her step, she walked purposefully out to the carriage waiting in the yard. She may not have decided quite what she was going to do but she knew one path that she wasn't going to follow.

In view of the arrangements and deceptions which they had agreed to be party to, it was small wonder that the Oliphants viewed their daughter's homecoming with some trepidation. Just supposing she refuses to participate in any of this," wailed Emily. "You know how impossibly obstinate she can be."

Her husband was no more sanguine about the prospect. Turning to face his pathetic spouse he addressed her sternly. "Now get one thing straight. A word out of place, a wrong move, a hint of coercion from us and the whole thing will be in tatters."

"I am only too aware of that," was the petulantly tremulous reply. "What you have failed to inform me is just how we should proceed."

Flouncing across to the deep window recess she continued with her tirade in an increasingly shrill voice. "You do realise that I shall lose any standing I have in the county if she sets against everything, don't you?" Twisting her already crumpled lawn handkerchief she rounded on him saying, "She must be made to see, made to comply."

"That just about epitomises your selfishness and your supreme lack of tact. In view of which I completely forbid you to broach the matter or venture one comment, unless, of course, it constitutes sweet reason. As that is a commodity in which you are totally lacking I will assume your utter silence."

Any further dialogue was disrupted by the sound of carriage wheels on the drive.

"Well, the moment of truth is at hand," George muttered. "And for heaven's sake leave things to me, Emily."

"Oh! I shall do that, never fear. Then, when things have all gone wrong, at least I can't be held responsible." Upon which she sailed across the room, in a flurry of bombazine, in time to greet the subject of their discourse.

Having bestowed a dutiful kiss on her mother's cheek and a slightly warmer one upon her father, Kate braced herself for the inevitable.

"Oh, my dear, you look so much better," trilled Emily. "Doesn't she George?"

And that gentleman had to admit that the sea air had wrought wonders. A previously pale, almost pasty, face was now becomingly tinged with pink, whilst the old sparkle had returned to her eyes. The auburn hair, which was undoubtedly her crowning glory, had regained its lustre, and her general appearance was really quite becoming. She may be no exquisite beauty but there was an unknown ingredient which made her a not completely unattractive creature.

Kate turned to her father with a smile and said, "I really am most grateful to you Papa for suggesting Cromer in the first place. It was, indeed, just what Edith and I needed and we enjoyed ourselves hugely. Old 'Fenny' was wonderful and made us so welcome. I think she actually liked having us."

Emily privately thought that the whole thing sounded unutterably boring but had the wisdom not to say so!

"I'll ring for tea and you can tell us all about it," she ventured instead. And, strangely enough, all three found the experience quite convivial.

The news of Major Masterson's visit was related in great detail and Kate would have been extremely obtuse had she failed to detect the arch interest displayed by her mother.

"I can scarcely recall what he looks like," she said, with some economy of truth. In fact, the details of that brief meeting did flash across the screen of her mind from time to time.

"Well, you must have made some impression on him," Emily persisted. "Men don't usually go out of their way to renew an acquaintanceship like that."

"Oh, Mother. Please don't let your imagination run away with you," she pleaded. "Anyhow, it's extremely unlikely that such a situation will occur again."

"Now that's just where you're wrong," her determined Mama continued. "He was so disappointed to have missed you that he is going to try for an extension of his leave in order to attend the Hunt Ball with the Pateleys. You may well be meeting him after all," she ended triumphantly.

George cast a warning look in his wife's direction, anxious in case her enthusiasm led her to be indiscreet. His attention was quickly diverted as he heard Kate say: "Hunt Ball! When is that being held? I shan't be going anyway. You know I have little interest in such occasions, besides which, I have nothing suitable to wear."

Before Emily could offer any further pronouncements, George

turned to his daughter with the suggestion that she go to her room and change in order to walk outside with him for a while.

"I need to talk with you on a certain matter and I also fancy a stroll, so we can kill two birds with one stone."

"Goodness," Kate teased, "that sounds ominous. Now what have I done?"

"It's nothing that you have done," smiled her father ruefully, "rather the reverse."

With which he made to leave the room, calling over his shoulder, "I'll see you in the stable yard whenever you're ready."

There Kate found him some fifteen minutes later, fondling the nose of one of his hunters and murmuring softly to it.

"Thank you for indulging me," he said, eying her a shade apprehensively. "Shall we wander down towards the stream at the bottom of Pitt's Meadow? We can talk as we go."

From her vantage point at the terrace window, Emily watched them set out with equal apprehension. Why, oh why did they have to be blessed with such an intransigent child?

For a while, father and daughter walked together in an uncomfortable silence which neither seemed inclined to break. Approaching a newly felled tree trunk lying on the ground, George gestured towards it. "Let's sit down shall we?" he suggested, and Kate duly complied in a state of total mystification.

"Did the holiday help to clarify things for you Kate? Have you decided on your next move?" her father asked.

"Not exactly," Kate replied, "but it did resolve one thing."

"And what was that?"

"Well, Edith is set upon following Miss Nightingale in London to help bring about the proposed programme of training for nurses. She was desperately keen for me to join her and, I must confess, it would be a temptingly exciting thing to do."

"So, what is stopping you?"

"St. Martha's is in a terrible state and isn't a particularly pleasant environment in which to work." She paused for a moment as though searching for the right words before continuing. "Yet, I suppose I do

51

have a certain fondness for the place, and I definitely feel a sense of loyalty towards Miss Upton and the Board. Then too, the people in growing cities like Morford need the best possible nursing just as much as the likes of London and Liverpool."

Kate got up and wandered off for a few yards before turning to face her father. "The truth is that I want to remain at St. Martha's and try to make use of the experience I have gained and improve the situation in which the patients are cared for. I know I don't have all the answers but I don't think I could bear to return in my previous role. Quite frankly, unless the Board is prepared to find the money to improve the place completely it will be impossible to make any of the progress that I would like to see."

Pausing for breath, she smiled ruefully at him and concluded, "In answer to your first question Papa, no, I don't know what my next move will be exactly. You may find that I'll be around for a while longer, I'm afraid," she added with a little laugh.

George sat silent for a while as the tide of hope began to surge within him. Eventually he rose to his feet and the two of them resumed their walk towards the beck.

"Thank you for sharing your feelings with me Kate, and now it's my turn. Believe me, I do not find this easy," he volunteered.

"Papa, whatever is the mystery? Has something happened that you have lost all your money and you're trying to tell me that we are about to face penury? Or is there something wrong with you or Mama that I need to know about?" she hazarded.

"No, no, nothing like that," he sighed.

"Kate, I know we haven't been the best parents and we've all certainly had our differences. You aren't the easiest daughter either," he smiled down at her. "I have long thought you to be a child born way ahead of her time. What you achieved in the Crimea was admirable and I admired your spirit and - yes, damn it - I've become proud of you."

He coughed and cleared his throat, not for any good reason other than the chance to gain some time. He crucially needed to find the right words. Taking a deep breath and fixing his gaze ahead, he resumed his thoughts. "I had dared to hope, indeed I like to think, that things have

52

improved between us since your return from the war, Kate."

She made as if to reply but was prevented from doing so.

"No, let me continue. Unfortunately, while you were in Cromer your mother and I allowed ourselves to become inveigled into becoming part of a scheme which very much involves you, but which will not meet with your approval, I fear."

Without further ado George appraised her of the activities and ambitions of Sir William and the Board of Governors and the part that she was expected to play in all this.

At last it was done, and mopping his forehead with a large handkerchief, he waited for his daughter to erupt. His outpourings, however, were greeted with a complete silence, a silence which he oddly found more unnerving than any indignant outburst. Suddenly, to his surprise and bewilderment he became aware of a rising tide of laughter issuing from the figure at his side. Clutching her arms around her body, Kate found a convenient tree against which to lean and fixed her bemused parent with a calculating stare.

"You are quite right Papa. Normally I would have considered your interference an insufferable personal exploitation and invasion of my privacy. I dislike fuss of any kind and I have never been drawn to the social whirl. Neither do I relish the prospect of becoming what will virtually be a public side-show. However, I think you may have unwittingly decided my future for me."

Shaking his head in disbelief, George announced in somewhat scathing tones, "I will never understand women. Never have and never will."

"Can't you see Papa? If I agree to be part of all this, I will actually be helping to further my ambitions for St. Martha's - a new St. Martha's which will be able to meet future requirements and capable of facilitating the proposed training plans for nurses."

Then, with a wicked twinkle in her eye, Kate fired her final shot. "You may tell Sir William that I agree to fall in with this scheme, but it comes with a price."

"A price?" he echoed, some of the relief he felt draining away.

"Indeed, that is only fair. If I am to be used in this way I insist on being consulted regarding any plans. Of course, I shall expect a nursing appointment commensurate with my status as well," she added pertly.

Now it was George's turn to laugh. "Kate, Kate, you drive a hard bargain but you are running too fast. This will all take time to achieve and between then and now, any manner of things can happen." Taking his half-hunter watch from his waistcoat pocket he announced that it was high time they started to make tracks for the house.

"Your Mama is already in a frenzy of anguish fearing your reaction. I think it would be kind to put her mind at rest."

Kate wrinkled her nose. She frankly couldn't give a toss what her mother felt for she was quite sure that the only thing worrying her was the possibility of losing face with her friends.

George noted the gesture and felt moved to say, "Don't be too hard on her. It is very difficult for her to understand your desire for independence and your lack of interest in the more gentle pursuits. I must warn you too that, in anticipation, she has arranged for her dressmaker to conjure up a gown for you to wear at the Hunt Ball. I might also add that it has cost me a pretty penny."

"Poor Papa, your womenfolk don't make your life easy do they? Never fear. I shall be suitably grateful and, I must own that, I am more than happy for Mama to busy herself with my wardrobe if it will afford her satisfaction. I can assure you that I have little interest in frills and furbelows."

In high spirits father and daughter completed the walk home in easy companionship, both more than happy with the outcome of their deliberations.

Chapter Three

New Experiences

The day of the Hunt Ball dawned bright with an autumn sun casting a mellow glow across the countryside. The harvest was nearly gathered in, most of the trees had been stripped of their colourful fruits, and bright berries sprinkled the hedgerows with vivid splashes of red and orange. Kate leaned out from her open bedroom window and breathed in the fresh air with appreciation. Since that memorable afternoon with her father, an aura of peace and accord seemed to pervade the old house. Once Emily learned that her daughter had not thwarted the proposed plans she became all sweetness and light, positively radiating serenity and affability.

Kate had to admit also to a frisson of excitement at the prospect of the forthcoming evening festivities which were to take place at the Assembly Rooms in Morford, and would mark the beginning of her foray into the world of public speaking and fund-raising on behalf of the new St. Martha's.

Her mother had tried to discover whether Major Masterson would be in attendance but without success, greatly to her annoyance. Apparently the Patelys were mustering a party numbering some nine people but as to their identities her source could not provide the answer. Wisely, she forbore from mentioning any of this to Kate.

After the years of comparative toil and deprivation, both at the hospital and in the Baltic, making the necessary preparations and titivations required for the evening's engagement was a whole new world. One of the maids was dispatched to attend and help her and such was her infectious enthusiasm that it became hard to tell who was deriving the most enjoyment from the occasion. Her toilette completed, the ball gown was slipped over her head and the row of tiny buttons fastened down the back, neat as a line of soldiers on parade.

Standing in front of the cheval glass, Kate had to admit that her mother's choice was impeccable. The holly green taffeta showed off her auburn hair to perfection and the material rustled satisfactorily around her legs as she moved, subtly defining a quite acceptable figure hidden beneath the swirling folds. Although hitherto professing a disinterest in her wardrobe, she would have been unnatural indeed to deny the pleasure afforded by such an exquisite creation. Meeting the eyes of her young assistant in the mirror, she needed no other confirmation to assure her that the picture she presented was more than adequate. Rejecting a proffered fan as being more than she was prepared to contend with, she allowed her helpmate to place a smart lined stole round her shoulders, picked up a matching reticule and, with a final glance in the mirror, swept onto the landing and descended the stairs to face the scrutiny of a still apprehensive Emily.

That lady, was, for once, completely silenced as she contemplated the results of her handiwork. Before she could summon forth an appropriate comment, George pronounced his verdict: "Kate, my dear, you look wonderful." Then added with a wry grin: "And it's worth every penny!"

Basking in the undoubted approval of both parents, Kate followed her mother into the waiting carriage and settled back to compose herself in readiness for the evening ahead.

The Assembly Rooms blazed with light and presented a hub of activity as the elegantly dressed elite of the county converged upon it to celebrate the opening social event in the hunting calendar. Fluttering mothers chaperoned demure daughters, who aspired to varying degrees of attractiveness, whilst keeping a surreptitious eye open in the search for possible eligible suitors. Husbands attended upon their spouses for the minimum time deemed acceptable before seeking out more robust company, whilst the younger male element congregated to survey any likely prospects under the pretence of animated conversation, fortified by the necessary liquid refreshment.

Sir William, accompanied by one or two hospital board members, anxiously awaited their arrival, greeted the Oliphants warmly, then turned his attention to Kate.

"I cannot express our gratitude to you enough for agreeing to promote the fundraising campaign for the new hospital."

"Indeed, Miss Oliphant, St. Martha's is fortunate to have gained such an illustrious champion," echoed the Archdeacon, favouring her with a monocled look.

Kate regarded each one quite deliberately before replying in measured tones: "Gentleman, this is a purely business arrangement. Under normal circumstances I would not have acceded to such a request for I abhor anything which hints of self-agrandiosement."

Ignoring the sharp intake of breath from an agitated Emily standing behind her, she calmly continued.

"These, however, are not normal circumstances. St. Martha's has been in serious want of improvement for too many years. I have good reason to know of the need following first-hand experience. Experience, I might add, which placed me in a position to be able to undertake my recent role in the Crimea."

"Quite so," interposed the Archdeacon, not relishing the development of a possible sermon which he clearly saw as his exclusive domain. "We had thought... "

Allowing a polite if decidedly cool gaze to pass over him, Kate continued as though impervious to his interruption.

"I consider, therefore, that I owe St. Martha's some debt of gratitude. More than that, however, I am keen to see that Morford has a hospital that will take it into the future. I would also like us to be in a position to embrace and implement the training programme for nurses which dear Miss Nightingale will be instigating as a direct result of the unfortunate conditions we were forced to witness in the recent troubles."

Sir William, who was used to Kate's self-composure and articulate, forthright manner, permitted himself a fleeting smile as he witnessed the slightly bemused discomfiture of his fellow trustees. If they had thought that in persuading her into this role they would simply acquire a decorative and silent advertisement, they were due for a shock. This young woman would never be manipulated and the sooner everyone realised and accepted that fact, the easier things would be.

Smiling sweetly, Kate concluded: "At any event which you wish me to attend, it must be clearly understood that I am not just to be a mere figurehead but a resounding voice on behalf of a cause I know we all hold dear. I thank the board for giving me just such an opportunity."

After ensuring that the chairman would introduce her and call upon her to speak during the course of the evening, she permitted her father to engage her in the first dance. Unaccustomed to such genteel pastimes Kate was forced to try to recall long forgotten dancing lessons. This required such concentration that any further conversation was momentarily curtailed.

There was no doubt that Kate's presence was the subject on everyone's lips and she soon found herself much in demand - for conversation if not for dancing! Many were the glances cast in her direction until she confided to her father somewhat ruefully: "You would think I'd got two heads!"

Emily, meanwhile, mingled with her friends and enjoyed the attention accorded to her as 'that wonderful girl's mother'. All the while, however, she was intent upon locating the party from Rosemount. It was not until halfway through the evening that they finally appeared, easily distinguished by the presence of two gentlemen in immaculate military dress uniform. Speedily extricating her husband from the company of a group of land-owning neighbours she propelled him firmly towards her quarry.

Settled comfortably at a table in an alcove, Roland Masterson scanned the ballroom but soon realised that the likelihood of identifying the object of his mission was quite remote amidst such a throng. Suddenly, an eager voice at his side brought him swiftly to his feet.

"Major Masterson," trilled an enthusiastic Emily, "how delightful that you were able to come."

The next few moments passed in a flurry of introductions and he permitted himself an amused smile as this determined lady appeared to effortlessly insinuate herself into the group around him. Addressing her resigned husband in a tone of voice that brooked no argument, George was commanded to find dear Kate immediately.

"She was quite beside herself at having missed your visit, Major," crooned his guileless spouse.

She was mercifully prevented from providing the assembled party with chapter and verse by the voice of Sir William craving silence for a few moments. With consummate skill he explained the unusual purpose behind the evening and thanked the hunt committee for being the first to come to the aid of the proposed new hospital. Emphasising the debt owed by everyone to 'our brave troops' he steadily worked his way to the climax of his speech. "We are privileged to have with us tonight Morford's very own heroine. Miss Kate Oliphant nursed here at St. Martha's before offering herself for service in the Crimea. After working alongside the indomitable and much admired Miss Nightingale, she has returned eager to do what she can to improve the hospital and nursing services here in the city. It is our good fortune that she has agreed to spearhead a fundraising campaign for that purpose. I have great pleasure in introducing Miss Kate Oliphant." Rather in the manner of a conjuror producing a rabbit out of a hat, he drew Kate onto the stage to the sound of wild applause.

Roland stared with interest and disbelief at the elegant and commanding figure as she silenced the audience and proceeded to give an articulate outline of the future plans. He may not recall the features but recognised the same energy of purpose and unaffected, plain outspokenness which had so captured his attention on that far-off afternoon in an alien land.

From her vantage point, Emily noted his reaction with interest whilst simultaneously preening herself in the light of the tribute being accorded to her daughter. Who would have believed that prospects could suddenly appear so hopeful, she thought.

Kate left the platform as people rose to acclaim her and Sir William took advantage of sending collectors out to receive their willing donations.

"Well done! Well done my dear! You were superb," said her father who had stationed himself in a position ready to acquaint her of the need to meet the party from Rosemount.

Somewhat taken aback by the enthusiastic reception she had

received, it was with mixed feelings that Kate faced the prospect of renewing her extremely brief acquaintance with the Major. To say that she had given the matter no thought would be untrue. Ever since being told of his visit to her home she had strained to recall the details of their one and only encounter but with limited success. Smiling politely to left and to right as she made her way across the floor she took a deep breath and prepared herself to acknowledge the introductions and plaudits of the group gathered in front of her.

Almost involuntarily, she found her gaze being drawn towards the comfortable face and soft grey eyes which were appraising her unashamedly. Extending her hand she took heart from the firm grasp in which it was taken and proffered a warm smile.

"How good to see you again Major, and looking so well after the ordeals of the battlefield," she murmured softly, aware of several pairs of eyes fixed on her.

"The pleasure is mine, Miss Oliphant," he countered. "And, may I compliment you on your oration just now; it was masterly."

Kate inclined her head and expressed her thanks before turning to greet Mr. and Mrs. Pately and the irrepressible Tom.

"Enchanted to meet you at last Miss Oliphant. I can understand why Roland has been so keen to make contact again!"

"Well, he has certainly chosen a better location than before," she retorted promptly, at which point everyone laughed and began to relax.

It had become obvious to the Major that if he were to have any chance of conversation with Kate they would need to take to the dance floor. Before she could either seat herself or move on, he gave a slight bow and requested the honour of the coming waltz. Without the least coquetry or affectation she accepted saying, "I hope you are prepared for your feet to be ruined for this is one of many graces in which I lack proficiency."

She need not have concerned herself, however, for he was an excellent proponent of the dance and she found herself whirling round as though completely accustomed to such an activity.

"Are you fully recovered now from your ordeals at Scutari?" he enquired.

"Oh yes, thank you, quite recovered. The memories will linger, however, for some time to come, although I don't dwell on them any longer."

He regarded her with pleasure before confiding, "You know, I would never have recognised you again."

"I should hope not," she chortled. "That ghastly uniform was scarcely becoming and would certainly have been out of place at an event such as this."

In a voice resonant with appreciation he said, "I hope you will not take it amiss if I remark how enchanting you look."

"Why, thank you," Kate replied. "Most people enjoy a compliment and I discover that I am no different."

The music drew to a close and as they prepared to return to their seats Roland asked whether she had found time yet to partake of any refreshment.

"Do you know," said Kate in some surprise, "I have been so involved since my arrival that there hasn't been the opportunity."

"Would you care to see if we can remedy that now?" he offered.

"I should relish nothing more," came her immediate response.

Upon which they disappeared together in the direction of the buffet, watched with considerable satisfaction by the constantly observant Emily. The success of the occasion was far exceeding her expectations.

***

Despite the lateness of their return, Kate was up and about at her usual time next morning. She had pleaded tiredness on the journey home and immediately retired to the privacy of her room. This manoeuvre was designed purely to avoid her mother's probing questions, causing great vexation to that good lady and amused satisfaction to her husband.

Greeting his daughter as she arrived at the breakfast table, George again congratulated her on her performance of the previous evening and enquired how she proposed spending the day.

"Actually, Papa, I received an invitation last night to visit the Pateleys at Rosemount for luncheon. They are kindly sending a conveyance to collect me."

George raised his eyebrows but merely expressed his pleasure for her. He certainly had no intention of querying the possible lack of a chaperone which his wife would certainly have done. He had long since accepted that this offspring of his was a free spirit and would constantly fly in the face of convention.

An hour later, Major Roland Masterson once more drew up at the front door of Painters Court, settled Kate comfortably into his gig and departed before the somnolent Emily had even left her boudoir. The leisurely drive to Rosemount provided a much better environment in which to develop their friendship and they used the time to discover more of each other's plans.

"So, you have abandoned any thought of returning to active nursing?" queried the Major.

"For the time being, yes," responded his companion. "I couldn't envisage that I would ever be content to return to St. Martha's in my previous capacity. Neither, I discovered, did I wish to join my colleague, Edith, in London to work with Miss Nightingale. Having thought the matter through, I have come to the conclusion that there is a role here in promoting improvements in a provincial hospital in order to put it on an equal footing with the teaching establishments. While I don't relish projecting myself in the public eye, it is too good an opportunity to miss if the goal is to be achieved."

He mused for a moment before asking, "How long is all this likely to take?"

"I have absolutely no idea," she said blithely. "I suppose it largely depends upon how successful we are in generating funds."

"Well, judging by the response last night, I don't think you are likely to have much trouble," he commented.

"I know that I am in very privileged circumstances," continued Kate. "I have an extremely comfortable home and Papa is happy to make me a generous allowance. There are not many who are in such a fortunate position from which to crusade."

Turning to grin at her he quipped, "I thought family relationships were one of the reasons that drove you to St. Martha's in the first place? I can't imagine you in the role of dependent relative again."

"Oh, things are much different now. My father, at least, has accepted that I am something of a law unto myself. However unorthodox that may be I think he has a sneaking respect. As far as Mama is concerned, it's amazing the difference a little fame makes, even if it is a five minute wonder," she said wickedly.

After driving for a while in companionable silence and drinking in the passing scenery Kate decided it was her turn to be inquisitor.

"What about you? Where will the future take you do you think?"

A short silence followed before Roland heaved a slightly despairing sigh. "Heaven alone knows. You have no idea how I have wrestled with that particular dilemma since returning to England."

"Is there a specific problem?" she continued to question.

"More than one," he ventured, "more than one. I don't really know how to explain it."

"Try," she encouraged. "I'm very good at listening."

He smiled at her, gratefully, before embarking on an explanation.

"For more years than I care to remember, the army has been my life. Now I find that events in the Crimea not only sickened me but made me question what I am actually doing. As if that were not enough, I have found things unutterably tedious since my return. The regiment was appallingly hit at Sebastopol and, by the time the war was over, it was utterly decimated. As a result I find myself tied to a desk with the prospect of becoming little more than a recruiting officer until we have rebuilt our strength. But, rebuild it for what? Just to be annihilated in some other campaign?"

Kate was unable to think of an immediate response and before she could do so, Roland let out an enormous groan saying, "The trouble is I simply haven't got the stomach for it any more, or the heart."

Nothing could have stirred more the natural depths of care and compassion which lay in the heart of the nurse seated beside him. In an automatic gesture of sympathy and understanding, which she had used so often before when tending the sick and wounded, she reached out and placed a hand gently on his arm.

"These things do have a way of sorting themselves out you know. It may not be possible to discern the path at the moment but it is there all the same. It is just a matter of finding it. The important thing is not to give up the search or allow yourself to sink into despair."

Fleetingly, her companion diverted his gaze from the road and permitted it to rest on this reassuring and totally unique young woman.

"You have an amazing sense and wonderful gift of perception, Miss Oliphant. Quite a distinctive brand of medicine for the soul in fact. I only wish I could share your optimism."

Quickly, Kate withdrew her hand saying, "Now you are mocking me sir, which is neither fair nor kind."

"I'm sorry you see it in that light," he countered swiftly, "for nothing could be further from the mark."

Contemplating the road ahead he forced himself to admit: "I suppose my response could be perceived as disparagingly cynical and must stem from living in an exclusively masculine world, I'm afraid."

"Fustion," retorted Kate spiritedly. "Army officers do not usually want for female company, I think."

Once more he was obliged to look at her lively face before considering his reply.

"You will have to believe me when I tell you that my whole life has been largely devoid of feminine influence - unless you count my old Nanny of course. My mother died when I was born. I have no sisters, only a considerably older brother who is a successful lawyer. He inherited the family home in Surrey on the death of my father a few years ago. There are no useful maiden aunts, nor married ones either for that matter. Although my brother seems contented enough in his marriage, I have never regarded his wife as a particularly warm person. They, in turn, have only managed to produce sons, so there aren't even any little nieces to redress the balance. I went to public school, followed by university, followed by the army so I think you will allow that there can scarcely be a more male-dominated existence."

He was startled by the gurgle of laughter emanating from the figure beside him and was forced to enquire sharply what he had said that was so amusing.

"Oh! I was just wondering whether you would care to borrow my Mama," Kate responded.

Whereupon they both joined together in unbridled mirth until Roland was forced to comment in amused tones: "You really are the most reprehensible character you know."

It was in high spirits, therefore, that they approached the farm in the quaint old village of Rosemount to enjoy a day of fun and companionship that Kate would long treasure. Tom, although younger than Roland and decidedly more extrovert, was clearly a loyal friend whilst his sister Agnes made no attempt to hide her admiration of both men. Mr. and Mrs. Pateley welcomed Kate with the minimum of fuss and treated her as one of the family. It was a novel experience to partake of a homely, informal meal in the large farm kitchen and join in the endless banter. She could quite see why Roland was so ready to avail himself of their constant hospitality. It was all in marked contrast to the relative formality of life at Painters Court.

Following lunch, the four younger members of the party went for a stroll by the river and back through the now bare orchards, in time to try their hand at a game of croquet completely out of season. This was played with mallets which had seen better days on a far from perfect lawn and involved much laughter and cheating. After doing justice to Mrs. Pateley's homemade scones with cream and jam, and with invitations to come again ringing in their ears, they set out to retrace the route to Shepherdstone.

"I cannot recall enjoying a day more," said Kate. "Thank you so much for bringing me."

"I can assure you that the pleasure has been all mine," asserted her escort.

"You won't think so when you are faced with the return journey in the dark," she teased.

"It will be a small matter compared with the trials of the Crimea," he retorted in return.

Kate paused for a moment before asking, "Do you often think of those days?"

Some time elapsed before he finally replied. "I don't dwell so much upon the action as I do on those who failed to return."

Ever since the Major's outburst that morning, she had been

65

wondering how to return to the subject of his future. Seizing the chance she pressed on.

"Yes, it was all so indescribably evil and such an appalling waste. I can quite understand your desire to seek a different way of life. Would it help to discuss it further?"

"Don't you think I have not already considered the possibilities?" he said, a shade of bitterness creeping into his voice. "I have been forced to the unpalatable conclusion that I am ill-equipped for any other career."

"I am sure you have," came the reply, "but you are merely looking at things from your own jaundiced perspective. I doubt you have discussed the matter with anyone else and it is well known that two heads are often better than one."

Seeing that he refused to be drawn, Kate persisted tenaciously, like a dog worrying a bone.

"You mentioned that you attended university. What was your subject?"

"History - with a strong emphasis on military history."

They had driven in silence for nearly a mile before Roland demanded to be party to her deliberations.

"Two prospects spring to mind. One is teaching and the other is writing. Have you thought of either of those?" she said triumphantly.

"Yes, to the first - and discounted it. No to the second - and what on earth would I write about?"

"Military history?" she proposed meekly.

At that, the Major threw back his head and let out a guffaw, quite startling the horse.

"Miss Oliphant, you are gloriously refreshing and a born optimist if ever there was one."

"You can write, can't you?" she said impatiently.

"I can physically put a pen to paper, if that's what you mean. As for earning my living by doing so, that is debatable to say the least."

"Well, you could do worse than consider it because I can think of nothing else to offer at this juncture."

Turning to look at his irascible companion, Roland could not but reflect on the stimulating effect she had. Here was a woman that he had known for a matter of hours yet with whom he felt completely comfortable and at ease. She was lively and intelligent, determined and independent and quite unlike anyone he had ever met before.

Her pleasant voice interrupted his reverie. "May I ask what you are thinking, Major?"

"You may indeed. I was simply considering what an exhilarating day this has been. I cannot believe that we have been friends for such a short time. In saying this, I hope I am not presuming too much, for we are friends aren't we."

"I do indeed pray so Major, otherwise I can't imagine what we are doing in this conveyance together," she retorted archly.

"As usual you have an answer for everything, Miss Oliphant. I am of the mind that life with you would never be dull. Unpredictable, perhaps, but never dull. I'm afraid I must appear a rather insipid individual by comparison. Nevertheless, may I dare to believe that you will look with favour on another meeting?"

With a gentle smile she announced her disappointment had he not suggested it.

"However, I would feel much happier if you could bring yourself to call me by my name. Miss Oliphant is so formal, don't you think?"

It was with considerable satisfaction, therefore, that the watching Emily observed the Major assist her daughter down from the gig and bow his head in order to place a kiss on her hand in farewell.

Chapter Four

Trials, Decisions and Triumph

The Christmas of 1856 proved to be the happiest Kate could remember. She found herself swept up in a whirl of activities which she willingly undertook, for each one meant that the building fund for the new hospital was further advanced. Ever since the ball money had been steadily accruing as the people of Morfordshire took the project to their hearts. From the great and the good to humble villagers; from children in schools and old folk in alms houses, all had pledged to make sure the venture succeeded, spurred on by the vital and inspiring young woman who tirelessly went from one event to another to further the cause. There were insufficient hours in the day to accommodate all that she would have wished to achieve and she found herself longing for spring with its promise of kinder weather and extended hours of daylight.

Following a lengthy, and not completely harmonious, discussion between members of the Board of Governors, Kate was invited to join their ranks to help formulate the plans for the new building. There were some diehards who felt that she was far too young for such a position. Sir William, however, was very aware that Kate's continued co-operation was crucial in the scheme of things, and that lady had made it quite clear that it would not be forthcoming unless she was accorded an adequate voice in the discussions and deliberations. Finally, it was agreed that she would take up a position on the board from the first of January.

Life at Painters Court was unbelievably serene, partly because Kate was usually only there to sleep. George had purchased a smart chaise which he put at her disposal so that she could fulfil her growing calendar of commitments with greater ease. If the distance to be covered was considerable one of the men would accompany her but she much preferred those occasions when she could be independent and drive herself.

"This new hospital of yours will bankrupt me before the first brick is even laid," he commented ruefully.

"Father, you don't have to do all this you know. I can manage I promise you. "

Casting a quizzical look in her direction he felt obliged to remind her that she would find it very difficult to execute the demands being made upon her time if she had to return to her post at St. Martha's in order to support herself.

Kate had the grace to lower her head. "I do know how much I owe to you and I am grateful, I assure you," and she placed her hand lightly on his arm.

"Call it conscience money, for all those years of neglect," George quipped. "Actually, if I'm honest, I'm getting quite a kick out of the whole thing. Added to which, I am undeniably proud of you."

Emily too was more than happy with the way things were progressing. There seemed to be a constant stream of visitors to the Court these days and a gratifying number of social invitations in which she delighted. Although she continued to foster fond hopes for the relationship between her daughter and the Major she was wise enough to keep her thoughts to herself. She had also learned to curb her tongue somewhat when Kate was around having at last accepted that there was nothing to be gained from confrontation. Consequently, the tenor of life was altogether more pleasant and the atmosphere greatly improved.

Roland returned to his regimental duties but letters to Kate arrived regularly and, to everyone's satisfaction, he was easily persuaded to join them for a few days over the festive season. George particularly welcomed the presence of another man and the prospect of some time together in the hunting field. Anxious for some fresh air and the chance to recover from a surfeit of rich food, the couple excused themselves after Christmas lunch and braved the crisp chill of a frosty day to wander in the surrounding fields and lanes. As they crested the brow of a hill and stopped to look back on the village nestled below, both were inevitably drawn to recall how different had been their lot a year ago.

"It isn't difficult to conjure up the memories of those terrible days," sighed Kate. "I can still smell that putrid, evil stench and feel the roughness of the skin on my hands from constant scrubbing, washing and disinfecting. "

Gazing unseeingly into the distance, Roland let out a heartfelt sigh. "It's the boom of the guns, clods of flying earth, the terrified whinny of the horses, the agonised cries of the men - all the ghastly trappings of war that assails my ears."

Turning to look at his companion he gave her a gentle smile and commented, "On those heights above Balaclava, if anyone had told me that in a year's time I would be standing with you here, bathed in the peace of the English countryside, I would not have believed it. Now that I am, it is with a feeling almost akin to guilt that I should be blessed in this way when so many paid such an appalling price."

She shivered involuntarily. "We can't do anything about that tragic past, Roland, but we can try to ensure that some good comes from it. "

"As indeed you are, my dear. I am so full of admiration for your crusading spirit. Your life has infinitely more purpose about it than mine, although I am working on that, you will be pleased to know."

"To what end?" Kate queried. "Have you reached a decision? I came to the conclusion that you were intent on maintaining the status quo, for there is never a mention of future plans in your letters. Not that I mean to pry."

"Rubbish!" he said gleefully. "It's the natural way of women to be curious and wanting to know everything, and you're not your mother's daughter for nothing!"

Kate rounded on him in indignation. "Oh, that is so unjust. I have never presumed to question you and I am certainly nothing like my mother."

"You are splendid when you get on your high horse and I just couldn't resist it," he countered. "I feel quite sorry for those noble citizens on the hospital board!"

Pulling a face at him, Kate began to move off down the hill. "That is something of a sore point you know, because I'm sure there are those who will make things as difficult as possible for me. I'm going to need all the support I can get."

"Well, you've got mine for what it's worth and I'm sure you will benefit greatly from talking things over with your friend Edith when she arrives the day after tomorrow. She will have all the latest news on developments in London, and when you attend your first board meeting you will be well prepared and one jump ahead of them all," he finished triumphantly. "Miss Kate Oliphant carries the day and reigns supreme."

"I do hope you're right, Roland. I do hope you're right. This means so very much to me and will help to make some sense of all that has gone before."

As the daylight continued to fade around them they made their way back to Painters Court in companionable silence, lost in their own private thoughts. Lights flickered from cottage windows and sounds of merriment spilled out into the world outside. Family carols sung around a piano stole across the ear and the pair quickened their steps as a chill wind sprung up ushering in the first flakes of snow.

"See how thoughtful your Christmas gift to me is," said Kate, clasping her hands firmly together inside an exquisite fur muff. "With such luxury, I may forget how to employ these usefully again."

"It is little enough, my dear, in view of all that you have given to me."

Somewhat puzzled, she thought of the mundane book which was all she had been able to think of as a present.

"No," he said, smiling, "I wasn't meaning the book, appreciated as that was. Your friendship has meant so much. To have someone with whom I can share my thoughts, my fears and doubts - that is priceless."

"So priceless that you still haven't told me in which direction your thinking for the future is taking you," she retorted. "You are quite happy for me to babble on, and I rather selfishly let you."

They had reached the stone driveway but before they entered the welcoming circle of light cast from the coach lamp above the front door, he reached out and took her arm.

"Kate, I'm still not certain but I am working on something and I promise that you will be the first to know when I reach a decision. You see, I'd like to think that in time you will come to be part of that future so I have got to make sure it is feasible."

Leaning towards her he allowed his lips to gently brush her forehead. "I'm hoping that this is just the first of many Christmases for us my dear. Am I being foolish to entertain such a thought?"

Hesitating only momentarily, she looked into the face which had come to mean so much to her before saying, "No, you are not being foolish but a great deal has yet to be accomplished before I can allow myself time to consider any personal future. I don't want anything to distract me. You do understand that don't you?"

Laughing ruefully, Roland fixed her with a fond look before asking, "Just how long does it take to build a hospital, Kate?"

"I only wish I knew," she answered as they burst in through the front door and into the welcome warmth of the hall.

Relaxed in their new found contentment together they proceeded to enjoy the rest of the holiday, revelling in a boisterous visit to Tom and his family, whilst the arrival of Edith afforded Roland the chance to avail himself of some hard riding with George. Altogether most satisfactory, observed Emily benignly with a relieved sigh.

***

"St. Martha's is an ill-ventilated, crowded, inconvenient and totally inappropriate building manifestly unable to meet the needs of an expanding industrial population, which is three times as large as when the hospital was founded." Sir William surveyed the Board members over the top of his glasses as he addressed them at the opening meeting of 1857.

"I don't think any of us disagree with that statement," ventured the Archdeacon. "What we require to know is just how much money will be involved to refurbish it."

Before the chairman could reply, Kate interrupted quickly: "Not refurbish Mr. Archdeacon, for that will achieve nothing effective, lasting or worthwhile. We have to completely rebuild."

The momentary silence was followed by some rumblings around

the table. Several pairs of eyes were fixed firmly and, in some cases accusingly, on the speaker.

"Would you care to enlarge on that statement, Miss Oliphant?" asked her mentor.

"There are huge changes ahead for hospitals in general, and nursing in particular, throughout the country as a whole. The next few years will prove to be a watershed in the history of provision of care, not only for the sick but those who minister to them. In view of this anything less than a structural rebuild will be a shortsighted compromise and one for which the people of Morfordshire will not thank us as we work forwards to the twentieth century."

Another silence ensued before a few hearty endorsements of this comment came from the doctors. Historically, relationships between the administrative members of the Board and the medical profession were usually parlous, therefore, the latter welcomed anything which would ultimately work to their advantage.

"Fine sentiments, but nobody has mentioned the cost," persisted the treasurer.

Kate caught Sir William's eye, whereupon he inquired whether she had any information that might assist them in their deliberations.

"The current air space of each bed at St. Martha's is 800 cubic feet whereas the new guidelines are advocating 2,000 cubic feet. A new building could not be put up for less than £120 a bed and that is over and above the cost of new land, which is unlikely to be under £5,000 to £6,000. I submit, therefore, that the probable cost of a brand new hospital comprising 200 beds, including the necessary supporting services, will be in the region of £30,000."

If there had been signs of disquiet previously, there was now virtual uproar.

"Mr. Chairman, such an undertaking is quite out of the question," interpolated the Archdeacon. "I must implore that common sense prevail and we consider a more prudent option."

"Quite right," boomed the haughty voice of Lady Bathmere. "The whole idea is preposterous. You talk about improving standards and providing training for nurses Miss Oliphant but where are they going to come from? It is difficult enough now to retain the inadequate staff currently in post to meet the needs of the present number of beds."

"Exactly so," interposed the Archdeacon looking down his beaky nose. "They will need to be of a considerably higher intellect and moral standing than most of those we seem to employ."

Seething with barely contained rage Kate sprang to her feet. "Mr. Chairman! I really must protest. You may be interested to know that records show that by no means all nurses are drunk and illiterate. Some have proved themselves remarkably devoted as has been witnessed in places during the cholera epidemics of 1847 and 1854. The conduct of those nurses was exemplary and they worked without respite, some themselves losing their lives to the fever. Much is made of 'dismissal for being found in liqour' at a time when water is contaminated and tea taxed at 100%. What would you have them drink? Beer and porter are virtually the only drinks available to the poor." Without pausing to draw breath she stormed on. "These unfortunates also succumb to pain and illness themselves at times, and the only means of assuaging physical discomfort or mental distress is alcohol and laudunum. I suggest that there isn't one person in this room who has not had recourse to these self-same props on occasion."

Voices raised in protest vied successfully with the very few in support of such an ambitious plan. Kate became more and more dejected and found herself being virtually ignored or sidelined. Matters finally became so heated that Sir William moved that the meeting be adjourned for three months. During that time a comprehensive statement of the general financial position would be prepared by the treasurer, their assets assessed, and the likely outcome of the current appeal projected.

Kate left the room with a heavy heart and hastened away unwilling to face any further criticism or pessimism. Arriving home she shut herself in her room to write a despondent letter to Roland. Little could she have foreseen what a difference three months would prove to make.

When the Board reconvened in April Kate had little expectation that the occasion would be any less stormy or more productive than those she had attended so far. It was the worst possible day. Far from a refreshing spring shower, driving rain beat against the misty window panes in horizontal sheets as an equally unseasonal wind howled around the building. The temperature outside was bitterly cold; a fact that seemed to be reflected on the expressionless faces gathered in a room which itself projected an atmosphere of unrelieved gloom. Sir William, however, maintained his customary aura of benevolence which was surprisingly echoed in the bearing of the normally precise, unbending and unsmiling treasurer who even seemed to exude a frisson of excitement.

Reaching into the pocket of her coat Kate's hand curled compulsively round the reassuring form of the mascot which had arrived in the post that very morning.

"I thought you might appreciate a lucky charm!" Roland had written on the accompanying note. "I found this whilst on a solitary walk in the hills when I was trying to wrestle with my own problems. I think it has worked for me, although I am not in a position to confirm anything at this stage. Nevertheless, I do hope to have something to tell you before too much longer. Meanwhile, perhaps its magic will settle on you. Hold tight to your dreams, my dearest Kate, and all will be well."

She had gazed with fascination at the heart shaped stone at the centre of which was a hole. Beautifully smooth, almost silky to the touch, and the most delicate shade of pink striated with diagonal bands in a darker shade, it fitted into the palm of her hand allowing her fingers to caress the comforting contours.

Painfully slowly the agenda was addressed until they reached the item occupying everyone's thoughts. Kate fiddled with her pencil while the Archdeacon leaned forward on the table and the assembled company prepared itself once more for battle. However, the broadside, when it came, caught them all completely unprepared.

"Ladies and gentlemen, I can contain myself no longer," said Sir William. "In the comparatively short time since we last met, there have been two major developments which will undoubtedly help to shape our thinking on the subject of the way forward for our hospital."

Twelve pairs of eyes fixed themselves unwaveringly on the speaker.

"As you know, the young Duke of Ashbourne is one of our patrons.

In an act of unparallelled generosity he has offered to donate a considerable area of land on the western edge of the city for the purpose of building a new hospital."

A tentative murmur rippled forth, but before it could become a vocal tide, he continued purposefully.

"In addition, a totally unexpected legacy has yielded the sum of £1,500 and pledges have been received from worthy individuals slightly in excess of £4,000."

Smiling broadly at Kate he informed them that this was in no small measure due to the impact made upon the community by Miss Oliphant whose hard work would never be fully appreciated. "Neither do these sums take into account the not inconsiderable donations to the appeal fund," he added. "Such support has caused one or two of us to take a long hard look at our current financial situation and our reserves."

This occasioned an immediate hum of voices which was swiftly quelled by the treasurer. "You will be interested to know that after careful appraisal of our assets it would be possible, with the Board's approval of course, to sell off some existing stock in the region of £10,000, to help boost the amount."

"In the light of this information," Sir William said, "I think we can safely say that the proposal for a completely new hospital is no longer the unfeasible prospect it once seemed but a very real and exciting possibility."

Kate waited for the voices of dissent to break forth. Instead, the announcement was greeted with enthusiastic response by the majority and grudging approval from the previous detractors.

The meeting finally broke up and as she made her way to the door Sir William placed a hand affectionately on her arm. "You see, Kate, all is far from lost! I know how downhearted and frustrated you have felt of late. Just have faith - and a modicum of patience, if that is possible - and all will come to fruition."

However, it was not until 1859 that building work was actually able to commence and another two years before Kate finally saw the fulfilment of all that she had worked for and dreamed of. By this time her personal life had taken a very different turn.

Following on from the favourable outcome of their Christmas celebrations, Kate and Roland maintained a regular correspondence interspersed with brief, snatched meetings as each juggled with the demands of their very different roles. The uniformed figure of the Major was sometimes seen at her side at important fund-raising functions, seeming to lend added weight to the occasion, whilst she became a regular visitor to the farm at Rosemount where he now spent most of his leave time.

That there was a true meeting of minds between the couple was never in doubt but the extent to which their hearts were involved was less clear. Any overt gestures of affection were reserved for occasions when they found themselves completely alone and no ripples betrayed any currents of uncontrolled feeling between the two. This was a considerable source of frustration to an increasingly impatient Emily. Much as she was relishing her role as mother and supporter of a heroine, she did not wish to countenance the prospect of her daughter returning to practical work in paid employment, no matter how prestigious the post was perceived to be.

Repeated lamentations and hand-wringing cut no ice with George, however, who constantly warned her of the likely outcome should she attempt to meddle.

He, in turn, frequently mourned all that he had missed from his lack of involvement in Kate's childhood but rejoiced in a fate which had allowed him, not only to come to know, admire and respect this girl of his, but to be affectionately accepted by her as well. There was no denying that he found the Major good company and would welcome him unreservedly as a son-in-law should Kate's heart lead her in such a direction. Nevertheless, he had far too much sense to bring the subject up, reflecting how much better things might have been had he himself taken more time over, and given more thought to, his own liaison all those years ago.

In the end events came to a head in the autumn. Once again, Roland arrived at Rosemount for the hunting which coincided with the annual harvest festivities celebrated by the Patelys in great style and tradition. The barns were swept and decked with flowers and produce. Trestles marched the length of the space groaning with home baked food - simple, homely, appetising fare prepared by the local wives, each with their own particular trademark contribution, secretly vying with one another to provide the best. In one corner, tables had been set up bearing barrels of beer and cider, whilst another catered for the needs of the women and children. The adjacent barn was cleared for dancing and here a lively musical group involved themselves in rehearsing their repertoire in readiness for the entertainment.

Now accepted as part of the family, Kate found herself swept up in the fun and the work involved. Harvests at Painters Court had never been anything like this and she threw herself into the spirit of things with her customary enthusiasm when tackling any project. Dressed in a simple gown of muslin floral print, deeply frilled at the hem, and with her hair swept up and caught in a bright ribbon, she joined happily in the country dancing, savouring with delight the informality of the occasion.

"This is such fun, isn't it," she ventured, as Roland sunk onto a bale of hay to sit beside her and relax with a cooling drink.

"Yes, and have you noticed the wonderful atmosphere of friendship and sense of community that exists with villagers and gentry mingling easily together?"

Kate pondered his words before saying, "I think it has something to do with Mrs. Pately, the squire's lady, and the vicar and his wife. They are clearly in considerable accord with each other and very active in the welfare of their workers and the inhabitants as a whole."

"I would have thought this might have revived childhood memories?" her partner probed gently.

"Goodness me Roland, can you really imagine my mother involving herself in anything like this? The Reverend Williams has always seemed as ancient as he undoubtedly is now, and the Squire is a very dour man whose wife died in childbirth. No; Shepherdstone was never like this."

"It could be, though," he pursued. "It only takes the right people with the right ideas and the necessary will to transform a situation. You are living proof of that. It must be a satisfying thing to be part of, and help to build up, such a community."

78

Kate eyed her inquisitor suspiciously. "Is there a point you're trying to get across?" she enquired somewhat waspishly. "I think you must own that this is hardly the time or the place for deep discussions. Let us return to the dancing and save these fascinating social theories for another time."

So saying, she sprang to her feet and headed for the centre of the barn where sets were forming for 'Strip-the Willow'. As she turned to give Roland her hand, he fixed a penetrating look upon her and said, "My dear, do you think you could keep tomorrow free for just the two of us? There is a subject to which we need to give some time and consideration, and you are quite right, we can't do it here."

"Well, if it has any bearing on your recent remarks, I am aquiver with curiosity," she laughed. "A tryst for the morning it is, although not literally at dawn, if you please!"

Without more ado the couple joined their friends to enjoy the rest of the celebrations for harvest home.

Although she would not have openly admitted it, Kate had been more than a little intrigued by the Major's comments the previous night. Consequently, by the time he had breakfasted and collected the gig from the stables, he returned to find his companion alert and quietly tingling with anticipation. Having helped her up into the conveyance and settled her comfortably, he headed out into the surrounding lanes at a leisurely pace.

Sensing that any lead into conversation must be instigated by the thoughtful figure at her side she, who was never at a loss for words, gave herself up to the delights of the surrounding countryside. Rich pastureland rolled in all directions where cattle, sheep and horses grazed peacefully in the rapidly vanishing early morning mist. Leaves on the trees and in the hedgerows flaunted their autumn colours as birds and wildlife darted about the serious business of food gathering.

She estimated that they had travelled some three or four miles in the direction of Morford before Roland pulled off the road onto a narrow track which led to a five-barred gate. Allowing the reins to hang idly, he leapt to the ground, retrieved a small nose bag from beneath the gig and fastened it over the horse's head to the accompaniment of softly murmured words. This completed, he resumed his place on the seat beside her and without further prevarication launched into speech.

"Do you remember Kate, that it was about a year ago that you and I shared our thoughts and hopes for the future? Except if I rightly recall, yours were much more formulated than mine. As the months have progressed, two issues crystallised into a certainty for me. That I could no longer countenance a career in the army was the first and I must tell you I shall be resigning my commission at the end of the year."

Wisely, the recipient of this confidence forbore to comment at that point, anticipating that much more was to follow.

"Naturally, the most pressing matter is to find an alternative means of support. Here again, two things helped to formulate my thinking. One was the considerable enjoyment I have gained from my frequent visits to Rosemount, which is now almost my home, and Painters Court which is different in many ways yet still manages to leave its mark upon me. Through my observations and general conversations with both Mr. Pately and your father, I have been drawn to the conclusion that life as a farmer is something which holds considerable appeal for me."

Pausing, he continued to gaze into the distance ahead of him before turning deliberately towards Kate.

"Whether I pursue this venture, however, hinges crucially upon another issue."

Palpably feeling for the right words, he continued in a firm yet almost pleading voice.

"It can be no surprise to you when I tell you how central you have become to my life, Kate. Above all things I want to take our relationship forward. Nevertheless, it would be unfair to entertain such aspirations without the practical means to advance them. These I feel are now within my grasp but I have no desire to pursue them to a conclusion unless I know that you will be a part of things."

Taking both of her hands in his, Roland held her look unwaveringly as he asked in a pleading voice, "My dearest love, will you agree to throw in your lot with me and consent to a marriage between us?"

How accentuated the birdsong seemed, Kate mused irrelevantly. Allowing her hands to remain within his, she bowed her head as though in prayer, and showed no inclination to burst into speech. A minute of silence, however, was all her suitor could bear before he asked quietly, "Is it really so hopeless? Have I misread things so badly?"

Eventually, she raised her eyes to his and with a gentle smile and a reassuring squeeze of his hand, said, "No, no you haven't. I suppose I knew, indeed hoped, that you would ask me to marry you one day. It is just the timing which creates the problem."

"No my dearest, timing has nothing to do with this. You have merely been hoping to defer the matter for as long as possible."

"But the new hospital... " she interrupted.

"The new hospital has been approved and will happen now, with or without you."

Rather icily, she was driven to remark, "There are many decisions yet to be made in which I wish to have a voice."

"And is marriage to me going to stop that?" he countered mildly. "You will still be able to serve on the Board."

"Gracious me, will I be able to find time for that alongside helping to build up a farm and my duties as your wife?" she commented tartly.

"Kate, Kate," he cajoled, "That is neither worthy of you nor fair."

"Fair?" She angrily snatched her hands from his grasp, swept the rug from her lap and struggled to reach the ground. "You dare to accuse me of unfairness; it is you who is being unfair."

Leaping from his seat to go to the head of the somewhat startled horse, he tossed the question over his shoulder. "Kate, how am I being unfair?"

"You've clearly spent months working all this out and thinking of little else. You've had time to get used to the idea. Now you spring all your plans on me; hint that you won't go ahead with your changed career plans without me, which is tantamount to emotional blackmail, and then wonder why I'm upset."

"Ah, but that isn't the real reason, is it my dearest?"

The subject of his intentions fixed him with a baleful look before commenting acidly; "You seem to have it all worked out, so pray tell me."

"Very well, I think there is a part of you that is reluctant to

81

surrender what you regard as your independence. Furthermore, when you returned from the Crimea, your mind filled with reforming ideas for nursing, the provision of a new hospital was only one feature. I suspect that you also cherished the notion that there would be a senior staffing role for you somewhere when it was all completed."

Not a sound broke the silence.

"Am I right Kate?"

Somewhat shamefacedly she turned to grin at him. "How well you know me, don't you?"

"Yes, I think I do; and I love what I know," he replied. "But it won't happen like that, Kate, and I suspect you recognise the fact but have been unwilling to confront it. Now, I have forced the issue."

"You're right, of course," she sighed wistfully. "If I ever have any aspirations in that direction, it will mean going to London to follow the course that Edith is pursuing. I rejected that in favour of campaigning for a new hospital, and even if I started now it is unlikely that I would be in a position to be considered for an appointment by the time the hospital is ready to open."

Watching her restless form pacing in front of him, he felt compelled to ask, "Will it be the most appalling disappointment and hardship for you?"

"Not really. I suppose I had secretly come to accept that it would never happen. You have merely made me face the reality and acknowledge it openly."

Going across to the gate she leaned against it with her chin in her hands and surveyed the scene in front of her. Close at her side, Roland posed his final question.

"So, where does this leave us, my dear?"

Alert as he was to every nuance of her behaviour, even he was unprepared for the answer when it came. With a delicious gurgle of delight she eyed him mischievously and said, "Half way to the altar and a farm by the sounds of it."

Absolutely shaking with relief he clasped her to his body, burying his head in her hair.

"Oh, my darling girl, you have made me the happiest man alive. I pray that you never have cause to regret the decision you have made today."

"I imagine I probably shall, from time to time, reflect on what might have been, because that's the way of the world. In the end, though, it is best to opt for the devil you know than the one you don't!"

Putting his hand under her chin, he raised her face to his and kissed her long and purposefully on the lips. Satisfied, he smiled as he said, "One thing is for sure, Kate. Life with you will never be predictable, orthodox or humdrum."

"No, but it will be very uncomfortable without anywhere to live," she chimed, "so I think you'd better expand upon your plans."

Rather sheepishly, he turned her back to face the gate. With one hand around her shoulder and the other pointing ahead, he managed to say, "You see the buildings to the left of that clump of trees down there? Well, I happen to know that the house, plus a sizeable portion of land, is for sale at a price I can afford."

Pounding on his chest with both fists, his intended proceeded to give indignant voice to her feelings. Laughingly he fended her off before roughly pulling her to him once again. "Kate, my Kate, we shall deal very well together, you and I."

George initially expressed his displeasure with his future son-in-law for not consulting him regarding his farming aspirations. Taking him to one side he confided that, on his death, Painters Court and its acres would come to Kate. He would, therefore, have been more than happy to guide his heir-elect into the intricacies of estate management. Much as such generosity was appreciated, Roland was at great pains to explain his need for independence and the opportunity to prove himself on his own. Such sentiments were not only admirable but even further increased George's respect for the young man.

Although Emily was generally enthusiastic, she was less ecstatic when she saw the size and state of the couple's new abode. In no respect could it be compared with the elegance of her own house but, as her daughter spiritedly informed her, there would be ample opportunity to make their own mark on the place. One or two rooms had already been transformed with furniture stored for Roland from his boyhood home which, coupled with some generous gifts from friends and contributions from Emily and George, gave the pair cause for considerable satisfaction.

The fact that the Patelys were so near to hand was another untold blessing. Tom's father was only too willing to help his farming protegé master the ropes and offer him the wise counsels of his considerable experience, whilst the friendliness and warmth of their farmhouse kitchen was always open to Kate as she developed her new role. The couple could have had no finer mentors.

Thus it was that on Easter Saturday 1858, Major Roland Masterson and Miss Kate Oliphant were married in Morford Cathedral which was filled with family, friends and supporters. Even Emily's outrageously extravagant hat could in no way eclipse the understated elegance of the bride in a stylish but plain dress with an impressive train held in place by a wreath of orange blossom. Walking confidently down the long aisle, on the arm of her undeniably proud father, she had no eyes for anyone but the increasingly dear and familiar figure awaiting her arrival at the chancel steps.

Whilst Roland was constant in his declaration of the love he felt for her, Kate was far more reticent.

"How do I know whether I love you," she had demanded, "when I'm not sure what love is? All I do know is that I admire, trust and respect you and want to be with you. In fact, I can't bear the thought of a life without you in it."

And with these sentiments her doting husband was more than content.

Whatever the fact of the matter, it was less than twelve months later when their union was blessed with the arrival of a child. Unlike George, who had so desperately wanted a son, Roland had set his heart on a little girl who would be just like her mother. After a relatively easy labour and delivery, to which Kate reacted in her customary, unflappable manner, little Sadie made her appearance in the first month of a new year just as a cold winter dawn was breaking. Moved almost to tears by the first glimpse of his daughter he could only keep saying, "She's beautiful, just beautiful."

Kate felt herself to be unimaginably moved by the experience and behaved towards the newcomer with a touching degree of gentleness and possessiveness laced with her inimitable brand of humour.

Emily's reactions were mixed with abhorrence at having to admit to being a grandmother coupled with an expectation that at least this whole unsavoury business had been accomplished and life could continue without any further disruption. Sadly, she was not only proved wrong but very much disconcerted when, within the space of fifteen months, a very angry and vocal John Masterson popped into the world just before midnight, and proceeded to keep everyone awake with his relentless bawls. To Emily's delicate mind such happenings indicated a severe want of restraint in the bedroom. To Kate, however, it was an intimation of a real understanding as to what it meant to love.

Meanwhile, sandwiched between these events, the new hospital began to take shape. Kate remained in constant attendance at all planning meetings, her mind as focused as ever and her ruthlessness relentless. A further decision had been approved to retain and update St. Martha's as a fever hospital which would remain under the control of Miss Upton. The addition of 200 extra beds on a separate site, coupled with Kate's determination to see the advancement of nurse education, created a pressing problem of adequate staffing.

Nurses were not the lowest paid workers in the nineteenth century. Sisters in London could sometimes earn up to twenty-seven shillings a week. However, by far the greatest disincentive to recruitment was the perceived lowliness of status and lack of respectability, which rendered it an unsuitable position for young ladies. Regrettably, there was to be no dramatic break with the past and reform would only come slowly and painfully. It required compromise between pioneering enthusiasts and hospital authorities, not to mention doctors who wanted to keep all staff accountable to them instead of to trained nurses. It was vital, therefore, to appoint a matron who would take the hospital and its aims bravely towards the next century.

Nurses who had received training in London were expected to go out and train others by accepting positions of responsibility in hospitals elsewhere. Thus, it was to St. Thomas's that Kate persuaded the Board to turn, and her delight knew no bounds when Edith was interviewed and appointed to the post as the first matron of the new hospital.

All that remained was to officially name the establishment. So, it was that on a summer's day in 1859 the Duke of Ashbourne officially opened the Morford Infirmary and Kate planted a sapling oak in the middle of the sweep of lawn which separated the two impressive wings of a U-shaped building. Each was 120ft in length and three storeys high. The transom comprised an impressive entrance hall with marble floor displaying the bust of Florence Nightingale. The administrative offices could be found to the left and a large Outpatient department to the right, where the Bishop of Morford held a short service of thanksgiving.

Behind an imposing pair of oak doors in the very centre of the building, the gracious dimensions of the wood-panelled Board Room looked out on to the grounds affording a commanding view of the new wards. The uppermost rooms provided accommodation for junior doctors and the nurses plus a flat for the matron. Miss Nightingale held strong views about the importance of female staff living in the hospital and in rooms opening off the ward corridors. "It promotes efficiency of the nurses and discourages dawdling and gossiping," she maintained.

Each of the six wards, containing 32 beds each, was given a name, rather than a number, often reflecting a person or community whose largesse had made a considerable contribution to the provision of such a facility. As a tribute to the two greatest benefactors, tablets inscribed in gold lettering pronounced the Ashbourne and Oliphant wings respectfully. If Kate was secretly elated by such recognition, an exultant Emily completely failed to hide her satisfaction at the thought of the extra prestige such an honour would bring to her standing in the county. Flanked by an undeniably proud George and Roland she graciously basked in the glory of the occasion. Kate could only marvel and give thanks that so much had been achieved in a comparatively short space of time.

The final touch to a truly memorable day came after the couple returned to their home, still flushed with triumph and reliving every moment. The children were safely in their beds and Kate was seated in comfort sipping a welcome glass of wine. Roland had left the room, shortly to return with an oblong leather box in his hand. To her surprise he knelt in front of her as he placed it in her hands.

As she raised questioning eyes to his, he said, "I wanted you to have a special memento of this day, Kate. I know just how much you have given up in order to be my wife and the mother of our children. I shall never cease to be grateful and I hope this will always serve as a token of my deep love for you and a constant reminder of the path you so courageously trod which led to your achievements."

Slowly Kate lifted the lid to find, nestling on a bed of satin a large, solid silver buckle. An intricate pattern of whirls, leaves, flowers and fruits seemed to chase each other in a dance of finest filigree workmanship, the two halves joining with scarcely a seam.

"It is meant to represent our love, my dearest; two halves made into a whole, each incomplete without the other."

Almost tenderly her fingers caressed the buckle and, to her husband's astonishment, tears slowly began to trickle down her cheeks.

"Tears, Kate? That was not the response I had anticipated. In all the time I have known you I have never seen you cry."

Taking his face between her hands she stroked his beloved features as she whispered, "I love you Roland above all things,"

Morford Infirmary became, in many respects, the model for a county hospital with light, airy and cheerful wards, tasteful furniture and a comfort too seldom seen in an English hospital. If Kate ever felt pangs of disappointment that she was unable to play a hands-on part in the brave new venture resulting from her endeavours, she didn't allow herself to dwell on what might have been.

She could never have imagined the happiness and contentment which stemmed from her role as wife and mother and would certainly not have exchanged it for any other post, no matter how exalted. Any lingering regrets were assuaged by her appointment to the weekly, in-house board which was controlled by the doctors and matron, responsible for the appointment of staff and the day-to-day running of the establishment.

It allowed her to share closely with her friend Edith the problems and successes of the enterprise and she became an astute and sympathetic intermediary between the medical committee and Board of Governors.

Kate became the matron's greatest ally in the early struggle to achieve the adequate staffing such an undertaking demanded if it was to succeed in its aims. Advertisements, placed in *The Lancet* and *The Times*, with the tempting offer of high salaries rising to £25 per year, brought forth good fruit. Probationers were recruited, from the newly formed Institution of Trained Nurses, to learn their skills at the bedside under the supervision of Matron and the Medical Officer. As the Institute contributed five shillings a week for the maintenance of each nurse it was a move welcomed by the Governors who were ever mindful of the enormous financial demands being made on them.

By far the biggest hurdle which Kate and Edith had to overcome was the insistence that domestic cleaning, other than light work, be kept separate from the nursing. Miss Nightingale had advocated that nurses should not be seen as housemaids. "For nurses to scour is nothing but a waste of power," she asserted most vigorously. This message took time to get through to some Board members before it was finally agreed that a staff of scourers would be employed.

Seated on the lawn outside their farmhouse, having tea with Edith, Kate could not but reflect on the good fortune of the past few years. She watched with affection and pride as the infant Sadie ran confidently across the grass, whilst the ever-growing John toddled energetically after her. In the distance she could glimpse Roland working with some of the men in one of the fields. Around her was evidence of the continuing success of their combined effort to make these acres into a viable working farm, and the house into a comfortable home.

Her hand crept to touch the silver buckle attached to the petersham belt encircling her waist which she wore constantly. For the briefest of moments Kate's mind ranged back over all that had happened since that day when she had left Painters Court, and decided there was neither time nor cause for regrets. God was in his heaven and all was indeed well with her world.

Part Two
Sadie Masterson

Chapter One

Farewell to Childhood

The funeral procession emerging from the entrance to Painters Court wound its mournful way along the lane leading to the ancient village church in Sheperdstone.

Four black horses sporting black plumes drew the glass-sided hearse, the coffin covered with white lilies. The frock-coated undertaker walked at the front in a top hat, followed by a stable lad leading a magnificent chestnut hunter with shiny leather riding boots reversed in the stirrups.

A sizable congregation, representative of a wide cross-section of the neighbourhood, awaited their arrival in sombre silence. Behind the seats reserved for the family sat the more affluent members of the farming and business community. The humble villagers huddled together at the back, the men looking somewhat uncomfortable in their unaccustomed formal dress.

The solemn organ music ceased. As one the assembled company rose to their feet and stood in curious but respectful silence as the polished oak coffin, borne on the broad shoulders of six ruddy-faced estate workers, proceeded slowly down the aisle behind the figure of the incumbent sonorously intoning the appropriate sentences.

Heavily veiled, the diminutive figure of Emily Oliphant leaned pathetically on the arm of her son-in-law. Following closely behind came the taller, composed figure of Kate, perhaps surprisingly for that age, flanked by her young children. Sadie, clearly distressed, clung to her arm while John gazed steadfastly ahead, intent on playing the man.

George Oliphant's sudden and traumatic death in 1873 on the hunting field had been a shock to everyone. At sixty-nine he remained vigorous and active, both mentally and physically, being regarded by those close to him as seemingly invincible.

Seated in a pew the fulsome words of the eulogy drifted somewhere above Kate's head as she lost herself in her own memories of the man whose body now rested on the draped bier just in front of her. Not one to openly display her emotions she found herself victim to a hollow sensation inside and felt the occasional urge to swallow deeply in order to maintain her composure. Whatever the vagaries of their early relationship may have been, she and her father had eventually achieved an easy rapport with each other and his passing would leave a considerable void. Not a week passed that he had not found his way to their now flourishing farm at Hollowdene where he took great delight in seeing all that they had accomplished in the last ten years. Always ready with advice when asked - and sometimes when not - she smilingly recalled, he was immensely proud of the home they had made. Thanks, in no small measure, to his periodic generosity it was now considerably larger and more suitably embellished than the day when a disdainful Emily first cast eyes on it. Roland had made a considerable success of his venture and he enjoyed an easy relationship with the older man who also took great pleasure in his two grandchildren, secretly cherishing a hope that he would see young John take an interest in agriculture and estate management. The two could often be found walking the fields together solemnly inspecting the cattle and admiring the crops. They would then return to seek home-made scones and jam in the warm and welcoming farm kitchen after which he would engage both children in a game of draughts or dominoes.

Now it was all over. Readily admitting how much she would miss him Kate, nevertheless, gave quiet but heartfelt thanks for the circumstances that had contrived to bring them closer together.

Aware that the congregation were now standing to sing the final hymn, she rose to her feet but found it well-nigh impossible to join in the poignant strains of 'Abide with me'. At last, with head bowed, she followed her husband and the now openly weeping Emily down the aisle and out into the small churchyard. A wintry sun struggled to cast its beams over the newly dug grave close by the perimeter hedge as the mortal remains of George Oliphant were reverently and finally laid to rest.

The formalities over they adjourned to the Court to be joined by family and close friends for the inevitable refreshment and polite conversation conducted in suitably muted voices. Eventually, it was over. Sadie and John were dispatched to the kitchen in the care of a doting staff while Emily, Roland and Kate, accompanied by the family solicitor, settled themselves in the lounge for the reading of the will.

Clearly George had been a shrewd and careful custodian for, quite apart from Painters Court and the surrounding acres, he was shown to possess a not-inconsiderable sum of money. Following the customary gifts to long-serving members of staff and a small donation to the Morford Infirmary, the remainder was spread between the family.

Emily was left the house in trust for her lifetime and a financial settlement more than sufficient for her needs. The land with any cottages, farm buildings and livestock was bequeathed to Roland with the expressed hope that he would continue to run it with the help of a manager for his lifetime. Upon his death the estate was to be passed on to John.

Kate would inherit any money remaining after the bequests had been settled plus Painters Court itself when Emily died. A desire was expressed that the house be kept in the family. If, however, the decision was taken to sell the property a set proportion of the money raised would be shared with Sadie. In the event of The Court remaining in Kate's possession then it must be left to Sadie on her death.

Removing his pince-nez the solicitor sat back in his chair. A smile betokened the end of the official business and a willingness was expressed to assist in the future should they be desirous of his services.

"I'm sure you will appreciate the care my client has taken to ensure the future well-being of the family and I trust that there is nothing in the will to cause concern," he said.

"On the contrary," said Roland finding his voice. "My father-in-law has been most generous." In truth he had not expected to be mentioned at all and was deeply touched to think that George considered him a capable guardian of the acres on which he had lavished such care and attention. It would also provide John with the most advantageous start should he decide to follow in his father's and grandfather's footsteps at some time in the future.

Turning to look at Kate he found her gazing worriedly in the direction of Emily. Throughout the proceedings she had sat, passively gazing into space, her face giving no clue as to her feelings. Indeed she appeared to be a million miles away and her daughter began to question just how much she had really taken in. For the past year, Kate sometimes had cause to wonder, on occasion, whether Emily's mental faculties were all that they might be. The acerbic tongue was gone along with the demands she was used to make. There were times when her mind seemed to wander beyond what could be considered normal, or she failed to register a remark made in conversation and her memory showed signs of becoming increasingly poor.

"Mother, did you understand what Mr. Bullock has been saying about Father's will, or is there anything you wish to ask him?" she queried gently.

The visibly aging lady gave every indication of genuine consideration then fixed Kate with a sad, unnerving stare before saying, "I didn't see Lady Baverstock at the service, did you? I felt sure she would come, you know."

Roland regarded her with bewilderment as Kate replied, "Yes, Mother, she was there but there were so many people that you couldn't possibly be expected to notice them all."

"Oh, that's all right then. Are we going to have something to eat now that everyone has gone? I do hope cook has prepared something."

Before Kate could respond to this, her mother went on in a tired, pathetic voice, "I don't think I'll dress for dinner tonight. Would you ask if I could have something light on a tray in my room dear?"

Looking apologetically in the bemused solicitor's direction, Kate took her mother's arm saying, "Of course that can be arranged and if you come with me now we'll see to everything."

"No dear, I want to go on my own," she asserted with a trace of her old petulance. "I'll ring for Clara to help me if I want anything. Goodbye Mr. er... so kind of you to visit," she said politely and wafted out through the door which Roland held open for her.

The two men stared at Kate in consternation.

"I had no idea, Mrs. Masterson, no idea at all," Mr. Bullock ventured in sober tones.

Roland was nearly beside himself. "Kate, whatever has happened? I know your Mama has been getting forgetful and seemed rather fey at times but this exhibition is extraordinary. Perhaps it is just the strain of the day and she's tired."

"I'm sure there is an element of that Roland but I think it goes much deeper. She and Father may not have enjoyed the closest of relationships but he was in fact her rock, although she would have died rather than admit it. He was always there to sort things out for her and she never had to think about a thing. I have worried for some time that she was beginning to evince signs of early senility and I think this little episode points strongly to such a diagnosis. Possibly Papa's death has been the final straw."

Sitting himself down again, the solicitor asked whether she had considered how to address the problem.

"Fortunately," said Kate, "the terms of Father's will are a great help. The worst thing would have been a need to sell the Court causing her to move somewhere quite unfamiliar. As things are, she can remain where she is and there is sufficient money to ensure that she will be admirably cared for by Clara who is more than used to her little ways."

Getting to her feet she volunteered in a voice which was considerably brighter than she felt. "I don't think we should attach too much importance to this episode. She will probably be totally different tomorrow. After all, this has been a long and emotional day for her."

Little could they know that it would mark the beginning of a rapid decline into an almost second childhood. Mercifully, Emily was spared any comprehension of her condition and she enjoyed every comfort that could be provided by her faithful staff despite the fact that she frequently knew neither them nor her family.

Kate visited as often as her commitments allowed but she frankly dreaded it. The maternal spark and those interfering habits, which had so irritated her in the past, were completely extinguished. If her mother had once been a distant but annoying thorn in the flesh, she sometimes thought that state would be easier to confront than the pathetic, mindless stranger facing her now who she barely knew. Kate was primarily a practical person of action and for once she felt completely out of her depth and lost as to what to do.

The one who took the situation completely in her stride was the young Sadie who seemed to delight in keeping her grandmother company for hours on end. She would sit beside the vacant figure and read to her tirelessly, playing games with her dolls or prattling away in her childish way quite undeterred by any lack of response. If Emily required help with her meals the little girl was more than ready to feed her and failed to be daunted by some of her rather unsavoury habits.

The domestic staff adored her and maintained that she not only had a good effect on the relentlessly aging lady but claimed that life was so much easier when she was around. This resulted in Sadie spending an increasing amount of time at Painters Court, even sleeping there when the school was on holiday.

Whilst thankful that her mother's life was as pleasant as possible under the circumstances, Kate frequently voiced her concern over the level of Sadie's involvement. It wasn't natural for a young girl to opt to devote every available moment in such a way. However, on reflection she had to admit that her daughter was quite different to her contemporaries in many ways.

Sadie had been the easiest of babies, especially when measured against the determined, noisy and outgoing John. Possessed with a gregarious character that was impossible to ignore, he completely overshadowed his quiet, amenable sister who patiently endured endless pranks and teasing at his hands without complaint. That he adored her wasn't in doubt but she simply wasn't interested in the games he wanted to play or the outdoor life which consumed his every waking moment. Revelling in his father's company, he could invariably be found somewhere on the farm with Roland quite absorbed in agricultural pursuits. Horse-riding had become a passion from the moment he first sat astride the reliable pony chosen for the purpose of teaching the rudiments of equestrian techniques. His constant plea was to be allowed to join in the hunt of which Roland was an expert follower. Despite several attempts, nothing would persuade Sadie into the saddle.

Both children attended a small private school, for their parents were determined to give them the best education possible and were keen that they should be in a position to mix with other children. Whilst John generally resented the hours of enforced incarceration in the classroom, and did the bare minimum to satisfy his teachers, Sadie applied herself willingly to her studies. Whilst she was liked by her peers and was content to join them in their pastimes there was no doubt that she was much happier in adult company. When Kate was busy in the kitchen baking or making preserves the little girl would contentedly stand alongside copying every move made. In just such a way she couldn't wait for the opportunity to spend time with Clara at Painters Court helping to prepare the bird-like portions of food which constituted all that Emily could be persuaded to consume.

Kate often wondered how she and Roland had managed to produce such a serious child. Petite and undeniably attractive as she was, there was no evidence of the rousing feistiness that coursed through her mother's veins.

"Thank goodness for that," Roland could be heard to say when his wife voiced her concerns. "I couldn't cope with two like you," he joked affectionately. "Don't worry about her. Just be thankful that she is so agreeable and accept her for the person she is."

"That's all very well dear," countered his wife, "but I do wish we could foster slightly more spirit in her."

"Why, for heaven's sake?" he persisted. "She is absolutely adorable and a peacefully refreshing soul to be with after John and his frenetic antics. Not to mention your boundless energy for committees and organising," he added with a twinkle.

For once Kate failed to rise to such good-humoured provocation, merely commenting rather pithily: "That is precisely the worry. Without a bit more persistence and determination she is liable to become just a delightful door-mat, happy to do everyone's bidding and hideously taken advantage of in the process."

Refusing to take his spouse seriously, Roland was content to retort good humouredly: "Exactly so. Just like her long-suffering father! Clearly she takes after me."

Realising that she was unlikely to make any further headway on the subject, Kate gave up any attempt at further discussion though little appreciating just how those prophetic words would return later to haunt her.

Contrary to everyone's expectations, Emily continued in her twilight existence for several years until, in the early hours of a June morning in 1877, she slipped away, almost imperceptibly.

Since completing her schooling Sadie had virtually moved into Painters Court in order to help the now aging Clara in the kitchen and to minister to her grandmother's needs. Her parents had insisted on rewarding her financially for such an act of devotion. They felt that the years she had so freely given to Emily's care were over and above anything that could have been expected from a granddaughter.

Kate, who had kept her company when they realised that the end was in sight, breathed a silent sigh of relief. Despite the fact that both she and her mother had mellowed with the passage of time, the circumstances of those early years were etched too deeply in her memory and prevented any great feelings of sadness.

For Sadie, however, it was different. She had never known a person other than the one whose fragile mind was always locked away within an equally frail body. Her love for the helpless invalid had been unquestioning and unconditional so, quite apart from the fact that this was her first experience of death, it was inevitable that the event should occasion considerable distress. She made no attempt to check the tears as they coursed down her pretty face. Kate rose hurriedly to her feet and went round the bed in order to draw her grief-stricken daughter into a comforting embrace.

"I know how upsetting this is for you, my darling, but try to be thankful too, that Grandma is now at peace." Quietly, she went on: "You didn't know the lively character that she used to be, nor how much she would have hated the hand that fate eventually dealt her. I shall always be grateful that she had no awareness of her condition."

Receiving no response from the silent but shaking girl, she continued: "However, the thing I am most grateful for is your unselfishness in caring for her so loyally. Without that she wouldn't have been able to stay in the home she loved for all these years. Take comfort from that, Sadie. You have done so well and we are all so proud of you and appreciative of the part you played."

Raising her tear-stained face she asked in a troubled voice: "What will become of this place now, Mother? You are right, Grandma really did love it you know and I can't bear to think of it being sold."

Smiling, Kate gently reassured her daughter. "Don't you worry your head about that now because it was all taken care of in the will Grandpa made. I haven't had time to work out the details yet but Painters Court will definitely remain in the family, I promise you."

So saying they pulled the curtains across the windows of Emily's bedroom and descended the stairs to break the news to the staff and to set about the tasks in front of them.

A week later, Emily was laid to rest beside her husband. It was no surprise to anyone when, shortly after, Sadie announced her intention to train as a nurse. The bewilderment came from Kate's attempts to deter her from pursuing such a course.

"I thought that at least you would understand and be on my side," the puzzled girl responded in bewilderment. "How you can possibly forbid me something which you yourself entered upon is beyond my comprehension."

Support came from an unexpected quarter when John chimed in. "It'll look a bit odd among your friends, Mother, in view of your constant crusading to encourage others to engage in the work. I thought you were always moaning about the shortage of suitable candidates, and here you are turning our Sadie down."

His sister cast a grateful glance in his direction but, having said his piece he lost interest and sauntered from the room.

Roland, ever the diplomat, went to place an arm round his daughter's shoulder and suggested that they listen calmly to Kate's explanations.

Casting her gaze on the unhappy young face that was regarding her somewhat sulkily she ventured to placate her. "My dear, it isn't that I am against nursing - of course I'm not. It's just that I'm not sure that it is right for you."

Swiftly interrupting, there was no mistaking the bitterness in Sadie's voice. "How you can presume to make such a judgment after all I did for Grandma, defies belief. You even commended me, if you remember."

"I'm not denying any of that for one moment," she affirmed. "You are a gentle, sweet, capable and caring young woman and I am very proud of you."

"Then why?" Sadie's tremulous voice trailed away as her father put his finger to his lips, indicating that she be silent.

Disregarding the interruption, Katy swept on. "You see, admirable as all those qualities are, to be a nurse requires a certain strength and stamina. It is one thing looking to the needs of one old lady in delightful surroundings and quite another matter contending with the demands made by a ward full of people, largely consisting of the deprived and the great unwashed. It imposes a huge physical, mental and emotional strain and I worry that it will all be too much for you."

She paused for a moment and Sadie seized the opportunity to challenge her once again. In tones of sweet reason she commented: "I just don't understand how the very self-same things that were right for you can possibly be so wrong for me. We have had the same upbringing, have we not?"

Mindful of her daughter's feelings towards her late grandmother, and not wishing to disillusion her in any way, she forbore to tell of the real reasons that lay behind her earlier desire to leave home. Instead, facing her squarely, she said: "Let us strike a bargain, darling. I will accede to your wishes but only if I have your promise that you will admit to me if you find things are too much for you. Don't think for one moment that you will have failed. I think it is a courageous step that you are taking so can we settle for a trial run?"

Before Sadie could say anything Roland said: "There now my little lass, I think that is an eminently fair compromise don't you? You see, I have some idea what is behind your mother's feelings. She went to hell and back out in the Crimea, and so did I. Because we love you so much we don't want anything like that for you."

"For goodness sake Father, I'm going to Morford Infirmary, not to war," his jubilant offspring countered as she flung her arms round his neck.

Hearing his sister's shriek of joy, John opened the door saying: "Thank goodness! I take it everything has been resolved to the mutual satisfaction of all and we can now have something to eat?"

Not even her son's far from dulcet tones could muffle Kate's sharply raised voice.

"Morford Infirmary, Sadie. You intend to nurse at Morford? I thought you would want to go to St. Thomas's in London."

Silence fell once more only to be broken by Sadie's uncustomarily sarcastic tongue saying: "What's the matter Mother? Afraid I'll let you down if I go to your precious hospital?"

"Don't be ridiculous," both parents chorused in unison.

"If that's what you want," said Kate, "I shall be more than happy and will follow your progress with interest."

"In which case," ventured her irrepressible son, "I'd opt for London!"

At this they all joined in the general laughter and repaired to the kitchen in order to satisfy John's constant demands for food.

Chapter Two

Changes and Difficulties

On a beautiful early autumn day in September 1878 Roland brought the carriage bearing a slightly diffident Sadie and her luggage to a halt at the imposing entrance to Morford Infirmary. Now that the arrangements were made and the actual moment had arrived she felt the first nervous fluttering rising in her stomach. To their joint relief her mother had decided to remain at Hollowdene thereby allowing her to present herself with the minimum of fuss. Kate was all too well known to most people at the hospital and the last thing Sadie wanted was preferential treatment. Not that there was any chance of that as the matron had been very quick to point out.

Edith, Sadie's godmother, had long since left after receiving a more prestigious post back in London. Two most unsatisfactory replacements had followed her in quick succession, both completely failing to maintain the standards of nursing or ward cleanliness that had been set. At last, on Edith's recommendation, a Miss Burton had arrived from Guy's Hospital to take on the mantle of matron and it was this rather formidable person who would oversee the training of the newest recruit.

Although, when talking to Kate, she had been adamant that Sadie would receive no favours, she was secretly delighted to welcome her. Nursing still wasn't regarded as suitable employment for young ladies and it was often quite a struggle to attract a good level of students. Therefore, the arrival of such a high profile addition to the ranks could prove to be a very useful local recruitment tool.

Bidding her father an affectionate goodbye, and with the assurance that she would come home at the first opportunity, she made haste to follow the porter carrying her belongings to one of the rooms allocated to nurses on the very top floor of the building.

A whole new world was about to open up in front of her but, with Kate's early reservations still ringing in her ears, she prayed fervently that she would prove capable of rising to the challenge.

The next few days passed in a confusion of sights, smells and experiences. Dressed in an ankle-length grey uniform dress, which was mercifully made of softer fabric than the previously irritant material, Sadie wrestled to attach the unbending stiff collar. Black leather ankle boots fastened with buttons encased a dainty pair of feet which would soon be aching beyond anything she could possibly envisage. Finally donning a white starched apron and cap, which made her look more like a maid, she prepared to be inducted into her chosen occupation. At the end of a week she was exhausted and her overriding impression was that there were an awful lot of patients, a prolific amount of work and not many staff.

The hours were long and there were no days off or weekends but, as her mother was quick to point out, they were an improvement on those which she had experienced. Starting at 8am she toiled away until 9.45pm having enjoyed a princely two hours respite at some stage and a part of each Sunday. Nine months of each year were spent on day duty followed by three months on nights when the hours ranged from 9.45pm to 8.30am and it was not unusual for one nurse to have thirty patients to care for. Provided with a candle, by the light of which she was expected to pad splints and turn sheets in her spare minutes, it at least reduced the chance of falling asleep on duty. Punishment for such an offence was instant dismissal.

Sadie very soon came to appreciate her mother's wonderful home farm cooking as never before and recalled with nostalgia those dainty trays she had lovingly prepared for her grandmother.

Nurses' meals were simple and certainly not lengthy affairs. Only fifteen minutes were allowed for breakfast, dinner and supper, although tea-time presented the luxury of a full half hour respite. There was only ever one course consisting of fish or meat, except on Sunday when a usually rather stodgy pudding would be produced.

Nevertheless, all the nurses found the chance to indulge in 'snapping time' for milk and bread and cheese between 10 and 11am. Indeed, the quantity of milk consumed became so vast that the Board Members were forced to enquire if the staff were bathing in it. However, the amount was not restricted for fear that, without it, many would fail to sustain the demands of the very heavy working day.

A register had been commenced of nurses employed at the Infirmary which told a salutary tale. Kate perused it with even greater interest than the other Trustees, for it showed just how many candidates proved to be unfit by temperament or lack of stamina for the gruelling work. Failure of health was often a reason for leaving but others quit simply because they couldn't settle to the discipline. Undoubtedly, physical strength was the greatest asset possible for any woman embarking upon such a career.

Although the hours worked made it virtually impossible for Sadie to visit her home at Hollowdene, she usually had a chance to exchange a few brief words with her mother during her frequent visits on hospital business. Kate observed that she was painfully pale and thin and she wondered just how long she would be able to sustain the pace. Each week she would bring with her tempting offerings from the farm kitchen and the old stool, that had once supported her own aching feet at St. Martha's, was retrieved from the attic, recovered, and given to her daughter.

If Sadie was finding the going tough, so were many of the others and one of the most valuable resources open to them was the mutual support system which evolved from shared adversity. From the very first day she had been drawn into a growing friendship with a newcomer in the adjacent room on the nurse's corridor.

Betsy was a typically outspoken Londoner and possessed a wonderful sense of humour. One of a large family headed by a father more interested in drink than work and a harassed mother forced to accept any chance that presented in order to support her brood, she was quite relieved to find an opportunity to put space between herself and her dysfunctional clan. When looking for an opening in nursing she certainly couldn't meet the elitist demands of some of the hospitals in the capital. Keen to discover whether the country roads were in fact better paved with gold she had willingly headed for the provinces.

Life around Betsy wasn't dull and her general air of irreverence and good spirits was a tonic for the soul. She was the complete antithesis to Sadie in every respect but they very soon became inseparable and both had different strengths to offer. Betsy's tirelessness and energy carried the frailer Sadie in its wake, whilst the latter's undoubted intellectual superiority helped the struggling Betsy to grapple with the intricacies of the job.

There were no lectures and all tuition was given on the wards. This teaching engendered in most a passion for further knowledge in order to understand better the problems and needs of the patients. Any spare minutes 'off duty' were often used to practise bandaging, and the application of dressings and poultices.

As professional nursing was established, important developments in medicine advanced alongside. In particular, two crucial breakthroughs began to revolutionise surgical practice.

Although Sir James Young Simpson had introduced chloroform as an anaesthetic in surgical operations in 1847, it didn't really take off at Morford until much later. The new recruits were fascinated to see a safer and more perfect reduction of dislocations and fractures being performed, as well as the relief of pain and suffering, resulting from this recent innovation. To Kate, it was an amazing advancement and she absorbed every detail of the changing trends in her discussions with Sadie.

The second weapon in the armour against disease was the introduction of antiseptic surgery. Prior to this there was very scant knowledge of asepsis and Sadie found her training was the first to incorporate Professor Lister's method of dealing with operation cases using an antiseptic spray and dressings. As a direct result of this, annual deaths directly following surgery were reckoned in single figures for the first time in the Infirmary's history.

This discovery also had implications for the work of the nurses. Suppurating wounds were required to be diligently cleaned and dressed and poultices applied four-hourly. Great attention was paid to personal toiletry needs. Patients were most conscientiously washed from head to toe with due frequency, clean linen was used unsparingly and every bed-ridden patient had their backs and hips washed and rubbed with methylated spirits and starch at least once a day. The iron bedsteads were carbolised each week until the whole hospital reeked of carbolic.

For Sadie, Betsy and their colleagues, life was steady but hard work all day long, but joy and love coupled with immense interest and satisfaction in the labour lent wings to it.

After almost a year both nurses were thrilled to be awarded a complete half day off together and arrangements were made to extract the maximum enjoyment from such an unexpected bonus. Promptly at two o'clock they descended the Infirmary steps to find John seated at the reins of the family carriage. Sadie hastily made the introductions and they both clambered in covering the distance in high spirits.

By the time of their arrival at Hollowdene, the normally irrepressible Betsy was steadily retreating into a state of utter bemusement. "It's all green," she said, "nothing but mile upon mile of grass and hardly any houses." Regarding her affectionately, Sadie just smiled. "Yes, isn't it lovely? I never realised just how much I miss it."

"But it's so quiet. Where are all the people, and whatever do you find to do?" her companion persisted.

John, who had opened the door to help them alight, caught the last remark and saved his sister the need to reply. With a wicked grin he quipped: "Come with me when I milk the cows and you'll find out!"

"Cows!" wailed Betsy. "I wouldn't know one end of a cow from the other."

"Don't worry; you'll pretty soon discover the difference," was his reply, heavy with meaning.

Roland and Kate, their arms affectionately entwined, stood eager to greet the party and hastened to welcome and reassure their clearly abstracted guest. Then, after enveloping their daughter in a loving embrace they filed into the house to enjoy the cool, refreshing drinks thoughtfully prepared in advance.

John declared that the endless babble of conversation was worse than the noise of the geese in the farmyard and soon tired of the constant stream of questions and answers. There was so much to cram into such a short time and they determined to make the most of every precious moment.

Betsy rapidly recovered her usual aplomb and entered wholeheartedly into the discussions. Both girls were eager to learn from Kate of proposals being considered for the future development of 'their' hospital. Until now children under the age of six had been excluded from admission but plans were afoot to build a dedicated children's block, furnished with cots. Some years earlier, under Kate's determined leadership, a 'Hospital League of Friends' had been formed. Thanks to their hard work and regular contributions the money was now in hand to finance this project.

"I'm even going to resurrect your pram from the attic and present it to them so that the babies can be taken into the grounds and get some fresh air," she enthused.

Roland laughed goodnaturedly before saying: "As you can see, your Mama has got the bit firmly between her teeth again."

"As you will have gathered Betsy, our revered mother is a great organiser," John chipped in.

"I thought you'd been uncommonly quiet," retorted his mother. Rising to her feet she suggested that they all go out for a walk around the farm whilst leaving her to put the finishing touches to a meal which, she said to her son rather pointedly, "will hopefully justify my so called 'organising abilities'."

Following her into the kitchen Sadie said: "Mother, can I ask if you have decided what is going to happen to Painters Court yet?"

Turning to face her daughter Kate smiled gently before saying: "Don't worry darling, I'm not going to sell it. The problem is in finding the right use for it. The place is far too big for anything we are ever likely to need. However, it certainly can't remain shut up for much longer because that won't do the fabric any good."

Vigorously whisking some cream in a basin she could do no more than reassure the anxious girl on whom the old house exerted such a pull.

"You really do love the Court, don't you?" she said.

"It's the nearest place to heaven I can imagine," her daughter responded somewhat extravagantly.

"Goodness me, I was hoping heaven would be a little less demanding in upkeep," Kate joked. "Now, off you go and join the others and don't fret yourself about Painters Court."

That night, closeted together in Sadie's room, and surrounded by a range of 'nourishing goodies', the two friends contentedly relived their day which had proved such a welcome oasis in an otherwise whirlwind of continual hard work.

Over the next eighteen months subtle changes evinced themselves in the tenor of the Infirmary. The festive season had seen the provision of Christmas trees with presents for patients and staff for the first time. This was symbolic of the feeling that there should be a little amusement and pleasure in hospital life. The grounds were used for walking, taking gentle exercise and the playing of games. A library was set up and people were encouraged to donate books and magazines, while approved ladies were invited to read to the patients. Carefully selected pictures were hung on the walls, courtesy of the Bishop. These were viewed with mixed feelings by the nurses who had to dust them!

Prayers were still said on the ward daily but, with the appointment of a Chaplain, there were now services in the hospital chapel and Bible classes for those nurses who could summon sufficient energy and enthusiasm to attend them.

Mercifully, financial contributions continued to match the demands made upon them. The Infirmary was regularly the recipient of various legacies and the funds gathered from regular Hospital Sunday collections which averaged some £2,000 a year. Some factory workers were also pledging one penny per week from their wages which yielded a welcome £1,500 annually and, by these means, Morford Infirmary continued to grow.

True to her word, Kate eventually found a use for Painters Court which met with ecstatic approval from her daughter. Many hospitals in the busy cities had found that some of their patients benefitted considerably from facilities provided by a more healthy environment in which to recuperate. A fortnight's rest in a country house often worked wonders to restore their well-being before they were forced to resume their work, often in ill-lit and poorly ventilated factories. Consequently a plethora of small country convalescent homes attached to larger city hospitals were coming into being.

When Kate approached the governing body with a proposal that they may like to consider the use of Painters Court for such a purpose there was almost universal approval.

The necessary legal contracts were drawn up whereby Morford Infirmary would lease the property from the Masterson family at a very modest rate for a minimum period of five years and, thereafter, renewable annually. The distance of the house from Morford posed no difficulty as the twice weekly visiting arrangements accorded to patients' families could be undertaken via the regular carrier.

Such a venture also proved popular with the local community for whom it afforded welcome employment as domestics and orderlies to assist the nurses who would be provided from the hospital on a rotation system. The very thought that she may one day find herself in the fortunate position of ministering to others in the very place that had played such an important part in her life filled Sadie with happiness. It would make all the hard work seem worthwhile.

Unfortunately, before that day came, clouds were looming on the horizon.

During the training all nurses were required to spend twelve weeks at the original St. Martha's which was now a designated fever hospital. The building had been updated since those days when the young Kate had walked the wards there but it still wasn't the most salubrious place in which to work.

Sadie had just completed a demanding stint in theatres, which seemed to involve a phenomenal amount of cleaning and boiling and carbolising, and was looking forward to returning to the familiar routine of a ward. Therefore, the news that her next assignment was to be the fever unit didn't exactly thrill her. "I don't know a thing about infectious diseases," she wailed to Betsy.

"Come on, love," her friend coaxed. "Just look on it as another of those hurdles you keep telling me we have to jump."

So, with uncustomary poor grace she vacated her familiar room and moved her belongings into St. Martha's.

Across the country fever hospitals were almost constantly full with cases of diphtheria and scarlet fever, typhoid and cholera, erysipelas and whooping cough. Bad drainage and water supplies, poor hygiene and housing caused many of the infectious diseases and resulted in severe epidemics on occasion. Similarly, any actual knowledge regarding cross infection was rudimentary and it was inevitable that staff would succumb themselves from time to time. Those who happened to be physically exhausted, or at a particularly low ebb, were especially vulnerable.

Sadie had scarcely been in post for more than a fortnight when she suddenly developed a sore throat which was soon accompanied by a feverish headache.

When the hands of the ward clock indicated the time for her to take her two-hour break she thankfully made her way to her room, undressed and sank gratefully under the covers. When she failed to return on duty a nurse was sent to investigate and found her shivering with rigors and chattering teeth. By the end of the day she was herself a patient in the hospital, a victim of scarlet fever.

Kate and Roland were beside themselves when the news reached Hollowdene and they set off for Morford in haste. A doctor assured them that everything necessary was being done and the best nursing care possible provided but there was absolutely no question of them being allowed to see their daughter. Thus, they were mercifully spared the sight of the red rash which eventually covered her entire body and roughened the skin, nor witness the vomiting attacks or her swollen, white furred tongue on which protruded bright red spots. Painfully inflamed tonsils made swallowing a torture and her temperature remained unusually high.

The news spread rapidly, for Sadie was well liked by her peers and highly regarded by the staff generally. Betsy was devastated and kept a close watch hoping to catch a glimpse of the Mastersons. Kate was similarly desirous to see her daughter's friend in order to discover details regarding the state of Sadie's health in the weeks leading up to this nightmare.

Betsy couldn't really shed any further light on the matter. "Was she overtired? Was she complaining of feeling unwell?" pressed the worried Kate, but the girl hadn't noticed anything out of the ordinary.

Turning to Roland she said: "This is just what I have always dreaded. Now do you see why I didn't want her to nurse. She isn't robust enough."

With a hand placed gently on each shoulder he sought to catch her gaze before saying: "Do calm yourself dearest. You're not thinking clearly. Remember all your colleagues in the Crimea? Are you saying that those unfortunates who contracted disease shouldn't have been out there? You know that's not true. This could have happened to Sadie at any time, my love,"

"Well, it's happened to her here and she was wide open to it poor child," she retorted petulantly.

Betsy, by now thoroughly alarmed, asked somewhat tearfully, "She is going to be alright Mrs. Masterson, isn't she?"

Kate either didn't hear or chose to ignore the question. Seldom had she felt so helpless but they could only wait.

Nobody denied that Sadie had undergone a most serious illness. Mercifully, by the end of three weeks she was sufficiently recovered to sit out of bed for short periods. The recommendation was made that she would be better off in a healthy country environment in which to recuperate and with thankful hearts her parents took her home to the farm. Kate delightedly returned to nursing mode and her greatly weakened daughter was quite content to be cossetted.

Nevertheless, the day came when Sadie decided it was time to return to the Infirmary. Once again, Kate tried with even greater determination to dissuade her.

"Mother, stop fussing," she said. "I was just unlucky but I am fully recovered and no harm done." So she faced the prospect of completing her training, little realising just how much this episode would colour the whole of her future life.

***

Sadie's return to the Infirmary coincided with the opening of the long-awaited Children's Hospital. Three wards had been built on a site adjoining the central wing of the existing building. Equipped with iron cots, mostly sponsored by firms or individuals, and each bearing a plaque to commemorate the fact, this new facility could accommodate sixty infants.

It was to prove a landmark in specific provision for the young who, until now, had invariably remained in their homes cared for by the family and supported by visits from a doctor if the parents could afford the fee. This accounted, in no small measure, for the high infant mortality rate which prevailed particularly among the working classes.

In view of her student's recent illness Matron decided to assign Sadie to the new unit. Certainly there would be no heavy lifting to tax her and it was felt that the whole ambience would provide a better and kinder environment in which to resume her duties. Kate was somewhat relieved by this news and thrilled that her daughter would be among the first to work on an enterprise to which she herself had once devoted so much voluntary time and effort. Her pleasure was as nothing to Sadie's excitement and the envy of poor Betsy who was struggling to cope with the manifest problems of demented geriatrics and the relentless physical demands resulting from the nature of the illness.

"Talk about the cradle and the grave," she quipped. "And I know which end I'd rather be. I don't think I've seen anything as sad and depressing as the ward full of old souls I'm working with at the moment. To think that I could come to an end like that," she shuddered.

"Then don't think about it," her friend advised.

So Sadie's training neared the end but the icing on the cake was her secondment to the convalescent home at Painters Court for the final three months. Despite the alterations and adaptations which, of necessity, had been made to the place, it still reflected the dreams of her childhood and exerted the same magical pull.

By dint of perseverance and hard work, against the odds Sadie achieved her goal, undeniably proud of all she had accomplished.

At about this time it became the custom for nurses who had completed the necessary training to be allowed to wear petersham belts fastened with ornamental silver buckles. A few hospitals designed their own which were presented to successful candidates, while some girls received them as gifts or bought one for themselves.

Sadie's cup of happiness, which was already full, had cause to overflow on the day Kate presented her with the silver buckle given to her by her beloved husband all those years before. It was a decision in which both parents were united, considering it a completely appropriate reward for all her hard work and ultimate success.

There was no doubt, however, that this triumph had come at a price as it became increasingly clear that Sadie's illness had undoubtedly left her with a less robust constitution. She tired easily and could become quite breathless on occasion, leading them to hope secretly that she would change her mind about continuing with a nursing career. However, nothing was further from Sadie's mind. The question was, what course should it take?

Back in 1867 Miss Nightingale had a vision for nursing which went far beyond the provision of good hospital care. In a letter to Mr. Henry Bonham Carter she wrote: "My view, you know, is that the ultimate destination of all nursing is the nursing of the sick in their own homes. I look to the abolition of all hospitals and workhouse infirmaries. But it is no use to talk about the year 2,000."

Even before that message had been conveyed, although there was no national formalisation or standardisation for the care of the sick in their own homes, there were some charitable organisations, such as the Quakers, the Anglican Oxford Movement, the Protestant Sisters of Charity and the Catholic Sisters of Mercy, which became associated with the concept.

However, it was the great philanthropist William Rathbone who first pioneered the embryo of a community nursing service in Liverpool following the death of his beloved wife. He had been extremely impressed with the services provided by a Mrs. Mary Robinson who attended his wife during her last illness, which had served to ease her discomforting problems immensely. He determined to do everything in his power to make this facility more widely available and to try to establish it on a recognised footing.

In 1861 he formed a society in that city which was able to train its nurses at the Infirmary and then send them out into the homes of the poor, and the private houses of those who could afford to hire them. He set the standards and provided the impetus. Prior to this there had only been 'Parish Nurses' whose names were held by the local clergy and were financed from parish funds or private donations. These were little more than well-meaning local women prepared to visit the homes of those folk, usually in childbirth or at death's door, who needed assistance, although family members were invariably the greatest providers of care at such times.

Once Sadie embarked upon her training her mother had followed her progress with a keenly observant eye, and a not-infrequent 'tut' of disapproval when a new, and in her opinion, unnecessary innovation, would be forthcoming on occasion. Indeed, it sometimes required the gentle, restraining imprecations of her more tactful spouse to stay that autocratic streak which lurked beneath her generally benign exterior. Now, she was to be faced with yet another advance.

She still maintained her connections with the Infirmary by serving on the governing body, and could vividly recall that earlier campaign to generate the necessary capital to establish an assured future for the hospital in Morford, which now took its place alongside the best in the provinces. Nevertheless, every penny raised was still needed to keep the existing medical services afloat.

It was with a measure of concern that she watched as developments began to take place which threatened to cause immense problems for the area. Toward the end of the nineteenth century people were beginning to make the connection between insanitary conditions, poor housing, poverty and disease.

Ironically, the urbanisation fostered by the industrial revolution, created growing misery for the poor in the midst of increasing affluence. As folk flocked into the city in search of better employment and the hope of improved wages, so the green landscape that had once virtually surrounded the Infirmary was giving way to an ever-increasing sprawl of tightly packed terrace houses in narrow streets. In Morford the drainage was still miserably defective and most sewers poured their contents into the sluggish stream which wound its way through the city. Privies and cesspools for collective use remained commonplace, for only a small number of homes were supplied with water closets. It would take the economic depression to pave the way for the Liberal reforms of the early part of the next century.

Therefore, when the news reached the Infirmary governors of the Liverpool plan to treat the poor sick in their homes, it inevitably became a local talking point. It was with great sadness that Kate had to bow to the general consensus that it would be impossible and improvident to embark upon any further such undertakings at a time when finances were stretched to the limit. Little did she realise the impact such a decision would have on her daughter.

Sadie, with the still-present memories of the demands that her grandmother's final illness imposed upon a family comfortably placed to meet them, could only chafe in frustration against the restrictions preventing the improved provision of any meaningful level of care for the poorer, and often uneducated, working classes in Morford. Closely involved as she was with this section of the community, who literally queued up to fill the available beds in the hospital, Sadie's tender heart ached for them. What hope was there for some of her patients once they were discharged into that world of social deprivation, inadequate sanitation and deficient nutrition, she constantly asked herself? Finally, she made a decision. If the Infirmary wouldn't establish a home nursing team, she would become a parish nurse attached to one of the charitable bodies. At least she would be able to put her training to good effect in an area largely populated by well-meaning lay people.

One of the local Parish Superintendents was quick to take advantage of Sadie's offer and, within a remarkably short space of time, she had left the confines of the Infirmary for greater freedom and independence in the city streets.

Chapter Three

Out Into Another World

Sadie pulled the folds of the long brown cloak more closely round her slender frame and navigated her way across the cobbles, all the while trying to avoid the rubbish strewn around. The other hand grasped a capacious carpet bag which carried an assortment of articles appropriate to the various nursing tasks that may be required of her. There was also a book in which to record the visits made and the care given.

By the 1880s the development of industry in Morford had resulted in a distinct hierarchy within the community. The labouring classes and the unemployed huddled in pockets of wretched poverty and inadequate housing in the back courts and alleys of the city. It was nothing to find two bedroom dwellings housing upwards of eight people, many of them adults. Possessed with the poorest of sanitation most were fit only for demolition. Water was frequently contaminated by the filthy oozings and drainings from slaughterhouses, muck heaps and overflowing middens and the resulting stench was nauseous.

The well-to-do working classes were amply provided with comfortable and healthy dwellings which had been built on the fringes of the city. However, through sickness, unemployment or bereavement, even the well-to-do could find themselves having to forsake these superior homes through want of the ability to pay the higher rents which they commanded.

Inbetween these two extremes were pockets of neat rows of affordable, functional terraces of five-or-six roomed houses, uniform in appearance, the majority being occupied by journeyman shoemakers. Morford had become a recognised centre of the footwear industry and those employed in it were proud of their craftsmanship which was largely handed down from father to son.

In nearly every street men could be found in huts in the yard, a spare room indoors, or sitting on a chair in the front doorway, working away at their trade. The shoemakers needed to live close to the source of their work so interspersed throughout the area were the warehouses, factories, and shops which they served.

Despite the slight chill in the early morning air, the doors to many of the terrace houses were open and men in leather, or white cotton aprons and women in pinafores, sat each busily occupied with their particular task, carried out over a muted hum of neighbourly conversation.

Sadie loved visiting these homes for they were usually cleaner and brighter and the standards of health and hygiene were in marked contrast to those in the poorer areas where it was virtually impossible to offer any but the most rudimentary care. Money was in short supply, therefore the necessary goods which would have made life more sustainable were unavailable. As a result, all attempts to educate these unfortunate individuals usually fell on deaf ears, consequently the mortality rates for both children and adults were high.

The shoe-workers were generally friendly souls who enjoyed a reasonable standard of living, welcomed a visit from the nurse and usually respected her advice and efforts on their behalf.

Although knowledge regarding the causes of disease was still in its infancy, doctors were beginning to recognise that certain occupations often seemed to spawn a proliferation of different illnesses.

Despite the absence of belching, factory chimneys and noisy machinery, shoe making was regarded as an unpleasant and often unhealthy occupation. The different processes undertaken in the production of footwear were numerous and each carried certain health risks.

'Finishers' constantly inhaled fumes from the gas used to heat their tools and were prone to respiratory problems and dermatitis.

'Hand-sewn' workers, seated for hours in a bent position on low stools, often fell victim to heart and lung disease only too visibly apparent by the classic deformity of the rib-cage known as 'boot-makers chest'.

Constant manipulation and tugging at the needles led to Reynaud's phenomena, known as 'dead hand' or 'white finger', and tenosynivitis resulted from strained fingers and thumbs.

By far the greatest scourge, however, was tuberculosis, or consumption, or phthisis as it was then called. It was usually the most common cause of death recorded and accounted for the demise of over one third of footwear workers which merely increased with mechanisation within a factory environment. Dust inhaled by finishers was a prime suspect but the disease was twice as common among the clickers.

'Clicking' - the cutting of the sections of leather for the uppers - was an exclusively male occupation. These were the top men of the trade commanding the highest wages, usually after a lengthy apprenticeship. Leather accounted for half the total cost of production, and skill in matching it and economy in cutting it were crucial to an employer's profits.

However, inhalation of the powder and fibres from the cut leather often wreaked a savage toll, not only in tuberculosis but in nasal cancer. The popular habit of snuff-taking, in order to keep awake, simply served to worsen the problem which was also exacerbated by a thorough hatred of open windows, which were considered to deliver death-dealing draughts.

As Sadie approached her destination she began to mentally prepare herself for what she would find when she finally reached 47 Inkerman Street. According to the instructions she had received her patient was a widow in the final stages of tuberculosis and required what care could be given to make her remaining days as comfortable as possible.

Sadie tapped on the open door and prepared to enter just as a middle-aged woman emerged from the kitchen to meet her.

"Oh, Nurse," she breathed a sigh of relief. "How glad I am to see you. The poor soul's that much worse and I'm at my wit's end to know what to do next for the best."

Putting her bag on a chair, Sadie removed her long cape and draped it over the back. Smiling reassuringly she asked to be brought up-to-date with the situation, although the sounds emanating from an upstairs bedroom told their own story.

"I'm Maisie from next door," she confided. "We've been friends for years and it's fair breaking my heart to see the state she's in."

"Has Mrs. Dane no family to care for her?" the young nurse enquired.

"There's only Herbert, her youngest son. The others fled the nest one by one and then, just a few years ago, her husband died from the same dreadful consumption as is eating at her now." Shaking her head sadly she went on: "Nursed him day in and day out she did. Nobody could have done more; and now it's happening all over again, 'cept that it's all happened so quickly. We've known she's been feeling poorly for some time but she seemed to keep going until these last few weeks when she got much weaker. Even then she somehow managed to wash and dress herself and get downstairs. Now, she's taken to her bed these last days. Gert, that's her other neighbour, and me have been taking turn and turn about to see after her during the day until Herbert gets home from work but she needs more than we can give her, Nurse, she truly does poor soul."

"I'm sure you're doing everything possible Maisie and the family are blessed for it. I'll go up and see what's to be done and, perhaps I can call on you for help if needed?"

The woman nodded her head and bustled off into the kitchen to ensure that there was an adequate supply of hot water on the range.

Climbing the steep, narrow stairs which gave onto a small landing Sadie noticed how well-cared for the little house was. The furnishings, though somewhat worn and humble, were clean while familiar prints of the time gazed down from the walls.

She had no need to wonder in which of the three bedrooms her patient would be found. From that overlooking the street came the rattle of a loose cough accompanied by retching sounds as the sufferer attempted to rid herself of the purulent sputum.

Kneeling by the bed, Sadie took a frail white hand into hers, gently introduced herself and explained that she was there to try to make the situation more comfortable and tolerable.

"There's not much you can do for me now but bless you all the same," the ailing woman whispered breathlessly. The mere effort brought about another paroxysm of coughing until she finally sank back onto the pillows exhausted.

Competently, Sadie set about her tasks. In a short space of time Mrs. Dane found herself blanket-bathed and clad in a clean nightgown. With the help of Maisie, she was assisted into the nearby armchair and propped up with pillows while the two women wrestled with the feather mattress and made the bed up with fresh linen.

"Now," smiled Sadie, "while you're sitting up I want you to try and take a little nourishment." Giving her patient no time to protest, she continued: "I know you probably don't feel like it but it really is important and it will give you a little more strength."

So saying, she drew a cane chair alongside, armed herself with a spoon and bowl of broth produced by Maisie and prepared herself to coax and cajole her patient into submission.

Returning later to the kitchen Sadie encountered the indefatigable Maisie wrestling with the soiled sheets.

"It's pitiful Nurse, and nothing short of a crime, that's what it is," she wailed. "Harriet was one of the best; a real buxom soul with a lovely skin and good colour and a heart of gold - now look at her, nothing but skin and bones."

"How long has she been suffering like this?" Sadie asked.

"Well, that's the thing! It weren't that long ago that she was still managing to do her housework and cooking and even a bit of work on the shoes. Mind, she didn't look all that special and she'd lost a lot of weight. Went right off her food and got tired very quickly so things steadily became more of an effort."

As she was finishing speaking footsteps sounded from the direction of the front door and into the room came a young man who had clearly been hurrying.

"Oh Herbert, you've timed that well," said Maisie. "This is Nurse Masterson whose been looking to your ma. Nurse, this is Harriet's son, Herbert."

"How is she?" he said, scarcely acknowledging the introduction.

"I'm sure Dr. Thorpe has already told you that your mother's condition is now very serious," Sadie replied quietly. "At the moment she is sitting out of bed and, with some reluctance, she has just had a little beef broth and arrowroot. At all costs it is important to try to get her to take sips of liquid as frequently as possible despite her obvious indifference."

"What about medicine? Isn't there anything you can give her?"

Shaking her head ruefully she said: "I know the doctor has told you that nothing can now be done to halt the progress of the disease but he has provided some linctus to help alleviate the cough."

"God, I can't believe this is happening," he said. "Well, I'd better go up and see her before it's time for me to be back at work."

So saying, he made towards the stairs.

Extending a hand to detain him Sadie asked whether there were other family members who needed to be informed and could possibly provide some help. She wasn't prepared for the vehemence of his reply. "They don't bother with her in health and I'm damned if I'll summon them now. If it's all the same to you Nurse, we'll manage thank you."

"Very well Mr. Dane. I, or one of my colleagues, will now be visiting each morning and evening and we'll see how things go."

Without a backward glance, or as much as a 'thank you', Herbert Dane took his leave.

"Don't mind his manner," said the hovering Maisie. "He's always been a bit different to his brothers and he tends to keep things very much to himself."

"That's as maybe," Sadie replied, "but they have a right to know."

"Now, don't you fret," comforted the older woman, "you know what families are like. Those lads are more informed than he likes to make out and they do visit when they can. They're scattered all over the country which doesn't help and they're married with families of their own and jobs to keep. They'll be here Nurse, you'll see. Not that him upstairs will thank them for it but it'll please Harriet."

As Maisie predicted the sons duly appeared in turn and arrangements were made for one of the wives to remain and take the household needs in hand. It transpired that her presence was not long required for, within a matter of two weeks, Harriet's life ebbed to its close in the early hours of a chill morning. Sadie was attentively at hand to provide care and support and carry out the last offices.

In the usual course of events this would have marked the end of her involvement. A few days later, whilst attending another patient, she had by chance seen the little funeral procession make its way down the street, the coffin hoisted on the hefty shoulders of the six eldest sons with Herbert walking emotionless behind as though slightly removed. A strange young man; part of the tableau, yet apart from it, was Sadie's assessment.

She was more than a little surprised, therefore, when responding to a knock at the door of the house provided by the parish for some of its nurses, to find Herbert Dane standing on the pavement. The light from the flickering street lamp played on his bare head as he fidgeted with the cap in his hand. Her previous attempts at conversation had always met with minimal response of monosyllabic proportions and she sensed that he regarded her almost as a non-person. Before she could make comment, he said: "I just wanted to thank you for all you did for Mum."

Smiling gently at him she replied, "There really is no need; I was glad that I could be of help."

Ignoring this, he continued somewhat awkwardly. "I'd like to give you something for your trouble and I've been thinking that your feet must ache a bit in your job." Taken aback, the young woman could only meekly agree.

"I've been looking at your shoes and I think you need something better. Anyhow, I've got permission from my employer to make you a bespoke pair. Would you like that?"

Completely taken aback, Sadie finally stammered: "That really is most kind but I couldn't possibly accept."

Brushing her words aside he replied, "I won't take 'No' for an answer. Can you be at the Waite's factory in Eleanor Road around lunchtime on Saturday, so's I can measure you up?"

"I suppose so," she said a bit doubtfully.

"Good!" I'll see you then." With which he turned and strode off.

Reflecting on the surprising unpredictability of folk, she returned to finish her supper.

It was with some apprehension that Sadie presented herself at the door of the well-known boot and shoe manufacturers. Gingerly pushing open a huge door, her ears were immediately assailed by a cacophony of sounds and voices and her nostrils became drenched with the smell of leather and resin. Uncertain what to do, she was relieved to see Herbert making his way towards her across the vast factory floor.

With no attempt at greeting, he simply said, "Follow me." Walking in his wake, she was conscious of curious eyes staring at her unashamedly as she picked her way towards a flight of wooden stairs. At the top of these was a small landing and a door with frosted panes of glass which prevented her from seeing inside. Herbert gave a smart rap with his knuckles and a deep voice bade them enter.

"So, young Dane, I take it this is the nurse who was so good to your mother?" said a white-haired man struggling to get to his feet from the chair behind a vast desk strewn with papers and samples of leather. Sadie took the hand held out to her as Herbert said, "Yes sir. This is Miss Masterson."

"Sit down my dear, sit down," he said, gesturing towards a chair. "Masterson, you say. Not a very common name. Don't suppose you're any connection to the Mastersons at Hollowdene by any chance?"

"Why, yes," she smiled. "Roland Masterson is my father."

"Well, you don't say. I've been making his riding boots for more years than I care to remember, and your grandfather's too, along with young Master John's. Got the contract for making officers' riding boots at the start of the Crimean campaign," he recounted. "Still, enough of that. Now, here you are to see for yourself what Waite's can do."

"What a coincidence," Sadie murmured politely, conscious of Herbert's figure standing behind her.

"I assure you, you won't be disappointed. Herbert here is a top-flight craftsman. He's told me what he wants to do and I think it's a capital idea."

"It certainly is a most kind gesture," she ventured, "although I really don't think I should accept."

"Nonsense my dear! Your feet have to last you all your life. Look after them and they'll do their bit by you. Your job must be pretty hard on those little feet of yours but I can assure you that, with the help of young Dane here, you'll soon be walking on air."

Barely pausing to draw breath he addressed Herbert. "Use my office, Dane. Nurse Masterson doesn't want to sit down there with that lot gawping while you go about your task. Anyhow, I'm off for some lunch. Delighted to make your acquaintance young lady and I'm sure we'll meet again."

Taking his crombie hat and walking cane from the hat stand by the door Elijah Waite strode from the room and the sound of his heavy tread on the stairs gradually receded.

Four weeks later, following two visits for fittings, Sadie was the possessor of a pair of the softest, supplest, highest quality shoes made from finest Italian, brown leather. Seated once more in the office she submitted her feet to the proprietor's close inspection.

"You've done a good job there, Dane. Couldn't have done it better myself. Excellent. Excellent. How do they feel?"

"It really is just like walking on air and such a difference," exclaimed the flushed and excited young girl. "I've never known such comfort, and they look so good."

"They do indeed, and they need showing off. I suggest you go and try them out properly by letting Herbert here take you somewhere for some refreshment," suggested Elijah.

"Oh no! Really, you've done more than enough already." Sadie gasped with embarrassment as she turned to look at her benefactor expecting to find him equally discomforted.

"I think that's an admirable suggestion. Nurse Masterson, will you allow me to take you out for tea?" With a rather awkward bow he extended a hand and drew her to her feet.

Elijah watched them go with a glint in his eye and an air of smug satisfaction.

Elijah Waite had employed all the members of the Dane family at one time or another but took a special interest in the youngest. In Herbert he recognised an exceptional talent and aptitude for the job, also admiring his single-mindedness, tenacity, diligence and attention to detail. He never ceased to be amazed at the depth of the lad's knowledge of the trade which stemmed not only from experience but the fact that he was an avid reader. Whilst possessing a fond respect for the old ways he was well-versed and up-to-date with the latest innovations. He may be something of a loner, rarely drawn to mix or socialise among his contemporaries, but this had its advantages for he was never distracted from the task in hand, unlike some of them.

Although the majority of men worked incredibly hard and for long hours they could also be somewhat feckless on occasion. It was not for nothing that the first day of the working week was commonly known as 'Shoemaker's Monday'. Many of them never used to work at all but just stood on their doorsteps talking, going up to the pub at dinnertime and for another in the evening. However, the rest of the week they'd work until ten o'clock at night, or later, to make up the time.

Monday was also the day when the pawnshop opened to take back the things which were redeemed on Saturday, such as suits and watches or anything that would fetch a shilling or two. Many things spent longer in the pawnshop than they did in their owner's possession.

It was also the day for attending local race meetings, rabbit coursing, bicycling and foot-racing. Men bet on everything from pigeons, dogs and horses to the results of local elections.

Herbert didn't join in with any of this and was definitely a young man to be encouraged in Elijah's eyes. His seniors may not warm to him particularly but they couldn't fault his work and promotion was swift in coming, with the result that he was now one of the youngest clickers in the trade for miles around. This was probably one of the things that didn't exactly endear him to his peers. Clickers often became manufacturers in their own turn. Clickers also supervised the distribution of work to outdoor employees and checked and approved the finished boots and shoes.

In any event, Elijah was anxious to keep him in his employ. Childless himself, he looked on Herbert rather as a protegé to be groomed for higher things. Although Waite's was now a limited company with a small board of directors, and Elijah's hand firmly on the tiller, he was acutely aware that he was the only one with any real in-depth knowledge or experience of the boot and shoe trade. In Herbert he saw a possible working director for the future but he would need a helping hand, and a favourable marriage would certainly be no hindrance. As a result of these machinations the young couple found themselves facing each other across a table in a local tea room.

Sadie had long decided that conversation wasn't going to be easy and was desperately searching her mind for a suitable topic when Herbert, having given their order to a young waitress, said: "Well now, how would you like me to address you? Will it be Nurse or Miss Masterson?"

Not having given any thought to this question, she hesitated before saying, "My friends call me Sadie."

"And am I a friend?"

"Oh, I do hope so, for you really have been most kind and generous."

"In that case you must call me Herbert," he returned.

"I'm surprised nobody has ever shortened it," she remarked. "I know several Berts but never a Herbert."

"Believe me, there are some as have tried, right from school, but I always insisted that Herbert was the name I'd been given and that is how I wish to be known," he replied, rather pompously.

"And did you go to school round here?"

"Yes, just up the end of our street. Truth to tell, I'm afraid I've never ventured much beyond the outskirts of Morford. Never really wanted to either."

"Well, Herbert, you don't know what you're missing. I was born and brought up on a farm in the country and I have to own that I do miss it at times," she said wistfully.

"No, boots and shoes are in my blood and it's my whole life. My father was what used to be called a cordwainer, and proud of it. He taught all his sons the craft and, from a nipper, I can remember watching him and running errands. If someone wanted a pair of shoes, he'd measure all the foot in detail and go through the whole process just like I did for you. There were seven of us boys - one for each day of the week me da' used to say - but no girls."

As if the bit were firmly between his teeth, he now pressed on with increasing enthusiasm.

"He taught us boys all he knew, then said what most fathers told their sons. 'You're on your own now, so off you go and 'follow the trade'. They'd up and tramp from one place to the next hoping to find an opening where work was plentiful. If it became slack then they'd move on. I've a brother in Coventry, two in Bedford, two in Rugby and one in Luton."

"And you never fancied following them?"

"Why would I? My whole life's been boots and shoes here in Morford. I've never known or wanted anything else, and I've been lucky to get taken on permanently at Waite's."

"Couldn't your brothers have got employment there as well?" the girl asked curiously.

"No. Waite's has only comparatively recently become a factory, now undertaking much of the work on site. Before that it was only a warehouse from which all the outworkers like my dad used to collect the orders and the materials to do the job. He used to work downstairs because all the bedrooms were occupied then, as my brothers left home one by one, he made the back bedroom into a little workshop. He even used to make his own tools, although he had some which his father had used before him. My mother worked alongside him. You see, the men depend totally on their womenfolk and if a wife dies it means a fall in the amount of money he can earn. Mum used to do the fetching and carrying from the warehouse then he'd craft and assemble the shoes, she'd take them back, book them in and bring home the money for what he'd done. She also hand-stitched shoes before Dad stitched the welts in and put the soles on. She could make five pence a pair so it was worth something to a large family."

Sadie opened her mouth to make a comment but her companion was in full flow.

"Do you know that they'd only leave off to have their meals and they'd be working until nine or ten o'clock at night? Because I'd been to school and could read, I'd sit upstairs of an evening and read the newspaper to them. It were a real blow when my dad died with the consumption but Mum was alright because I kept her supplied with hand sewing. She even had to make her own thread though at one time, you know."

"Goodness Herbert, I've learned more about the shoe trade than I thought possible," Sadie said with feeling, wondering whether he actually had any other topic of conversation.

"That's the trouble with folk. Everyone wants shoes and they moan about the price of them without ever giving a thought to all that is involved," came the slightly pious rejoinder.

Glancing at his watch he frowned and informed her that he really would have to go as he still had some work to complete.

More than a little irritated by this somewhat terse termination to their outing, and his egotistical assumption that he was the only one subject to the pressures of work, Sadie felt driven to retort: "Actually, I shall have to fly because I still have a number of patients to see and visits to make. Pleasant as this interlude has been, I'm afraid it has made a heavy inroad into the day's busy schedule."

Once outside she turned to thank him again for all he had done and prepared to take her leave. To her surprise she heard him say, "Are we going to meet again then?"

Slightly taken aback she replied, "Do you want to Herbert?"

"Yes," was the monosyllabic response.

"Then, what do you suggest?"

"I'm not much of a hand at this sort of thing," he owned. "What day is best for you?"

"Sunday afternoon," Sadie replied promptly. It was the one day in the week when she could usually guarantee some free time.

That agreed, they each went their separate ways.

There were no shortage of distractions on offer or things to do in Morford in the 1880s. Although the shops weren't open on a Sunday, and nothing of a sporting nature allowed, it was possible to while away a pleasant few hours.

Sharman's was a popular venue with beautiful grounds, ornamental lake, bear pit and zoological garden. During the week it attracted many who were becoming devotees of the bicycle, gathering around a newly laid cycle track where riders of penny-farthings and the very latest velocipedes raced and generally showed off their prowess. A cricket ground and swimming tank were also available.

The old Abbey ruins stood in some five hundred acres of park, and the river running through it provided tow-path walks where a procession of cargo-laden barges could be seen wending a slow course. Less than a mile away were the remains of the ancient castle, both features bearing testimony to the historic importance of the city. On the fringes, Alderman's Common offered healthy walks for the more adventurous and the water meadows invariably froze completely in the winter months permitting ice-skating to take place while the vendors of roasted chestnuts conducted a roaring trade.

There were cricket and football clubs for the athletically minded which attracted a regular following of supporters, while Working Men's Clubs catered for the more sedentary where, for a subscription of a half penny a week, members could enjoy a drink and play bagatelle, billiards and draughts.

On Bank Holidays, fetes and fairs were held, while brass band concerts were popular along with the ubiquitous Punch and Judy shows for the amusement of the children. Locals vied at the horticultural shows, and folk thronged to the Saturday market in search of bargains. At the beginning of the nineteenth century the Theatre Royal had opened its doors and provided a diverse range of entertainment while regular dances were held at the Assembly Rooms.

In light of so much choice, Sadie could be forgiven for thinking that her escort would have some plan in mind when the time came for their meeting. It rapidly became clear that this was not the case.

"Well, what do you like doing?" she questioned, striving not to sound exasperated.

"Truth to tell, I'm not much of a one for going out. I'm very content with reading and working out possible designs and plans for the business," he confessed.

"You know, Herbert, 'all work and no play, makes Jack a dull boy,' is how the saying goes."

Ready to take offence he retorted: "Are you telling me that I'm dull."

Thinking quickly she said, "Of course not, but I do think you work too hard and it's good to have a change, relax and get some fresh air on the rare occasions when we get the chance. Let's start off by exploring the Abbey Grounds or the Castle ruins. Perhaps we can find somewhere to have some tea."

So a pattern was established and gradually Herbert began to enjoy these excursions and Sadie looked forward to his company. After a while, he would occasionally make the odd romantic gesture by bringing her flowers and encouraging her to take his arm on their walks. Generally speaking, acts of impractical spontaneity, or tenderness, let alone passion, didn't appear to be on his agenda. However, he was extremely possessive of her time which Sadie merely chose to interpret as a sign of affection.

In fact, time was a very precious commodity. There didn't seem enough hours in the day to accomplish all that needed to be done. The Parish Nurses were only too aware that they were merely scratching the surface regarding the welfare needs of the community especially in the deprived areas of the city. Here, the infant mortality was extremely high and those that did live were often puny, sickly children who succumbed easily to the numerous infections which abounded. Although the condition wasn't understood, it was poor nutrition and lack of sunlight which caused the crippling deformities many had to contend with. Rickets was a common complaint which resulted in shortened bones, which were prone to bend under pressure, a crooked spine and barreled ribcage. The teeth had a tendency to fall out easily and if affected children managed to survive infancy they grew up to be severely crippled. This, in turn, generated a multiplicity of problems especially among rachitic women who rarely survived the anguish of childbirth due to a flattened and misshapen pelvis. It was nothing for such victims to endure over a week of exhausting and painful labour at the mercy of untrained women, often of questionable practice and dubious hygiene. Few could find the fee of a guinea required to summon the services of a doctor whose skill in such cases was not high.

It was not uncommon for destructive procedures to be carried out to remove the foetus in order to try to save the life of the mother. If she didn't die as a result of the trauma she was likely to surrender to the almost inevitable infection.

Although obstetric cases rarely, if ever, came the way of the Parish Nurses, a doctor would sometimes seek their assistance to offer care when nothing further could be done. Sadie dreaded these calls. Often confronted with an emaciated, feverish girl, younger than herself, facing almost certain death by the time she arrived, she felt completely helpless to do anything but make her suffering as bearable as possible. The trouble was that nobody evinced much surprise if a woman or baby died in childbirth because it was so commonplace and life was still cheap, even in the latter half of the nineteenth century. However, such an experience could leave Sadie in the depths of depression for days afterwards.

It was not surprising that she looked forward to the rare moments when she could get right away from everything and recharge her batteries. Although she couldn't share her work with Herbert in any great detail, he was sufficiently aware of some of the sights and tragedies she had to encounter. Gradually, he seemed to become more sensitive to her needs and, although feeling in no personal need of the diversions which Sadie enjoyed, he did try to provide the escape from reality she so often craved.

Elijah constantly questioned him about Sadie and encouraged him to pursue her ardently. "You want to snap her up, young man, before someone else does," he advised with a twinkle. "She's a lovely, intelligent woman, from a good background, and can only be an asset to you."

Sadie had secretly been longing for the time when she would be able to visit her old home again. Although she managed the odd meeting with her parents or John, if they had cause to come to Morford, the limited free time available to her was rarely long enough to make the journey to Hollowdene. Therefore, great was her excitement when she realised that a whole half day would be at her disposal one Sunday.

"Come with me," she implored Herbert. "I'd love you to see the farm and meet my folks. It will be a whole new experience for you."

Herbert wasn't quite so enthusiastic. "Oh Sadie, I shall feel like a fish out of water."

"Rubbish," she replied, which was a sentiment endorsed by Elijah on hearing what was proposed. With some reluctance the young man was eventually persuaded.

After completing her morning visits, changing out of her drab uniform, and snatching a hurried lunch, Sadie sallied forth on Herbert's arm to catch a ride with one of the carriers plying a regular route to the outlying areas of the city. Transport was not always easily come by. A local undertaker had founded a firm of cab proprietors in 1860 and horses, pony traps and furniture removals were also available. Nevertheless, it was generally cheaper for the average person to travel with the carrier.

Sadie fidgeted impatiently in her seat as the horse and wagon proceeded along at a sedate pace, her pale face alight with anticipation. As the city gave way to green fields dotted with hedgerows and trees, she gave a contented sigh. "Isn't it wonderfully fresh and clean," she said, "and can't you just smell the healthy air?"

Herbert's reaction was less rapturous. "There's nothing happening. Where are all the houses and people? What's to do?"

"Aren't you enjoying the ride?" she enquired, somewhat crestfallen.

"It's not that, Sadie, but don't expect me to react in the way that you do because this is completely alien territory for me. It certainly takes a bit of getting used to. Apart from which, it's so quiet."

"Exactly! Complete heaven and you can actually hear the birds calling."

Unable to see what was so wonderful about that, Herbert remained unconvinced.

Eventually, they drew up outside the local pub and Sadie's excitement was unrestrained. "We're nearly there. Just down this lane and you'll get your first glimpse of Hollowdene." True to her word, as they rounded a bend, she took Herbert's arm and led him towards a five bar gate. There, nestling in a hollow was her childhood home so full of happy memories.

"Come on. Let's take the short cut through the fields," she trilled gleefully. "Look out for the cow pats though!" Her companion, whose knowledge of cattle derived primarily from the end products which appeared on a meal table, viewed the expedition dubiously. Arm-in-arm they made their way towards the house.

Kate, standing at the kitchen window, spotted them. Calling excitedly to Roland she dashed into the yard and was soon holding her daughter in a warm embrace.

After greeting Herbert hospitably, but not without a degree of curiosity, they went inside to be joined by John and the conversation was soon flying backwards and forwards. Sadie, ever conscious of the uncomfortable figure seated beside her on the sofa, went to considerable pains to try to include him in the chatter but with little success. Roland, however, soon found the means of releasing Herbert's tongue by asking him about his work. As her paramour launched forth on his favourite topic, she watched the somewhat bemused look that stole across the faces of her family, and recalled the occasion of their first outing. On the subject of footwear Herbert, in full flow, assumed the guise of a non-stop train.

"Goodness me, how fascinating," breathed Kate when she could finally get a word in. "I think I'd better go and see about something to eat, if you'll excuse me," and escaped to the kitchen.

Searching for another subject, Roland suggested that Herbert accompany them into the farmyard to view the latest acquisition in machinery.

"That's a good idea," said Sadie. "You three men go and I'll help Mother."

Although the first separate classification with reference to mechanised farm and industrial implements appeared in local directories in 1841 it was many years before they began to come into regular use. It was a move which had met with considerable opposition on some fronts, primarily from a fear of job losses among the labourers.

Mainly at John's instigation, Roland had recently taken delivery of a steam-operated threshing machine and they were justifiably proud of their acquisition. As they demonstrated its many benefits they also catalogued the string of obstacles that had to be circumvented, and assurances given to the work force, before it finally became accepted. There had been numerous incidents of machines being vandalised by men fearful for their livelihood.

Not to be outdone, Herbert launched forth on a detailed discourse regarding the progress which had been made in his own industry. The introduction of the Blake sole-sewing machine in 1864 and the Goodyear welting machine in 1872 had led to considerable reductions in total manufacturing costs but the resulting protests had caused many highly skilled workers to seek work in other areas. By 1870, some 1,500 'Howe' sewing machines were being used in the town and hand-stitched closing, except for high quality work, gradually disappeared.

"It's these and other similar machines that have created the need for the modern factory," said Herbert warming to his theme. "It's no longer feasible for most of the work to be done at home by outworkers so some warehouse owners set up machine shops. Waite's was way ahead of some," he declared proudly. "Mind you, all of this led to the founding of the National Union of Boot and Shoe Operatives in 1874 and that was a good thing in some ways. It has stopped young children from working fourteen hours a day in small, overcrowded, ill ventilated rooms, all for the princely sum of one shilling a week. Do you know I had to work my six months apprenticeship without any pay?"

Both men made what they hoped were appropriate noises. Seemingly heedless, he went on. "The other benefit is that the working day is now from seven in the morning to six at night with an hour allowed for lunch. The downside is the threat of strike action of course. We've already had a few hot-heads making ripples and posters keep appearing clamouring for a minimum wage. Have your lot got a union?" he asked.

"Thankfully no," John replied.

"We actually pride ourselves on treating our men very fairly. That we succeed is shown by very few moving on and we've had members of the same families working for us in succession," Roland added.

Casting a somewhat disparaging eye around him Herbert commented: "Well, there isn't much else for them to do out here, is there?"

It was plain that John was becoming impatient and irritated by their guest. Before he could say anything his father quickly intervened. "There are quite a few benefits you know. They enjoy tied accommodation at very reasonable rents. They also have access to fresh produce, cheap milk, butter and cheese and as much wood as they care to gather for their cooking and heating purposes. I daresay the families have much better health than their counterparts in the city, so there is a lot to be said for it."

With some relief he welcomed Sadie's voice calling them in for a meal and they settled themselves round a table groaning with an array of delectable fare which did more than justice to Kate's culinary skills. "There will be plenty left for you to take some back with you," she beamed, "and I've put together a basket of dairy produce plus a chicken which John killed and dressed for you yesterday."

"That will be a real treat for the three of us who share the parish house. Thank you so much. Mind you, I think old Mrs. Roberts who cooks and cleans for us will be even more grateful. "

"Well, we must try and put some colour into those cheeks of yours. You are looking positively wan."

Conversation then turned to the forthcoming annual harvest barn dance and celebrations. "You will try to get that evening off, won't you Sadie?" her parents voiced in unison. "It would be just like old times," Kate remarked wistfully, "and some of your old friends will be there."

Having agreed to do her utmost to attend, Sadie turned to Herbert. "It's such a fun occasion, you'll love it."

"Aw Sadie, I'm not much of a one for dancing."

"Rubbish. It's all very informal and free and easy and anyone can barn dance even with two left feet, and that's certainly not your problem, I'm sure."

On the first Saturday evening in October, John drove into Morford in the trap to transport the couple to Hollowdene. Despite Sadie's high spirits she thought she detected a slight tension in the rather desultory conversation which flowed back and forth but determinedly pushed it to the back of her mind.

On arrival, she excitedly took Herbert into the gaily decorated barns, happily greeting old friends with whom she exchanged cheery chatter on the way. Eventually they made their presence known to her parents who advised them to help themselves to refreshment before the crush started.

Grabbing Herbert by the hand she whisked him off. Having filled their plates with a greater variety of food than that young man had ever experienced, they perched themselves on a hay bale. Meanwhile the instrumentalists prepared to launch into their repertoire for the evening.

Whilst Herbert was content to listen to Sadie as she pointed out different things and people to him, on the occasion when she indulged in conversation with the many people she knew, her attempts to include him were fruitless and he became his old, monosyllabic self.

The situation deteriorated further once the dancing began. Sadie's feet were beating a rhythmic tattoo to the music and positively tingling with the urge to take part. No amount of persuasion or playful coercion could coax Herbert from his seat. John, guessing there was a problem, sauntered over to claim her as his partner in the Dashing White Sergeant. Happily she tripped through the old familiar steps and when the dance finished everyone joined hands for the Circassian Circle. Finally, flushed and slightly out of breath she flopped down beside Herbert.

"Oh, I did enjoy that; I haven't danced for ages."

"Well, it wasn't much fun for me sitting here on my own."

Stung to indignation Sadie exclaimed: "So am I just supposed to watch, simply because you don't want to join in?"

Before he had a chance to reply one of John's friends arrived to whisk her off to Strip the Willow and retained her hand to make up a set for the Cumberland Square Eight.

By the time she returned Herbert's face resembled a thunder cloud.

"How much longer does this go on for?"

Looking at him somewhat reproachfully she sighed: "For my sake you might at least try to make an effort. If you'd only let yourself go and join in you might be pleasantly surprised and find that you actually enjoy it."

The musicians struck up the tune heralding the Gay Gordons and

Sadie extended her hand to the glowering man in one last entreaty. Reluctantly Herbert got to his feet and allowed himself to be dragged towards the group where John and his girlfriend, Christine, were forming a line. Placing an arm round Sadie's waist he painfully tried to follow the steps but his whole demeanor bore testimony to the fact that he found the whole exercise far from enjoyable.

Eventually, Sadie cornered John and, pleading an early start for work next morning, asked if he would mind taking them back to Morford. The journey was lightened by the presence of Christine who, rather than be left on her own, opted to accompany them. The two girls talked happily together recalling the days when they were at school. Herbert, realising that he would have to redeem himself somehow if he hoped to have any chance of a future with Sadie, felt for her hand and held it firmly in his until the trap pulled up outside the modest nurses' house. Leaping down he turned, attentitively helped her down and, placing an arm possessively round her waist, stood and waved as John took his leave of them.

Moving away from Herbert's hold, Sadie turned, politely thanked him for accompanying her and, withdrew the key to the front door from her reticule. Before she could locate the lock he turned her round to face him. "Aw Sadie, don't be mad. I know I haven't been much company this evening, and I'm sorry. I can't help it if I find such occasions difficult but I'm just not used to them the way you are."

"No, and you never will be if you aren't prepared to try."

Sighing heavily she looked up at him. "Herbert, I truly don't think there is much point in our continuing to meet... " Quickly placing a hand over her mouth he breathed, "Don't say that Sadie, please. I couldn't bear it if I thought that we couldn't share any more time together. I've got used to you being there for me."

"That's exactly it. Perhaps you have become too accustomed Herbert. I'm not simply here to do the things that you want when you feel like it. Unless we can enjoy sharing different experiences then there is little point to our friendship."

Hastily taking a deep breath, he blurted out: "Sadie, don't you realise that I want to share the rest of my life with you?" Without giving her a chance to reply he pulled her roughly to him and tentatively kissed her on the lips. Sensing no resistance he continued with ever-increasing feeling. Suddenly, Sadie wriggled free saying, "Please Herbert, I need time to think."

"Think about what, Sadie? For heaven's sake woman, I want to marry you."

Caught completely by surprise she frantically sought for words.

"Marriage is a very big step. Your proposal has come like a bolt from the blue and I need time to take it in. And we both need to take time to talk things over."

"To hell with talking," said the young man preparing to take her in his arms again, but she neatly evaded his embrace and firmly said: "We will meet again next weekend when we have both had sufficient time to consider the matter. Now, I really must go in." Having placed a fleeting kiss on his cheek, she inserted the key into the lock with a shaking hand and, quietly entering the hall, closed the door gently behind her and leaned back on it while she brushed her fingers over her lips.

If Sadie had been left feeling somewhat uncertain following the Harvest celebrations, she little realised the disquiet which her relationship with Herbert was causing among her family. On the day following the barn dance a clearly troubled John confronted Roland and Kate demanding to know what they intended to do about the situation.

"Calm down," said his father. "We don't know that Sadie is contemplating actually marrying him. I think he is just someone she has met through her work and for whom she feels sorry. You know how soft-hearted she is in fostering lame ducks."

"And that," interjected his wife, "is precisely the problem. I've said it before and I'll say it again, that girl is too kind and too long-suffering for her own good."

"That's as may be," Roland interjected, "but don't overlook the fact that she has also got a stubborn and determined streak if obstructed. She's also twenty-five and not exactly a child. And let's not forget another thing. Here we are voicing all these concerns, but why are we concerned?"

"I'll tell you why," interrupted John. "I simply don't like the chap.

Didn't take to him from that Sunday when she first brought him here."

"For what reason?"

"He's got no conversation unless it involves boots and shoes, which he goes on and on about as if there's nothing else of importance. He showed no interest in what we are doing. In fact, I found him incredibly boring and self-engrossed. He evinced absolutely no sense of humour and I don't think I've ever seen him smile," said John with increasing vehemence.

"Not everyone can be blessed with your fun-loving rumbustiousness," his father said with a grin. "At least he doesn't seem to be work-shy."

"No, but I know what John means," Kate sighed. "I can't exactly put my finger on it. He was perfectly polite and well-mannered enough but there was no spark in him, unless talking about his work. Rather dull, I suppose."

"Do we have the right to condemn someone merely for being dull?" Roland queried in a reasonable tone, "because I think we shall need more than that with which to confront Sadie. It was clear from his demeanour at the harvest supper that he was in an environment where he didn't feel comfortable. I suspect he was only there to please her, for which he should be commended rather than censured."

John leaped to his feet impatiently. "For heaven's sake, we're her family, Dad. That sort of attitude doesn't bode well for the future. Don't tell me that you actually like him?"

"I don't feel that I know him well enough to have the right to give an opinion."

As John once more prepared to give voice, Kate, attempting a laugh, said, "Goodness, here we are talking about a future when there's probably nothing of the sort to be considered. Apparently his mother was one of Sadie's patients who died and, likely, she feels sorry for him."

"All I can say is that someone had better find out which way the wind is blowing before it's too late," her son commented.

Meanwhile, Sadie's mind was in a positive whirl. In the days following that last memorable encounter she went about her tasks in a haze. Although she had sometimes wondered what Herbert's real feelings towards her were, his proposal had caught her off guard and begged more questions than answers. Did she really want to marry him? What were his true feelings for her? Did he love her, and did she love him? What sort of life could she expect if she married him? It was with a mixture of excitement and apprehension that she awaited their next meeting.

Promptly after the nurses had finished Sunday lunch, Herbert knocked on the door of the house in Brewer Street to be greeted by a slightly flushed Sadie.

"Shall we go for a stroll in the Castle grounds and find a nice quiet spot where we can ponder our future?" he said with a smile. Shyly she agreed and, slipping her hand through his arm, they set off.

Morford was enjoying something of an Indian summer and it was pleasant to be out and about in the balmy warmth. Finding a shady spot under a large, spreading cedar tree, Herbert removed his jacket and spread it on the ground for her to sit on. Once settled he wasted no time in coming to the point. "Well, Sadie, have you decided whether to throw in your lot with me?"

"I've been thinking of nothing else all week."

"And?"

The question hovered tantalisingly in the slight heat haze but it required an answer.

"Herbert, why do you want to marry me?" she half whispered.

"What an odd question," he said. "Over these past months I've grown accustomed to being with you and I've come to rely on our meetings. There's something missing when you're not around, besides which I admire you tremendously."

"Is that all?" she persisted.

"What do you mean?" he asked with a puzzled expression on his face.

Sadie fidgeted with the buttons on his jacket and plucked uneasily at a tuft of grass. She was vaguely aware of other couples strolling leisurely along the footpaths and the sound of children's voices raised in laughter.

"Come on Sadie, tell me what you mean?" he repeated impatiently.

"Well, you could have been talking about a housekeeper or a pet dog rather than someone you wanted to marry," she replied somewhat petulantly. "Do you actually have any real feelings for me?"

"Heavens, I thought I made that very clear the other night when I kissed you goodnight. Of course I've got feelings for you."

The silence lengthened between them. Finally Herbert said, "What about you, then? How do you feel about me?"

"That's just the trouble," she said; "I'm not really sure that I know."

He made as though to interrupt but she went on. "Like you, I enjoy the times when we are together and I look forward to them. I admire and respect you and I'm proud of you but are those sufficient reasons to get married?"

"My dear, you really do believe in making things complicated don't you. Here I am telling you that I want to make a home with you, to raise a family together... "

"Well, you certainly haven't mentioned that before," she chipped in.

Looking at her in surprise he said, "Don't you want to have children Sadie?"

"Of course I do," she muttered in exasperation.

"Then, I can't see what the problem is."

She looked at him wearily saying, "Suppose I'd said that I didn't or, for some reason, couldn't, have children, would you still want to marry me?"

"Lawks, I don't know Sadie. The thought never crossed my mind."

"Exactly. We neither of us really knows enough about each other's true feelings to make this sort of commitment at the moment."

"So, what are you proposing? What have I got to do to convince you for heaven's sake?"

"Just let's give ourselves a bit more time Herbert," she pleaded. "After all, there's an awful lot at stake - the whole of the rest of our lives in fact."

With that Herbert had to be satisfied.

As it transpired, Sadie found herself with plenty of time to consider the situation. Laid low with a severe respiratory infection in late

November, the doctor recommended a short respite in the country. Thus she was forced to seek recovery at Hollowdene to the relief of her parents who had been looking for some way to get their daughter on her own.

Once more, Kate was up in arms. "This is yet another indication that the work really is too much for you."

Wearily, Sadie responded: "Stop fussing Mother. The early harsh onset of winter has resulted in the usual seasonal illnesses and what started as an irritating cough very quickly turned to bronchitis. I have to own that it is taking a while to shake off and has left me feeling rather weak. Doctor Spencer is quite convinced that this break is all that is needed to set me up."

Avoiding the subject that was uppermost in their minds, her family gave her time to relax before broaching the matter in what they hoped was a casual fashion. Gathered round the table in the homely warmth of the farm kitchen, before father and son set about the business of attending to the evening milking, Roland looked fondly at Sadie.

"How is that young man of yours getting on?"

"Herbert? Very well I think, although this wretched infection means that I haven't seen him for a while."

"Is this a serious relationship then?" queried Kate.

Aware of three pairs of eyes fixed upon her she tried to laugh the matter off. "Goodness, what's this, the inquisition?"

"Of course not, although you can't blame us for being curious, my dear."

"Herbert assumed responsibility for his mother after her husband died and his brothers had already left home. Obviously her death affected him greatly. I was quite surprised when he contacted me some weeks later wanting to repay me for the care I had given her. He offered to make me a pair of shoes. Imagine me with bespoke footwear," she said, giggling like a young girl. "I have to say they are wonderfully comfortable too."

Sensing a slight unease, Sadie looked from one to another before saying: "Is there something wrong?"

Easing his position in the big, old carver chair, Roland cleared his

142

throat. "Clearly things have progressed since then, otherwise why would you bring him home?"

Now very much on her guard, she retorted: "Why wouldn't I? You've always welcomed my friends here."

"Come off it Sadie," her brother chipped in. "It's one thing turning up with Bessie but this is an eligible young man."

"Oh, so you do think he's eligible then?"

"I don't know. None of us do. You haven't deigned to confide in any of us," he said irritably.

"And I wonder why that is? Well, I'll tell you. I knew how you'd react and your whole attitude now shows that I was right."

Quickly intervening, Roland reached forward to put a hand on her arm. "That's not quite fair, young lady. It would be negligent parents indeed who paid no heed to their only daughter or failed to take an interest."

Ignoring her father she turned instead on John. "This is all your doing isn't it? You took against Herbert from the start. Well, it's none of your business. I'm twenty-five years of age and old enough to make up my own mind who I choose for friends. I notice nobody is criticising your precious Christine."

"Now Sadie, that's enough," her father intervened. "Christine is an entirely different matter. You all virtually grew up together and her family are well known to us. It's only natural that we are keen to find out more about someone who is clearly becoming important to you."

"That's as maybe, Father, but I want to know exactly what my dear brother has got against Herbert," and she glared in his direction.

"Alright, I confess that I found him boring, completely wrapped up in footwear, totally humourless and socially inept."

Kate gasped in dismay. "John, that was unkind and uncalled for," but Sadie forestalled her.

"In that case, it's a good job that I'm the one going out with him. I see a person deserving of admiration not condemnation. Herbert hasn't enjoyed your privileged upbringing or financial advantage. He is a prodigiously hard worker who is succeeding through his own effort and self-education. He is already climbing the ladder at Waite's and I happen to know that Elijah Waite thinks very highly of him. He doesn't drink or smoke or gamble. In fact, until I introduced him to some of the attractions of Morford he never went out much. If that constitutes dullness in a person, so be it. Now he is learning that there are things out there beyond work and reading. He is polite, kind and attentive to me and that is what matters."

And there the matter might have been left except that Sadie, probably for the first time in her life, chose to lie. "I have absolutely no idea where this friendship is heading, if anywhere, because the subject has never been raised. Neither do I know what my response would be if it was. Now, if you will excuse me, I am feeling very tired and will go to my room." With which Sadie gathered up the sewing on which she had previously been working and walked quietly from the room.

Silence prevailed in the kitchen, except for the rhythmic tick of the grandfather clock and the crackling of the wood on the fire, to be broken eventually by Kate.

"Oh dear, that wasn't very pleasant and I don't think it's actually got us anywhere."

"No, and I fear it may have done more harm than good," replied her husband,

Without a word John went out into the yard to lose himself in the work of the farm.

Resting unhappily on her bed, a confusion of thoughts and emotions raced through her mind. What course should she choose?

Women of the 1880s mostly had very few choices. The vast majority came from the poor or working classes and lived in a state little better than slavery. They had to obey men, because in most cases men held all the resources and women had no independent means of subsistence. A wealthy widow or spinster was a lucky exception; nevertheless, the woman who remained single attracted social disapproval and pity. She could have no children or cohabit with a man: the social penalties were simply too high. Unlike Sadie, hardly any could follow a profession, since nearly all were closed to women.

Women's sole purpose was to marry and reproduce so they had little choice but to comply. Upon doing so everything they owned, inherited and earned automatically belonged to their husband. If an offence was committed against her, only her husband could prosecute.

Furthermore, rights to the woman personally – that is, access to her body – were his. Not only was this assured by law, it was enshrined and written into the marriage service as a vow before God. Every man had the right to force his wife into sex and childbirth. He could take her children without reason and send them to be raised elsewhere. He could spend his wife's inheritance on a mistress or on prostitutes. That was the background and way of life Herbert came from. Although Sadie didn't think for one moment that he would be like that, was she prepared to risk such treatment?

If a woman was unhappy with her situation there was, almost without exception, nothing she could do about it. Except in extremely rare cases, a woman could not obtain a divorce and, until 1891, if she ran away from an intolerable marriage the police could capture and return her. All this was sanctioned by church, law, custom, history, and approved by society in general. The Divorce Act of 1857 merely emphasised the moral inequality. Mere adultery was not grounds for a woman to divorce a man; however, it was sufficient grounds for a man to divorce his wife. The law even permitted men to administer 'moderate correction to disobedient wives'.

Sadie pondered all the implications of marriage to Herbert and finally reached a decision.

Chapter Four

Trials and Tribulations

The attitude of her family was the catalyst that determined Sadie to finally accept Herbert's marriage proposal, although it was with some misgiving that Roland acceded to that young man's formal request to marry his daughter. When everyone was gathered at Hollowdene on the evening of Christmas Day, the couple officially announced their engagement but not all those present found it easy to express genuine pleasure and delight.

Once the decision had been made neither of them could see any reason to delay and they resolved to have an Easter wedding. In the resulting flurry of preparations and planning Kate managed to push any misgivings into the background.

A major consideration centred around the matter of finding a home. An offer of financial help from the bride's parents to acquire a modest property in the city was met with a curt refusal from Herbert who professed himself quite able to provide for their needs. He had absolutely no wish to be beholden to his future in-laws in any way. His employer queried the wisdom of this. "It's a golden opportunity to really establish yourself, lad," Elijah counselled. "After all, a lass from her background deserves the best. If you sow well now, you will reap a harvest later," he said with a knowing look. His protegé was having none of it. "We shall fare well enough. After all, we are both working."

His last announcement came as unpleasant news to Kate who had hoped that marriage would at least relieve her daughter from the physical strains her job imposed on her.

"Why ever would I not continue to nurse, Mother? I can hardly sit around at home all day twiddling my thumbs. Besides which, it wouldn't be fair on Herbert. After all, his mother managed to run a tidy house, bring up seven children and still play her part by taking in work."

"She probably had a far more robust constitution than yours," Kate countered, only to be silenced with an impatient retort from Sadie. "When will you stop fussing about my health? I'm absolutely fine."

With that Kate had to be content though secretly hoping that an early pregnancy would put an end to the matter.

In the event, both parents were pleasantly surprised when the day came that they were taken to inspect the couple's future home.

As Morford continued to expand, new properties were constantly being built. In a pleasant road some two miles from the city centre Herbert and Sadie had come across a new development of basic but functional three-bedroom terraced houses which were nearing completion. Purchase of one was out of the question but they had discovered that a few were for rent and they speedily staked a claim with the landlord.

There was, of course, the matter of furnishing it, at mention of which Kate could hardly contain her excitement. "Just think my darling there is still so much stuff from The Court stored at the farm, some of which will have such happy memories for you." Turning to Herbert she implored, "Do at least come and have a look." And in this respect her future son-in-law was agreeable to accept an offer of help.

Not to be out-done, Roland also made a proposal. "I see there's a small patch of ground for a garden at the back which is in a bit of a rough state at the moment. How would it be if I got one of my lads to come across and dig it over? Perhaps we could even put some turfs down." Herbert, whose experience with a spade was limited to filling coal scuttles in the backyard, and whose acquaintance with a fork was non-existent, was more than ready to acquiesce. Sadie clapped her hands in undisguised delight and her betrothed regarded her obvious happiness with satisfaction whilst basking in a clear mellowing of relations all round.

Easter Saturday 1885 dawned crisp and bright and fanned by a gentle breeze. By midday the village church was filled with family,

147

friends and villagers, all arrayed in their finery, and straining to see the bride on the arm of her father as she moved to take her place alongside the man who was to become her husband.

Sadie appeared almost wraith-like with a pale beauty which was accentuated by her ankle length dress of ivory silk overlaid with exquisite lace which, at her request, had been adapted from her mother's gown, much to Kate's pride and delight. Her copper-coloured curls were topped with a circlet of real flowers securing a delicate lace veil and a trembling hand clasped a trailing bouquet of lilies, ivy and smilax.

Herbert, standing rigidly to attention, uncomfortable in the new suit and stiff white collar, managed to cast an appreciative glance at her before turning to face the vicar as he prepared to go through the old familiar marriage rite.

Sadie's old friend Bessie had returned from London to take her place alongside Christine as bridesmaids, while one of the groom's brothers filled the role of best man.

Seated just behind the groom was the upright figure of Elijah Waite whose countenance bore token to the approval and immense satisfaction he was gaining from the occasion. This had been marked by an increase in wages for Herbert and his generous wedding gift to the young couple.

One of several Leather Fairs which took place during the year was held in London on Bank Holiday Monday. The old man decided to kill two birds with one stone by requesting Herbert to attend with a view to assessing the samples, which came from all over the world, and using his judgment in placing orders where appropriate. It was a responsibility which would test his mettle even further and hopefully serve to justify Elijah's faith in him. In return the old man had arranged for them to spend three nights at a modest hotel in the capital for their honeymoon.

Sadie was ecstatic for neither of them had ventured that far afield before and it was an exciting new experience which they could share. It would certainly provide Herbert with another topic of conversation.

As soon as the wedding breakfast had finished, and Sadie appeared dressed in a new ensemble suitable for travelling, John drove them to Morford station in the trap.

Following Elijah's advice, on arrival in the capital Herbert summoned a horse-cab from a nearby rank. Peering out from its confines the young couple gazed wide-eyed at the bustle and sights which they could just glimpse in the rapidly fading light.

Initially, neither of them were totally comfortable with the new-found intimacy into which they were thrust. Herbert was awkward, clumsy and seemingly lacking in any finesse. Sadie with her usual patience submitted to this new assault on her body with good grace, assuming that things could only get better.

Their delight in the sights of their new surroundings pushed everything else into the background as they marvelled at the various landmarks previously only heard about.

When Herbert left her to attend the Leather Fair she was more than happy and excited by the chance to explore the amazing shops and gaze with wonderment on the latest fashions.

By the time they came to leave the capital both were elated by the experience and beginning to adapt to each other's company.

On their return they quickly settled back into the daily routine while revelling in the thrill of their first home. Within a short time Sadie had been given the responsibility for the sick in that particular area whilst Herbert took everyone totally by surprise with the purchase of a bicycle.

Although various two and three-wheeled conveyances had been appearing on the scene for a few years with varying success it wasn't until 1885 that John Starley created the Safety Bicycle which would become the prototype for the modern day bike. It was pedal and chain-driven, had a cross frame which changed little over the years, a saddle, handle-bar grips and, initially, sported solid rubber tyres. Three years later the pneumatic tyre was developed providing an even smoother ride. Within five years, mass production of reasonably priced bicycles allowed working class men to use them for work and leisure.

Sadie was both amazed and delighted by her husband's seeming new-found determination to embrace this contemporary form of transport and was quick to compliment him and express her approval.

Kate and Roland were relieved that their earlier doubts regarding the relationship appeared to be unfounded and rejoiced in their daughter's happiness.

Elijah Waite was similarly satisfied with the results of his faith in Herbert's judgment at the Leather Fair. Within a year the works manager retired and he had no hesitation in appointing his protegé to the post. This move did little to endear him to his former neighbours and workmates who felt that he was becoming a bit too big for his boots.

By the end of the first year the only cloud on the horizon of mother and daughter was the lack of any sign of a forthcoming pregnancy. However, they were soon swept up in the preparations for John's forthcoming marriage to Christine. For Sadie, any pleasure gained from the event was shortlived when, within a few months, the couple announced the news of an impending birth. She watched enviously as her sister-in-law blossomed with the healthy glow of imminent motherhood and tried to accept with grace and delight their invitation to be godmother to a lusty son to be called Ted. All the while she prayed constantly that her time would come.

Finally, after three years of marriage, the waiting was over but her dreams were dashed when, within a matter of weeks, she suffered a miscarriage.

Miscarriage was more dangerous for the majority of women than giving birth at full term. In the days before blood transfusions and antibiotics, miscarriages could cause the death of the mother, or involve prolonged illness.

Research at the beginning of the nineteenth century showed that out of four hundred pregnant married women, one hundred and twenty eight had miscarried one or more times, giving birth in ten years to five hundred and fifty six live children and three hundred and five dead embryos. By 1894 eight women out of ten miscarried one or more times.

The perceived solution for prevention was to keep absolutely flat, stay calm and, importantly, not worry as any kind of stress or tension was considered injurious to the developing pregnancy. Pregnant women would spend days on a couch or weeks confined to bed as a means of taking precautions against miscarriages. It was hardly surprising that the incidence of depression among them was high.

Altogether, miscarriage was a painful, traumatic experience often culminating in high fever, pain and intermittent bleeding indicating an incomplete miscarriage, when some of the products of conception were retained which could result in septicaemia due to infection. The regime for management of such an event was one of poultices, laudanum, bromide, brandy, quinine, morphia, castor oil and ergot and, when all else failed, a doctor would perform curettage under chloroform.

Despite taking every care, to Sadie's distress and despair she experienced four such devastating disappointments but amazingly escaped any complications, probably due to the short gestation of each pregnancy. Kate secretly began to wonder whether her daughter would ever manage to carry a baby to full term.

Against all the odds she eventually succeeded and on a stormy night in 1890 went into labour. Herbert wasted no time in summoning the local midwife, and his mother-in-law, to come and attend her.

The term midwife in those days was a euphemism. Every locality had some experienced women who were ready to be in attendance at a confinement. Their skills and knowledge were often shared and passed down from one generation to another. However they were completely lacking in training and possessed no formal qualifications, hence their levels of competence varied enormously.

The concept of Lying-In Hospitals was first adopted about one hundred years previously. The intention was to provide a safer place for delivery, but any purported benefits were far outweighed by the high levels of infection and the risk of death from sepsis. As a result the vast majority of women gave birth at home in overheated rooms devoid of fresh air. Pain was dealt with by recourse to herbal remedies and age-old rituals, few of which had any value.

Delivery took place in whichever position the woman found most comfortable. This could be sitting on a birthing stool, squatting, kneeling, standing, or lying on a bed propped up with pillows.

Those gathered in the little terraced house prepared themselves for a long wait.

One day turned into two while Sadie struggled to cope with the contractions which, although initially bearable, were now coming relentlessly. Her nursing colleagues took it in turns to be with her and to support Kate but it soon became clear that the young woman's strength was fading as her body strove to withstand the onslaught. The local doctor, also in attendance, expressed his grave concern to Kate. Worried beyond measure, she sent for Roland who needed no bidding to provide the financial inducement to seek out the obstetrician at the Infirmary to request his help and advice. By the time that gentleman arrived Sadie was thrashing around the bed barely able to draw sufficient breath to call out in her distress.

After his examination the consultant agreed with the doctor's tentative diagnosis that the baby's head was lying in a posterior position. It was felt that the best means of dealing with this was by the use of instruments.

Obstetric forceps had been introduced into the country from France. Although their use was becoming accepted and commonplace there were still many who regarded them as a last resort due to the risk of maiming the infant or injuring the mother through careless or unskilled application of the blades.

Caesarean sections were being performed more frequently but with appalling results. At the end of the century, maternal mortality from this procedure was 75% and it was not surprising that pregnancy and childbirth became the subject of increasing concern and inquiry by the medical profession.

The tension in the bedroom was palpable as one of Sadie's friends flew to the kitchen to boil the instruments in the fish kettle. Herbert had been tasked with ensuring a constant supply of hot water while Roland sat on a chair with his head in his hands. The midwife cleared the surface of the chest-of-drawers to accommodate the necessary paraphernalia then hastened to help Kate place a clean sheet on the bed underneath the perspiring figure of her daughter, now completely drained by the remorseless strength of contractions which were achieving nothing.

The head of the bed was pulled away from the wall and the

consultant requested the doctor to administer chloroform, but sparingly in view of the patient's weakened state. Chloroform, which had been made so fashionable following its use by Queen Victoria, could render a person totally unconscious. Mercifully the distressed figure became less agitated and the obstetrician indicated for Sadie's legs to be placed into the lithotomy position and held there, supported by two former colleagues. Carefully he examined her internally then, after lubricating the blades, inserted them carefully but firmly either side of the descending head and locked the handles together.

The two men downstairs paled and flinched when, despite the chloroform, Sadie's muffled scream rang through the house as the consultant applied steady traction on the forceps whilst imploring the uncomprehending patient to 'push'. As he pulled, at the same time endeavouring to rotate the head, very gradually it began to appear.

Commanding the midwife to be ready to receive the infant into a towel, which had been warming for the purpose, he exerted one final tug and the limp, moist, blood-stained body of a baby girl was unceremoniously hauled into the world. After deftly cutting the cord he returned his attention to his patient.

Kate gazed anxiously at the tiny scrap, now being suspended upside down by its ankles in an attempt to clear the airways and establish respiration, but with no signs of success. Pressing the back of her hand across her mouth, she watched as the midwife laid the child on her back in the old-fashioned, hooded, oak family cradle on rockers, which had been brought back into service. Leaning over it she inhaled deeply and blew a blast of air onto the inert form. Straightening up she watched as two little arms suddenly jerked spasmodically into life, a pair of startled eyes stared wildly at her assailant, and an extremely annoyed young lady gave a cry which could even be heard downstairs in the kitchen. Roland jumped to his feet and with a smile of relief clapped Herbert on the back.

Having given voice, the infant clearly had no intentions of stopping. Swaddling her firmly in a towel she was placed in Kate's arms as the obstetrician abruptly demanded help. Looking towards the bed she was in time to see the afterbirth emerge followed by a seemingly unstoppable flow of blood. Under his breath the doctor at its head could be heard saying to his colleague, "Her pulse is very slow and weak and she's not responding."

Sadie had fallen victim to post partum haemorrhage, one of the biggest dangers following childbirth and every doctor's worst nightmare. She fulfilled the whole range of predisposing factors having undergone a long labour with resort to instrumental delivery and the use of anaesthesia. This scourge was one of the major causes of maternal death and the difficulty still pertained that little was possible in the way of effective treatment.

Those in attendance looked on helplessly as an extreme pallor descended over the patient's face, the respirations became shallow and the extremities cold.

"Don't just stand there. Get me plenty of hot water and any material I can use to pack this uterus with heated swabs, and pile some blankets on her for warmth. Doctor, you try to rub up the uterus into a state of contraction for it is essential to keep it contracted if we are to have any chance. Nurse, look in my bag, find the bottle marked Ergotinine and a syringe and needle and draw me up a measure, while I try bi-manual compression of the uterus. Doctor, we'll also try some digitalis if you please in the hope that it will strengthen the pulse and help to stem the bleeding," the consultant requested urgently.

All was frenzied action.

Although the number of drugs available to a doctor were few the uses of Ergot had been recognised for at least two centuries. Found to originate in the spurs from rye wheat its administration narrows the arteries thereby restricting blood flow, but it was only since 1875 that its use in the treatment of post partum haemorrhage had come to the fore. Ergot came to be called "the powder of birth", one of the great benefits being the speed with which it was absorbed after giving it either orally or by injection.

A syringe for the purpose of dispensing medication first appeared in 1853 and this was becoming the preferred method.

After what seemed an unconscionable time the two medical gentlemen came downstairs to face Sadie's family, who gazed at them with anxious expressions.

"She is going to be alright, isn't she?" Roland implored.

"I have to tell you that your daughter's condition is grave. Quite apart from the strain imposed by a normal delivery she has been traumatised by the necessary use of instruments compounded by considerable blood loss. Indeed, there was a point when my colleague and I feared for her life."

Kate gave a low moan and held onto Roland's arm. Herbert stood uncomfortably trying to make sense of it.

Regarding them with compassion, the consultant continued. "Against all the odds she is still with us. The haemorrhage appears to be under control at the moment although that doesn't mean that it won't recur. Naturally all this has left her in an extremely weak and parlous state. Indeed, at the moment she is completely unaware of anything. She has been given a sedative because it is essential that she has total rest if she is to recover."

"Believe me, she will want for nothing," said her mother fervently.

Smiling gently he nodded his head in approval. "I'm sure she won't. However, I have to warn you that there seems to be another problem." Looking from one to the other he posed a question. "Can I ask whether Mrs. Dane has ever suffered any serious illness?"

Kate glanced quickly at Roland before replying. "Towards the end of her nurse training at the Infirmary she was a patient in the hospital with severe scarlet fever, although she ultimately made a good recovery."

Eying his medical colleague the consultant went on: "Ah! That undoubtedly explains something which was noted immediately before delivery and is now giving cause for concern. We observed at the time that her heart beat was irregular and it remains so. Mr. Dane, does your wife ever show signs of becoming breathless on exertion?"

"Well, she certainly seems to tire easily although, as to breathless I couldn't really say. Perhaps she does puff a bit if she takes the stairs too quick but I've never really given it much thought."

"What is the significance of all this?" Roland asked.

"I think the signs point to the fact that your daughter has sustained permanent damage to her heart as a direct result of the scarlet fever infection. If she pulls through this ordeal, I would like her to see one of the physicians at the infirmary. He will be better placed to give an opinion and prescribe appropriately. Meanwhile let us concentrate on getting through the next few days."

Sadie's recovery was painstakingly slow but steady, thanks in no small measure to the ministrations of her mother. Although the nurses took it in turns to visit daily to give general care, it was inevitable that the main burden would fall on Kate who had moved in. Kindly neighbours provided some meals, for Sadie had been well-liked, and Roland arranged to collect and return all the washing so that it could be laundered by the staff at Hollowdene. There was no way that the new mother was able to undertake any care for the baby which meant that Kate was plunged into the endless round of feeding, bathing and changing day and night.

Herbert had regarded the new arrival with an amusing mixture of surprise and bewilderment. Beyond gazing at her periodically any physical contact was negligible which was very much in keeping with the times. Babies were women's work.

It had been several days before Sadie even became aware of her baby's existence or had any opportunity to forge a bond with the infant. Later, each time the child was placed beside her, she gazed at her with an expression of such love that it moved even the practical Kate to tears. The first time her presence had really registered, and she fully understood that she had a little girl, she stroked the tiny hand, looked at Herbert and in a weak voice said, "She's Lucy, isn't she?"

Truth to tell, he had never thought for one moment that the baby would be any other than a boy. He was, therefore, quite happy to agree with Sadie on this occasion and he would have his say with the next one. Any such ideas were brutally crushed within a short space of time.

In deference to Kate, who knew the consultant physician well, that gentleman paid a visit to the recovering Sadie at home. His careful examination only served to confirm the obstetrician's suspicions.

Addressing them all he explained: "The significance of serious infection upon the heart is only now being recognised. Unfortunately, young lady, it would seem that your brush with scarlet fever resulted in rheumatic fever, which is a not uncommon complication. This inflames the heart and impairs its ability to circulate blood around the body. In turn this affects the response of the heart muscle to any extra demands made on it, and also causes progressive degeneration."

Sadie and Kate gazed at him in dismay but Herbert seemed incapable of grasping the impact.

"Naturally, now that you know what the problem is you will be able to treat it?"

"Unfortunately, as I suspect your wife is only too aware, there is no magic remedy. With care and no undue stress or exertion, she will be able to live a reasonable life within the limits imposed by the disease but her constitution will always be weak. However, we are finding that people suffering from shortness of breath and fatigue due to heart failure experience improved symptoms by taking the herbal medicine hawthorn. It appears to have a beneficial effect on the workings of the heart by dilating blood vessels, thereby increasing the heart's energy and pumping capability. It also prevents further weakening of heart muscle and treats any irregularities in rhythm."

"Hawthorn!" exclaimed Herbert. "Is that the best you can do because it sounds positively pagan?"

Not used to having his experience questioned, the older man regarded him somewhat witheringly before delivering the final coup de grace.

"I also have to tell you that, following consultation with my colleague and your doctor, there must be absolutely no more pregnancies."

Herbert's head shot up and Sadie let out a clearly audible sob but, before they could say anything, the stern voice continued.

"There is definitely no doubt that any more will kill you for two reasons. The internal damage sustained by your body at delivery coupled with severe haemorrhage renders it extremely dangerous to contemplate a repeat performance, which would assuredly not have such a happy outcome. Even were you obstetrically fit, there is no way that your heart will survive another such onslaught on it."

Devastated by this latest news the family convened to try to plan the way forward.

The normal lying-in period following a birth was one month but it rapidly became clear that it would be considerably longer before Sadie would be able to cope with the demands of a baby and a house. Kate too was feeling the strain and needed to return to Hollowdene. Finally, faced with the reality of the situation, it was with relief that Sadie welcomed the suggestion that they should move into the farmhouse for the time being. Unable to come up with any suitable alternative Herbert consented, although with considerable reluctance and little grace.

So began the lengthy period of cosseting the young mother back to health surrounded by all the care of loving family and old friends. From her bedroom window she watched with envy as Christine pushed Lucy out in the old pram, while the sturdy Ted happily ran ahead.

"Be patient," her mother encouraged gently, "it won't be long before you can join them."

Sadie wasn't the only one forced to exercise patience. Herbert, now faced with a lengthy bicycle ride each morning and night, was chafing to return to the convenience of their old surroundings. On occasions when the weather was bad, or if he wanted to work late, he would stay at the little house in Morford.

Meanwhile, after discussing the situation with Kate, Roland quietly went about plans of his own. They were both firmly of the opinion that their daughter would be better off in the country air and close enough to receive help when needed. Within sight of the old Painters Court stood a solid grey stone farmhouse which had been part of the original estate and was now standing empty. Within weeks builders were brought in to enlarge and modernise the property whilst still retaining its old character.

Realising that they would have to handle the matter with the utmost skill the couple finally decided that, as Sadie's health was now greatly improved, the time was right to unveil their proposal.

Sitting back in his chair after they had all enjoyed a satisfying meal in the farm kitchen, Roland indicated the young couple to remain seated.

"I know these past months have been a testing and difficult time for both of you but thankfully Sadie has pulled through. Naturally you are keen to return to your home to be a proper family which is something Mother and I want for you. However, my lass, you have still not fully regained your strength and, if you are honest, you will have to admit that you will require help with the heavy work in the house for some time to come."

"We'll manage somehow," Herbert asserted.

"I'm sure you will. The trouble is that I know my daughter only too well. If she sees something that needs doing while you're at work, she'll get on and do it without thinking."

"Well, we can't stay here any longer," he replied firmly.

After pausing in order to choose his words carefully Roland went on to say: "Before either of you says anymore, I would be grateful if you will just hear me out as I have a proposition to put to you."

Looking at Kate he asked, "Do you want to explain about your father's will, or shall I?" She indicated that he should continue.

Addressing Herbert directly he said, "When we got married I bought this farm. George Oliphant had a considerable landholding in and around Shepherdstone which he worked with the help of a farm manager. When he died the estate was left to me in order to run it in tandem with my own for the benefit of John if he decided to follow in his grandfather's footsteps, which he is doing. My wife was left Painters Court and the contents in trust, plus a sum of money in her own right, on the understanding that in the event of her death this would pass to Sadie. The Married Woman's Property Act of 1882 now allows a married woman to retain ownership of property received as a gift from a parent."

"But The Court has been sold to the Infirmary," Sadie interrupted.

"That's right, and the money was put into a trust fund, the interest from which currently goes to your mother. The principle itself is untouched and will, in due course, come to you and then to Lucy." Twinkling at her he was quick to assure her. "Don't worry, you're not a wealthy heiress or anything and your mother is still very much alive, praise be."

Herbert had been struggling to see where this was going until his father-in-law said, "The Painters Court estate included several tied farm cottages and a rather nice old farmhouse, which has been empty since the last manager left. John prefers to live in Hollowdene so had no use for it. If and when anything happens to me the estate of course passes to John but I would naturally want to give you something, lass."

Pausing in order to choose his words, he then went on. "This year a further act of parliament has granted women legal control of all property of every kind which they had owned at marriage or acquired after marriage by inheritance or by their own earnings."

As this disclosure progressed, Herbert's lips pursed tighter and his countenance positively glowered. His wife, appearing impervious to any of this, moaned out, "Please don't talk like that Father, I can't bear it."

"I am merely being practical and realistic. What I am proposing is to gift the farmhouse to you on the understanding that it becomes part of the trust. As beneficiary of the trust you will receive the income from it. There are two trustees who have the power to assist you at any time. One is John and the other is the family solicitor."

Kate said impatiently, "Never mind about the details, tell them about the house."

"I have recently had it extended and bought up-to-date and it's ready for occupation. If you moved there it would fulfill three criteria. Sadie would be nearer to us so that we can provide support if needed. It will be possible to get help for her in the house from someone in the village. It will ensure that her health will benefit from fresh country air."

Sensing that Herbert was preparing to put an immediate veto to the idea he hastened to add, "I know you have reservations and I appreciate that but before you dismiss it out of hand, would you at least do me the courtesy of coming to have a look at it?"

"It will hardly be convenient for me to get to work," he commented somewhat truculently.

"I grant that, although it is two miles shorter than the journey you have recently been making, with the added benefit of being on a hackney carriage route to Morford. Look at it in another way. You will be saving the money you are currently paying in rent which will enable you to put it aside toward the day when Sadie is hopefully stronger and you will possibly be able to purchase a house of your own in the city."

"Alright," he agreed reluctantly, "there's no harm in looking, I suppose."

"Good man," said Roland. "It's a lovely evening and there's no time like the present so I suggest we seize the moment."

Sadie's excitement mounted as their conveyance entered Shepherdstone and bowled along the high street, past the church towards her beloved Painters Court. A quarter of a mile before that they came to a halt outside a substantial mellow stone house set back from the road. One by one they clambered down and walked up the path to the solid oak front door. She held her breath as it swung open to reveal accommodation beyond her wildest dreams. Roland had spared nothing in renovating and modernising the property with many up-to-date innovations. Leaving mother and daughter to complete their explorations he turned to Herbert saying, "I would like to show you something which I think you will appreciate."

Placing a hand lightly on his shoulder he ushered him into the back garden, where stood a small stone building.

"This used to be a store for farm implements," he explained. "I thought that maybe it would make a useful workshop for you. There's a long wooden bench providing space on which to spread your designs, with shelves above for your tools and catalogues. In fact, it could be developed in any way you wished to give you your own freedom."

He watched the young man's face intently as he slowly absorbed the possibilities.

"What my old Dad would have given for something like this," Herbert breathed. "My Ma too, come to that, instead of having their work take over the house."

"Anyway, it was just a thought," said Roland, who had in fact contrived quite hard to make it a selling point.

Returning to the house Sadie looked at him anxiously. "What do you think?"

"I don't have to ask what you want so I suppose I'll have to agree," came the rather ungracious reply. "I can see some benefits attached to such a move," he allowed, "but it is only going to be a temporary measure until you're completely better."

With squeals of delight she flung her arms round his neck while Kate and Roland exchanged satisfied looks. Another hurdle had been accomplished.

Even before the harvest had been gathered in a vehicle, hired from a recently founded firm of cab proprietors and furniture removers in the city, conveyed the couple's possessions from Morford to Shepherdstone. Willing hands transferred and dispersed them into place under Sadie's direction while extra furnishings were spirited over from Hollowdene. Standing on a chair in order to hang a pair of bedroom curtains, Christine laughingly confided her envy. "It's just perfect, Sadie. With you being so near we're going to have such fun and so will Ted and Lucy."

As they happily planned the future, from the window they caught sight of Herbert busily shifting boxes into his garden retreat.

"I don't think you're going to see much of your husband," Christine laughed.

Sadie smiled, little realising how true that would prove to be.

When everyone had finally left, Lucy was tucked up in the nursery and they were seated at the table having a meal, Sadie put her hand over her husband's saying, "Thank you so much my dear. I know what sacrifices you have made for my sake and you will never know how much I value your thoughtfulness on my behalf."

"Well, there weren't that many alternatives at this juncture. I must own though that this is something we could never have aspired to," he said looking round appreciatively.

After the washing up was done and tired from the activities of the move they made their way upstairs. Turning into the master bedroom, Sadie heard the door open into the spare room.

"What are you doing, Herbert?"

"Well, I take it this is mine."

"I assumed that we would once more resume our old pattern. I thought you had been relegated for long enough since my illness."

Looking at her askance he replied bitterly, "How can we? You heard what the doctor said. We can't afford to take the risk."

"That doesn't mean that we have to sleep apart," she replied.

"Aw, Sadie love, we're both tired now. Just go to sleep and we'll talk about it tomorrow."

So saying he disappeared into the back room and shut the door.

Going into the nursery to check on Lucy, tears began to trickle down her cheeks as she desperately sought to find a way out of the dilemma.

Various attempts at contraception had been around for over two thousand years with erratic and unpredictable outcomes. Methods differed according to prevailing cultural and religious attitudes varying from ingestion of herbs, douching with vinegar, primitive pessaries, or tampons of lint soaked in honey and tips from the acaia shrub which contained the spermicidal agent lactic acid. There were those who held that it was impossible to become pregnant whilst breast feeding and although that myth was disproved it often led to the prolonged nursing of infants.

In Victorian England contraception was regarded as obscene. Abortion was prohibited by law unless performed in order to save the life of the woman. This left only condoms, coitus interruptus and the rhythm method, both of which were notoriously unreliable, the latter primarily due to ignorance regarding the actual mechanism of the menstrual cycle. Meanwhile the illicit back street abortionists who plied a bloody and dangerous trade flourished.

Condoms had been in use for several thousand years. Originally made of impregnated linen, the sixteenth century saw the application of animal tissue and intestines to make sheaths. However, they were expensive thus subject to re-use. This type of condom was described at the time as "an armour against pleasure, and a cobweb against infection." In 1855 the Goodyear tyre company began to mass produce vulcanised rubber condoms quickly and cheaply but they were as thick as bicycle inner tubes and had big seams down the side so were not particularly pleasant to use. Although they were more economical the skin condoms offered better sensitivity, thereby remaining more popular.

At about the same time a law came into force making the advertising of condoms illegal. Opposition to any form of birth control was voiced by the moralists and by the late 1800s the growing feminist movement was decidedly anti-condom. They wanted this area of life to be exclusively in the hands of women. However, a lack of anything more effective meant it remained the most popular method but the failure rates were high.

It was against this background that Sadie and Herbert were forced to confront their problem. Whichever way they looked at it abstention was the only course open to them.

"I managed without before we wed and I'll manage again," he said tersely, "so let's have no more talk on the matter."

Privately, Sadie had to admit a feeling of relief for she had secretly been dreading a return to their previous physical relationship. Coupled with that was a sadness and concern that the loss of intimacy was placing on their marriage. Although on the surface they each went about life as usual, deep down she acknowledged that their marriage was not as it had been.

Consequently she drew solace from her surroundings, the joys of motherhood and the closeness and warmth of her family. She made friendships in the village and joined in the various activities while constantly striving to ensure that Court Farmhouse became a homely and welcoming place. Her old interest in cooking revived and she revelled in the country pursuits of making preserves and chutneys and bottling fruit, greatly aided by the constant supplies of fresh vegetables and dairy produce from Hollowdene. Christine and Ted became constant companions as they visited each other's homes and it was an endless pleasure to watch the youngster's antics as the small boy tolerated Lucy's emerging bossiness and energetic high spirits.

Nevertheless, Sadie came to dread the onset of each winter which invariably occasioned bouts of bronchitis. Every time she was forced to accept willing help as she struggled for breath, while the fits of coughing took a toll on her energy and her heart. Gradually her husband came to accept that the likelihood of ever moving from Court Farmhouse was remote.

As his daughter began to develop beyond babyhood so Herbert took a greater interest in her. Sadie watched in delight on the day he emerged from his workshop proudly bearing the seat he had made for a swing, which he suspended from the bough of an old oak tree at the bottom of the garden. No sooner did she progress into needing footwear than a stream of beautiful boots and slippers constantly appeared.

Much to Sadie's surprise her husband approached her one day to ask whether she would be prepared to entertain Elijah Waite for a meal.

"Why, of course. We should have thought of it before. Whenever he cares to come will be fine."

In the event he elected to share a Sunday lunch with them and a great success it turned out to be. The old gentleman cast an admiring eye around their home, all the while nodding his approval. He professed himself to be enchanted with the young Lucy who, to everyone's amusement, was equally fascinated by his white beard.

After the meal, which was beautifully cooked and presented, and earned the cook the praise of both men, they retired to Herbert's workshop. There they remained in deep discussion until tea time. Fortunately Sadie had foreseen this possibility. After fortifying Elijah with her famous farmhouse scones, jam and cream, the lightest of Victoria sponges and the richest fruit cake he went on his way back to Morford impressed and heartened by all he'd seen.

In a rare demonstration of affection, Herbert put an arm round his wife's waist and complimented her on her skills as a hostess.

All was not lost, or so it seemed.

However, Herbert was experiencing problems from another quarter. In March 1895 the great lock-out began. Posters calling for a minimum wage and the abolition of low paid piece work appeared. Increasing mechanisation continued to threaten those outworkers and handworkers who didn't actually work in the factory. Although they didn't want it, they were all members of the union and strike action seemed the only way open to them in order to secure their jobs at a reasonable rate.

When Herbert, as works manager, defied the strike call he was hooted and booed all the way up the street.

Elijah decided that the time had come for Herbert to take the place within the firm which the old man felt he had earned by merit and hard work. His appointment to the board as a working director was announced and did not pass without comment in several quarters, not all of it favourable. If Herbert was aware of this he evinced no concern. At last he had proved himself and shown them all, especially his in-laws, that he was a person to be reckoned with in his own right.

Sadly, his moment of glory was shortlived as, to the shock of everyone, Roland suffered a fatal heart attack whilst out working on the farm and died at the age of sixty four. When John arrived to break the news Sadie was heartbroken for she had always regarded her father as her champion.

Kate was utterly devastated but, following the funeral, she began making decisions in her old independent manner. Addressing her son she suggested that he, Christine and Ted should take their rightful place in the farmhouse at Hollowdene.

"It's far too big for me now. I shall just rattle round like a small pea in an overgrown pod," she said.

John was equally certain that she would be very unhappy exchanging it for their modest cottage. In the end she was persuaded to remain at the farm but with her own private rooms.

"How do you feel about that?" Sadie asked her sister-in-law.

"Quite honestly, it won't be a problem. The place is so large and I've always got on well with your mama. Added to which Ted will help to take the edge off things for her. He's very fond of his grandma and it's impossible to remain sad for long when he's around."

Within a couple of months while still grieving the loss of her adored father the day arrived that Sadie had secretly been dreading. It was time for Lucy to start school.

By the end of the Victorian era all children under thirteen had to go to school. Day schools sprang up in most villages, many organised by churches and charities. The school could be quite a grim building. The rooms were warmed by a single stove or open fire and there was little fresh air because the windows were built high in the walls, to stop pupils looking outside and being distracted from their work.

Lessons lasted from 9am-5pm with a two hour break for lunch. They were concentrated on the "three Rs" – Reading, wRiting and aRithmetic. The inclusion of the fourth "R" of religion was simply assumed as right. Children learned by reciting like parrots, until they were word-perfect.

At Herbert's insistence Lucy was sent to the newly opened school in Shepeherdstone rather than undertaking any form of private education.

"If she's got it in her she will succeed," he told Sadie. "She must take her chance with the others."

He proved himself right. A bright, outgoing and popular child, Lucy took to school as the proverbial duck to water. It came as no surprise, therefore, when the head teacher recommended that she be allowed to continue her education beyond the age of thirteen.

In the late Victorian era, the ancient grammar school system was reorganised to provide secondary education for a larger and wider cross section of pupils.

Most of the original schools were attached to cathedrals and Morford already boasted one dating back to the sixteenth century.

The Endowed Schools Act of 1869 saw grammar schools re-invented as academically orientated secondary schools offering both a literary and scientific curricula. Across the country, schools endowed to offer free instruction to boys were re-modelled as fee-paying schools for both sexes, but also provided a few competitive scholarships. A girls' grammar school established in a town or city with an older boys' grammar school would often be named a 'high school'.

Herbert and Sadie were both proud and delighted when the equally excited village teacher announced that their daughter had won a place at Morford High.

Lucy accepted the heartfelt congratulations of her grandmother and uncle with grace and her cousin Ted's merciless teasing with her customary feistiness.

"Just because you were too dim and lazy," she mocked, "you will be tied to a pitchfork and manure for the rest of your life."

"Which is all I've ever wanted," he shouted as he picked up the aforementioned tool and proceeded to chase his cousin round the farmyard.

Sadie and Christine watched in amusement, affectionately commenting on the close bond which still existed between the two youngsters.

"What career do you think Lucy will choose to follow," her sister-in-law asked.

"Herbert is secretly hoping that she'll opt for teaching but who knows."

"Openings are appearing for women in fields that neither you nor I could have dreamed of," said Christine wistfully. "After all, look at Elizabeth Garrett Anderson and her successful struggle to break into the male-dominated medical profession."

"What about the telephone and typewriter?" Sadie volunteered. "According to Herbert there is a growing need for competent women with the appropriate knowledge and secretarial skills to be employed in the business world."

Sighing, she went on to add, "The recent death of the dear Queen truly has marked the end of an era. What this new century will bring forth you and I can't even begin to imagine."

Overhearing her mother's last comment, Lucy was quick to respond.

"I can tell you one thing that is going to be different, for sure, and that is the position of women in society. You have all accepted that a woman's place is in the home and her body a temple to her husband, so that he can simply concentrate on making money."

Sadie flinched. "I can't imagine where you get hold of these ideas, Lucy."

"I read, Mother and I tell you now, reform is coming."

"Well, you'd better not let your father hear you talking in such a way, is all I can say."

However, as time went on, and Lucy's knowledge and awareness grew and her thoughts developed, she became even more confident and outspoken about her views. By the time she changed schools she was seeing less and less of her father whose work seemed to occupy him more and more.

At the turn of the century Elijah Waite had died. To the chagrin of the other members of the company he had left the majority of his shares to his long-time protegé. Herbert's ego and authority increased proportionately. There were frequent late nights and visits away on business matters, all of which Sadie accepted with patience and understanding. Her daughter had no such tolerance and secretly deplored the fact that her mother didn't ever seem to stand up to him.

Indeed, Lucy displayed no such fine feelings when the time arrived to reveal the path she had decided upon for her future career. Seated round the dinner table on one of the increasingly rare occasions that her father graced them with his presence, she suddenly announced: "By the way, I've decided that when I leave Morford High at the end of the school year, I'm going to do my nurse training."

Sadie raised her head in surprise while Herbert gave a suitable impression of a whale having apoplexy.

"Stuff and nonsense," he exploded when he had regained his composure. "What a complete and utter waste of a fine secondary education. You could choose any number of things and you are content to settle for that."

As Lucy prepared to launch forth he addressed his wife saying with a sneer, "I suppose this is all yours and your mother's doing."

For once Sadie rounded on him. "How dare you think such a thing even for an instant. For your information this news has come as much of a surprise to me as it has to you."

Turning to her daughter she questioned, "Are you really sure about this because it is a role which I never once imagined you wanting to fill?"

"Well, let's put it this way. Nothing else really seems to appeal so I intend to give it a go. If I find that it isn't for me, I can always try another avenue," she finished gaily.

Looking at her father's scowling face she grinned. "Cheer up Papa, it may never happen."

Scraping his chair back from the table he shot one last look in her direction before leaving. "Don't come crying to me when it all goes wrong, as it undoubtedly will, for I completely wash my hands of you. Anyone less suited to such a profession is hard to imagine."

With which he took himself off to his workshop, leaving mother and daughter to discuss the matter in a more rational manner.

Later, tossing and turning in the large double bed, Sadie could only reflect that for all Lucy's talk, some things never seemed to change - at least, not for the women of their family anyway.

Part Three
Lucy Dane

Chapter One

New Horizons

" You will be provided with board and lodging plus a starting salary of eight pounds a year. The training will last for three years at the end of which you will receive your final certificate if you are found to be proficient. It is not mandatory but I hope that, once you are qualified, you will remain for at least one year so that the Royal may benefit from the considerable time and effort that will be expended on your education."

"Yes Matron. Thank you Matron," murmured Lucy dutifully and with uncharacteristic meekness.

Inclining her head in acknowledgment Matron continued. "The date set for your entry is September 1st when you will present yourself to Home Sister. Please bring the minimum of luggage making sure that you obtain all the required items for which you will receive a list before you leave."

"Yes Matron," she uttered respectfully.

"Now, Miss Dane, you are in something of a unique and fortunate position in that you already have some knowledge of the life of a nurse and the demands which will be made. However, I wish to make it quite clear that, despite your family's long and illustrious ties with this establishment, you will be shown no preferential treatment."

"Neither do I want any," Lucy replied. "Indeed, I'd rather be as anonymous as possible."

Not for the first time she pondered the wisdom of her decision to train at the Royal. Had it not been for her mother's frail health and her father's seeming antagonism, she probably would have set her sights on London, but it was too late now - the die had been cast.

To mark Queen Victoria's Golden Jubilee back in 1887, buildings and statues, fountains and charitable institutions had sprung up across England in tribute to her long reign. Morford had marked the occasion by building an imposing, red-brick nurses' home in the grounds of the hospital, in which to house the steadily increasing number of young girls seeking what they hoped would be a satisfying career in the brave new world where previously unheard of opportunities for women were tentatively, oh so tentatively, becoming more acceptable. This act of philanthropy had been duly recognised when the right was conferred upon the hospital, henceforth, to be styled as Morford Royal Infirmary, affectionately known to the staff as the MRI.

On the appointed date in 1908 Lucy duly presented herself at the door of this impressive residence. An indifferent maid led her upstairs and along interminable corridors decorated in the customary uninspiring brown and cream institutional paint. Stopping outside a solid varnished door she unlocked and opened it and gestured the girl inside, then handed her the key and left without a word.

Loosening her coat and exhaling deeply Lucy took stock of her new surroundings. Although by no means large the room had been carefully but plainly furnished and contained a corner wardrobe, a heavy chest of drawers and mirror, a small table and hard, upright chair. The floor was polished wood on which stood a single bed covered with a rather insipid beige cotton spread. However, her eyes lighted appreciatively on the unimagined luxury of a small, corner washbasin with hot and cold running water. She grinned as she thought how incredulous her mother and grandmother would be after all their dire warnings. The late Victorian and early Edwardian era saw technological changes which enhanced lifestyle. With the installation of bathrooms, central heating and electricity significant improvements were being achieved. When building the nurses' home, the Infirmary governors had clearly considered such things a wise investment.

Moving to the window her eye was immediately drawn to the spacious area of garden bounded on three sides by the walls of the home. In the very centre a small lawn tennis court had been marked out. 'Wonders will never cease,' she thought, eyeing the large French windows giving access to a lawn and flowerbeds and wooden seats which had been strategically placed. "Perhaps life will actually be quite tolerable."

Heaving her modest luggage onto the table, Lucy set about unpacking and started to stamp her mark on the room with the few personal knick-knacks brought from home. This finished, she turned her attention to the uniform laid out on the bed, in which she was required to present herself in time for tea. A long heavy duty cotton dress in a shade of lilac, which buttoned down the front, appeared acceptable at first sight until she felt the unforgiving boned bodice. Struggling into its spotless confines she searched for the required studs with which to fasten the starched collar, cuffs and belt. Next followed the bibbed and starched apron topped with a Sister Dora type cap with fluted pleats down the back, which sat somewhat awkwardly on her springy copper curls.

"Hmm! Not half bad," she acknowledged, viewing her trim figure in the mirror with some satisfaction. Stuffing a clean handkerchief into her pocket, followed by a small notebook and pencil, she set out to navigate a course to the dining room and a meeting with the rest of her companions in this new venture. They proved to be quite a mixed group of largely middle-class girls all intent on forging a career which would provide them with some kind of independence.

It didn't really matter what ailed a person. If sickness befell anyone at the beginning of the twentieth century, a doctor couldn't do much more than provide limited medicinal comfort until the body defeated the illness, or succumbed to it. He had few goodies in his little black bag beyond morphia and aspirin to ease pain, quinine to fight off malaria, digitalis for heart failure, ergot for post-partum haemorrhage and smallpox vaccine. Tincture of benzoin, or Friar's Balsam, provided two medicinal uses: as an antiseptic treatment for damaged skin and as an inhalant and decongestant, while arnica aided care of bruises and abrasions. In the last years of the eighteen hundreds Roentgen discovered x-rays and the Curies revealed the possible usefulness of radium but these were in their infancy. By 1903 it was possible to obtain an electrocardiograph and, two years later, the invention of the sphygmomanometer enabled the recording of blood pressure.

Against such a backdrop it was easy to see the importance of good nursing ministrations, which could be the only thing to make a sufferer's life bearable. As a result the training was still fairly basic and heavily slanted towards physical care and procedures.

Facing the latest intake of nursing recruits the Sister Tutor began to deliver a well-rehearsed discourse.

"At the centre of nursing is a core of hard, day-to-day work. It bears no resemblance to the popular conceptions of 'the soothing hand on the fevered brow'. There is no place for romantic nonsense in this profession," declaimed that awesome figure in a forbidding voice.

"There will be no intimate contact between nurses and patients or nurses and doctors," she went on. "During your training some lectures given by hospital consultants will be made available to you. This is an honour unknown to your predecessors and it is up to you to make the most of these opportunities. Should such instruction chance to fall during any time off, including sleeping hours whilst on night duty, you will still be expected to attend."

"I don't think much has changed," Lucy informed Kate and Sadie on a visit home.

"Except that you get considerably more time off," her grandmother commented with asperity.

"Thank goodness and I should think so too. I think I'd go mad cooped up indoors day after day with all that regimentation."

"Do I detect signs of misgivings with your choice of career?" Kate quizzed.

"Heaven's no! I'm really enjoying it and, without wishing to sound smug, I'm finding it a lot easier than many of them. So far the theory is fascinating and easily digestible, which is more than can be said for the food."

"So how do you spend your spare time?" her mother enquired.

"Well, there's so much to do in Morford that we're spoilt for choice," she responded non-committally.

What she omitted to tell them was of her passionate interest in, and fascination with, the steadily growing suffragette movement. The struggle for women's suffrage, affording them the right to vote, wasn't just a national concern but one which had been experienced in other countries, many of whom had already succeeded in achieving their aims. New Zealand was often said to be the first country to grant the right, although Sweden acceded to the demand as far back as 1718, but only for property-owning women. In 1906, the year before Lucy commenced training, Finland accorded them not only the vote but permission to stand in elections regardless of wealth, race or social class.

In 1903 Emmeline Pankhurst, with the help of her two daughters, Christabel and Sylvia, formed the Women's Social and Political Union (WSPU) with the intention of forcing the matter in Britain. Initially fairly low key it soon escalated and by 1908 extreme activism, with street marches and cases of criminal damage and affray, regularly resulted in violent clashes with the police. This resulted in prison sentences being handed out to the unrepentant perpetrators which marked the first incidents of hunger strikes and led to the controversial and obnoxious practice of force feeding.

It was during her final years at school that Lucy became aware of the importance and significance of this cause and avidly read any accounts that appeared in the newspapers. It wasn't long before her intelligent grasp of the subject, coupled with a growing talent for articulate outspokenness, brought her into conflict with her father.

Her early years had been spent between Shepherdstone and Hollowdene where she enjoyed happy times, running wild with her cousin Ted and the warmth of family life. Her father's frequent absences she had regarded as the norm. By the start of her secondary school education, Herbert had become an increasingly distant figure in her life. She felt sorry for her mother, without fully understanding why, and with the egocentricity of youth was too busy pursuing her own friendships and interests to devote any real thought to the matter. Nevertheless, her new-found interest had sparked some increasingly heated exchanges with her father on the subject when she did see him, and his attitude began to cause tensions and extreme annoyance.

The WSPU had adopted the colours purple, white and green as their insignia, which represented dignity, purity and hope. Banners, flags and rosettes proclaimed the message and it was only a popular myth which maintained that the colours were really green, white and violet with the acronym GWV spelling 'Give Women Votes'.

Feeling it would be imprudent to overtly proclaim their allegiance for fear of reaction from the hospital hierarchy, Lucy and her friends surreptitiously sported the enamel badges on the inside collars of their coats. Nevertheless, when public meetings were arranged in the city it wasn't long before they were showing both interest and support.

In 1896, to the wonderment of the local population, the first car was driven in Morford at an average speed of around 10-12mph. Although the first model had been demonstrated abroad as far back as 1879 it wasn't until 1885 that the petrol-fuelled internal combustion engine made its appearance, spearheaded by German inventors. In Britain a four-wheeled model was produced in nearby Coventry in 1895. The city was already a world leader in cycle manufacture and motorising it was simply a natural progression. The first production line began in 1900 with the aim of creating a vehicle for the middle classes at a cost of just under two hundred pounds. However, it wasn't until 1905 that motorised transport really began to replace the horse and, in 1908, the first motor taxi cab made its appearance. Before petrol filling stations opened in the early 1920s motorists had to buy petrol in two-gallon cans from the chemists, hardware stores and garages.

Amidst great excitement Herbert, ever keen to promote his standing in the community, had recently purchased a motor car. Heading for a locally organised meeting of the WSPU one evening, Lucy happened to be passing her father's Club and spotted his car parked on the forecourt. Mentally thanking her lucky stars that he wasn't there to quiz her as to what she was doing, she swiftly reached the turning into the next side street and, looking along it, to her great surprise spotted the unmistakable gait and figure of Herbert Dane walking briskly past a neat terrace of reasonably new houses. Drawing back behind a convenient hedge she furtively peered around it in time to see him stop, draw something from his pocket, mount the flight of steps and insert what had to be a key into the lock. The next moment he had passed inside and closed the door behind him.

How odd she thought. Curiosity getting the better of her she prepared to casually saunter past the residence in question in order to ascertain the number. Having done that, she retraced her steps. Noting the plate bearing the name of the road, she consigned to memory 15, Mayors Walk. Quickening her pace so as not to miss the opening speech, she tried to work out what he could have been doing there. A very modern woman with a fertile imagination and a realistic mind didn't have too much trouble in putting two and two together. Proving her suspicions to be correct, however, was another matter.

Over the next few weeks her nursing duties prevented any further sallies into town but afforded her plenty of time for thoughtful planning. As a result, at the first opportunity, she presented herself at the house in question at an hour to coincide with the usual tea-time. Taking a deep breath she grasped the knocker and rapped smartly. Almost immediately the door opened and she found herself confronted by a young lad of about nine or ten. Scarcely able to suppress a sharp gasp, she stared in amazement at the boy bearing an undeniable resemblance to her father and blurted out her prepared words. "Could I speak to Mr. or Mrs. Farmer please?" she asked.

"There's no one of that name living here," he answered politely but expressionlessly.

From a room at the end of the hall the figure of a woman emerged and a well modulated voice said, "What's to do, Billy?"

Turning towards her he shrugged his shoulders. "This lady wants a Mr. and Mrs. Farmer."

Coming to stand at the door, Lucy had the chance to study her closer. Simply but tidily dressed with an apron covering her skirt she presented a perfectly ordinary picture of someone about thirty-five to forty years old, of medium height with medium brown hair - in fact everything about her was unremarkable.

"Are you sure you've got the right address?" she suggested.

"This is 15 Mayors Walk, isn't it?"

"That's right, but there's no one of that name here."

Trying to look puzzled, Lucy ploughed on. "Well, those are the details I've been given. They're an elderly couple," she offered. "The gentleman is quite badly crippled."

179

"I'm afraid I can't help you. I don't know of anyone round here fitting that description."

"Have you actually lived here long?" she persisted.

"Ever since the houses were built," she replied.

"Goodness, you should know if anyone does," Lucy laughed. "I'll have to try and get some more details. I'm so sorry to have bothered you Mrs. er... " she said leaving the question hanging in the air.

"Mrs. Burton," came the helpful reply.

"Thank you so much, and I'm sorry for the trouble."

Managing to maintain her composure, Lucy descended the steps onto the pavement and with a final acknowledgment made her way back up the road, her mind racing.

Without doubt the mystery was resolved. The question remained, what to do with the information?

For days Lucy pondered her dilemma while feelings of pity for her mother and an intense loathing of her father grew. Finally she plucked up courage and left a note for him at his Club. 'Dear Father, I really need to see you urgently. I am off-duty from 6pm on Thursday and will meet you by the bandstand in the park within half-an-hour unless I hear from you to the contrary. Please don't mention this to Mother.'

Herbert's surprise on receipt of the note was quickly overtaken by suspicions as to what predicament had befallen his daughter. As a result, he set out for the rendezvous quite prepared to play the heavy father. He was somewhat taken aback, therefore, by Lucy's response to his opening gambit.

"Well young lady, what kind of a mess have you got yourself into?"

Never had she felt such anger. Regarding him unflinchingly, she said, "On the contrary Father, it isn't me that's in a mess but you, and I felt you should know."

"What on earth are you going on about, girl?"

Without deflecting her gaze she answered quietly, "I think there is something that you need to tell me about 15 Mayors Walk and Mrs. Burton and Billy, don't you?"

For a brief moment she actually felt sorry for him. The broadside had caught him completely off guard. Even had he managed to find

180

immediate words with which to counter the attack, his face would have betrayed him. Sitting hunched forward with his hands clasped between his knees he stared intently at the ground as though searching for inspiration.

"You don't deny it then?" she persisted.

When no response was forthcoming, she continued.

"I suppose you thought and hoped that no one would ever find out."

"May I ask how you did?" he enquired in a subdued voice.

"It doesn't matter how. What is of importance are the terrible consequences this could have wreaked on future generations if I hadn't."

Looking up in surprise and with a trace of belligerence in his voice he said, "What in God's name are you talking about?"

Impatiently she spat out, "You're the clever one. Think. Suppose, in years to come I marry and have a son who happens to meet and marry Billy's daughter?"

"Highly improbable," he muttered.

"It is unlikely though not impossible. But it wouldn't be your problem would it? Frankly, the selfishness and moral irresponsibility of your actions appall me. Quite apart from any future generations, what about Mother? Does she know about any of this?"

"No," he mumbled, "and neither must she."

"Oh, don't worry, your sorry secret is safe with me because I know that, in her state of health, the shock and the shame would likely kill her - or doesn't that bother you? And what about me?" she persisted. "Did you once spare either of us a thought?"

With a remarkable return to his usual bullishness, Herbert quickly retorted. "Did either of you give a damn about my situation? Can you imagine what it's like to be trapped in a marriage with someone whose health renders her so frail that it is virtually impossible to lead any kind of normal married life?"

"That is hardly Mother's fault."

"Maybe not, but it's my misfortune," he countered.

"It's all about you Father, isn't it? Your feelings, your needs. How do

181

you think Mother feels, making a lovely home for us all yet being treated without any noticeable affection, like a second-rate citizen, a non person? And you wonder that I am joining in the fight for women's rights?"

Regaining his usual pose he jeered: "I thought it wouldn't be long before this suffragette nonsense was brought up."

Before he could continue, Lucy interrupted. "This particular revelation is a prime example of the need to pursue women's rights. As it stands a husband can divorce his wife on the grounds of her adultery. However, the unfortunate wife has no such entitlement if her husband is unfaithful, as you have been. And you think that is fair?"

When she saw that no response was forthcoming, and sensing an opportunity, Lucy warmed to her theme.

"Why should there be different moral standards for men and women? Why should women be nothing more than mere chattels?"

"That's hardly so now," he interrupted swiftly. "What about the comparatively recent Married Woman's Property Act? At one time her wealth and assets were passed to her husband, now she holds them in her own right as I know only too well. How do you think I feel living in a house that isn't mine and never will be?"

Seeing her puzzled look he said, "You didn't know that, did you? Thanks to the machinations of your grandparents, everything is beautifully tied up in favour of you and your mother. What do you think that does for a man's esteem?"

"Under the circumstances, Father, I can think of no more prudent a move and I'm relieved that, while you are busy supporting your other family, at least I know that Mother is secure."

"I might know you'd take her side. I'll have you know that your mother has never wanted for anything materially. Agnes works hard at a job in order to contribute to 'that other family' as you put it."

"Mum may have all that she needs materially but she hardly enjoys much of your affection or company. This isn't about taking sides Father. It is about rights and wrongs and blatant unfairness. One of the reasons I am such an adherent of the suffrage cause is the hope that through political equality it may be possible to establish domestic equality."

"It's all absolute poppycock and if you persist with this you are going to find yourself in trouble. And don't expect me to come and bail you out."

"Believe me, I wouldn't dream of asking or wanting you to."

"A little more respect from you wouldn't come amiss," he said, the old pompous tone emerging once more. "After all, I'm still your father."

Regarding him with irritation she replied, "Respect isn't an automatic right. Respect has to be earned."

An uncomfortable silence developed between them as though neither knew what to do next. Finally, Herbert got to his feet and stood looking down at her before saying: "So what happens now?"

"Father, that is entirely up to you. I can only repeat that Mother will never learn of this from me."

"Thank you," he grunted grudgingly, before quickly adding, "and we won't mention this subject again, eh?"

"Not unless something happens that will have a fundamental affect on Mother's well-being."

And with that he had to be content.

***

Eventually the day arrived when Lucy completed her training. To both Kate and Sadie's delight she had not only passed with flying colours but was awarded a certificate for outstanding achievement. To mark the occasion, the whole family were invited to attend the first-ever prize giving ceremony in Morford Civic Hall which, thereafter, was to become an annual event. Although her mobility was becoming impaired, Kate was determined to be present. In a rare gesture Herbert collected her in the car and conveyed her in style. Afterwards they all assembled in the drawing room at Court Farm to drink a toast to Lucy which was followed by cheers and applause. Sadie fastened round her daughter's slim waist the belt with the Victorian silver buckle that was about to see service with a third generation.

Reminiscences of experiences flew back and forth between 'the three Nightingales', as they were referred to by the others. Even her father presented her with an exquisite pair of shoes, which he had crafted himself in the latest fashion, plus a small cheque. As she dutifully planted a kiss on his cheek she couldn't help but think of it as a conscience offering, knowing that it was only a temporary truce in an ongoing skirmish. Nothing, however, could destroy the total pleasure of that never-to-be-forgotten evening.

Although she returned to the Royal to undertake her assignment as a staff nurse in the Casualty Department one thing was very obvious to her - at some point in the not-to-distant future she would simply have to get away from Morford, but where to go and what to do?

As a result of her experiences in the Crimea, Florence Nightingale had recognised the need for a permanent medical facility to be established specifically for the training of army surgeons and nurses. Her written reports and recommendations received considerable support from some politicians and men in high places, also capturing the interest of Queen Victoria herself who directed that a hospital be built specifically for the purpose. In May 1856 Her Majesty laid the foundation stone of what would become The Royal Victoria Hospital at Netley, Southampton. Erected in twenty seven acres of parkland, on the site of a thirteenth century Cistercian monastery, the location was specifically chosen so that hospital ships from around the British Empire could safely dock and disembark patients.

It was a magnificent brick edifice dressed with Portland stone and topped by a dome affording stunning views out across Southampton Water. Sadly, it was neither convenient nor practical and not at all the design envisaged by Miss Nightingale. There were three floors with corridors a quarter of a mile long comprising 138 wards with one thousand beds. Reputed to be the largest Military Hospital anywhere in the world it was finally opened in March 1863. Three years later a railway line was laid connecting Netley directly with the docks, almost immediately to be followed by a spur line extending into the grounds themselves so that it had its own station. Out of sight, tucked away in a corner, a military cemetery was established a year later to cater for the small proportion of patients who would not survive.

Finally, in 1881, the project was given the official title of The Army Nursing Service.

Following the death of Queen Victoria, her daughter-in-law continued her interest in the work being carried out with the result that, in 1902, Queen Alexandra's Imperial Military Nursing Service was established by Royal Warrant at a time of relative peace in the British Empire. The salaries of army nurses were increased so that they were above the rate of civilian nurses and each trained nurse carried the title Sister.

In view of her ever-worsening relationship with her father, and a desire to explore the world beyond the confines of Morford, Lucy resolved to leave the Royal as soon as the statutory year of post-registration service had been fulfilled. After studying the options open to her she decided that a career in military nursing afforded the best opportunity of meeting her aims.

At this time there were only around 250 regular trained members of Queen Alexandra's Imperial Military Nursing Service, mainly because of the strict rules. Personnel had to be single, fully qualified general nurses and of good social status.

Resolutely Lucy set about researching the requirements and possibilities, and was pleased and excited when she finally heard that she had fulfilled all the conditions and standards and would be accepted for training. This then was Lucy's aspiration for the next stage of her career.

News of her decision was received with mixed reactions. Her grandmother was immediately encouraging. Vivid memories of her time at Scutari flashed through Kate's mind. Now she would have a firsthand opportunity to see just how much progress had been made as a direct result of the appalling suffering and chaotic conditions which had prevailed in that campaign. Sadie, although pleased to offer her support, was apprehensive for two reasons. Fearful as she was of the possible implications for the safety of her only child in the unlikely event of hostilities breaking out somewhere, she was also acutely aware of the huge gap that Lucy's departure would leave in her own life. Recognising the selfishness of this thinking and mindful of the times when she had flown in the face of her own mother's wishes, she did nothing to stand in the girl's way.

Her father, however, was a completely different matter.

"I have never heard anything so preposterous in all my life," he spluttered.

"May I be permitted to ask why?" his daughter enquired icily.

"For a start, the army is no place for women."

Lucy groaned. "I am not enlisting to brandish a gun, merely learning to deploy my skills in another direction."

"Stuff and nonsense!" he disagreed. "You've filled your head with all this irritating suffragette baloney and you're merely out to prove a point. What about your mother? Have you given a thought to her feelings?" he persisted.

Sadie, who had been sitting tensely on the edge of her chair, quickly intervened.

"Lucy isn't responsible for me in any way, Herbert. She has her own life to lead within the profession which she has chosen."

"That's right, you stick up for her. Anything to do with nursing would be alright by you."

Before his wife could find words to reply, Lucy calmly responded. "Don't you think that's a bit rich, coming from you?"

Striking a somewhat affected pose, with his feet apart and his fingers stuck in his waistcoat pockets, he puffed out his chest, saying: "Your point being?"

"From a little girl I can remember you saying how the business of boots and shoes was in your blood - something handed down through the family."

"And so it is," he retorted proudly.

"Well, in just the same way, nursing happens to course through my veins. Unfortunately, you didn't have a son to follow in your footsteps, although I'm sure you're grooming someone to fill the role," she said slyly, "yet you resent me pursuing mine."

Casting a baleful look at her, Herbert seriously began to wonder whether it would be any bad thing to have this outspoken daughter conveniently situated away from the environs of Morford. He was irritated by her subtle, snide comments which threatened his secret, and the lack of respect she now accorded him.

Thus it was with a feeling of liberation, and a positive spring in her step, that this determined young lady took her leave of old haunts in 1913. As the train bearing Lucy south drew into King's Cross station she removed her bag from the rack, straightened her clothes and prepared to alight. The next hurdle was to accomplish the journey to Waterloo station.

The beginning of the century had seen the emergence of a growing underground train network in the capital. The carriages were small, cramped and windowless and the ride unpleasantly rough. To Lucy it was a whole new experience and her heart skipped a beat as she consigned herself to the cavernous depths below the city streets.

Surfacing unscathed she made her way to the platform from which the Southampton train departed. There were only a few passengers awaiting its arrival and she studied them with covert interest. Her gaze was drawn towards a young woman of about her own age and she smiled to herself inwardly. Approaching her she gave a grin and said: "Excuse me, would I be wrong in thinking that you are heading for the military hospital at Netley?"

A pair of slightly startled grey eyes turned to meet her greenish-amber ones.

"Goodness. Are you blessed with second sight or something?" The words were uttered in a muted but unmistakable London accent.

"Not really, though it seemed a reasonable probability. It takes a nurse to know one, or words to that effect."

Sizing each other up, Lucy took the initiative. "By the way, I'm Lucy Dane, fresh down from the Midlands."

"And I'm Alice Penrose, native of this city, and you don't know how good it is to meet a kindred soul."

By the time they finally reached their destination they were still chattering nineteen to the dozen and the seal on their future friendship had been firmly set. Clutching their belongings they approached with awe the imposing edifice that was to be their home.

"It's absolutely huge," Lucy breathed.

"My feet are already aching at the thought of all the miles of floor," her companion groaned.

On the first morning they presented themselves for inspection in their smart new uniforms consisting of a grey dress with a square-bibbed, white apron, white muslin cap and short scarlet cape. The cape was supposedly designed to keep the sisters warm and the officers cool! Fixed to the back of this, between the shoulder blades, was a stiff Alexandra rose.

In the event, the daily routine on the wards was not greatly different from that of the hospitals they had so recently left and their training stood them in good stead. However, it had not prepared them for the extra demands of their new roles. Day after day they were grounded in the arts of establishing emergency field clearing stations and makeshift operating theatres, or transforming unlikely looking premises into efficiently functioning wards. Throughout it all was the constant exhortation to maintain the highest possible levels of cleanliness and hygiene.

"The key to being an excellent army nurse is resourcefulness, adaptability, improvisation, initiative and the capacity to keep a clear head. These are skills which you will need in abundance in a battlefield situation," the forbidding-looking tutor declared with her no-nonsense approach. "Remember, the enemy isn't only the man wielding a gun, it is also the elements," she exhorted them as they battled to erect bell tents in the wind and rain. "You're not in a drawing room now, Sisters."

When their backs were breaking and every muscle ached, they were dispatched back to the wards with their taskmaster's final words ringing in their ears. "The men who are your patients are dependent on you at all times and their needs are paramount. All these other things will be fitted in around those needs."

"They didn't tell us that entrants needed six pairs of hands, the strength of a lion and the constitution of an ox," wailed Lucy as she demonstrated her impressive biceps to anyone interested.

Another day found them being driven round the grounds in motorised vehicles as they lurched from side to side whilst attempting to dress wounds or administer first aid.

"The troops will arrive covered in lice and you will often get infected after caring for them. These lice are nick-named 'the grey backs' and they are the very devil to get rid of. There's a shortage of water and you find yourselves having to wash the men in a canvas bowl in a tent. How are you going to manage the situation?" rapped the relentless voice of their tormentor.

"Phew! This is a long way from the women's gynae ward," whispered Alice with feeling.

Before Lucy could respond the voice of their commanding officer called out: "Sister Dane, your patient has lost a leg, is suffering from severe abdominal wounds and is bleeding to death. What are you doing about it?"

"Praying hard," she muttered under her breath.

However, there were more restful periods when they found themselves seated in the relative comfort of the classroom facing a theoretical range of issues, some of which would have caused their genteel relatives to throw up their hands in horror.

"What do you think is one of the biggest medical problems facing any army?" one Medical Officer asked at the start of his lecture.

Lucy put forward a good argument for trauma and blood loss but they were all somewhat startled when he bellowed: "Sex, ladies, pure and simple. Only, the sex I'm referring to isn't pure. In the sixteenth century it was called 'the great pox'. Today we refer to it as 'the immoral disease' or VD. Venereal disease down the years has decimated armies, lost battles for a nation and wreaked suffering which may last a lifetime."

Some rather delicate eyes sought a convenient spot on which to fix their gaze while their speaker warmed to his theme.

"So, what is the army doing about it, you may ask? To date, in all areas where servicemen tend to congregate, and prostitutes ply their trade, treatment centers have been set up."

Peering round at them he continued. "Yes, I'm afraid it is you good ladies who are largely responsible for this contagion with your wiles and charms."

Shuffling uncomfortably in their seats they waited for the next fusillade.

"Nasty diseases these, especially syphilis, and until recently there wasn't much to be done although arsenic has been used in the attempt. Now, thanks to one Dr. Paul Ehrlich and his research, there is a 'magic bullet' that will hopefully target and destroy the organism responsible. Only three years ago the drug Sarvasan was added to the doctor's ammunition and we are very optimistic," he announced with satisfaction.

Pacing back and forth across the front of the room he suddenly spun round to face them.

"So, I can hear you thinking. Where do you come in? Sisters, you must be vigilant at all times and keep one eye open for the tell-tale sores and signs indicating the disease, which may present themselves in the course of your general care of the patient. If this wretched abomination isn't recognised, caught early and speedily dealt with, untold havoc can be wreaked. Men could pass it on to their unsuspecting wives and innocent mothers to their children. If untreated, the germ can lie dormant for years ultimately causing irreversible damage to the brain, nerves, eyes, heart, bones and joints."

If this homily was aimed to shock it had certainly hit the target. To most of those listening any previous knowledge, or experience, would have been peripheral and not within their remit.

Striding towards the door, the lecturer turned to deliver one last salvo. "In the event of a war, Sisters, we shall be fighting it on two fronts, namely military might and disease. If the latter is allowed to overtake the former, then all will be lost. It has been suggested that Napoleon lost the Battle of Waterloo because his mind was distracted from military strategy by the discomfort being experienced from his haemorrhoids. Remember that vigilance on your part, plus active pursuit of this enemy, is the key to any success in overcoming it."

Following his exit they sunk into a somewhat more comfortable pose and finally acknowledged that, indeed, this was a nurse training like no other. At the end of it they prepared to be disbursed to other military nursing establishments around the country. Many of the garrison towns, such as Colchester, boasted their own army hospitals, and the Royal Herbert at Woolwich had been purpose-built in the pavilion style recommended by Florence Nightingale.

"I do hope we can get a posting somewhere together," said Alice wistfully one evening as they were settling down with a hot drink before turning in for the night. "We've been through so much together right from the start that I can't bear the thought of having to start all over again with someone new."

It transpired that the matter was taken right out of their hands and any ideas they may have harboured as to the unlikelihood that they would ever be called upon to put their new found talents to the test, were crushed almost immediately. By the middle of 1914 it became increasingly clear that war storms were gathering across the European continent. By the end of August seventeen million men from eight nations were involved in a colossal conflict, the magnitude of which had never before been witnessed.

'Your Country Needs You' was the cry of the Secretary of State for War, Lord Kitchener, which blazed forth from every billboard and hoarding in the land in September 1914.

True to the Medical Officer's predictions, Lord Kitchener immediately issued another message contained in his instructions and given to each soldier.

'It is discreditable, and even dishonest, that by contracting, through self-indulgence, a disease which he can avoid, a man should render himself incapable of doing that work for his country which he enlisted to do. Every man can by self control restrain the indulgence of those imprudent and reckless impulses that so often lead men astray, and he who resists is a better soldier and a better man than the man of weaker will who allows his bodily appetites to rule him and who lacks the strength of character to resist temptation.'

For that closely knit group commissioned in the service of Queen Alexandra's Imperial Military Nursing Service, who had finally found themselves retained at Netley, the hour was fast approaching.

Chapter Two

On Active Service

The September day was grey and damp as the troop ship heaved and rolled its way relentlessly across the Channel. The mass of soldiers crammed on the decks joked and sang 'It's a Long Way to Tipperary' and smoked endless cigarettes. Some, unable to disguise their nausea hung wretchedly over the sides.

The team of nurses on the top deck, surrounded by numerous items of medical equipment, perched wherever they could find a space. Never before having given the matter a thought Lucy was vaguely surprised to discover that she was in fact quite a good sailor. She watched with sympathy as the faces of some of her colleagues changed from white, to a greenish-grey and the sweat broke out on their foreheads. As their shoulders began to heave so they hastily tried to find their way to some corner where they could give vent to their problem in a modicum of privacy.

Suddenly a shout went up and eyes strained towards the shard of coastline which loomed faintly out of the mist and spray. "Not much longer now, old thing," she said encouragingly to the woebegone looking figure at her side. "Just try and hang on a few minutes longer. You'll feel tons better once we've set foot on dry land."

In no time the vessel nosed into a berth on the pier-head at Boulogne where hands waited to catch the ropes which would make her fast whilst others scrambled to set the gangplanks in place. To the skirl of pipes a detachment from one of the Scottish regiments started to disembark and Lucy watched as they marched proudly and confidently away along the quay and out of sight behind some ugly buildings. Soon it was their turn as, clasping their hand luggage, the little group of

Queen Alexandra's Imperial Nursing Service Sisters followed behind their senior officer, their grey bonnets and long cloaks only adding to the drabness of the day.

The town was a hive of activity and the dockside area seemed to be a seething mass of ambulances, wounded men, doctors and nurses, appearing and disappearing in a never-ending stream. The Sugar Sheds on the Gare Maritime, long since emptied of their familiar cargo, had been converted into a Stationary Base Hospital. It was an indescribable spectacle. In the first shed were hundreds of troops euphemistically classified as the walking-wounded. In torn uniforms, with hardly any wearing caps, and blood-stained bandages much in evidence they presented a sorry sight. The slump of their shoulders, their obvious disabilities and the pain etched on haggard faces told a grim story. In fact it was as much as some could do to shuffle or stumble along with the help of their mates. Nevertheless, as long as a man could crawl, he was deemed to be a walking case. At one end wooden partitions had been erected behind which some iron bedsteads carried the stretcher cases. Many of the occupants had legs off, some had sides simply blown away and all were wounded in several places. To that little band of nurses it was a chaotic spectacle.

Bearing purposefully down on the scene appeared the unmistakable figure of Dame Maud McCarthy, Matron-in-Chief to the BEF in France and Flanders.

"Thank heaven for some more trained staff," she greeted them. "I must warn you that things here are in a pretty desperate state. Never mind, first things first." Beckoning imperiously to a harassed-looking passing orderly she issued instructions for the group to be taken to their place of accommodation. This proved to be rooms in a hotel in the town, most of which were in the process of being requisitioned for military use. Lucy and Alice opted to share and gazed in amazement at the facilities which were far superior to their quarters at Netley.

"What a crazy world we're living in," Lucy remarked. "If we hadn't witnessed those scenes at the harbour we could be forgiven for thinking we had arrived for a holiday."

"Somehow, I don't think this is going to be a seaside vacation," smiled Alice wryly, "so don't bother to get your bucket and spade out." Sporting their familiar short scarlet capes and white muslin caps the group reconvened.

With the arrival of reinforcements the nurses set to and the Sugar Sheds were gradually transformed until they became a well-ordered medical facility. However, unlike the normal hospitals they were accustomed to working in this was more of a transitional staging post. As many as three thousand casualties were dressed, fed and passed onto waiting boats in a day, and it was not uncommon for three different lots of men to occupy the same bed in the space of twenty four hours.

All incoming troops were met by an NCO who drafted patients according to the degree of their wounds. They were then seen immediately by a doctor who prescribed for them, the treatment being written down by a sister. A band of nurses followed to carry out the procedures required. The men were then sent to long tables for food and a mug of tea after which they passed out on the far side of the ward, collected 'Blighty' tickets and orderlies helped them to the evacuation ship which would take them to England. Thus room was made for the next convoy of wounded to arrive.

Ironically, after all the hard work, within a matter of weeks the Sugar Sheds were taken over by the army post office and the nurses found themselves establishing a permanent Base Hospital in huts on the road between Boulogne and Wimereux. It was destined to become one of many. A converted seafront hotel became No.4 Stationary Hospital Wimereux, on the top floor of which were the nurses' quarters. Operating theatres were established there and surgery went on unceasingly night and day.

Following a major onslaught the place would be full to overflowing with terribly injured men, many dying of gangrene and tetanus. Stretchers lay on the floor between the beds and the nurses had to step over them in order to carry out their tasks. It was no easy matter to get once wet clothes, now dried and caked with mud, cut off and the men washed and fed - a drink being all that the majority were able to take.

Lucy wrote: *'My Dearest Mother, I am at a Base Hospital which is part of the evacuation chain, further back from the front line than the Casualty Clearing Stations, so you have no need to worry for my safety. They are generally located near the coast and close to a railway line in order for casualties to arrive and leave quickly for repatriation to Britain for long-term treatment. They are often situated in former hotels although that doesn't mean that my room is exactly the Ritz! We are frantically busy the whole time so I can only send the briefest of notes which I hope you will share with Gran and the folks at Hollowdene. How far away that seems from the reality with which we are faced here. If we stopped to think the work would seem hopeless. Not a word comes from the injured men all the time they see us so busy. Some, who are horrifically injured, wave us in the direction of a comrade they seem to think is in greater need. Their wonderful patience and unselfishness never cease to amaze me. In fact, the worse wounded often seemed to feel less pain than those who have slighter injuries. The shock of a shattered limb appears to destroy the nerves in that part of the body. '*

Despite everything, by the time Christmas Day dawned, red quilts adorned each bed, the men all wore red jackets, red screens rendered a modicum of privacy when needed and even vases of flowers appeared. A service was held in one of the wards at 6am and a present given to each man. The place had a constantly changing population and it was wonderful to see how happy they were, their wounds and hardships forgotten in the joy of being en route to 'Blighty'.

So, notions of a war that had been predicted to be of short duration faded amidst the only too real evidence of continuing blood-stained carnage and the enormity of the death toll.

In the New Year Lucy managed a longer letter to the family.

'Thank you all so much for your cards, gifts and goodies, especially the cake which was greatly enjoyed by all the nurses. Would you believe there are now more than fifty thousand assorted nurses deployed throughout the war zone? We are the most senior but are supported by the Territorial Force Nursing Services and a wide range of auxiliaries such as the Voluntary Aid Detachment. The First Aid Nursing Yeomanry is a great help. Their training involves learning to drive an ambulance and basic engine maintenance, plus map reading. At least we aren't involved in any of that which leaves us free to concentrate purely on the nursing. Mind you, they've got an astonishing

uniform. Just imagine a scarlet tunic with a painfully high collar and white braid facing; a navy bell-shaped skirt; a scarlet flat cap with a shiny black peak; black patent riding boots, white gloves and a riding crop. More like something out of an opera!

'There is very little let-up in the volume of work, but we are given a few hours off when possible. However, I don't really get the chance to spend much money so please don't send me any as I have enough for my needs.'

The flow of casualties from the various theatres of war soon overwhelmed the recently established bases in France and Flanders with the result that existing facilities in England became inadequate. Some general hospitals were pressganged into service to take the overflow, while a hutted area was built at Netley to accommodate an extra one thousand five hundred men.

At the end of January 2015 Lucy was granted home leave. Not even the news that a German U-boat had sunk two British ships in the Channel could quell the delight she felt at the prospect. Her mother greeted her with fervent relief and pleasure which only superficially masked the undertones of restraint and coolness evident between father and daughter.

"I can't believe it's only four months since I left for France," she confided. "So much has happened and I have so much to tell you and Gran. How is she, by the way?"

"Amazingly well for a lady of her considerable age," Sadie replied. "She finds it difficult to get about now but her mind is as sharp as ever."

"As is her tongue," grunted Herbert from behind the cover of the newspaper he was reading.

Shaking her head she went on to say, "I have arranged for us to spend the day at Hollowdene tomorrow. Mother's simply longing to hear all your news."

"I hope I'm not expected to be in attendance," came her husband's distinctly sullen voice.

"Of course not, dear," his wife replied quietly. "I assumed you'd be far too busy at the factory, as usual."

"Someone's got to keep the wheels of industry turning," was his somewhat pompous reply before leaving the room. "I've got a business meeting this evening and probably won't be back until late."

"I bet you have," Lucy muttered under her breath as she looked pitifully towards her mother.

Kate greeted her granddaughter with unmistakable pride and affection. "It's so good to see you and I can hardly wait to hear what you've been up to," she said.

"It's hard to know where to begin Gran, but one thing I will say, I am finding it almost impossible at times and I cannot begin to imagine how you ever coped all those years ago."

Kate simply smiled as her mind wandered towards scenes from never completely forgotten events.

"After all you told me about typhoid and cholera you'll be pleased to know that advances in medicine and hygiene have greatly reduced sickness rates among the troops. We now reckon that ten men die from enemy action for every one that dies of disease, simply because of the new vaccines at our disposal."

Kate nodded her head in approval.

"I don't see what's so good about that," Sadie cried sadly. "It's all an appalling waste of life for whatever reason."

"Well, I'm afraid that's the way things are, Mum. Better to die at the hand of the enemy than from some disease which, in a better environment, may have been treatable."

Casting round in her mind for further snippets of information, Lucy went on to say: "We've also got something which you had never heard of, Gran. Saline drips administered intravenously, which reduce the damage caused by shock, are becoming routine and the new blood transfusions are something you didn't have the benefit of either. So today's soldier has some advantages although gas-gangrene and tetanus are not uncommon, largely due to the fact that the men are fighting in prime agricultural areas where the soil has been heavily manured."

She paused to take a drink from the cup of tea standing forgotten on the occasional table by her side before continuing.

"Something extremely new, which we have only just started to try, is a method of treating wounds by irrigating them with a liquid called Dakin's Solution. This is a germicide which is supposed to prevent gangrene and sepsis, but we shall see how effective it really is."

"What about all the shattered bones?" her grandmother enquired. "They always presented such a problem and resulted in rather too many amputations, I felt."

"I'm afraid we still get our fair share of those, too. However we've also got a contraption called a Thomas's splint which has practically halved the death rate for fractures of the femur."

"How different all this is to my experiences," Kate sighed.

"Maybe," Lucy replied, "but I'm sure one aspect never changes and I don't see how it possibly can. I think the truly awful thing is the impact these dreadful experiences have on the minds and emotions of the troops, yet little attention is paid to them. Some are reduced to quivering wrecks and I can't imagine how long it will take for them to get over their experiences, if ever."

"Oh dear," Sadie said, "hearing this at first hand makes us feel so helpless sat at home here."

"Well, I've been thinking," Lucy continued. "There is going to be a huge demand in this country for places where troops can go to recuperate. Apparently, one or two big houses and estates are already starting to open their doors for this purpose. I was wondering whether either of you still has any influence with the Infirmary Board because Painters Court would be ideal for the purpose. The local people would feel they were contributing to the war effort if it was used in this way."

Kate met Sadie's look and they spoke almost in unison: "That would be wonderful."

"Of course, the place is officially nothing to do with us any longer," her grandmother said, 'but I'm still not without some influence. Who knows what a word in the right circles might achieve." With that she settled herself back in her chair in order to hear more of Lucy's exploits.

"I seem to spend hours writing letters and postcards to wives and parents back home every time one of their loved ones dies in my care," she went on.

"Some things don't change then," Kate replied. "Dear Miss Nightingale had to fit in copious amounts of correspondence amongst her other duties."

Smiling fondly at her daughter Sadie questioned, somewhat tentatively: "And is there a dashing young officer in your life yet?"

"Shame on you, match-making in the middle of a war, Mum," Lucy laughed. "The answer is 'no' but I'm working on it, although anyone I find won't possibly match up to Grandfather in your eyes, will he?"

So the three generations whiled away a pleasant afternoon until John Masterson and young Cousin Ted with his girlfriend, Maureen, taking a brief break from their work on the farm, burst in on them to share in the high farmhouse tea Christine had prepared. It was a short idyll in a world which seemed light years away from the horrors of war.

With something akin to relief Lucy returned to join her colleagues and, within an hour, found herself swept up once more into the now familiar world of relentless toil and unspeakable suffering. Alice welcomed her back enthusiastically, anxious to fill her in with the latest developments and the news that the remit of their work had extended beyond the confines of the Base Hospital.

"We are now expected to take our turn serving on the Ambulance Trains," she volunteered.

"Ambulance Trains?" echoed her friend. "Does that mean we'll be going up to the front?"

Alice nodded her head. "Well, certainly closer to the scene of action than we are here," she confirmed, "although I haven't had to go yet. Perhaps we'll be able to work together when the time comes."

These trains had first featured following the First Battles of Ypres and Arras in October 1914, although they were operating sporadically in other areas. In the early days, for reasons of speed and to avoid the delays caused when fleeing refugees clogged the roads with their carts, railways became the high-roads of war. Anything that ran on wheels and could be attached to an engine was brought into service. Sometimes the trains were just holed up waiting but this could rapidly change when called to a Casualty Clearing Station.

Each train carried three Sisters and the Sisters' mess and bedrooms which although originally somewhat primitive, eventually became quite comfortable. The front half was comprised of sleeping berths for stretcher cases, while the rear coaches had hard wooden seats reserved for the walking wounded. These coaches were not interconnected and climbing from one to another by way of the footboard was strictly forbidden. This, like more than one rule, was honoured in the breach more than in the observance, for this means of passage was often a necessity in the interests of the patients.

Ambulance Train life never lacked excitement as there were frequent air raids and the clearly visible red cross on the roof in no way exempted them from the fury of the enemy. On the night of October 31st 1914 No.7 Ambulance Train had the misfortune to be standing in Ypres station when the First Battle there commenced. The train received a baptism of fire as shells made holes in her sides and broke windows.

It was during WW1 that the system of triage assessment and casualty evacuation was developed which did so much to prioritise and streamline treatment efficiently. However, trying to care for the mass of injured troops on these trains was far from easy. Soldiers who had first passed through a Casualty Clearing Station, which was often nothing more than a collection of tents were, where possible, cursorily cleaned up, fed, given the minimum of emergency treatment, and transferred onto a train with reasonable rapidity and ease. The nurses then had to carry on the good work although it was no simple matter to tend to wounds and undress soldiers sitting on a bench in a swaying railway carriage. Once loaded, all medical cards were inspected, basic nourishment offered if required, any treatment due was administered and cigarettes, sweets and books were handed out. Sometimes the nurses even had time for a chat.

The patients were finally unloaded at Base Hospitals after which the train was scrubbed and beds remade ready for the next journey. Stores were taken on board and the stopover was usually long enough for the nurses to go shopping for their own mess requirements. Then it was up-line again or reload with patients for England.

However, any interest in this new project rapidly receded into the dim recesses of Lucy's mind when, in the middle of the following morning, she came face-to-face with, quite frankly, the most divine-looking man ever to cross her path. Dressed in immaculate officer's uniform he stood hesitantly at the entrance to the ward casting an eye around for someone to come to his assistance. Lucy finished straightening the sheets on the bed of the soldier whose dressing she had just changed before approaching him.

"Can I help you?" she asked.

"I'm certainly hoping so. I'm Lieutenant Appleton of the Intelligence Corps and I've been told you have some German prisoners among your patients. Is that right?"

She nodded. "That's correct, although there are only five here at the moment. The rest were moved out yesterday."

"Are they in a fit state to be questioned?" he asked.

"Yes," she replied, "athough their command of English isn't up to much, I'm afraid."

"That's not a problem," he smiled. "My German is fluent."

Moving in the direction of the ward door, Lucy indicated for him to follow. "We pride ourselves on giving the same measure of care to all the troops no matter what side they're on although, for obvious reasons, we do keep them apart." She stopped by a small room that, in better days, had seen service as a hotel lounge but was now equipped with the customary beds. Beckoning to an orderly, she explained the Captain's purpose bidding him to offer any help required.

"I hope your mission is successful," she said and went to resume her duties.

Somewhat to her surprise he later sought her out to thank her for her assistance.

"Are you stationed here in the town?" she asked by way of conversation.

"Not really. Mine is something of a roving commission and I rarely have the luxury of a regular billet, although St. Omer is my supposed HQ. That said, I shall be in Boulogne for the next few days unless things go wrong - and they often do," he grimaced wryly.

He appeared to hesitate for a moment before saying: "Is it too much of a cheek to ask, if you would be prepared to take pity on me and come out for a meal this evening?"

"Goodness, that would be a treat," Lucy exclaimed, "but I shan't be able to get off until eight o'clock I'm afraid."

"Right then, eight fifteen outside the main entrance it is."

With mock horror she looked up at him with a twinkle in her eye: "You don't believe in giving a girl much time to get ready, do you?"

"You don't need time, you're fine as you are, so until tonight," was the response.

Fraternisation between nurses and military personnel, which had been strictly forbidden in peace time, was still frowned upon. Yet there now seemed neither time nor heart for petty rules and regulations and many romances flourished and came to fruition against the grim backdrop of conflict.

It was one of the incongruities of the situation which pertained that, despite the war and the fighting which might be taking place at any given time, life went on much the same as usual in the towns and villages which were not directly affected. The shops and cafes still opened for trade and restaurants tried to offer a reasonable cuisine while wine flowed in abundance. Sometimes, if they weren't too tired, a group of nurses would make their way into Boulogne and try to relax and forget the traumas of the day although it inevitably felt somewhat unreal.

Although Lucy's looks and vivacity had ensured that she had never been short of male society in Morford, no one captured her interest for long. When she emerged, promptly on time, her waiting escort somewhat sheepishly commented: "I don't even know your name, which would have made me look pretty stupid if you hadn't turned up as I wouldn't have had any idea who to ask for."

"Lucy Dane if you please, kind sir," she quipped as she offered a mock curtsey.

"Marcus Appleton at your service," he responded gravely with a small bow. "Now we've got that over, where do you suggest we head for? I imagine you know this place better than I do."

"Do you like fish?" she asked.

"Positively love it."

"Well, there's quite a presentable place that serves the most exquisite seafood just a short walk away," said his companion.

"I'm in your hands, Lucy. Just lead on."

"Goodness, are you usually as trusting as that? After all, you don't know where I might take you," she laughed.

"I'm not in the least worried," he assured her. "I reckon I'm a pretty fair judge of character so I'll take the risk."

With that they set off in the direction of the old town and within a remarkably short space of time were ensconced at a table for two, set with a red cloth and sparkling cutlery. From the very outset the conversation never flagged, both eager to find out as much as possible about the other. Seldom had she felt so instantaneously comfortable in a man's company.

"You know what I do," Lucy ventured, "but I'm afraid I'm very ignorant as to your place in the system. What exactly does the Intelligence Corps do?"

"Nothing very glamorous I'm afraid. Nevertheless, it is something of a sensitive organisation so I can't go into things in any detail I'm afraid. Let's just say that, in the scheme of things, we're the proverbial Jacks of all trades and masters of none."

"It actually sounds quite exciting," his companion ventured.

"Don't run away with any romantic notions," Marcus replied. "There's not a lot of cloak and dagger about what I do. After all, in civvy street I'm a schoolmaster, although that life now seems an eternity away. There's certainly nothing remotely exciting about this rotten war. The whole thing's a shameful disgrace. "

Initially, when Britain went to war no Intelligence Corps even existed. Suddenly, hapless officers, who just chanced to be visiting the War Office, found themselves being seconded for Intelligence work. By the end of August, fifty individuals had been commissioned as Second Lieutenants including a number of selected university lecturers, masters from public schools and assorted others, chosen chiefly for their knowledge of the Continent and proficiency in foreign languages. In addition, some volunteers were taken on as scouts, many of them having previously worked for the police force.

Its main sphere of work was centred along the Western Front and consisted largely of train watching behind German lines in order to trace enemy troop movements. Other duties ranged from acting as interpreters, interrogating German prisoners, gathering information, organising civilian working parties, obtaining food for retreating infantry, translating claims for damages from French and Flemish peasants, to supervising parties of saboteurs. Many of the train watchers recruited were local women living in houses overlooking railway lines who covertly sent their information to agents. It was a job that required brilliant if unconventional improvisation and the ability to work in isolation.

Lucy was quite content to accept the limited information which Marcus gave her but tentatively suggested that such a peripatetic existence must surely mean that any further visits to Wimereux would be extremely unlikely. To which her escort commented that there was no way of telling. "In such a crazy war predicting events virtually consists of sticking a needle in a map. Anything is possible, and we simply have to be prepared for it and cope with each event no matter how unpalatable."

Before many months passed his words were proved only too true when, on October 15th 1915, the world was shocked and angered by the news of the execution of Nurse Edith Cavell. She had saved the lives of soldiers from both sides without discrimination and was arrested for helping some 200 Allied soldiers escape from German-occupied Belgium. Accused of treason, she was found guilty by a court-martial and sentenced to death. Despite international pressure for mercy, she was shot by a German firing squad.

The staff at Wimereaux went about their work in subdued silence. It came at a time when morale generally was at a very low ebb. Only the day before, the British troops had suffered defeat at Loos, just weeks after experiencing the appalling loss of life at Verdun for the gain of a mere four thousand yards of ground.

"What's the point of it all?" Lucy wailed as she and Marcus sat in a bar snatching a few unexpected moments together.

"I must confess things are pretty dire," he replied and the Generals don't seem to be achieving much by throwing wave after wave of men into a bloody fray. If they go on at this rate there won't be any troops left."

"What on earth is going to happen, do you think?"

"You may well ask, Lucy. According to General Joffe he is 'nibbling away at the enemy and in the end the side with the most men left standing will win.' Whatever kind of remark to make is that, I ask you?" he said in disgusted tones as he finished the last of his wine.

Lighting another cigarette he inhaled deeply and leaned forward with both arms on the table. "Do you know that the latest estimates put the cost of this war at three million pounds a day?"

"Surely that's impossible," she gasped. "Where's it all coming from?"

"The coffers must be running pretty low which is why I think the 'powers that be' are hoping the Americans will pin their colours to the mast, although they don't show much inclination at the moment."

Twirling the stem of her glass between her fingers Lucy looked up at him and said, "All this seems a bit unreal doesn't it? I mean, here we are enjoying an evening out and around us life looks pretty much as normal. Yet, it's far from normal and this is reflected in our conversation. What other couple would spend time talking about battles, and casualties and strategies for heaven's sake? Yet that's all we can think of. We breathe, eat, drink and sleep this wretched war."

Marcus shrugged his shoulders and grinned ruefully as his frustrated companion leapt to her feet saying: "How much longer must we endure this madness?"

Getting up he grabbed her hand and pulled her to him. Holding her close he looked down into her upturned face and said: "Quite right! No more talk of war. From now on it's only about you and me," a sentiment with which she was only too happy to concur.

Chapter Three

Casualties of War

Abruptly, only a few days later, her thoughts were channelled in another direction with the arrival of a telegram informing Lucy of her grandmother Kate's death. Sitting with the piece of paper in her hand, she tried to work out how she felt. There was no doubt that she had been extremely fond of her and she had provided a sort of constancy over the years. Now, surrounded, as she was by so much carnage and mortality, which was claiming the lives of once strong, fit and vital young men, the natural demise of one elderly lady almost seemed to pale into insignificance. Yet it marked the end of an era and a vibrant strand in the tapestry of the family had faded.

Nevertheless, knowing how devastated her mother would be, Lucy approached the authorities with a request for compassionate leave which was duly granted. Twenty-four hours later she found herself bound for home once more. Sitting on the train as it rattled its way between London and Morford she stared disinterestedly at the passing scenery and listened to the jovial banter and ribald comments of the soldiers travelling to their homes on furlough.

Alighting at her destination the chill wind struck as she pulled her uniform more closely to her, giving thanks that earlier in the year the traditional grey bonnets and long cloaks had been withdrawn in favour of a more practical coat and felt hat. Preparing to cast around for a cab she was stopped in her tracks by the welcoming sound of Cousin Ted's hearty voice.

Lucy greeted him with enthusiasm. "Gracious, I didn't expect to see you."

"Well, I had to come into town for some spare parts for the tractor and Dad thought that if you were granted leave to come there was a good chance it might be on the afternoon train, so I timed things accordingly on the off-chance."

Scooping up her modest travelling case in one hand and taking Lucy's arm in the other he guided her towards the waiting farm truck.

"Not exactly a state coach m'lady but better than Shanks's pony," he said, helping her up into the passenger seat. "I'll take you to Hollowdene first because your mum's there with Dad planning the funeral, then one of us will take you back to your place later."

"When is the funeral?" Lucy asked, gazing out at the uninspiring terraces of houses lined in serried ranks around the ugly factories.

"Day after tomorrow. Thankfully it's going to be a fairly modest event although several people have tried to press for a service in the cathedral in recognition of all that Gran did for Morford. "

"Saints be praised for that," Lucy said in heartfelt tones. "The last thing I feel like is being on show."

"Well, you won't have to worry on that score. Apparently, organised as ever, the old lady left implicit instructions that the service is to take place in the local church with the burial alongside her beloved Roland, and that's what is happening."

Easing herself into a more comfortable position as the vehicle bumped and shook over the potholes in the country lanes, to which the urban streets had given way, she ventured to enquire tentatively after her mother.

"Of course she's upset," Ted replied, 'but being very sensible and relieved that, at least, she didn't suffer."

"Gran wasn't ill then?"

"Lord no. She had supper with us as usual, went to bed and when Mum took her tea up in the morning, she was dead. She died quite peacefully in her sleep."

"Good, I'm pleased it was like that for her. Would that the poor devils I'm trying to help could know such peace instead of the hell they have to go through. It's all so jolly unfair Ted, it truly is. They don't deserve any of this. Nobody does."

The funeral of Kate Masterson passed off with suitable dignity. With due regard for her wishes it was a quiet affair, although there was a considerable representation from among those who wanted to honour all that she had done for the Infirmary in Morford. However, most of her contemporaries had predeceased her and it was the family, villagers and estate workers from Shepherdstone and Hollowdene who formed the greater part of the congregation and lined the churchyard as her body was laid to rest beside her husband and her parents.

Returning to the home of Sadie and Herbert for the customary 'tea', it was inevitable that conversation should turn to the subject of the war, for only that week John Masterson had learned that two of his farm hands had been killed in action.

"For all that's being printed, as far as I can see it's a pretty disastrous state of affairs, " he said. "So much for talk of the war being over within months."

Not wishing to have the conversation monopolised by anyone else, Herbert was quick to respond in his customary self-important manner.

"You'll soon see that things will change. The appointment of Field Marshall Haig as CinC to the British Forces in France and Belgium was the best thing that could happen."

"That was months ago," said John, "and there hasn't been any really significant breakthrough yet."

"Of course there hasn't," his brother-in-law blustered. "He's got to find his feet, feel his way and test the water. According to the press he has a force of over one million men holding seventy miles of front. His conduct of the retreat from Mons won him high praise," he finished with the knowledgeable flourish of a military strategist.

"That's as maybe, but remember what he said," ventured the young Ted. 'Wars aren't won by retreating, and there's been more of that than we'd bargained for."

Not wishing to be so summarily dismissed, Herbert was quick to interpose. "You just wait and see! Once the men can sense a superior hand at the helm things will be very different. A soldier responds to good leadership and good equipment and he's got both. The British Tommy will be feeling greatly heartened and more determined than ever, and we'll soon see the wind change for the better."

To the surprise of the assembled company Lucy, unable to conceal her fury, entered the fray with all guns blazing. Casting a scornful look in the direction of her father she spat out her words.

"How can you possibly presume to know what the average British Tommy feels or thinks? While you're pontificating on the progress of this war, situated in the relative comfort and safety of your blessed factory, he's being subjected to unspeakable horrors the like of which you can't even begin to imagine. Those wonderful boots from your production lines don't prevent him getting trench foot or frostbite. Can you just stop and try to visualise what it is like to sit with your toes in the air while an officer walks along tweaking them? The frozen ones snap off, which is a good thing because it prevents them going gangrenous."

Some of the assembled company shuddered involuntarily but Lucy either didn't, or refused to, notice. "I often have the job of trying to remove footwear that is caked in dried-on mud after being immersed in water and slime and hasn't been taken off for weeks."

Not pausing to draw breath she ploughed on. "Here you are in your dapper suit, dining comfortably in your pleasant home while Tommy, as you call him, exists on a meagre diet of bully beef and hard biscuits which he consumes standing in a filthy trench while the rats run over his feet and the lice nest happily in his uniform."

A white-faced Sadie reached out a hand in an attempt to suppress any further comment.

"No Mum, I won't be quiet. Father, you really have absolutely no idea."

His face becoming perceptibly redder by the moment, Herbert Dane almost shouted, "I will not be spoken to in this way in my own home. Just remember that I'm doing my bit for the war effort by making sure that this army goes well shod. I can't help it if the footwear is subjected to conditions beyond my control."

"Maybe, but it isn't exactly doing you any harm financially, is it? The more boots Tommy gets through the better off you'll be. And the more injuries he sustains which necessitate the provision of surgical boots will also swell your coffers. It's nice to know that someone's benefitting from this ghastly hell," she said bitterly, "but it certainly isn't Tommy."

"Now just you see here, young lady. I'm keeping the factory going night and day under difficult circumstances. I even have to employ women to do men's work in order to fill some of the gaps left by my young hands who have signed up."

"And you don't like that do you, Father? Goodness me, what with women driving ambulances, maintaining vehicles, manufacturing ammunition, operating machinery and now working for you, whatever next. I hear that thousands of them have marched in London in order to demand jobs and good for them. I'll tell you now, when this war is over things will never be the same again. Women have proved that they can be the equal of men and they won't take kindly to being subjected to a subordinate role. And why should they?"

John Masterson had been listening carefully. Much as he disliked his brother-in-law, even he was surprised by the obvious degree of antipathy between Lucy and her father.

"Still got your head stuffed full of that suffragette nonsense, I see," spluttered Herbert, by now almost apoplectic with rage.

Before Lucy could launch another broadside, John said gently: "She does have a point you know. I've got several women working like Trojans on the farm filling the gaps left by my chaps who have enlisted. And a jolly good job they're doing too. It's heavy work and dirty, out in all weathers, but you never hear them complain. We really must give them their due."

"Oh, I might have known you'd be on her side although I don't recall asking for your opinion," Herbert almost sneered.

Sadie, becoming more agitated by the minute, looked at him imploringly. "There's no need to be rude, dear," she said gently. "Everyone is entitled to speak their mind."

"Something your family are very good at doing," he countered. "Your mother was a prime example and Lucy's inherited it in double measure. It was doubtless her who filled the girl's head with this army nursing nonsense."

"That simply isn't true and you know it," retorted Lucy swiftly.

"And I don't know how you can upset everyone by being so insensitive as to speak of Gran like that at this time." So saying, she placed a protective arm around her mother's shoulders as if defying him to say any more.

Striding towards the door her father turned and glared at the assembled company. "As my presence is so obviously irritating to you all, I am taking myself off to my club in Morford in the hope of passing the rest of the evening more congenially. It's a poor thing when a man isn't welcome in his own home."

Sadie's attempts to dissuade him fell on deaf ears and he departed saying, "Don't wait up for me. I shall spend the night at the club. At least I'll be ready to make an early start on my work for the war effort," he added sarcastically.

"Very well, Dad, at least I shall know where to reach you in the event of an emergency," Lucy responded, fixing him with a meaningful look. Herbert scowled balefully at her and stormed out, slamming the door behind him.

An uncomfortable silence descended which was hastily broken by Lucy. "I'm sorry you had to witness that. I'm afraid it is my fault. Dad made it plain from the beginning that he didn't want me to pursue the course I'm doing partly because he feared for my safety and partly because of the effect the worry would have on Mum." Squeezing Sadie's hand she continued, "Perhaps I have been selfish. Perhaps I should have stayed and done my bit here. However, I know I've made the right decision serving in the way I am. In the scheme of things I suppose my efforts are small but I do know they're worthwhile and that between us nurses over there, we are making a difference. Gran understood that only too well and so does Mum."

"Don't you worry yourself," her uncle replied. "We're one hundred percent behind you and full of admiration and pride."

"Please, don't say that," Lucy checked him. "Save your admiration for Tommy."

It wasn't much longer before the folk from Hollowdene made their farewells. Going into the hall Lucy managed to take her uncle to one side. "I hate to ask you this Uncle John, but can I crave a favour?"

"You don't need to ask," he smiled. "What is it?"

"This war is going to last much longer than any of us thought and it will probably be some considerable time before I can get home again. The journey alone takes up valuable resting time and there are good opportunities to stay in small towns and villages in France out of the war zone, which some people opt to do. Apart from which I undoubtedly inflame the situation when I'm here," she said ruefully. "The problem is I find it well nigh impossible to curb my tongue where Dad's concerned."

"I had noticed," he grinned, "but sometimes it's necessary to stand up for what you think and believe."

"That's just it," she said gratefully. "The trouble is that I do worry about Mum and I do care about her. Will you keep a good eye on her for me, or is that too much of an imposition?"

"My dear girl, of course it isn't. Sadie is my beloved sister and I do drop in as often as possible during the week when your father's at work. Then, once or twice a week she'll make her way to Hollowdene to spend the day with Auntie Christine. Anyway, the two of them will have plenty to keep them occupied now. I don't expect Ted's told you but he's decided to get married before Christmas."

"No! Well, good for him. I take it he is marrying Maureen?"

"Who else? There was never really anyone besides her. In fact, it feels as if she's been part of the family for ages as she's always in and out." Gazing around the old familiar room, he gathered his thoughts. "I do think that this war has propelled many young couples into marriage earlier than expected. It's the uncertainty that's so unsettling, people are trying to find an element of permanence in a shifting world."

"Goodness, that sounds a bit profound, Uncle John."

Smiling at her he put out a hand to stroke her cheek. "Don't take any notice of me my dear. You just go and carry on the good work and, rest assured, I'll keep an eye on your mother. You will have absolutely nothing to worry about on that score, I promise you."

"Bless you," Lucy said, reaching up to plant a kiss on his cheek. She hesitated momentarily, as though considering saying something more but thought better of it.

With everyone gone, mother and daughter headed for the kitchen to set about the washing up. Initially a silence hung over the proceedings until Lucy, giving a huge sigh, said: "Mum, I'm truly sorry if my outburst upset you but, quite frankly, I find Dad's whole attitude insufferable."

Studiously drying a crystal wine glass, Sadie sought for the right words. Finally, after placing it on a tray she ventured cautiously: "I know that for some reason, you and your father don't enjoy the best of relationships and, rightly or wrongly, I've kept out of it; but don't be too hard. Things aren't easy for him at the moment."

"Things aren't easy for any of us Mum, but there is no need for rudeness or unpleasantness," she retorted.

"Well, altercation isn't the answer either, I'm sure."

Lucy drew a breath and tried again. "Look, I know you hate confrontation but you really mustn't let him walk all over you - and he does, you know."

"That's just his way, dear. Anyhow, thanks to the pressures as a result of the war I seem to see less and less of him at the moment so it isn't a problem."

Lucy gritted her teeth but wisely forebore to say anything further.

"Shall we have a hot drink?" Sadie offered.

"Good idea. You sit down and I'll put the kettle on."

Seated at last in the comfortable old chairs either side of the range, Lucy cast her eyes round the room as though committing every detail to memory.

"What are you thinking, darling?"

"Oh, I suppose it suddenly hit me that these are the things I miss most at the moment. There's something undeniably warm and comfortable and permanent about a home kitchen, isn't there?"

"It's quite my most favourite room in the house," Sadie smiled. "All the while I can potter round here I'm quite content."

"Hardly the peak of excitement," Lucy quipped.

"I'm not looking for excitement, for heaven's sake. It's quite enough for one of us to live life dangerously. Anyway, ever since you arrived I've been dying to tell you the news but there hasn't been a moment."

"Don't tell me! You've got a secret admirer," grinned her daughter.

"Shame on you, my girl but you're not even close," Sadie replied. "No, when you returned to France last time Gran didn't let the grass grow under her feet and, the upshot is, that Painters Court has been given over to the rehabilitation of soldiers injured in the war."

"Mum, that's really fantastic."

"Ah, it doesn't stop there. I now go in every day to help out. Not nursing or anything like that," she hastened to add, noticing the look of surprise on Lucy's face. "You see, some of them have lost their sight and I read the newspaper to them and write their letters home at their dictation. If the weather's nice I take them out into the garden and I do little bits of shopping for them. This frees the staff up to do all the important things."

"Well done," Lucy exclaimed sincerely.

"To tell you the truth I love every minute of it. Oh, not the fact that those poor men are so terribly maimed - that is horrible. No, it's the feeling of being useful and needed and the sense that I'm playing some part in the war effort, however small and insignificant."

"You don't know how pleased and relieved that makes me," Lucy said. "I do worry about you, you know, and it makes what I am going to say slightly easier."

"Is something wrong?" her mother asked anxiously.

"Quite the reverse," she laughed. "You see, I think I've met my dashing officer. No, I'm not saying any more or going into details because nothing might come of it. However, it does mean that, as things are at the moment, I shall be looking to spend my leaves in France in the vain hope that we can at least enjoy some snatched moments together as and when they present. I can't tell you how difficult it is for us both to get our off-duty to coincide. Added to which he has something of a roving commission and never knows where he'll be next so it's a matter of seizing every opportunity."

"How exciting my dear and of course I understand," Sadie replied with her customary grace. "Just as long as you drop me the occasional line, however brief, so that I know you're alright."

"Thanks for being so understanding Mum. You're an angel."

A day later, and feeling much happier about things at home, Lucy eagerly made her way back to France. Marcus greeted her return with a suitably ardent response and within an incredibly short time it felt as if she had never been away. Almost immediately she had to learn to contend with yet another horror.

Gas was first used on the Western front by the Germans at the Seond Battle of Ypres in April 1915 but Lucy had been on leave at the time. One morning she found herself being sent to provide extra help at a hard-pressed field clearing station only to come face to face with the most pitiable scene. In a letter to her mother she wrote:

'It was quite terrible. There was this field full of blindfolded and gassed men, and new cases kept coming in led by an orderly. They trod gingerly, along duckboards, towards the dressing station, truly the blind leading the blind. They sat or lay down on the grass clearly suffering a great deal.

'Severe mustard gas poisoning is usually fatal and invariably disabling. The symptoms begin with a runny nose, nausea and vomiting. After a day the eyelids close and by the second day blisters form, the ears swell and the victim coughs up his own mucous membrane. Death often occurs within two to ten days. And the awful thing is that there is virtually nothing we can do. I have never felt so helpless, and that is the bleak reality of this hell we are in.'

In June 1916 the British invented an exciting armoured weapon. The new vehicle was code-named 'tank'. Within weeks it received a baptism of fire at the Battle of the Somme. This great Allied offensive launched in the morning was halted at night with only marginal British advances and sixty thousand casualties in one day, the highest number reported in this costly war.

Large numbers of German prisoners were also taken, all of which put an intolerable strain on the medical personnel. Nevertheless, a small force of British tanks did make what were classed as important gains in one sector. As a result of this the top brass claimed this was proof that a strong mechanised force was the key to unlocking the seemingly fruitless form of trench warfare. So the order was given to continue to press home a precarious advantage.

Eventually, on November 13th the Battle of the Somme ended after only an eight mile advance which took four months and claimed four hundred and twenty thousand lives. Base hospitals everywhere were working beyond capacity almost to breaking point.

Christmas arrived but there was little to be cheerful about. Parcels appreciatively received from home brought nostalgic reminders of festive times past. Every member of QAIMNS was sent a gift from the Queen herself, consisting of a canvas bag laced up with ribbon in the colours of the Service. The bags contained a photograph of the Queen, a Christmas card, notepaper, acid drops, a tin of chocolates and a fur-lined cape, hood and muff. British newspapers also contributed parcels of food and clothing. It was good to know that they were being remembered.

Attempts were also made to decorate the wards and to provide little extra comforts for the injured men.

Marcus somehow made sure that he would be in Wimereux and he became an immediate hit when he took his place at the piano to lead some impromptu carol singing. This inevitably gave way to those songs so beloved by the troops.

Despite their appreciation he was sad to think that Lucy wasn't actually standing beside him. Although she could hear everything, she was totally committed to performing those tasks so vital and relentless for the wellbeing of the latest arrivals. He was mindful too of the lights burning from the windows of the operating theatres and the staff who manned them almost non-stop.

"We shall probably never forget our first Christmas Day together," Lucy murmured as she finally managed to nestle in his embrace to bid him 'goodnight'. Kissing her gently, he agreed. "Let's just pray that we will be able to enjoy many, many more festive seasons together in the peace and safety of our own home."

"Amen to that," she sighed with feeling.

So spring arrived once more. Contriving at very short notice to meet up in their favourite café, Lucy greeted him fondly then eagerly said: "Have you read the latest in the newspapers? Apparently the end of the fighting is practically guaranteed?"

Covering her hand with his he leant forward saying, "Please darling, we agreed no talk of war. Remember?"

"I know, and I'm sorry but I so desperately want this war to end so that we can get back home to some degree of normality."

"Well, don't pin your hopes on some journalist. Words, words, words but no action, that's all it is."

Seeing her downcast face Marcus reached across to take her hand again. "Cheer up my love, our time will come, I promise you."

"Our time," she said dreamily. "It's difficult to imagine that it will ever happen, or what it will be like?"

"I know exactly," said her companion. "It will be a job out of uniform for me and a place in the country for both of us, with roses round the door and a baby crawling on the grass. Oh, and a piano!"

"A piano?" she shrieked, attracting smiling glances from the other patrons.

"Didn't I ever tell you? I am passionate about music and I play both piano and organ at any opportunity."

Seeing how quiet she had become Marcus asked somewhat tentatively, "Is that a problem, Lucy?"

"What, the piano? No, of course not, though it does underline just how little we really know about each other."

"But we know the most important thing don't we?"

"Such as?"

"Well, for my part I can't imagine life without you and I was rather hoping that you felt the same."

"Are you asking me to marry you?" she simpered coquettishly.

"You may be sure I am and I've never been more serious about anything in my life."

"You know," she mused, "I always imagined that for a proposal the setting would be utterly romantic, the lighting subdued and we'd be togged out in our best. Yet here we are in a pretty ordinary cafe in a war zone and it feels like heaven. And, yes of course I will."

***

Nineteen seventeen proved to be the turning point in the war. The arrival of American troops boosted the morale of the Allies while American industrial and financial aid definitely tipped the scales against Germany. It also saw Marcus frequently being deployed to different territory, so that the opportunity to meet became less and less easy and correspondence more and more erratic. One evening he was forced to tell her that the situation was such that he was being positioned much further away.

Lucy looked at him aghast. "How are we going to be able to keep in touch and, worse still, how can I ever be sure that you are alright?"

"I'm afraid it is probably going to be quite difficult if not impossible. I have managed to come up with a measure which will tide us over for a while. As you know, my base is nominally at St. Omer and all my correspondence goes there for forwarding on. I have a very good friend who was wounded earlier in the war and now can't be used in the field so he is permanently posted. His name is Lieutenant Angus MacDonald and he is now in my confidence. Send your letters to me at that address and he will forward them whenever viable. I will continue to try and write to you but please don't be surprised if they are infrequent. In the event of a complete emergency, contact Angus and he will do what he can. Cheer up! Hopefully it won't be for long."

Lucy refused to be downcast and clung to the special memories of those wonderful times when they had been able to escape and completely lose themselves by slipping away together into another world. They had both discovered the fulfillment of a passion beyond belief, and cherished the odd occasions when they managed to give full, unbridled rein to their feelings. So be it if people wouldn't approve. They loved each other beyond doubt or reason, and this was war. Anyhow, it was a matter for them and them alone.

Only it wasn't. Three months after Marcus's last leave the blow struck. Lucy's inkling that she might be pregnant became a reality she could not ignore. Try as she would to convince herself otherwise the sneaking doubt refused to go away. Damn and blast, this wasn't supposed to happen and, probably for the first time in her life, Lucy found herself plunged into uncertainty as to what she should do. Desperately she prayed that Marcus would get some leave, but his irregular letters weren't hopeful. How she longed to be able to confide in him but there was no way that such stupendous news could be conveyed in a letter. He would worry himself sick. No, there was nothing else for it but to hang on for as long as possible and pray that things would work out.

Although by the end of June Lucy was feeling fine and the pregnancy didn't show she knew that something had to be done. She reluctantly accepted that Marcus had now been positioned miles away and was unlikely to return imminently. Decisions needed to be made.

As fate, or fortune, would have it her turn came round to take a week's leave which also coincided with Alice's. With no Marcus about and future arrangements requiring urgent attention, she decided to accompany her friend back to England. Importantly, it would give her time away from the daily pressures in which to think and plan with a clear head. Suddenly, the enormity of the situation hit her and she knew that she must confide in someone. On the train journey between Folkestone and Victoria Lucy revealed her plight to her incredulous friend. Alice, whose thoughts were focused on the pleasure of a week's complete rest with her family, turned in her seat and regarded her companion with a look of sheer horror.

"Lucy, why didn't you tell me before?" Then, after eyeing her surreptitiously, she commented, "You don't look pregnant. When is the baby due?"

"Sometime in November by my reckoning."

"What on earth are you going to do? Do your parents know? Does Marcus know?" Still in shock, the questions tumbled from her lips.

"The answer to the last two is 'No'. As to the first, that is what I've got to address during this week's leave."

"Have you any ideas?"

Lucy thought for a moment before replying. "Alice, one thing I do know is that I can't possibly tell my parents. Mum has enough problems of her own and as for my father he'd probably be delighted to have a reason to disown me. I can't go into details but simply believe me that they are the last people I will approach for help."

"So where are you going when we get to London?"

"Well, as you say, the pregnancy isn't evident yet so I intend to go to Morford for a couple of days, just so that I can put Mother's mind at rest and she will see that I'm OK. I will then tell them that I have to attend some further nursing exercise in London. Once there, I shall make enquiries regarding Mother and Baby homes and the like. There must be somewhere that caters for women in my situation," she sighed.

"And where will you stay?"

"Fortunately, I've saved a commendable amount and money isn't a problem, so I'll book into a small hotel somewhere."

"Indeed you won't," her friend exploded. "You're to come to us. My folk have heard so much about you and would absolutely love to meet you. Furthermore, I shall be able to help you. Two heads are better than one you know." After much demurring and protestations from Lucy, the matter was finally settled and she sank back into the seat to prepare herself for the next hurdle on the course.

It was with considerable surprise, and no little gratitude, that by the end of the week everything she had set out to do had been accomplished in the most extraordinary way. Her family had been thrilled to see her with frequent comments made as to how 'well and bonny' she looked despite all the deprivations. Sadie's observation that she actually seemed to have put on a little weight despite all the exertions, was put down to the stodgy nutrition and a surplus of bread and potatoes thereby giving her mother every excuse to produce the most tasty and tempting meals. Even her father had been more amenable and made the effort to spend time with her. Doubtless trying to impress her with the energy and skill he was devoting to the phenomenal increase in the demand for widely differing ranges of surgical boots, he even took her to the factory and sought her advice on certain aspects of their design from a medical perspective.

She also managed to visit her uncle and aunt who were relishing their new role as grandparents. Ted had wasted no time and, to the surprise of everyone, he and Maureen had produced a pair of bouncing baby boys. Lucy found herself placing a protective hand across her abdomen as she was urged to find herself a husband before she was left behind.

Unbeknown to Lucy, Alice had confided in her parents. Consequently, their initially tentative welcome steadily increased in warmth, and the impending predicament was resolved when Mrs. Penrose offered to provide shelter for her daughter's friend when the time came for her to leave France. Having produced and reared four children of her own, she generously agreed to see the girl through her confinement and care for her and the baby until such time as Lucy and Marcus could regularise the matter. Stating that she would actually enjoy the company, she privately acknowledged that the financial contribution the young mother-to-be had proposed would not come amiss in these straightened times.

Rarely given to displays of emotion, Lucy wept copious tears of gratitude.

Casualties were appalling in 1917. In April British and Canadian troops gained a hollow victory at Arras with the loss of eighty four thousand men, once more putting the medical and nursing resources at Wimereux under unremitting strain. Immediately following the return of Lucy and Alice from their leave, July heralded the start of the Third Battle of Ypres which was to last until November ending with the British taking Passchendaele Ridge. Just five miles of territory gained in three months and at a heavy cost.

However, by the time that moment came Lucy was no longer there for she had long since been sent back to England in disgrace. On 12th November 1917, as the Battle of Passchendaele finally came to an end, a healthy baby girl took her first breath in the back bedroom of a house in Sydenham. An exhausted but radiant Lucy cradled her closely, wishing with all her heart that Marcus could share in this moment.

"Your daddy would be so proud of you," she crooned softly, stroking the downy head already showing a tinge of auburn.

"She's a fine little lass," said Mrs. Penrose with satisfaction. "What are you going to call her?"

"Just Mary. That way she will have the first three initials of her father's name."

The older woman smiled her approval. "You are going to be the most loved baby," she said, taking her and placing her in the cot. "And you, Lucy, must rest and get your strength back if you are going to persist with this ridiculous plan of returning to the fray."

So another bitter-sweet Christmas came and went while, all the time, Lucy schemed and planned with only one end in mind.

She decided that her best chance of succeeding in her aim to be reinstated in QAIMNS lay in being completely open and honest. Nevertheless, her request to be allowed to return to France was categorically refused and her relentless persistence resulted in an unpleasant and nerve-wracking interview with the authorities. It took all of her powers of reasoned argument in the attempt to persuade them to re-instate her. Initially, those pleas fell on adamantly deaf ears. Reluctantly, after consulting her records which included a glowing testimonial from the Chief Officer at Wimereux, and listening to her story, they began to soften. Even the most battle-hardened souls were becoming war-weary and there was a limit to the number of tales of grief and suffering that human hearts could sustain. More importantly, trained nurses, especially those who already knew the ropes, were a precious commodity in increasingly short supply.

The restrictions governing entry into the service had already been removed and over ten thousand nurses had joined the Queen Alexandra's Reserve which, for the first time, included married women, younger women and those of lower social class. Casualties among them were inevitable. Two hundred assorted army nurses had been killed in action and the supply was running dry. Finally, only after the most rigorous medical examination, and written evidence of a proposed agreement of care for her child, confirmed by Mrs. Penrose as foster mother, was her wish granted.

Lucy's return to active duty at the beginning of summer coincided with yet another tragedy about to unleash itself onto a devastated and unsuspecting universe. As a new year gathered pace an unforeseen and alarming enemy emerged to further decimate already debilitated forces. Early in 1918 Britain, and indeed most of the world, was under attack from an influenza epidemic. This soon became a particularly aggressive strain which raged across the globe with unprecedented speed and virulence. By June it had begun to decimate the German ranks and the following month France was reported to be in its grip. Seeming to have started in Spain, 'Spanish flu' spread rapidly through the ranks of both armies and created havoc among civilian populations weakened by the stress and poor nutrition caused by the war. The medical resources of most nations were strained beyond belief. Worldwide, the influenza epidemic claimed more lives than were lost in a war in which more than ten million died. A whole generation wiped out. Mercifully few cases presented at the Wimereux clearing centre but England and her troops would not escape its insinuating tentacles.

Alice and her colleagues still at the base hospital welcomed Lucy back with open arms, none of them quite believing that she had actually managed to sway the authorities.

"Under normal circumstances you wouldn't have stood a hope," said their senior officer. "As things stand now, the situation is far from normal but there must be no more getting carried away. We are here to do a job," she added pointedly.

"Have you heard anything from Marcus?" another asked sympathetically.

"I have received nothing but the infrequent and obviously hastily scribbled notes which he sent here and Alice has forwarded on to me," she replied. "Heaven only knows where he is."

At the earliest possible opportunity Lucy determined to try and make contact with Angus MacDonald which elicited nothing other than the fact that 'Lieutenant Appleton is alive." With that she had to be content.

On 12th September the Second Battle of Havrincourt commenced. At the time it seemed to be simply yet another offensive in an endless list. Although nobody could possibly foresee, it actually signalled the beginning of the final German retreat but inevitably occasioned another outbreak of fighting. Once again Lucy and Alice found themselves deployed to the Ambulance Trains.

It had long been felt in some quarters that the quicker a man could be operated on the greater his chance of survival. At the peak of the Third Battle of Ypres there were some twenty-three Casualty Clearing Stations, situated immediately behind the lines, each with three surgical teams working sixteen hours on and eight off and each capable of dealing with over a thousand cases a day. This was both physically and mentally demanding of the doctors, nurses and orderlies who manned them. It set the pattern, however, for the future handling of the seriously wounded but depended heavily on the trains to move the cases on to base hospitals following emergency surgery.

Returning to the base hospital one evening in the first week of October, following a particularly gruelling day, Lucy found a letter awaiting her from St. Omer. Opening it with trembling hands she read:

'Dear Sister Dane, I have to inform you that we have recently lost contact with Lieutenant Appleton. I do not wish you to become unduly alarmed as we are at a crucial and hectic phase in operations at this time. If anything serious had happened I feel sure we would know by now but he has been officially reported missing.

'I am so sorry and assure you that I will contact you as soon as there is any definite news.

'Sincerely, Angus MacDonald.'

Alice discovered Lucy in her room sobbing as if her heart would break. Seeing the crumpled letter she picked it up and read it. Kneeling beside her friend she put her arms round her, saying: "Lucy, I know this is awful for you but just listen for a moment. It doesn't mean the worst has happened. Angus is right. If Marcus had been taken prisoner, injured or killed, they would know. He's probably holed up somewhere waiting for things to subside. He always told you he would never take unnecessary risks. You've come this far so don't give up now."

Although she made a brave attempt at optimism, there could be no doubt that, for Lucy, this was a bitter blow. Not even a long letter from Alice's mother giving happy news of Mary's progress could lift her spirits. Returning to the train next morning, Lucy was grateful for the concentration and focus which the work demanded as they loaded up the latest consignment. Many of the patients had come straight from the battlefield and it was packed to full capacity with stretchers on the floor, in the corridors, kitchen and mess.

"Do you think life will ever be the same again?" mused Alice, as they scurried to make the vehicle ready for the next intake of casualties. "Will we ever settle back into the old routine of hospital life?"

"I certainly shan't," replied Lucy. "Neither have I any intention of doing so. When this awfulness is finally over my only ambition is to make a home for Marcus and Mary and me and grow flowers and keep chickens and have scones and jam for tea." With which she let out a sigh of near contentment and allowed herself the luxury of gazing dreamily into the future.

"It will be wonderful Alice, just wonderful."

There was no time for dreaming, however, as the war continued to run its relentless course.

On an autumnal morning in October 1918, Lucy and Alice alighted from the Ambulance Train to which they had been assigned on what was now a familiar mission. A short distance away stood a cluster of hastily erected tents. Weary-looking stretcher bearers ferried their grotesquely injured cargos, setting them on the ground to wait their turn with the surgeons.

The girls smoothed down their skirts, straightened their shoulders and prepared themselves for the onslaught of human flotsam and jetsam that would be looking to them for relief from the hell in which they found themselves. All the while, the distant guns kept up a seemingly never-ending barrage.

Alice turned her head in the direction of the sound. "Is it my imagination or do they seem closer than usual?" she asked.

"Heaven knows," Lucy replied, her mind on other things. "I keep thinking how wonderful it would be if this proves to be the day when Marcus appears."

"Oh, Lucy please don't keep getting your hopes up so. Let's just concentrate on the matter in hand, shall we?"

"I shall never give up, Alice. I simply know in my heart that he's still alive. I don't care how badly injured he may be, I only want him with me. Is that too much to ask for?" she finished wistfully.

"No, of course not, but don't set your heart on it happening today. Goodness, we'd get neither sense nor use out of you if it did," she grinned.

At that moment a worn-looking ambulance which had been trundling slowly towards them drew up and opened the rear doors to reveal the tiers of stretchers to be disgorged onto the waiting train. For the next hour the nurses went about the task of settling the patients down, reassuring and calming them ready for the journey which would at least offer them some hope for a future.

"Bloody hell!" exclaimed one of the drivers, "those bloomin' guns are getting a bit too close for comfort. That last shell burst almost overhead."

"The blighters have probably got our range," his companion replied, pulling the ends of a stretcher towards him. "This is the last one Sister, so you're only waiting for the walking wounded to finish filing down and you can be off."

"And I wish we were coming with you," said his mate in heartfelt tones.

Alice emerged from the train bearing a large box. "We mustn't forget these supplies of surgical instruments, Lucy."

"Gracious, no! More than our lives are worth," she grimaced at the men. "Give her a lift up with that little lot and I'll finish off here."

"Be back in a jiffy," Alice called from the swaying ambulance lumbering over the rough terrain.

Lucy disappeared inside the middle coach.

Only minutes later an explosion rent the air, the ground shook and smoke and debris hurtled into the air. Alice stared in horror. Their train with its precious cargo had suffered a direct hit. The central carriage was nothing but a wreck. Men were groaning and calling out. The walking wounded stopped dead in their tracks.

Overhead the sky darkened and rain began to fall softly.

Chapter Four

Picking Up the Pieces

Alice Penrose paced the rather worn carpet covering the floor of her parents' shabby but comfortable home, her lips pursed and her hands working feverishly over the material of an old, well-loved skirt. It was an indescribable relief to be able to relax again after the untold horrors and awfulness of France yet she felt like a coiled spring and the tension in the air was palpable.

Her mother, seated in an armchair, whilst applying herself to the unwelcome but necessary task of repairing some bed linen, regarded her with concerned affection.

How wonderful it was to have her home for good and, mercifully, safe and sound. Yet, there could be no real peace for any of them until a certain matter had been resolved.

As if on cue, an indignant wail was heard from the old pram positioned under the apple tree in the garden as the occupant struggled to reach a sitting position. Finding this impossible, thanks to the linen restrainers designed to prevent any hapless accident, the cries became even more persistent. Mrs. Penrose automatically laid aside her needle and thread and wearily rose to her feet, only to be stopped in her tracks.

"It's alright Mum, I'll fetch her." With which Alice swiftly left the room, only to reappear a few minutes later with a now smiling infant neatly clothed in a white cotton pin-tucked pinafore over a similar dress, from beneath which protruded a pair of chubby little feet working themselves into a positive frenzy of excitement.

Straightening herself up, the older woman indicated a blanket spread out on the floor and said, "Put her down here and she'll play quite happily for a while".

This done, she indicated a nearby chair, saying, "It's no use my dear. The matter cannot be put off any longer and you have to decide on a course of action".

Sensing a possible interruption, she pressed on. "I know how fond you were of Lucy and admit that the whole situation is absolutely tragic. It was bad enough that she found herself in the condition she did and, whilst I agreed to care for Mary until the war was over and she and the father could regularise matters, the circumstances have changed."

Chuckling out loud as she observed the antics of the tiny mite at her feet, she continued, "Obviously I have grown fond of the little soul but I never envisaged my involvement as more than a temporary measure. Furthermore, there is absolutely no way that I can consider a more extended commitment."

Before she could say more, Alice swiftly interposed. "Mum, I'm not expecting you to. I'm filled with admiration at the way in which you have coped. Since I've been home I can see what a time-consuming business it is caring for such a little one. I feel horribly guilty that you look so exhausted and had I foreseen the way things would turn out I would never have put you in such a position."

"I know you wouldn't, and under normal circumstances I wouldn't have been party to such an arrangement."

Sighing deeply, she went on, "But then, war isn't normal is it? Nevertheless, we've all got to try to get back to some kind of normality. You will doubtless need to return to your nursing, consequently Mary must be placed in her rightful home as soon as possible and, in view of all that has transpired, that place is with Lucy's parents".

The silence that fell was broken by Alice's anguished voice. "Mum, how can I possibly go to Mr. and Mrs. Dane, and drop the bombshell on them that they have a granddaughter? Lucy was concerned for her mother's indifferent health and knew just how her father would react, which is why Mary is with us. I hardly think they are likely to regard the matter more sympathetically now that she is dead."

"Nevertheless, Alice, they have a right to know. You may well find that they will take some comfort from the news once they have got over the shock."

The babyish gurgles of contentment scarcely disturbed their private thoughts until the older woman, with one accomplished movement, swept the delighted child into her arms. Having settled her comfortably onto her ample lap she fixed her daughter with a look full of pathos as she groped for the right words.

"Heaven knows what I would have done had anything happened to you, and I can't even begin to imagine how that unfortunate couple are enduring their loss. One thing I do know, however, is the bitter sweet feeling of joy that must result from the knowledge that a part of the person you loved so much is continued as the result of a new life."

"Even one born out of wedlock?" questioned Alice wryly.

"Even that," rejoined her mother unhesitatingly.

Gazing at this remarkable woman with renewed love, respect and surprise, the words came rushing out. "Oh, Mum you are the most exceptional and wonderful person. I really don't deserve you." With which she got up and placed an arm fondly round her shoulders before placing a light kiss on the lined forehead.

After pondering things in her mind for a moment she ventured, "Lucy didn't talk much about her home, you know. She was clearly fond of her mother but I think there was some difference between her and her father. From what she did say, however, I didn't get the impression that it was as warm and loving as this."

Mrs. Penrose responded thoughtfully, saying, "You know dear, all the while she was staying here, I never managed to engage her on the matter of her family. She was always evasive, deliberately changing the subject or just wandering off without answering. It really was quite awkward at times and I simply gave up in the end. Do you really know nothing at all about them?"

"Her home is a village near Morford in the Midlands. I think her father is something to do with manufacturing footwear but she never spoke about him and became quite tight-lipped if anyone asked. Apparently both her mother and grandmother had been nurses. From the little Lucy did say, I think she seemed to feel quite sorry for her mother, although I don't know why. She certainly wrote to her regularly and was always pleased to receive her replies."

Shifting herself into a more comfortable position, Mrs. Penrose declared firmly, "There you are then. Who could be more suitable to cope with Mary? What better solution can there be?"

Walking slowly away in the direction of the window, Alice paused reflectively before turning to say, "There is the matter of the child's father to consider".

This elicited an exclamation akin to exasperation. "For goodness sake girl, what on earth do you expect him to do in the state he's in?"

An attempt to locate Marcus's whereabouts had resulted in Alice paying a visit to the War Office, visiting various departments and consulting numerous lists. Despite all her experiences in action, she was totally unprepared for the news when it came.

"We regret to inform you that Lieutenant Appleton has sustained serious injuries," said a weary-sounding clerk, inured by now to being the bearer of bad tidings. "He was initially posted as missing presumed dead, which you will be relieved to know is not the case," he offered.

On inquiring as to his whereabouts, any relief she may have felt was dashed when she was told that he was in the Royal Herbert General Army Hospital at Woolwich, awaiting transfer to St. Dunstan's Home for the Blind once his wounds had healed.

Reeling from the shock she had made her way home as though walking through a mist. Visions of that gentle, handsome face periodically floated in front of her entwined with that of the vibrant, laughing Lucy. Once again her grief was renewed threatening to overwhelm her as she recalled the couple's love and their eager hopes for the future.

Mentally shaking herself out of her reverie, Alice turned to her mother once more saying: "Marcus has as much right, if not more, to know of Mary's existence. Surely, out of consideration, he should have some say in what happens to her?"

In a quiet but firm voice, back came the reply, "Which means you will have to visit him and tell him. If you don't, no one else is going to."

So saying, and with the infant's arms clasped trustingly round her neck, she rose to her feet and swept out of the room to engage on yet another task requiring her attention.

The gaunt bulk of the vast army hospital confronted Alice immediately she descended from the fourth tram she had been forced to take in her journey across London in order to accomplish a mission which she was frankly dreading. Searching in her bag she brought out the piece of paper on which she had painstakingly written down a block and ward number. Familiar as she was with hospital routine and organisation, there was an uncomfortable pit in her stomach as she followed the numerous signs, each one bringing her relentlessly nearer to the end of her quest.

At last she was confronted with a short corridor at the end of which was a pair of oak doors with panes of frosted glass in the upper half. These swung open to reveal a glimpse of the customary row of beds running down neatly either side of a very long ward, before closing again behind the figure in nursing uniform which had emerged bearing a covered tray towards one of the rooms leading off to the side.

Quickening her pace, Alice was able to intercept the young girl who, with a compassionate smile, pointed her in the right direction.

"Through the doors, dear, and Lieutenant Appleton's is the last bed on the righthand side before you reach the balcony. He's a bit brighter today and is sitting out in a chair, so isn't that good?" she beamed brightly.

Squaring her shoulders, Alice opened the doors and stepped firmly into the ward.

Recumbent shapes, many heavily bandaged, lay in some of the beds. Other figures in dressing gowns, or the familiar navy jacket and trousers issued to the wounded, sat around in desultory groups talking and smoking cigarettes. Men having to adapt to life without a limb struggled to balance as they exercised warily on crutches, whilst a couple of limbless victims slowly propelled themselves around in wheelchairs. In and out amongst the beds nurses carried out their tasks, expertly fielding the occasional cheeky comment or outstretched hand.

The memories came flooding back of desperately wounded men with no hope of recovery, men waiting patiently for repatriation out of the hellhole that was France. Young boys, for that's all they were, who wanted nothing more than the comfort of a mother's presence. For a few blissful days she had been able to walk free of all this but it had only been an illusion for the reality was all too clearly still there.

A few visitors were scattered about on chairs as she made her way towards the end of the ward, her eyes becoming fixed on the form seated beside the last bed, his bandaged head staring unseeingly in her direction. Propped beside the chair were the unmistakable crutches. Swiftly her gaze flew to his limbs and she took an involuntary breath - they were all there, although one was substantially padded and strapped.

Coming quietly to a halt in front of him she thought to stand and regain her composure but with apparent perception Marcus lifted his face and in a flat, expressionless voice said, "Whatever is it now, Nurse? You've done my dressing, I've had my eye drops and medicines, and the bed's made."

Stooping forward she took his hand in hers and said, "Marcus, it's Alice, Alice Penrose."

She felt him stiffen, the hand tensed within hers and a seeming age passed until he said, "Alice. Lucy's friend isn't it?"

"Yes," she whispered. Dear God, she thought, please let him know about Lucy. I can't bear to have to break that news as well. "Is it alright if I sit down?"

"Please do," he said woodenly. "You'll have to forgive me for not pulling a chair up for you - a bit incapacitated I'm afraid."

Deliberately she dragged it across the floor and sat down alongside him. Having settled herself she turned towards him, hoping that he would open the conversation. Instead, she found herself plunging in: "Marcus, I am so sorry to find you like this. I had absolutely no idea until three days ago."

"That's alright," he replied unemotionally. "How long have you been back?"

"Only about a week." Desperately she cast around in her mind for something to say.

"I managed to get sent home on one of the hospital trains at the beginning of December and was told I needn't go back, thank goodness! I'm afraid it's all taking a bit of getting used to."

"Yes, it must do."

Damn it! How difficult it was to engage in any way with this man who was incapable of making eye contact. His voice wasn't giving anything away either.

Still she pushed on. "I've brought you some oranges. Some shops have managed to get a few for Christmas, and I've got an uncle who's a greengrocer so we were lucky."

With no perceptible change in inflection the reply came back: "Thank you so much, I shall enjoy such a treat."

A passing nurse called out cheerily, "How lovely that you have a visitor, Lieutenant." This evoked absolutely no response from the once vital but now impassive frame blindly intent on some unknown point ahead.

Abruptly, the near-despairing Alice found herself saying, "What happened to you Marcus? Can you bear to tell me?"

Suddenly leaning forward and gripping both arms of the chair, he almost hissed, "Never mind me. What happened to Lucy?"

There – it was out. There was no ducking the issue now. Before she could respond, he said in a voice ravaged with pain, "It's alright, I know she's dead. I've managed to discover that much, also when and where it happened but not why and how. I understand that she's buried at Wimereux so I assume it was all quite quick, otherwise she'd have been brought home. It's the very devil being tied like this and I couldn't find the right person to ask. So, you see, you're coming here today is almost like an answer to prayer even though I know it doesn't sound as though I mean that."

Alice breathed a sigh of relief and leant to take his hand again. "I guess it's difficult for both of us. For a start, I had no idea whether you knew or not. Added to which, we both loved her so much that it is bound to be painful."

"Oh, believe me," he assured her, "it's nowhere near as painful as not knowing and letting your mind wander freely over all the hideous possibilities. Well, that's what I've been driven to. A mixture of anger, impotence and grief constantly fill my eyes with tears that can't find release."

With this he snatched his hand away, passed it helplessly over the bandages round his head and face and ejaculated through clenched teeth, "Damn and blast this bloody war".

Searching for the right words, Alice eventually said, "Marcus, I will put your mind at rest over one thing right away. There is absolutely no way that Lucy suffered. In fact she wouldn't even have been aware of anything. I promise you that."

"Thank God for that," he voiced in heartfelt tones, "Thank God for that."

"You see, we were both on one of the Railway Trains transferring the wounded from a Casualty Clearing Station. It was a routine thing we'd often done before."

Excitedly he gripped her hand exclaiming in a relieved voice, "So you were actually with her, Alice? She wasn't on her own?"

"Quite the opposite. She was amidst people she knew and liked. We were very near the front. There was plenty of bombing and shelling just as there invariably was, although it did seem to be closer than usual. Suddenly there was a whistle and roar and the next thing we knew one coach of the train had taken a direct hit. I was in one of the ambulances at the time. I jumped out and started running back and by the time I got there they were bringing out the bodies. The whole carriage were killed outright with the exception of Lucy and she was deeply unconscious."

She was only too aware of that unseeing gaze fastened on her face and felt the tide of emotion welling up from this unfortunate man.

"Go on," he urged, visibly swallowing, and she braced herself to continue, all the while reliving in her mind each vivid detail which, she knew, was etched in her memory for ever.

"A surgeon appeared but decided there was little that could usefully be done in those surroundings and ordered us back to a base hospital. I won't forget that journey. We couldn't use the train so I sat with her in the back of an ambulance and you would have thought the driver was transporting the most precious load in the world. You know how ghastly and riddled with potholes those roads are? I swear he managed to miss every single one."

"And did they operate?" he persisted. "Did they try to save her?"

234

Pausing for a moment, in order to find the right words, she eventually continued. "Closer examination revealed that she had sustained numerous abrasions and fractures, none of which would necessarily have been life-threatening. Unfortunately there was also an appalling wound to the back of her skull which defied any active treatment. We all knew that it was simply a matter of time. In fact, she barely survived another twenty four hours."

Like a fish gulping for air, Marcus relentlessly pursued the interrogation, his fists tight clenched all the while.

"Were you with her at the end, Alice?"

"Yes," came the whispered reply. "I held her hand, but I don't think she knew. Her life effectively ended at the time of the explosion."

Vainly trying to think of something to give him some small crumb of comfort, she was drawn to say, "Lucy was always beautiful. All the girls envied her looks, and she never lost those. Despite her injuries, there wasn't a mark on her face itself. She just looked as if she had fallen asleep."

A silence fell. Alice could think of nothing else to say and she watched sorrowfully as this helpless man, chin sunk on his chest and shoulders quietly heaving, struggled to master his emotions.

Totally oblivious to the life of the ward being acted out around them, they both sat immersed in their thoughts.

Suddenly, aware that Marcus had put a question to her she was forced to ask him to repeat it.

"Did you go to the burial?"

"Of course," she said. "Everyone went and I managed to find some flowers which I put on the grave. It was very dignified."

"Good," he mouthed, "and thank you Alice. This can't have been easy."

Once again they lapsed into a thought-filled silence which was only broken by the approach of an orderly pushing the inevitable tea trolley.

Alice accepted a cup of the welcome refreshment and began to sip it automatically as she watched the handle of a beaker being placed in her companion's hand, and a plate bearing a slice of seed cake on his lap. She admired the confidence and lack of fuss with which he dealt with this everyday event despite his handicap.

During this time she learned briefly of the intelligence exercise which had resulted in a badly injured leg and a head wound which had deprived him of his memory for days, and his sight permanently. He exhibited a considerable reluctance to talk about any of this but was finally led to remark bitterly, "I was behind enemy lines. I must have lain where I fell for some considerable time. Apparently, I was eventually found by a local peasant family who took me in and nursed me as best they could with the help of the local doctor. How long I was with them or how they managed to eventually get me out I don't know. I have absolutely no recollection of anything so I'm merely guessing. I was hospitalised before my memory returned slowly, bit by bit."

Burying his chin deep on his chest, he muttered, "I just wish they had let me die so that I could have been with her instead of having to endure this living death." Quickly looking up, he went on, "In a way it's good that Lucy didn't survive because I couldn't have borne for her to see me like this. All our plans blown to smithereens Alice, because there is no way that I would have agreed to our marriage in this state".

"You are reckoning without a very determined lady who loved you deeply. She would have wanted to be with you no matter what."

The Lieutenant grunted quietly to himself before remarking, "Well, it's all academic isn't it because she's gone and as far as I'm concerned the future can go hang. I've certainly nothing to live for now."

She began to protest only to be cut short. "I'm truly grateful to you for taking the trouble to seek me out, Alice. I must admit that your visit has brought a measure of peace as well as pain. However, I am not likely to be good company and I'm sure you are anxious to get back to your folk. I seem to remember that you lived in Sydenham? Lucy spent part of a leave with your parents I recall. She wrote to me regularly you know and I received a couple from there."

Looking in her direction he finished gloomily, "I haven't even got those reminders now. Most of my stuff seems to have gone missing."

Alice had been fidgeting nervously for some time and, before she had the chance to lose her nerve, she blurted out, "I can't leave yet Marcus because I'm afraid I have only told you half the story. You mentioned just now the odd letters you received from Sydenham. In actual fact there were considerably more because Lucy stayed for quite some time with my parents."

As he made to interrupt she placed a hand firmly over his saying, "No, please let me finish because I am finding this somewhat difficult".

"Alice, if you have anything to tell me that will destroy my memories of Lucy, please don't. They are all I have left now and... "

"No, no, it's nothing like that," she hastened, "and I'm afraid you really need to know. Some weeks after the last occasion that you were in Boulogne, Lucy discovered she was pregnant." Ignoring the astounded gasp which erupted, she pressed on. "Amazingly, she managed to conceal this and remain in her post well past the time that would normally be possible. All the while she was hoping that you would reappear but, when it became clear from your communications that this wasn't going to happen, and every passing week made it more difficult, she was eventually forced to reveal her plight. As you can imagine, it created several ripples in certain quarters and she was dispatched back to 'Blighty'' with all speed."

"But why didn't she tell me, for heaven's sake?" Marcus almost shouted, causing several heads to turn in their direction.

"I think Lucy reckoned that you had enough to contend with. She didn't want to have to give you the news via a letter, and what could you have done anyway?"

"But why was she staying with your family, Alice? Why didn't she go home to Morfordshire?"

Despite the time of year, it seemed to be getting increasingly warm in the ward, even though it was only heated by the meagre stoves around which the ambulant patients gathered in social groups. Running her finger round the collar of her dress in an attempt to loosen it, she drew in a deep breath before picking up the threads once more.

"I don't know whether Lucy ever discussed her family with you Marcus, but it would seem that she didn't enjoy the best of relationships with her parents, or more specifically her father. From the start she made it quite clear that there was no way she could tell them what had transpired. Faced with the uninspiring prospect of going into a home for unmarried mothers, I persuaded my parents to take her in. My mum is an absolute saint and not only agreed to this but also consented to care for the baby until such time as you both returned to retrieve the situation."

"But what about the letters I received from the hospital?" pressed her stunned listener.

"Lucy posted them to me in a separate envelope and I forwarded them on, as I did the ones to her mother as well. Eventually, many weeks after the baby was born, she was successful in her attempt to be reinstated at the hospital. Things were so hectic, and skilled hands in such short supply, that the powers that be would have accepted a monkey if it could jump through the right hoops. All the while, she was desperately hoping that your paths would cross again. Then your letters stopped completely and she began to fear the worst, fuelled by the fact that it seemed absolutely impossible to get any reliable information. Then, so near the end of the worst of the hostilities, she had to lose her life," she finished lamely.

A silence developed which seemed destined to continue indefinitely as Marcus withdrew into a world inhabited by a swirling kaleidoscope of jumbled thoughts and images. Alice perched uncomfortably on the edge of her seat, completely unable to free herself from the constricting bands of physical tension which had built up. The next move had to come from the helpless figure slumped deep into the armchair.

At last, as though mentally forcing himself to recognise her continued presence, he gave a long sigh before saying, "Alice, this has come as the most incredible shock. I hope you will understand if I ask you to go now and leave me to my thoughts."

Quietly but in measured tones she gave her reply. "Marcus, I understand how you must be feeling. Nevertheless, I'm afraid we have to talk further because things can't just be left in this way. There are decisions that have to be made and I need your guidance in the matter."

"Can't they keep for a while?" he countered wearily.

"Unfortunately, that isn't possible. Mary is now more than a year old. My mother isn't exactly a young woman and, while she was prepared to care for her until the end of the war, there's no way that she can continue to undertake this task indefinitely. I shall have to return to nursing very shortly and this matter must be resolved before I do so."

"The baby was a girl then?" he said.

"Yes. Lucy gave her only one name, Mary, when she registered the birth."

"Does she look anything like Lucy?"

Alice considered for a moment before replying. "Not specifically. She has the same colour hair but the shape of her face is more like yours, I suppose. Oh, I don't know! She's just Mary, developing into a real character. A lovely, healthy child in every respect and one whose future has got to be decided."

Marcus shifted irritably in his chair and said with some bitterness, "Well, I can't imagine why you're asking me? I am hardly in a position to do anything for her?"

"Of course I realise that, but you are her father and you have a right to be consulted. I can't just go ahead and place her anywhere I choose. Lucy wouldn't thank me for that and neither, I'm sure, would you."

Their deliberations were interrupted momentarily by an orderly collecting the tea things and Alice was forced to pass a few desultory comments before she moved on. This brief interlude gave the unhappy man a chance to martial his thoughts.

"Have you considered any possible solutions, Alice?"

"Believe me, I've done nothing else but think. My mum is firmly of the opinion that Mary should be placed with her own kith and kin. Given Lucy's seemingly parlous relationship with her parents I don't relish the thought of having to confront them with this situation. I certainly can't face it on my own. Someone will have to give me some support. Furthermore, what am I to do if they refuse to accept things and just wash their hands of it?"

A heartfelt groan was emitted by the figure at her side. "God, how damnably helpless and useless I am stuck here like this. I just don't know how to offer you any practical help."

Vainly grasping at straws she said, "I did wonder whether perhaps you might have family who would be prepared to help?"

Somewhat cynically he retorted, "Alice, you see before you the proverbial orphan of the storm. Parents both dead, no brothers or sisters, or any other accommodating relatives for that matter. You are the only visitor I've had except for my commanding officer and another army friend. I have no family home - the school where I taught was my family, indeed my whole life until I met Lucy. I have a small amount of money but nowhere near enough to meet the needs of a growing child for an indefinite number of years. Neither is my future earning capacity exactly brilliant. As soon as I am deemed fit enough to leave here, I am to be transferred to the care of St. Dunstan's. There, it is hoped and intended that they will train me in some way that will make it possible for me to eventually find some kind of employment to enable me to live as independently as possible within the constraints this whole bloody mess has placed on my life. I think you'll agree, it is hardly a scintillating outlook and certainly not one which takes account of a baby." Thumping both arms of the chair the frustrated occupant was led to exclaim, "What a damnable, impossible plight this is and I'm so sorry that you have been made to carry such a burden. It has placed you in an intolerable predicament, of that I'm quite aware."

Touching his hand lightly and looking for some words to ease his agitation Alice remarked, rather ineptly, "I'm so, so sorry Marcus. None of this is of your making."

Turning his head towards her he commented, somewhat dryly, "I rather think that it is all my bloody fault! Oh Lucy. Why did you have to die? All those plans we made, but none of them took account of anything like this. How can fate be so cruel, Alice?"

This was a question to which that young lady had no ready answer and caused them both to sink back into silence again.

A bell being rung vigorously at the end of the ward signified the end of visiting. Alice stooped to gather up her bag and stood up with a heavy heart. Nothing had been decided and she was no wiser than when she came.

From his position Marcus put out a hand vainly groping to make contact with her, eventually clutching at a fold of her coat. Looking up he said, "Can you possibly come and see me again? I realise I have been of no help today. You must own it has all been the most tremendous shock but I promise that over the next few days I really will apply myself to the utmost and try and sort this out. I do need a bit of time though. Christmas will shortly be upon us and there is little likelihood of being able to make any kind of arrangements before then."

"I wasn't envisaging that possibility," said Alice. "However, something must be settled as early as possible in the New Year."

"Can you leave me with an address where I can reach you?"

"Of course," she said, taking a pencil and hastily writing on the back of an old envelope. "I have put it on the top shelf inside your locker."

"I appreciate that and I can only thank you for all that you have done and for your courage in coming here today. Please convey my deep gratitude to your mother as well. It doesn't bear thinking what would have happened without her unselfish help. I'm just so sorry that by our actions Lucy and I inadvertently placed you in such a position."

"Nobody could have foreseen any of this, Marcus. I'm just sorry that I have added to the considerable problems you already have."

"Don't be sorry," he said. "You have also brought me a kind of release from my tortured thoughts and certainly something else to keep my mind occupied with," was his rueful parting shot.

With which Alice retraced her steps out through the main entrance of the hospital and into the raw chill of the evening. Bracing herself she prepared to navigate her way back to Sydenham. The matter hadn't been resolved - how could it be? Nevertheless, she felt as if the burden had shifted slightly and the wheels set in motion. Thus it was with a veritable wave of mixed feelings that she grasped the rail of the tram, as it rattled to a standstill, and swung herself into its dubious warmth.

Marcus proved to be true to his word for, within a week, a letter arrived addressed to Alice bearing an official stamp. Thinking it to be news of her next nursing appointment she was rather startled to read the signature: Donald Denison, Chaplain to HM Forces, Woolwich.

The helpless man had clearly sought assistance from possibly the only source available to him. As a result the writer, being fully conversant with the unexpected problem facing Lieutenant Appleton, was desirous of arranging a meeting with both of them at her convenience.

Glancing quickly at the calendar hanging on the parlour wall, which was already adorned with a spray of holly, Alice confirmed that there was little more than a week to go before Christmas Day itself. After hasty consultation with both her parents she sat down to compose a swift reply.

Ever since their meeting an idea had been formulating in her mind whereby she could perhaps kill two birds with one stone - a means of ensuring that Marcus would have visitors at the festive season coupled with a surprise gift in the shape of his tiny daughter.

These thoughts she explained to the Chaplain hoping that he would be able to persuade the ward sister to allow them a place of privacy for the purpose and he didn't disappoint her.

After enjoying the first Christmas dinner of the peace, and certainly the first to have any meaning for an excited little child, Alice and her mother climbed into Uncle Ted's greengrocer's van to be transported across London. The young Mary, suitably wrapped up against the cold, took turns at sitting on their laps clearly stimulated by the experience.

As they approached the ward door at the appointed hour Alice became aware of a tall, lean figure in military uniform clearly loitering for a purpose. Closer inspection revealed the deep white circle of a clerical collar beneath the khaki jacket and the welcoming figure introduced himself." I certainly don't have to ask who you are," he smiled and tickled Mary playfully under the chin. "I think I've been able to set everything up satisfactorily, as you requested and I can assure you that Lieutenant Appleton has absolutely no idea of what is in the wind." So saying he ushered them through a door into a small office which normally saw service as an interview room but now bore token evidence of an attempt to cheer up the stark decor with seasonal additions.

"Come in and settle yourselves down whilst I fetch the patient."

Turning to him Alice conveyed her thanks for making it all possible expressing the hope that such a request had not disrupted his own plans. "Far from it, " he replied. "I am officially 'on duty' all over Christmas and am delighted to be able to help."

With that he disappeared in the direction of the ward reappearing some five minutes later expertly propelling Marcus through the doors in a wheelchair.

"This contraption isn't really necessary but I thought it would be a bit quicker," he volunteered breezily, parking it neatly next to Alice's chair. "Now, who's going to effect the introductions?"

Placing a hand on the clearly bewildered man's arm Alice said gently, "Hello Marcus, it's me again and I've brought my mum along so that you can meet her." On cue, Mrs. Penfold transferred a puzzled Mary to her daughter's lap while she knelt in front of the wheelchair.

"Good afternoon Lieutenant Appleton and a very Happy Christmas. I'm delighted to have the opportunity to meet you at last and we hope you will like this small gift," she said, placing a gaily wrapped box of assorted fruit and nuts and sweets on his lap.

"I just don't know what to say," came the reply. "It is me who should be giving you a present after all that you have and are doing. Fancy putting yourself out by sacrificing your Christmas afternoon to come and visit me. I am most touched," and he gestured broadly with his hand.

Turning to Alice he asked, "Who is looking after Mary while you are both here?"

All the while, the child had sat quietly but with eyes fixed somewhat questioningly on the bandaged head of this strange person who had suddenly appeared from nowhere. Hearing her name mentioned she let out a gurgle of delight and proceeded to jig animatedly up and down.

On the other side of his chair he heard the padre's voice as it said, "The time has come for you to meet your daughter, Marcus."

Getting to her feet, Alice turned and deftly placed her charge on his lap saying, "Mary, this is your Papa."

"Heavens, I don't believe it," said Marcus in a choked voice as he moved to position his hands correctly to accommodate his burden. "Won't she be scared?"

"At this age it really wouldn't matter if you had two heads," replied Alice, "because she has no idea what is normal and what isn't. So don't disturb yourself on that account."

"It's a pity everyone can't react to disability in the same way," Donald commented, "It should provide a lesson for us all."

All the time they were speaking two bright eyes surveyed the strange face and two little hands crept up to probe the bandages. With very moist eyes Alice and her mother watched as Marcus instinctively fielded the extended arms and enfolded them tenderly within a gentle grasp. Squealing with pleasure Mary determinedly attempted to escape their confines but showed no inclination to reinstate herself elsewhere.

There could be no doubting the depth of feeling this visit had stirred within the heart of the lonely, troubled and isolated man. Tiring of her game Mary nestled happily against him to play contentedly with the buttons and tasselled cord of his dressing gown.

Raising his head Marcus addressed them all in a voice thick with emotion. "What a Christmas present you have given me. Thank you, thank you so much. You cannot imagine what this means. It's almost as though I am holding part of my beloved Lucy once more," and he lowered his chin to nuzzle the silky softness of the child's hair.

"I'm glad you have gained pleasure from our planning," said the chaplain, "but we mustn't lose sight of the other purpose of this visit."

Looking at Alice he continued, "Following your visit to Lieutenant Appleton he contacted me and put me in possession of the facts surrounding the dilemma with which you are faced. Since then I have busied myself considerably on the matter and, with his permission, would like to put a proposal to you."

"Please, do go ahead," said Marcus.

"Having discussed the limited avenues open, we have come to the conclusion that you are right, Mrs. Penfold, and Mary should be placed in the care of her own family if at all possible. I understand that relationships were not particularly good between Lucy and her parents but it is clear that they must be acquainted with events as they stand. One stumbling block emerged immediately as none of you seem to know their exact address, except that they live near Morford."

Pausing for a moment to survey the faces watching him intently, he continued, "Well, someone must be smiling on our quest! I have a cousin who is a Canon of Morford Cathedral. I managed to contact him and, without divulging the reason for my query, discovered that the Dane family, who lost a daughter in France come from a family who are, in fact, quite well known in the area and he was able to furnish me with the details I required."

"But I can't possibly face them on my own," Alice rushed in.

"Lieutenant Appleton isn't expecting any such thing of you, Miss Penfold. What I suggest is that you write to them as a friend of Lucy's recently returned from France expressing a wish to see them. If possible try to tie them down to a morning in the first week of the New Year when you will call on them whilst visiting friends in the area. As soon as you receive a reply, let me know and I will arrange to drive you up there. It will be impossible to accomplish this in one day, or even two, because of the distance. However, my cousin will be more than willing to accommodate us."

There was a silence for a moment whilst the two women digested the information.

"Are you proposing to take Mary with you?" asked Mrs. Penfold, already mentally assessing the preparations which would be involved.

"No. We did discuss this but I think it is better to defer that until we find out how the land lies. It is a long journey for a little one to make."

"Well, you seem to have considered everything and it all seems eminently sensible," said the older woman. "As soon as we get home Alice will write the letter, won't you?"

The relief was palpable in her daughter's voice as she said to the chaplain," I can't thank you enough for all this. It seems an awful imposition on your time but there truly is no way that I could face this hurdle on my own."

"Neither will you have to, so that is settled. Two heads are better than one, you know," he said with a smile. "Speaking of which, why don't you and I disappear for a moment and draft a suitable letter to be dispatched to Lucy's parents immediately?" a suggestion with which Alice was more than happy to comply.

At that moment there was a knock at the door and Sister appeared with a tray of tea and some Christmas cake, providing a pleasant ending to a most heartening occasion for all concerned.

***

A few days later, Alice received a fairly curt note signed by Herbert Dane inviting her to partake of coffee with them on the third of January. Upon contacting Donald Denison he announced his readiness to collect her from her home early on the morning of the previous day, upon which they would make their way to Morford at a fairly leisurely pace.

Alice confessed to viewing the occasion with a degree of apprehension tinged with a measure of excitement. It would certainly be a different start to 1919 and what many people hoped would be a brave new year.

The journey to Morford proved to be easy and enjoyable. The chaplain's car, whilst not in the top flight of motor vehicles, was far more comfortable than most forms of transport Alice had experienced. She settled herself into the front passenger seat and appreciated the driver's thoughtfulness as he solicitously wrapped a warm rug around the lower half of her body to stave off the rather biting chill of the otherwise bright day.

Donald Denison himself turned out to be an interesting and considerate companion with whom she quickly formed a rapport. Possessed of a broad range of knowledge and information he was a good conversationalist and the miles flashed by most pleasurably.

After partaking of a most satisfying lunch at a congenial roadside hostelry outside Dunstable they arrived in Morford in time for tea.

Donald's cousin Robert and his wife Evelyn proved to be a delightful couple who welcomed them warmly to their pleasant house in a quiet corner of the cathedral precincts. After unpacking and refreshing themselves they were more than willing to allow their host to take them on a guided tour of the spectacular building upon which earlier generations had lavished so much care and artistic workmanship.

Later in the evening, their hunger once more assuaged, they sat around a roaring log fire enjoying a convivial drink together. It was a world which seemed to be light years away from the one which Alice normally inhabited yet she felt completely at ease.

During a lull in the conversation the Canon took the opportunity to enquire as to their plans for the following day, prepared to offer directions and advice on time needed for such an excursion.

"Alice has received a letter from Mr. and Mrs. Dane to the effect that they will expect us for coffee at eleven in the morning," said Donald.

"Have you met them before, by any chance?"

"No," replied Alice, "I really know nothing about them. Their daughter, Lucy, was my greatest friend throughout the war. We experienced so much together, especially during the time spent nursing in France."

"Donald tells us that she was killed most tragically as the result of enemy action. We heard news of this of course, for Morford and its environs is still quite a close knit community despite the inroads being made by industry and new housing. However, I do have to say that Herbert Dane is not exactly one of the most liked or popular people in the neighbourhood so I haven't heard chapter and verse as it were."

Alice and Donald exchanged a surreptitious look as this piece of information was imparted but their attention was drawn back in time to hear his wife comment feelingly, "It's his poor wife I feel sorry for".

"Now then Evelyn, I think we've said enough on this subject. Alice and Donald must be allowed to formulate their own impressions. Apart from which they are going there on an errand of mercy, as it were, for which any grieving couple must surely be grateful."

Once again the younger couple were forced to cast a furtive glance at each other. If only they knew the truth, thought Alice.

"Anyhow, you'll enjoy the drive out to Shepherdstone," said Robert. "It's a pleasant little village. Our local hospital has a convalescent home there in Painters Court which, I believe, used to be Mrs. Dane's family home. They now live almost adjacent to it in a rather nice converted farm property constructed from local stone. Yes, yes, I think you will find you will be made welcome."

I only wish I could share your confidence, Alice mused to herself as she made her way up to her bedroom shortly afterwards.

Thus it was that, the following morning, just as the village clock was striking eleven, Donald turned his car in through the gates of Court Farmhouse and came to a standstill in front of the oak front door.

Having assisted Alice from the car he pulled firmly on the wrought iron bell hanging to one side, stood back and took a deep breath. Before the peals had ceased to reverberate within the house, the door was opened by a middle-aged woman dressed completely in black, with a white apron, who had clearly only been expecting Alice and was somewhat taken aback to be confronted with a military gentleman of the cloth.

"Miss Penfold?" she queried tentatively.

"Yes," responded Alice, "and this is the Reverend Denison."

"If you would care to come in I will let Mr. and Mrs. Dane know that you are here, although they were only expecting a Miss Penfold." She disappeared into a room leading off the hall, shortly to reappear and bid them enter.

A slightly balding, thick-set man of average height and unsmiling face, stood to greet them but Alice's eyes were drawn toward the frail-looking woman lying on the chaise longue, propped up on pillows and covered with a rug.

Extending a hand towards Herbert Dane, Donald apologised for his unforeseen presence. "I am currently based at the military hospital in Woolwich and offered to drive Miss Penfold rather than leave her to contend with the vagaries of public transport at a rather inclement time of year. I also wished to visit a relative in Morford so it has worked out rather well."

Herbert briefly nodded his head before indicating the figure on the couch. "This is my wife who, as you can see, is not at all robust. Lucy's death has affected her badly and I had grave misgivings in acceding to your request," he said rather pompously. "Anyhow, you'd best sit down and I'll arrange for coffee to be brought in."

Alice stationed herself as close as possible to Mrs. Dane in a low seat that made for easy eye contact. In a gentle voice she said, "Believe me, the last thing I want to do is to cause you further distress. Lucy and I were such close friends from the moment of our first meeting at Southampton, and we have been through so much together that I felt I must at least try to see you."

Sadie Dane sent her a look of almost pathetic gratitude but was

248

prevented in whatever she might wish to say by her husband.

"I hardly imagine you can tell us any more than those who have already visited. Some army welfare person brought us her personal belongings, although there were precious few of those, and one of your chaps came - for what good it did," he commented, casting an almost disdainful look in Donald's direction.

"Please Herbert, please don't. They were very kind and... "

"Simply doing the job they are paid to do - no more, no less," he interrupted disparagingly. "Doing it all the time, aren't you Padre? Same pat phrases, same meaningless words."

Noting Sadie's growing distress, and unsure how Donald would react to such a broadside, Alice speedily intervened.

"That is one of the reasons I have come," she said. "You see, I worked alongside Lucy throughout the war and I was with her at the very end. No one is in a better position to give you the real facts."

"You were actually beside her when she died?" asked Sadie. "Please tell me all that happened, please tell me the truth."

Just as she had done for Marcus only a few weeks previously, so Alice now sought to bring a measure of peace to a mother's troubled and unhappy mind. Oblivious to the cold, unfeeling form of Herbert Dane, who continued to drink his coffee with seemingly little interest in what she had to recount, she drew her seat close alongside the invalid's couch and took her hand tenderly in hers.

When she had finished there was a momentary silence before a heartfelt voice said brokenly, "Thank you Alice, thank you so very much. You will never know how much your coming today has meant." With which she reached under her pillow for a handkerchief to stem the threatening tears.

"Now see what's happening," spat her husband regarding her with exasperation. "I warned you that nothing but grief would come of all this."

Donald, who had been quietly sitting in the background, clearly felt it was time for him to intervene.

"That your wife is upset is only natural but such outpourings often prove to be an aid to mourning a loss and very therapeutic in the end."

Before Herbert Dane could draw breath he went on, "Forgive me, though, if I remark that you yourself appear amazingly controlled and stoical in view of the tragedy that has befallen you. I cannot even begin to imagine what it must feel like to lose a daughter."

"I consider such a remark a great impertinence," Herbert erupted. "Our family business is none of your concern but, as you have raised the matter, let me say that I grieved for the loss of my daughter a long time ago. There was no need for anything like this to have happened if she had remained here, which she could have done. But she would have none of it; flouted every rule, showed no respect for her parents, completely headstrong and determined to have her own way without thought for others. That is the child I have lost, Padre."

"Mr. Dane," came Alice's voice, "that is not a picture of Lucy that I or any of her colleagues would recognise. She was an excellent nurse. Full of fun and laughter certainly, and that is what endeared her to everyone, but totally committed, caring and dedicated. She demonstrated common sense and the strength and confidence to use her own initiative when necessary - qualities that were invaluable in the situations in which we often found ourselves, and there are many beside me who would stand testimony to this."

She felt Sadie's hand seeking hers and heard a voice once again whisper, "Thank you my dear, thank you."

Clearly determined to get rid of these unsought visitors, Herbert Dane rose from his chair saying, "I don't think there is anything further that needs to be said on this subject and my wife will be getting quite exhausted. Thank you for giving us your time." With that he began to walk towards the door only to have his progress halted by Donald's calm but firm voice.

"Unfortunately sir, much as I am sure you will find it distasteful, there is another issue that must be touched on before we leave. Perhaps you will do me the kindness of sitting down again whilst I endeavour to explain?"

With great reluctance that gentleman complied and Donald launched forth in an attempt to deal with the delicate matter in hand as sensitively as possible.

That he had patently failed was evident as an irate Herbert Dane leapt to his feet and with a face almost puce with rage yelled, "Now we know why you have really come." Indicating the openly weeping Sadie he continued contemptuously, "Bringing comfort and solace to my grieving wife be damned; you have simply twisted the knife further."

Ineffectually, his wife raised a hand and opened her mouth in an attempt to get him to listen to her but he was like a traction engine hurtling out of control.

"If anything justifies the words I used with regard to Lucy earlier, I think you will agree that this sordid tale is more than adequate proof. Now I really must insist that you leave. As far as I am concerned I have not heard a word of this story and a child by the name of Mary Dane simply does not exist. You have the birth certificate Miss Penfold and you will simply have to sort things out with the father. Neither my wife nor I wish to hear another word."

"But Herbert... " protested Sadie weakly trying to prevent a further flood of tears.

"Enough, the subject is closed."

So saying, he flung open the door into the hall, strode to open the front door, determinedly ushered the visitors out then slammed the door shut.

Hastily getting into the car they sat for a moment in order to try to regain a measure of control. Alice was nearly beside herself and incredulous with disbelief.

"No wonder Lucy left home with little if any fond memories. That man is impossible."

Turning to Donald she said in heartfelt tones, "Thank heaven you came with me. I cannot imagine how I would have coped on my own."

"Well, I'm afraid I didn't manage to achieve anything," he said ruefully. "Almost within minutes of our arrival I could have told you how things were going to end. Don't distress yourself my dear, we did our best. I have to say, whatever decision is made concerning Mary's future it has got to have a brighter outlook than a life in that place."

Having become somewhat calmer, Alice said pensively, "That poor, poor woman. I'm sure she would have been more sympathetically inclined towards Mary. She didn't stand a chance though against that hectoring bully. If that's an example of married life then spare me."

With eyes smiling gently at her, the chaplain said, "Marriage doesn't have to be like that at all, and well you know it. Just look at your own parents. Anyway, I'm pretty sure I've come to know you well enough to be certain that you would never allow things to reach that state."

Breathing a heavy sigh his companion was drawn to say, "It seems so incongruous to live surrounded on all sides by material comfort and so much beauty, yet to be inwardly composed of so much sadness, unhappiness, bitterness and hatred." And she looked round at the tranquillity of the setting all the while reflecting on the discord within the four walls of the mellow old house beside them.

"Before you immerse yourself into any further philosophising, professor, I think we should make our escape."

As if on cue the front door suddenly opened and a still irate Herbert Dane hurried towards them waving a box. Upon lowering her car window the object was tossed disdainfully into her lap.

"You might as well give that to this by-blow of Lucy's when she is older and see what she makes of it, if anything. It's certainly no use to us anymore."

Having delivered this last fusillade he went back into the house from which they could hear Sadie's voice crying piteously, "No Herbert, oh please, no."

Lifting the lid they saw, nestling inside, the exquisite tracery of Lucy's silver buckle.

The return journey to the cathedral precincts was an unhappy one. Alice had been more shaken than she thought possible by the encounter with Lucy's parents and her mood fluctuated between outbursts of frustrated anger, complete disbelief and desperate worry and unhappiness.

Donald was only too aware of the steady trickle of tears staining her cheeks which she unsuccessfully tried to mask by blowing her nose frequently into the inadequate, screwed-up handkerchief clutched tightly in her hand.

Eventually, when within sight of the rooftops of Morford, he pulled in to the side of the road and turned off the engine.

"Do you want to get this out of your system first, before we face my cousin?" he suggested kindly.

"No," she hissed fiercely. "I just want to collect my things and get home."

Before he could comment she swiftly turned to face him, her face distraught. "Donald, I do apologise; that was absolutely unforgivable. I was only thinking of myself. I am in your hands and will, of course, do whatever you think best."

Placing a hand on her arm he gently replied: "My dear, there is no forgiveness necessary. You have every right to feel as you do. Indeed, there are some far from Christian thoughts coursing through my mind as well."

Firmly grasping the steering wheel while simultaneously easing his body in the seat, he went on to affirm her wishes.

"I agree with your suggestion. There is positively nothing to be gained by remaining here a moment longer." Following a deep sigh he continued: "Apart from which we, or I, have the unpleasant task of acquainting Marcus with the facts, an assignment I don't relish, I have to confess."

Bravely, Alice assured him of her continued presence. "Of course I must be there. I set this whole wretched train in motion and I shall not rest until I have seen it through to the bitter end - and bitter I feel it is going to be."

"Thank you," her companion replied with heartfelt sincerity. "I will value your help in all of this."

So saying, he put the car into gear and swung out into the road towards the city.

Robert and Evelyn were on the point of opening their front door as the vehicle entered the Close and they prepared to greet the couple. One look at Alice's face and the stern set of Donald's shoulders relayed the outcome of the ill-fated visit.

"May I take it that things have not been a success?" said the Canon shrewdly.

"That is an understatement to say the least," replied his cousin as he placed an arm protectively round Alice's shoulders. "We've just come to collect our things and we'll be on our way.'

"Oh dear, I'm so sorry," ventured their hostess. "I can quite understand if you want to be off, but at least have some soup or something before you go."

Looking at Alice, her companion briefly inclined his head before replying: "If it won't be too much trouble that would be greatly appreciated, Evelyn."

With which that lady scuttled off towards the kitchen and within a remarkably short time managed to produce steaming bowls of soup, cheese, crusty home-baked bread and a dish of fruit.

"I'm afraid we normally eat in the kitchen if it's just the two of us," she said looking at them somewhat apologetically. "Quite frankly, it's the warmest room in the house."

Without demur and with suitable murmurs of approval, Alice and Donald sank gratefully onto the rush-bottom chairs set round a scrubbed wooden table and settled themselves to fortify their flagging spirits. After some attempt at desultory conversation, Robert looked them both square in the face and said: "Look, it's quite obvious that matters have not gone well for you. I have no wish to pry but is there any way in which I can possibly be of help?"

Alice averted her gaze to the plate in front of her and devoted herself steadfastly to her meal, leaving Donald to reply.

"Thank you for the offer but I'm afraid there isn't."

Then, feeling that there was a need for some comment, he offered: "I'm afraid we were both taken aback by the total lack of warmth or response engendered by our visit. We both found the whole thing rather upsetting."

Unable to contain herself Alice interrupted him. "What you mean to say is that the attitude of Lucy's father defied belief. He was positively loathsome."

Before her husband could comment, Evelyn promptly interposed a question.

"What about her mother? Surely she was pleased you had taken the trouble to visit?"

"Pathetically grateful," said Alice. "At least, she was when she was allowed to speak for herself."

Readily she let Donald take up the saga. "Mrs. Dane is a frail, broken, gravely unhappy woman. She is all too clearly in a state of deep grief and bereavement as a result of her daughter's tragic death. Unfortunately she appears to be totally at the mercy of a man who I can only describe as cold and unfeeling. I don't think I've met anyone quite like him before. He truly was extraordinarily unpleasant."

There was a short silence as his cousin helped himself to some cheese before thoughtfully saying: "In the light of what you have told us, I think I can now tell you the little I know. I do have to stress, however, that it is all second-hand knowledge, which is why I was unwilling to apprise you of it last night."

"There's no smoke without fire," countered his wife pithily.

"Be that as it may my dear, it was not for us to prejudice these folk before they had a chance to make their own judgment," Robert reproved mildly.

"So, what is the problem?" Donald pressed.

"I'll tell you what the matter is," persisted Evelyn. "It's what happens when you marry outside your class, that's what it is."

Fixing his irrepressible spouse with a quelling look, the Canon continued. "Sadie Dane is the only daughter of a fairly comfortable landowner and farmer. Her mother was an extraordinary person whose fame is legendary in the city and was, in fact, the major inspiration behind the Hospital here. Sadie followed in her mother's footsteps as a nurse. Many say that she was a gentle, caring soul but she failed to inherit the maternal fire and spark."

He paused to consider before proceeding. "I don't know the details but it would seem that Herbert Dane came from typical working-class stock. I think Sadie met him through her work in the homes of the poor. Anyway, she ended up marrying him although her family tried to dissuade her. I suspect he thought he was on to a good thing, although it hasn't worked out like that. True, he has a managerial position and a seat on the board of one of the large factories here and has insinuated his way into some of the more high profile local organisations.

Unfortunately, people never really warmed to him. As a result he has failed to gain the entry into society that he thought would come with such a marriage. This has meant that Sadie too has suffered for she is rarely seen out socially."

There was a pause while this news was absorbed before Donald replied: "I suppose much of that must account for his behaviour. It does not, however, excuse his insufferable attitude towards his wife."

"Rumour has it that he's got a mistress in the city," Evelyn interjected.

"That is pure hearsay," her spouse cautioned. "We have no proof."

"No wonder Lucy spoke so little of her home or family," said Alice reflectively. "It also answers her reason for spending most of her leaves elsewhere, too."

Sensing that Evelyn was quite ready to pursue the matter, Donald looked at his watch and took the opportunity to bring the matter to a close. "Goodness, if we are to reach London at a reasonable hour we must take our leave at once. You have been more than kind to us but we really can't afford to delay any longer."

With that they made their way out into the close, bade their farewells and headed out through the magnificent old cathedral gateway into the bustling High Street and on to the London Road. Once the car had cleared Morford, Alice turned towards her companion and said: "This visit may not have accomplished what we hoped for but it has indeed answered some questions. The thing is, what are we going to do now and whatever is to become of little Mary?"

Casting a brief smile in her direction he gently counselled patience. "I think we both need time to assimilate the outcome of this visit; apart from which we can do nothing until we have talked with Marcus."

The grey afternoon light gradually faded as dusk descended and Donald needed all his concentration to contend with the hazards of the road in that gloomy, in-between world of shadows.

"It's been both a trying and a tiring day," he ventured. "Why don't you try to catch a little sleep?"

Despite her protestations Alice found herself succumbing to the sound of the engine and the rhythm of the vehicle on the road and was soon curled up into herself with head lolling on her chest. So she remained until the chaplain's quiet voice roused her and she gradually became aware of the sulphurous glow from the street lights and the rattle of trams.

"We're well into the suburbs of London now, Alice. I'm going to run you straight home but I have been thinking. Would it be possible for you to come to my office in the hospital tomorrow morning so that we can approach Marcus together?"

"Of course," she said, tidying her hair and attempting to straighten her coat. Addressing him directly the words came tumbling out. "Donald, I am so grateful for all that you have done. I couldn't have coped on my own under the circumstances and you have made it both possible and endurable."

"Thanks aren't needed, my dear. I am only doing what is, after all, part of my job. Besides which, Marcus is a brother officer and it could have been me lying there in his place."

Looking at him in surprise she said: "Were you in France as well? Somehow, it never occurred to me to ask. "I don't know why not."

"Yes, I was. Now is not the time to go into it, though. Some other time we'll swap experiences if and when we both feel up to it."

"Of course," she said, and there was no mistaking the depth of understanding in her voice.

Following a fitful night's sleep Alice once more presented herself at the hospital. Together she and Donald broke the outcome of their abortive trip to Marcus.

"My poor, beloved Lucy," he sighed. "Small wonder she glossed so lightly over any mention of home."

"Yes, it definitely wasn't the happiest of experiences but at least we know where we stand," said Donald. "Which means that we must now consider the options open to us. As I see it there are three possibilities, namely an orphanage, a foster home or adoption."

With a shudder in her voice, Alice whispered: "Please, not an orphanage. Mary is used to being at the centre of a family and neither my mother nor I could bear to think of that for her."

"No, I wouldn't condemn her to that," Marcus responded quickly.

Swivelling round in his wheelchair he continued: "Quite frankly I think adoption would be the best and kindest thing for the child. There is no way I will ever be able to provide even half a life for her. Better that she should go where she is wanted and will be loved. What do you think Padre?"

Regarding the destroyed figure of the man facing him he replied in the gentlest but firmest of voices: "You have decided wisely. That is the conclusion I hoped you would arrive at, and I'm sure Alice will agree," he said, casting a searching glance in her direction.

"Yes, of course," was her rather reluctant response, "but I do hope we can be absolutely sure that she goes to a good home."

"Don't worry on that score, either of you. Many people only associate the Church with pious prayer, pomp and ritual, tea, buns and good works," he said, somewhat wryly. "However, among other things there are some very *bona fide* Church adoption agencies. I think this is something that you can safely leave to me."

Standing up he addressed them both saying: "I'll get on to it right away and keep you informed."

With that the party broke up leaving one to pursue a definite course of action and the other two to their thoughts.

Only a matter of days later Alice found herself once more en route to the familiar military hospital at Netley where she and Lucy had first met. Was it really a mere handful of years ago? What high hopes they had cherished then as they proudly donned their smart new uniforms, keen to experience a new life.

Well, they had certainly done that, she mused, but at what price? The cost had been in the thousands upon thousands of lives lost. Did the thirst for excitement and adventure always exact such a toll? Had it all been worth it?

The train rattled on its way as these thoughts and questions danced through her mind in rhythm to the wheels, although her heart was heavy as lead. This time there would be no Lucy at the station. That vivacious figure, with a head topped by a cloud of glorious copper hair carelessly confined beneath the muslin cap, and the sparkling green eyes so full of life, had gone forever.

Reluctantly she pulled herself to her feet as the platform slid alongside and, firmly gripping her battered case, she strode off in the direction of the hospital to face yet another hurdle. In the days that followed there was no time for reflection, personal sadness or sense of loss. That vast medical institution had become the repository for the inevitable human wreckage which stalked in the wake of battle. Men, their bodies and minds sacrificed on the altar of war, now looked to the nurses with anxious and pitiful eyes beseeching help, relief and restoration following their unspeakable ordeal. Once again, life had entered a new phase and she squared her shoulders to meet this new challenge which she soon found left little time to think of anything but the task in hand.

A few weeks later a surprised Alice looked up from the report she was writing to find herself gazing at Donald's welcome face. Scrambling to her feet she queried breathlessly, "Goodness, what on earth are you doing here?"

"Now then, do I take that remark as one of pleasure or dismay?" he quipped.

"You know that I'm delighted to see you," she said sincerely, "but you must allow me to express some surprise."

"Clearly then, you haven't read the in-house orders," he countered with mock severity, "otherwise you would know of my posting to Netley."

Alice found herself giving a very good imitation of a goldfish gasping for air which caused great amusement to the chaplain who was eventually drawn to ask how long she intended to stand transfixed with her mouth open. In a trice she regained her composure and the inevitable catalogue of questions came tumbling out.

"All in good time," he said, "all in good time. I was wondering whether we could meet up when you are off duty and I can bring you up-to-date with all that has happened at leisure."

Grasping the moment Alice found herself informing him that it so happened she had a rare evening off and it took only a moment to arrange a time and venue.

So it was that, as darkness fell, she found herself once more seated in Donald's car as they drove off through the hospital gates towards the centre of Southampton in search of a restaurant.

In the end they settled on a small hotel but, once inside, it was clear it had seen better days. The dining room proved to be somewhat drab and uninspiring although none of that appeared to matter one jot to the couple seated at a secluded table.

Toasting their reunion with a pre-prandial drink, Donald wasted no time in bringing his eager companion up-to-date with the situation which had, in fact, served to bring them together in the first place.

"I think you will be absolutely delighted with the outcome of our efforts," he said. "Indeed, events have taken a most satisfactory and surprising turn."

"I can't bear the suspense a minute longer. Just tell me what is to happen to Mary," his companion urged impatiently.

Resting his arms on the table, Donald leant towards that flushed and excited young lady and launched into a veritable chronicle.

"The first thing to tell you is that, within a week of our abortive and unhappy visit to Morford, I received a letter in the post from Lucy's mother." Ignoring Alice's gasp of surprise he continued.

"In it she thanked us both for taking so much trouble and apologised for her husband who, she hastened to inform me, had no knowledge of this communication. The purpose of her writing was to make me aware of certain information which will have a profound bearing on Mary's future."

Pausing to take a sip of his sherry, he went on. "Apparently the house we visited was once part of her family's estate and is owned by Sadie Dane as part of a trust established by her grandfather. On her death this would have passed to Lucy as her only child. Under the circumstances it seems that little Mary could well eventually become the beneficiary. That is supposing that circumstances don't require it to be sold, or the money needed for Mrs. Dane's own care and well-being."

"But how on earth can we be sure any of that will happen when the family hasn't any knowledge of her existence? I'm perfectly sure Mr. Dane will keep everyone in the dark and see that it doesn't leak out. And how on earth is the child to be kept track of once she is adopted?"

Smiling rather triumphantly the Chaplain patted his clerical collar with his forefinger. "I can assure you, my dear, that it will be possible and this strip of white can open doors at times. After discussion with Marcus we agreed that it might be better to try to arrange a private adoption. I contacted Roger Chapman, a friend I met at theological college, who is vicar of a parish in Hertfordshire and heavily involved in social work with unmarried mothers in the diocese of St. Albans. Really it was just to sound him out and ask his advice. However, 'Someone Up There' was directing my footsteps in the most remarkable fashion. Three years ago he married Pam in the knowledge that it was impossible for her to bear children."

"He must love her very much," interrupted Alice, "for I can't imagine many men prepared to do that unless they possibly loathed the thought of fatherhood."

"That's not the case here I can assure you for they had decided that, in the fullness of time, they would try to either foster or adopt."

"I don't believe it," shrieked Alice, causing several heads to turn in her direction. Hastily putting her hand to her mouth she whispered: "They're going to adopt Mary?"

Nodding vigorously he persevered with the rest of the details. "Mrs. Dane had instructed her solicitor to contact me and, to cut a long story short, I paid another visit to Morford as I really felt a face-to-face meeting was best. He is now fully in possession of all the facts and is liaising with Roger's legal advisors who are in charge of the adoption proceedings. And Sadie Dane's will is to be redrafted with all the relevant details. She also made two requests. The first was for a photograph of Mary to which there have been no objections. The second was to ask that Lucy's silver buckle be handed to the adoptive parents to be given to Mary on her 21st birthday, and this will gladly be done."

Flopping back in her chair, Alice shook her head. "I am in a complete whirl, Donald, and you must be exhausted. What a marathon you have accomplished."

"Well, I had a few days' leave between postings and, truth to tell, my dear, it has provided an outlet from some of the ghastly post-war problems and emotional and physical traumas of the wounded troops, many of whom are destined to be years in the healing, I'm afraid. At least Marcus has been able to move on to St. Dunstan's with a measure of peace of mind for he accepted that the outcome is the best we could have dared to hope for."

Pausing for a moment he continued rather as an afterthought: "By the way, Mary is destined to become 'Catherine Mary'. Roger and Pam prefer that and as the child is so young I don't think it really matters, does it?"

Before she could respond a rather elderly waiter placed some decidedly indifferent-looking soup in front of them and shuffled off. Donald pulled a face. "I'm afraid this isn't going to be the Ritz, is it?"

Unfolding her serviette Alice replied: "I wouldn't be disappointed if it turns out to be stewed grass! I am completely full to overflowing on a diet of contentment. No meal on earth could equal the satisfaction which your news has brought."

This joyful outburst was followed by a perceptible silence and he looked up to see her gazing distantly into space. "Is something bothering you?" he asked.

"I was just thinking about Lucy and hoping that she would be pleased with what we have decided for her child." Looking at him with misty eyes she murmured: "Do you think she knows?"

Reaching out he placed a hand warmly over hers and struggled to find the words to satisfy her. "I don't think this is either the time or the place for a theological discussion on 'the life hereafter' but, for what it's worth, I'm sure she does," he smiled.

Anxious to lift her from her reverie, he quickly went on to say, in the manner of a magician pulling yet another rabbit out of the hat: "Incidentally, there is an added bonus in all this because we shall be able to keep in touch with Mary's progress over the years. Roger and Pam have suggested that we consider becoming Mary's, or rather, Catherine's godparents after everything has gone through. Think how happy the thought of that would be to your friend."

But they don't even know me," protested a bemused Alice.

"Ah! They know all about you," twinkled Donald, "and such a satisfactory arrangement will at least ensure that we have ample

262

opportunity to advance our friendship, won't it?" he added nonchalantly.

Colouring slightly at the implication of his words, she didn't quite know how to respond.

"Look at things this way, my dear. Although neither of us wished any of this to happen, circumstances ordained that it did. The consequences of tragic events conspired to bring us together and I believe there is a purpose behind it all. Call it fate, destiny, good fortune, the hand of God or what you will, it's up to us to seize the moment when it presents itself."

For the life of her, Alice still couldn't bring herself to say anything.

Determinedly holding her gaze, Donald spoke in low but firm tones: "There's a road out there for both of us to travel and we can either make our own way along it or explore it together. Shall we give it a try?"

"It sounds a bit inadequate," his companion replied shyly, "but, yes please!"

Chapter Five

Revelations and Choices

The group of people seated on the lawn, enjoying the last of the day's sunshine, presented an attractive picture. Two women in simple cotton dresses lounged comfortably in deck chairs, one sipping a glass of homemade lemonade, whilst the other speedily manipulated a pair of knitting needles from which dangled a piece of work destined to become a pullover for her husband. Both men sprawled on a large rug puffing contentedly on their pipes, smiling at the antics of a seven-year-old girl trying to perform acrobatics on a swing suspended from the sturdy branch of another tree. Crawling happily nearby was a fair-haired baby in a romper suit, intent on trying to uproot the grass. In the background loomed a large Victorian house.

"How on earth you manage to keep that place clean I'll never know," said Alice. "Thank heaven the army doesn't provide such huge properties for their chaplains to live in or I'd be sunk."

"I'm afraid that most vicarages were built to accommodate enormous families plus the servants," Roger laughed, "and we have to make the best of it. Things aren't too bad because we've shut off the second floor and just pretend it isn't there."

"And I do have some help," confessed his wife. "It's also been easier since the diocese replaced the old range and installed a modern gas stove."

Tapping out his pipe on the heel of his shoe, Donald stretched his arms and with considerable contentment replied: "Whatever the drawbacks may be, it's a fantastic place to come and stay - much better than any hotel. The food's good and the service is quite passable!"

"Careful, or you won't get another invitation," warned his hostess.

"Seriously though," said Donald, "it's fantastic to catch up with

264

Cathy's progress and we don't have to ask how things are because everything speaks for itself."

Pam laid aside her knitting and, turning to her friends, assured them that they would never fully appreciate the debt that was owed to them by bringing this child into their lives.

"Rubbish! You would have taken the plunge at some stage. The particular crisis with which we were faced merely hastened matters."

"Maybe, but that 'later stage' couldn't have produced a Catherine you know. She really is something special. I mean, you only have to look at her to see how blessed we are," Roger enthused. "She's pretty, bright, affectionate, happy, even-tempered and... "

"Sometimes naughty, you will be pleased to hear," Pam hastened to add. "Anyhow, what about that gorgeous little fellow of yours? We were thrilled when we heard the news of his arrival."

"So was I," groaned Alice. "I'd had more than enough of floundering about like a beached whale. It took such ages to conceive that I sometimes wondered whether I'd find myself in your position. I can't say I enjoyed being pregnant, and the birth wasn't a load of fun either, so I think there's something to be said for adoption."

"But he's surely worth all the effort. Just look at him," Pam said. "Isn't he adorable?"

"He has his moments I can assure you, although you're quite right for we couldn't imagine life without him now, could we Donald?"

Casting a wistful glance in Cathy's direction, Pam let out a sigh. "The only regret I have is not knowing her as a tiny baby."

Addressing Alice she asked, "Is she anything like her real mother?"

Roger checked her instantly. "You are her real mother darling. She will certainly know no other."

"I'd still like to hear Alice's response, if she doesn't mind."

"Of course I don't. Well, the copper curls are definitely inherited from Lucy, and from what I've seen she is happy and constantly on the go. Lucy was immense fun and seldom still."

Donald intervened. "Pam, those things are purely superficial. I firmly believe that nurture is the true cornerstone in shaping the person a child eventually becomes. Catherine is lucky to have you both."

Addressing Roger, he went on to ask: "Out of god-parental interest, have you decided what you are going to tell her about her adoption?"

"Funnily enough, we were greatly helped in this matter. Last year a member of our congregation had a baby which Catherine made a tremendous fuss of. We got the inevitable questions about how and where it came from," he smiled ruefully.

"I suppose we gave the classic answer that it's what happens when two people love each other and marry. She then latched onto the conclusion that we had her for the same reason."

"Yes, it was a bit of luck," said Pam, taking up the story. "We simply explained that although some people love each other very much, and no matter how much they want a baby, they just aren't fortunate enough. This makes them very sad but they are sometimes given a chance to choose a baby instead."

Roger chuckled, "Before we could say anything else, her ladyship wanted to know why that baby's mother didn't want to keep it for herself. There are no flies on that one I can assure you."

Chipping in, Pam continued. "Thanks to the number of funerals Roger has to conduct, we have already had all the questions about death. So she appeared to accept, quite matter of factly, that this occasionally happened to a young mother as well. After giving it a bit of consideration, I suppose it was inevitable that she should ask us whether she was 'just born or chosen' as she put it."

"So, in answer to your question," Roger said, "she has been told and seems to have swallowed it without much ado, because she hasn't mentioned it since. However, it will undoubtedly come up again, but at least the seed has been sown and we have something to build on when the time comes."

"Well, I take my hat off to you both," Donald responded. "It isn't an easy thing to have to do."

Alice had listened to all of this with great interest and delight at the outcome. However, her natural curiosity got the better of her. "Have you heard any more of Mrs. Dane, by any chance?"

"Not directly of course, since she obviously doesn't know the identity of the adoptive parents. However, each year on Catherine's birthday, we send her photograph to the solicitor who gives it to her personally. Via him we then receive a reply. Poor soul, she is clearly so pathetically grateful. Nevertheless, I don't think we can continue now that the child is getting older."

Alice reached out to place her hand on Pam's. "Thank you for such a thoughtful gesture. I'm so pleased she has had that comfort at least."

Gathering numerous bits and pieces together, she called out, "Cathy, would you like to bring Richard indoors because I'm going to bath him and get him ready for bed?"

The girl leapt from the swing saying eagerly, "Can I do it Auntie?"

"I was hoping you'd say that. He's such a wriggler and I need all the help I can get."

The girl swooped on the unsuspecting infant and bore him purposefully away.

"Do you want a hand?" Roger asked.

His wife replied, "Not yet. You two just sit there and put the world and the Church to rights, while Alice and I beaver away."

Casting a sly glance in her direction he ventured good humouredly, "Donald, have you noticed how insufferably impudent these women have become since they got the vote?"

"And not before time," Alice interjected.

With mock groans, both men adopted attitudes of suitable subservience before hastening their respective partners away.

An easy silence descended leaving each to his own thoughts. After a while Roger said, "If you think about it, we've come quite a long way in a remarkably short space of time. Only seven years ago the country was involved in a horrendous war."

"You don't have to remind me," his friend muttered fervently. "I'm still surrounded by the fall-out from it, and I have to disagree with you. Things haven't moved speedily enough for the unfortunate victims of it all. They returned home, supposedly as heroes, but what recompense is there for them? A scarcity of work with low wages for the fit and able, and virtual obscurity for those left with appalling physical injuries and mental scars that will haunt them for a lifetime."

With the bit well and truly between his teeth he ploughed

267

relentlessly on like a steam roller. "Did they really go to hell and back, only to find that there's no place for them and they can't provide for themselves or their families? How can we dare to sit back comfortably whilst ex-servicemen are still seen begging on the streets?"

Realising that he had touched a very raw nerve, Roger was quick to apologise. "I'm sorry Donald, I wasn't thinking straight. You're right of course. It's easy to become so immersed locally that we fail to see the bigger picture. I suppose that living in pleasant, leafy Hertfordshire has blunted my perspective a bit."

He paused to reflect before continuing: "I look at Catherine and desperately want a bright and happy future for her. That makes it easy to throw every ounce of energy into building for tomorrow that we forget yesterday and fail to meet the needs of today."

"If we had a pick-me-up Roger, we could drink to a happy and peaceful future for all of us," his companion stated pointedly.

Grinning broadly he replied, "Message received loud and clear."

He promptly made off in the direction of the house from which came sounds of excited squeals of laughter. Leaning back in the deckchair, his eyes closed against the setting sun, Donald was left wondering what did lie in store for them in the years to come.

***

Ten years elapsed, and 1935 found a teenage girl avidly pouring over the newspaper spread out in front of her on a large table in the middle of an equally large kitchen. Without looking up she tossed a remark to the woman standing by the cooker.

"Have you seen that Lawrence of Arabia has died?" she remarked. "He was quite a romantic figure don't you think? We've been reading his book 'Seven Pillars of Wisdom' in English Literature."

"I'm afraid your ignorant mother isn't qualified to comment on the subject."

Gazing dreamily into space, the gym-slipped figure continued. "He had such a poetic way with words. In his book he said that he 'wrote his will across the sky in stars'. Don't you think that's powerful?"

"Not nearly as powerful as your father's comments will be if he arrives home to find the meal not ready. Catherine, be a dear and set the table for me."

As if on cue the door from the hall opened and a distinguished-looking man, with hair greying at the temple and clad in a long. black cassock, came in and collapsed onto a chair.

"The Lord preserve me from Diocesan committees," he said with feeling. "And thank heaven for the opportunity to come home to my two beautiful women. You don't know how much I've been looking forward to this moment."

Deftly placing a plate of steak and kidney pie in front of him his wife suggested he would feel altogether different after a reviving meal. She had heard it all before. In the relatively short time since Roger had been appointed a residentiary canon at the cathedral, she had come to wonder whether it would have been better had he remained a humble parish priest. It wasn't that he lacked the necessary qualifications to fulfil the role but he was already missing the steady, day-to-day pastoral care of a parish. At the same time, having once exchanged their first large, unwieldy vicarage for the compact delights of something more modern, Pam was once again having to come to terms with an altogether different residence. An ancient, mellow pile, rich in history and teeming with character, but short on labour-saving facilities, was no consolation. Yet there were compensations to be had from the seclusion of its position in The Close yet so near to the throbbing streets of the city, plus the opportunity for their daughter to complete her education at the highly acclaimed grammar school.

As though on cue, Cathy's voice wafted into her consciousness. "Have you got to go out again this evening, Dad?"

"Afraid so my love. Why? Do you want me for something?"

The girl gazed at him with obvious affection. "Only that I need to discuss my future with both of you when you've got a moment."

"Gracious, that sounds ominous," he quipped.

"I'm being serious. You know I've been trying to make my mind up what to do when I leave school."

"And?" her mother interrupted curiously. "Have you found something that interests you?"

Pausing to reach for the gravy boat, she helped herself liberally before replying.

"As a matter of fact, I think I have. I want to be a nurse."

Husband and wife simultaneously stopped with their forks poised midway between plate and mouth.

"Nursing. Are you sure?" they questioned as one.

"Well, there's nothing else that appeals. I don't want to be a secretary, nor occupied in an office or a shop. I did wonder about teaching but the thought of working with just children doesn't enthrall me. I mean, although I like them, I wouldn't relish being around them all the time. Anyway, I don't want to go on to any further education - I've had enough of school."

"If you take up nursing you'll still be subject to lectures, essay writing and exams you know."

"Yes, but at least I'll be working and getting paid at the same time."

Roger decided to probe further. "Is this decision in any way related to the fact that your mother was a nurse?"

As Cathy had grown older she had accepted their honest explanation of her adoption and the little they could relate of her earlier background. They sometimes wondered what went on inside her head for she never tried to pursue things further.

"My mother is right here at this table," she responded fiercely.

Visibly touched, Pam whispered, "Thank you darling, thank you so much."

"I couldn't wish for better parents - even when you do get on at me," was the impish retort.

Roger suddenly slapped his hand on the table making them jump. "How stupid. I know just what we should do. We'll phone and invite your godparents for a weekend. They can provide you with far more information and experience on the subject of nursing and hospitals than we can."

Pam seized on the suggestion immediately. "That's an inspired idea. If you're really set on this career their advice will be invaluable."

Within a fortnight Donald and Alice had responded to the summons. Following one of Pam's memorable meals, five heads joined together in animated conversation. Despite being regaled with Alice's dire reminiscences of hard work, long unsocial hours, unsavoury tasks and relentless discipline, Cathy refused to be deterred.

"Why you would want to subject yourself to all that, I can't imagine," her mother sighed. "It's bad enough having one member of the family going around wearing a hair shirt."

"That's a bit strong," Roger responded indignantly, to hoots of laughter.

Cathy left the room to fetch the information she had already gathered on training schools and their requirements, keen to hear Alice's thoughts on the subject.

Donald seized the opportunity to ask a question. "Have you got Lucy's silver buckle here?"

"Of course," said Pam.

"Well, do you think it might be a good idea to show it to Cathy now and tell her a bit about it?"

"Why?" Pam queried rather defensively.

Gently placing his hand on hers, he replied: "Look, I know she is aware that she is adopted and it hasn't given rise to any problems so far. I think that if you can refer to the coincidence of her choice of career quite naturally, it could have two benefits. First, she will see that the parents she clearly loves so deeply don't feel threatened in any way by the course she is taking. Secondly, it will provide a valuable chance for her to voice any thoughts she may secretly have wanted to but hasn't in case it causes hurt or discomfort to the pair of you."

Alice watched as the couple exchanged diffident glances. Finally, Roger got up, placed one hand on the end of the stone mantlepiece and momentarily closed his eyes before turning to his wife.

"I know you're apprehensive my love but I think it's a reasonable suggestion. What do you say?"

As she simply nodded her head he turned and made for his study, almost colliding with an excited Cathy bearing an assortment of papers.

"Now where's Dad disappearing to?" she wailed in exasperation.

"It's alright," soothed Pam, "he's only gone to fetch something."

Cathy perched on the arm of her godmother's chair while Pam

busied herself topping up the coffee cups.

Roger returned bearing a blue leather case very familiar to Donald and Alice. Sinking onto the settee he patted the place beside him.

"Catherine, leave what you're doing for a moment. There is something we want to show you and this seems as good a time as any."

Full of curiosity, the girl settled next to him and he placed the case in her hands. "Whatever's this Dad?"

"Why don't you open it and see?" he said softly.

Four pairs of eyes watched intently as the lid was raised to reveal the silver buckle. Cathy looked up in bewilderment.

"Sixteen years ago when we adopted you darling, we were instructed to hold this in safe keeping for you, until your 21st birthday. Under the circumstances, we thought it would be nice to show it to you tonight, especially as Alice is here as she knows far more about it."

Alice leaned forward ready to take up the story. "I think you know that Lucy, your birth mother, and I were great friends and nursed together in the war until she was tragically killed?"

Cathy simply nodded.

"When nurses successfully qualified they were entitled to wear silver buckles to fasten the petersham belts which are part of most uniforms. This one belonged to Lucy. I'm afraid I can't give the exact details, although I do know that it previously belonged to her mother, your grandmother, who was also a nurse at one time."

For once, the normally chatty teenager was unusually silent. Then, gently caressing the delicate silver tracery, she said: "And this is to be mine?"

"Yes," her father replied, "but not until you're twenty one."

"Just think! With a history like that, what better incentive could you have?" ventured her godfather.

Still she didn't say anything.

"Are you alright, Catherine?" her mother was driven to ask anxiously.

"I don't quite know how I feel," she whispered. "It's all a bit unreal."

Turning, she threw her arms round her father's neck and buried her face in his jacket, saying: "Thank you so very much."

"Hey! You haven't got the buckle yet, young lady," her father teased, "and my word, haven't you got something to live up to?"

"A bit scary, isn't it?" she said, reverting to her normal self.

At this, they all laughed and the mild tension in the room began to ease. "There is just one thing I'd like to ask, providing Mum and Dad don't mind."

"Why don't you go ahead and find out?" came the reply.

Looking at Alice she said, "Do you have a photo of Lucy at all?"

"Only of a group taken when we were in France. It's in the wallet in my handbag. If you give me a minute I'll find it."

"More like half an hour," joked Donald, keen to keep things as light as possible. "The amount of stuff you cart around is incredible."

"I'll treat that remark with the contempt it deserves," she responded, retrieving from the cavernous bag the item she'd been searching for.

Cathy stared intently at the four smiling figures in uniform standing outside a canvas bell tent on a sunny afternoon.

"Lucy is second from the right, next to me," her aunt volunteered.

"That's the buckle she's wearing, isn't it?"

"Yes, she was never without it."

"When was this taken?" Cathy asked.

"Soon after we'd arrived in France and had set up a base hospital in a seaside town called Wimereux. In fact, Lucy is buried in the military cemetery there."

Donald took the chance to butt in. "Have you studied the works of the war poets at school?"

"Siegfried Sassoon and Wilfred Owen you mean?"

"Yes, that's right. Well, there are others, among them a Canadian army doctor called John McCrae."

Cathy sat up excitedly. "I know, I know. He wrote the lines: 'In Flanders fields the poppies grow Between the crosses row on row.'

"Well done. What you probably don't know, however, is that he is buried in the selfsame cemetery as Lucy. I always think the last two lines of that poem are the most poignant:

'If you break faith with us who die We shall not sleep, though poppies grow in Flanders fields.'"

It was possible to hear a pin drop in the sitting room that evening as the adults watched carefully the effect this was having. But there were no tears, no great display of emotion, no silent withdrawal, simply a matter-of-fact display of natural curiosity, accepted quite equably. The young girl continued to gently stroke the buckle, while her thoughts were indiscernible. Those watching her with loving concern seemed momentarily at a loss as to how to break the spell which appeared to have engulfed them all. Finally, Donald rose languidly to his feet, making a great play of patting his pockets for his pipe and tobacco pouch. This had the effect of stirring the others.

"How about a night-cap?" said Roger. "I think we can run to some half-decent brandy, courtesy of a grateful lady who seems to like the cut of my cassock."

This remark was sufficient to rouse Cathy from her reverie. "You aren't blowing your own trumpet by any chance, my beloved pater?"

"Well if I don't, it's certain no one else will."

Turning to her godparents she raised her eyes to the ceiling saying: "He has the constant adoration of his harem in this house, yet he needs the adulation of a positive army of godly matrons out there, who seem to think he's the bees knees."

"Blasphemy, blasphemy, all is blasphemy! No respect Donald, not even in my own house. I will assume my role as humble waiter and get those drinks."

"Not for me, Roger," said Alice. "At the risk of sounding ungrateful, I'd be happier with a cup of tea."

Relieved to be given a reason to busy herself, Pam leapt to her feet and made for the kitchen.

When they had both left the room, Cathy took one last look at the silver buckle before consigning it to the case, and gently closed the lid. Placing it on the mantlepiece she turned to Alice and commented: "We didn't get very far in sorting out a training school for me, did we?"

"There's always tomorrow," came the comforting reply.

"Where did you train?"

"St. Monica's, in the poorer part of London. Although I retain a fondness for the place, I think we can find somewhere better for you."

"Did Lucy train there as well?"

"Gracious no! We didn't meet until we joined the QA's."

"Do you know where she did do her training?"

Alice cast a look in Donald's direction but, for once, there was no help forthcoming.

Deciding that honesty was the best policy, she said, "Morford Royal Infirmary."

"What, in the Midlands?" Cathy paused for a moment before adding: "Isn't it funny? Because I was born in London, I never thought of her coming from anywhere else."

"Do you think about her much?" interposed Donald, comfortably drawing on his pipe.

Putting her head on one side as though giving the matter careful thought, she replied, "Not really. More subconsciously I suppose. Mum and Dad are super. They've always been honest with me, so it feels disloyal to ask anything else. I don't want to hurt their feelings, or give them the impression that I'm discontented, because I'm not."

"That does you more than credit my dear, but I think you underestimate them. They really won't mind, I'm sure."

As if on cue, Roger swept into the room bearing two brandy goblets and a decanter.

"Won't mind what?" he queried.

"Please Uncle Donald, it doesn't matter. It truly isn't important."

Depositing the drinks on a small table, he went to sit by Cathy and, enfolding her in an embrace, ventured to say, "This evening has been quite an emotional one for all of us. Naturally it must have given rise to many questions in your mind, and you mustn't try to shut them away because that isn't healthy. You can never be a whole person, or hope to understand yourself, if there are things you need to know and have never been told."

Arriving with the tea tray, Pam saw his hand stroking the hair of the child who meant so much to them and heard him say, "Mummy and I love you more than words can describe, and all we want is your happiness. Over the years we have tried to explain things to you as simply as possible, and to deal with your questions as and when they arose. You never really asked much, did you?"

Gently holding her away from him, he continued. "With Alice and Donald here, it's the ideal opportunity to ask all those niggling things that perhaps you never even admitted that you wanted to know."

Flopping into a nearby chair, Cathy leaned back and closed her eyes. Then, quickly sitting up straight and alert, said, "Ok! But only if you're sure."

"Trust us sweetheart, we mean it," Roger reassured her. Taking his wife's hand firmly in his he smiled and said, "Fire away!"

"Well, I know Lucy was killed in the war, and my natural father was so badly wounded he could never have looked after me, but is he still alive?"

Donald sat forward in his chair contemplating his clasped hands.

"I am probably the one who should be able to answer that question Cathy and, to my shame, I'm afraid I can't. After your adoption had been arranged and the papers signed, Marcus was discharged from hospital into the care of St. Dunstan's Home for the Blind to be trained for some kind of employment. It coincided with my transfer to Southampton and we lost touch."

"What was he like?"

Here Alice was quick to take over. "Tall and very handsome. Lucy was the envy of the other nurses. He was quieter than her with a strong inner character, but gentle and he adored her."

The girl waited for a moment before saying, somewhat shyly, "I know they weren't married... "

"That was simply because of circumstances," Alice interposed swiftly. "As soon as the war was over everything would have been regularised."

"Yet she left me with your mother rather than stay here to look after me. I find that a bit odd."

A silence fell on the assembled company, eventually broken by Alice.

"Cathy, war does some funny things to people and they don't always behave rationally. Who knows how any of us will react when faced with a given situation? She was so in love and desperate to make contact with Marcus to tell him about you. Perhaps she was rather headstrong and impulsive, some might even say selfish, but try not to think too badly of her. She did what she felt was right at the time. Besides which she knew you would be well cared for. It never crossed her mind for one moment that she might be killed."

Once more there was a gap in the dialogue until Cathy asked, in a slightly belligerent tone, "Weren't there any grandparents or other family members who wanted me?"

Not for the first time her godparents exchanged glances before Donald replied, "Marcus had absolutely no family at all, although Lucy's parents were both alive at the time."

Recalling the distasteful meeting with them he was forced to pause but Alice quickly stepped in.

"Lucy was an only child and her mother a chronic invalid who would have been quite incapable of caring for a baby, whether she wanted to or not. Neither would it have been fair to any child to be foisted onto anyone in those circumstances."

Roger's calm and steady voice broke in saying, "It was she who made sure that the solicitor instructed us to hold the silver buckle in trust for you. She loved you and cared enough to want you to have some tangible reminder of your roots."

Much to the amazement of everyone the girl, who had been quizzing them so closely, suddenly flashed a grin and said, "Goodness, I really was an orphan of the storm, wasn't I?"

"More another casualty of war, I think," was Donald's wry reply.

"Well, whatever! It certainly looks as if I have to thank my guardian angel for watching over me. Just think, if you hadn't taken me in there's no knowing where I might have ended up. I could have been sold on the white slave market," she added impishly.

Her father flung up his hands in mock horror. "You, my young lady, are quite incorrigible and have obviously been reading too many of those trashy novels you seem to find so irresistible."

While the others laughed, Pam gazed at her lovingly, "I wonder if you can imagine how empty our lives would have been but for that amazing chain of events which presented us with such a heaven-sent gift?"

"Has that helped to clear things for you, Catherine?" her father asked, "or is there any other burning issue because it's rather late and, while you lucky folk can lie abed, it's my turn to say the Morning Office in the cathedral at half-past seven."

"Never mind," said Donald. "I'll come and keep you company."

"And if I think of anything else, I'll save it until breakfast," Cathy offered. Upon which the party broke up, although sleep didn't come readily to any of them as they pondered the events of the evening.

Next morning, following their shared devotional service, Roger and Donald returned to The Canonry to find Cathy bubbling with excitement. Her father's gaze shifted from one eager young face to take in the clearly less certain nuances emanating from the two older women. Calmly removing his jacket and draping it over a chair, he unhurriedly took his place at the table.

"Now, what's afoot?" he asked. "What dark plans have you all been hatching while our backs were turned?"

"Please Dad! Oh please say that we can."

"Can what?" he asked without taking his eyes off the boiled egg he was neatly decapitating.

"Catherine remembered your promise that, if it was a reasonable day we might possibly go for an outing," his wife volunteered.

"Yes, and while I was in bed I had this absolutely fabulous idea of going to Morford."

"Morford!" the men echoed in unison. "Whatever do you want to go to Morford for?"

Alice thought it time for her to interrupt. "It is merely that, in the course of our discussions last night regarding the merits of various hospitals, Cathy wanted to know where Lucy trained."

"Dad, it's only about an hour or so by car, and I really would like to see the place."

Sensing that Alice was none too keen to revisit the scene of previous unpleasant memories, Donald attempted to dissuade her. "I can't see what you actually hope to achieve, Cathy. You won't be able to simply walk in and look around and the outside won't tell you much."

"Uncle Donald's right," said her mother, mentally relieved at the prospect of being spared another emotional switchback ride.

However, she had reckoned without her husband. Seeing the dejected slump of the shoulders and the downcast young face, he took everyone by surprise.

"Why not? Catherine's quite right. We can stop off somewhere for lunch, then get a general impression of the place."

Grinning at his daughter, he added, "Perhaps if we throw in the chance to do some serious shopping they may be tempted. I understand there are some pretty good department stores in Morford."

"And how on earth would you know that?" Pam questioned somewhat tetchily.

"Trust me," he responded. "We'll have a wonderful day out together."

The early June weather was at its best and matched Cathy's infectious high spirits. Between them they found plenty to comment on as Roger drove his comfortable Rover saloon car along. Taking a detour off the major road they meandered through quiet, grey-stone villages, where humble cottages rubbed shoulders with the splendour of the occasional manor house, or the brash modernity of more recent constructions. Ancient churches stood as firm bastions of the faith against the intrusion of red-brick, non-conformist buildings, erected during the religious evangelism of the nineteenth century. Welcoming hostelries, offering nourishment for the body, took their place alongside those temples to the soul.

After stopping to satisfy their hunger, the party found themselves on the main arterial route leading to the city of Morford. The pleasant, mainly agricultural landscape began to give way to urbanisation. A proliferation of uninspiring rows of terraced houses started to emerge and, far away on the skyline, the occasional outline of a pit-head with attendant slag heaps, stood out. Long factory sheds jockeyed for position beside the snaking railway line, whilst tall, unattractive chimneys bore token to the smoke which would belch forth on a normal weekday.

"What do you think of this Cathy?" her father asked. "A bit different to our pleasant neck of the woods, isn't it?"

"It may not look as attractive but at least it's helping to provide some people with employment and roofs over their heads, and that's what matters."

"Well said," her godfather commented. "I think we may have an embryo social reformer in the making, Roger."

"Never mind that. We're fast approaching the city proper, so keep your eyes peeled for any signpost to the hospital."

In the end it was Cathy's eager eyes that spotted the words Morford Royal Infirmary. Banging her father heartily on the back brought forth an expletive not quite befitting a gentleman of the cloth. Within minutes the bulk of the unmistakable Victorian building came into view.

"It's a pretty impressive place from what can be seen," Donald commented.

"And certainly bigger than I'd imagined," added his wife.

Parking the car by the kerb, Roger suggested taking a stroll to work out the lie of the land. Cathy needed no second bidding and swiftly made off up the road, only to return to inform them that she'd found the main entrance.

"Please don't get your hopes up," begged her mother, "because we won't be able to see inside."

She had reckoned without the pull of two 'dog collars'. People seemed to be passing through the doors in a steady flow and Donald quickly realised that it was afternoon visiting. Joining the human stream they found themselves in an uncluttered entrance hall where they came face to face with a bust of Queen Victoria atop a pedestal. Hanging on the wall on either side were two impressive oil paintings. A sign informed them that the Casualty Department was to the right and all wards to the left.

"Come on Dad, let's see if we can just have a little peek."

They were unaware that their hesitancy had been observed until a voice coming from behind an inconspicuous, glass-fronted office marked Porters Lodge enquired whether they needed any help. Roger decided to be quite frank.

"In actual fact I'm afraid we're being nosey. My daughter here is interested in pursuing a career in nursing. We don't come from this area and were just passing through, saw the hospital and wondered whether we could obtain some information regarding the School of Nursing."

Their inquisitor smiled broadly. "Always anxious to get more nurses we are. Unfortunately I can't help you, but if you bear with me, I think I can find someone who can."

"No really, we don't want to cause a problem."

"It's no trouble your Reverence, no trouble at all. If you care to sit on that bench I'll see what I can do."

It seemed no time at all before he returned in the company of an attractive, slim woman wearing a smart, long-sleeved, dove-grey uniform dress, with white piping round the mandarin style collar, and topped with a white, lace-frilled and pleated starch cap.

"Good afternoon. My name is Sister Charles. How may I help you?"

Roger once more repeated his tale. As it unfolded a pair of clear blue eyes came to rest on Cathy's face.

"How old are you?"

"I shall be eighteen in November," came the breathless reply.

"Have you visited any others? And how much do you actually know about hospitals?"

"Not visited as such, but I have sent off to several for details."

"And how much do you actually know about nursing as a career?"

"Well, my godmother here was a nurse and I've discussed it with her."

"How interesting. Where did you work?" she asked Alice.

"In London first, then with the QA's in France during the war," Alice responded, with just a slight note of pride in her voice.

"My goodness, that must have been some experience. Two of our staff were similarly involved and their accounts are unbelievable."

Addressing Cathy once more, she said. "While you're here, would you like to have a quick look around?"

"Oh, yes please, that would be wonderful."

Appraising the porter as to her whereabouts, she turned her attention to the little group and, with obvious pride and enthusiasm, proceeded to enlighten her captive audience.

"The original infirmary was founded on a different site in the eighteenth century but the present building largely owes its existence to the efforts of the lady you see in that portrait. Her name was Kate Oliphant, who actually worked with Florence Nightingale in the Crimea, and one wing of the hospital is known as the Oliphant Wing. The gentleman is the Duke of Ashbourne and a major financial benefactor. The second wing bears his name and it is to him that thanks are owed for obtaining our 'Royal' status. This part of the building is known as the Victoria Memorial Wing, hence the bust of Her Majesty."

Turning smartly to her left she bade them follow her. After walking along a lengthy, marble-floored corridor, and climbing two flights of stairs, she drew them to a standstill by a large window.

"This is a very good vantage point from which to gain an overall impression of the Infirmary. This and the two wings which you can see are the original building in the shape of a 'U'. Earlier this century this corridor was extended, as you can judge if you look to the right. At the end an identical wing was added so that the plan now resembles an 'E' shape comprising nine wards, each containing 36 beds. Medicine is advancing at such a rate that we are finding it difficult to keep pace. As a result, several smaller specialty wards have been created elsewhere, wherever a space presented itself. We now have approaching six hundred beds and are fast running out of options for further expansion."

Pointing from the window she continued: "If you look beyond that large tree, which was actually planted by Kate Oliphant when the hospital opened, you will see the new Outpatients and Phhysiotherapy departments which were only completed recently. They have made a vast difference as their relocation has enabled us to extend the rather cramped Casualty department which leads off from the main entrance hall where we met. This has also allowed us to create a new operating theatre suite above it."

"It is certainly much bigger than I ever expected," Alice ventured.

The Sister smiled. "We are now one of the largest provincial hospitals and proud of the fact that we were amongst the first recognised training schools for nurses outside of London."

"Did you train here yourself?" Roger asked.

"I did indeed, so I'm afraid I'm naturally biased. However, you will go a long way to find a better place."

Turning to Cathy, she said, "I must warn you that it's jolly hard work and you'll need good physical stamina. In the course of a day your feet will walk many miles on these hard, unforgiving floors. The hours are long and unsociable, although nothing like those undertaken by our forebears, as our senior members of staff never cease to remind us."

Drawing her attention back to the window Pam asked, "What is the rather imposing building partly visible to the right of Outpatients?"

"Oh, that is the nurses' home. It is a requirement that all staff 'live in' during training and the accommodation is really good - all single rooms with their own wash basin."

"Goodness Catherine, that's more than you get at home," her father commented.

As a nicely judged sop to the two ecclesiastical gentlemen, Sister Charles said, "In the heart of the hospital we have a rather lovely chapel. The earliest founding father was a clergyman and prayers are still said on the wards each morning before work commences."

"At least that hasn't changed since my day," said Alice.

"Poor Cathy. No escape from the cloistered life it would seem. I'd think twice about coming here," her godfather teased. "However, I do think we've taken up more than enough of your time."

"To be honest, it makes a nice change, so don't feel guilty. However, if you like to return with me to the general office I will give you a rather nice illustrated brochure full of information, plus a set of application forms in case you wish to take things further. We have four intakes a year but I must warn you that if you wish to be accepted in November there isn't much time left."

Eventually, when thanks and goodbyes were over, Cathy left clutching the proffered literature.

"Well," said Roger, easing his body back into the driving seat of the car, "that's given you something to think about, young lady."

Unhesitatingly she replied, "Oh I don't have to think. I'm going to Morford Royal Infirmary, if they'll have me."

Part Four
Catherine Mary Chapman

Chapter One

Following a Well-Trodden Path

F eeling conspicuous and uncomfortable in their unfamiliar uniforms, the twelve young girls who had been considered fit to undertake nurse training at Morford Royal Infirmary in 1935 drifted in ones and twos from their rooms in the nurses' home to gather, as requested, in the classroom.

In many ways it was little different from the school environment which most of them thought they had waved goodbye to with glee. Single desks faced a floor length blackboard and the walls were lined with charts, pictures and models of body parts whilst in one corner, dangling helplessly on a chain suspended from the ceiling, the condemned form of a skeleton leered toothlessly at them from sightless eye sockets. The light was harsh and unforgiving and reflected off the glass-fronted bookcases which, beside the expected weighty tomes, seemed to host an array of specimen jars containing a motley display of human organs neatly labelled.

"Not quite like my mother's preserves but I suppose it's all the same sort of thing," muttered an unmistakably broad Scottish accent emanating from the tall figure standing beside Cathy. She turned and grinned weakly but was prevented from responding further by the arrival of a dapper little woman in a smart navy blue dress topped with a crisp white collar and lace cap.

Unsmilingly she surveyed the occupants of the room and in a firm voice and manner, which clearly denoted someone who would brook no nonsense, she bade them to stand at the front and be seated as and when they heard their names called.

"You will sit in alphabetical order starting at the front left and that desk will be yours throughout your stay here. "Nurse Cameron, Nurse Chapman... "

Without allowing the group time to settle, and before they could even contemplate embarking on any tentative conversation, she continued relentlessly.

"I am Sister James, the senior Sister Tutor here. There will be plenty of time for you to get to know each other later so, for now, I want your undivided attention because I don't expect to have to repeat myself."

Clearly getting into a very familiar stride she launched forth.

"You will notice that I have referred to you by the title 'Nurse'. That is a mere euphemism at this stage because it is going to take unremitting hard work and time to transform you into anything remotely worthy of the name. However, that will be your title from now on. The use of Christian names whilst on duty will not be tolerated. Matron is 'Matron', sisters are 'Sister', staff nurses are 'Staff Nurse', or 'Staff' if you must. Consultants are addressed as 'Sir', junior physicians as 'Doctor' and junior surgeons as 'Mister'. It is unlikely that you will have any contact with medical staff for some time and I must warn you that any liaison between you will be strictly in the course of duty."

Scarcely pausing for breath she continued her diatribe.

"I and my staff have little over three years in which to transform you into safe, responsible, knowledgeable and respectable nurses. On the desk in front of you is a book entitled 'Practical Nursing Schedule'. Open it and you will see listed inside every single procedure in which you are required to become proficient. At any time during your training period, when you feel that you have mastered a particular skill or technique, you may ask to be tested on it. Providing you prove successful, the examining Sister will place her signature in the right hand column. Nothing may be missed out and I advise you to apply yourselves to the completion of this as quickly as is practicable and not leave it to the last minute. I have no intention of chasing you on this matter. You are now deemed to be adult and responsible. It is you who want this nursing qualification, not me. However, I must stress that I do not tolerate failure. It is totally unacceptable in a trainee from this hospital."

Out of the corner of her eye Cathy became aware of a covert sideways glance from Nurse Cameron to her left but dared not allow her gaze to wander from the stern face of the Tutor.

"For one week you will be excused ward duties while we acquaint you with the hospital, the numerous facilities and some rudimentary classroom instruction in hygiene, cleanliness and the most basic elements of nursing care. At the end of this you will each be allocated to a ward where you will normally stay for a period of three months. Following this you will undertake your first spell of night duty. During this time you will be expected to attend lectures and to study. While every effort is made to arrange these during reasonable hours, at times you may find yourself having to give up your sleep or free periods. This may seem hard but remember, some of us never enjoyed such a luxury. If you are desirous of success you will need to be totally committed and to practise, practise, practise - there is no substitute for it. To that end, the teaching rooms are always open to you until ten o'clock."

Although the weather outside was murky and grey, Cathy began to feel decidedly warm and uncomfortable under the starched stiffness of her collar. The least movement of her head seemed to cause unremitting chafing of her neck and there was certainly nothing soft into which to sink one's chin. Refocusing her attention she heard the words 'Rules and Behaviour'.

"It is absolutely impossible for any organisation to function properly without discipline, much of which will be learned as you go along. However, all rules are there for a reason. For instance, lights out is at half-past ten although you will be permitted the occasional late pass on application to Home Sister. This isn't because we wish to curtail your activities, but out of consideration for our patients who are dependent on you and will not get proper treatment at your hands if you are tired.

"Similarly, you are required to sign in for breakfast each morning and midday lunch. Nurses cannot hope to have the energy to function properly on an empty stomach.

"Uniform will be worn correctly and smartly at all times and never outside the hospital. Jewellery and make-up are forbidden on duty and please see that hair is off the collar and stocking seams are straight. An untidy nurse is indicative of an untidy mind and untidy practise."

Their mentor appeared to be running out of steam at last and the assembled company drew silent breaths of relief as she announced, "I will leave you now to get acquainted with one another and will meet you here at eight o'clock sharp in the morning. Bad time-keeping is not tolerated."

With that, she picked up her papers and made for the door which one girl had the foresight to open before further remarks regarding manners, or the lack of them, could be voiced.

"Phew! Welcome to prison," quipped someone in the back row.

"Don't worry, she's always the same," her neighbour commented. "My sister trained here and almost repeated that little homily to me verbatim. Apparently it never varies. According to her, although she seems a bit of a tyrant she is an excellent Sister Tutor and manages to achieve good results, and I suppose that's what counts."

Cathy's Scottish neighbour had been idly turning the pages of her schedule and expostulated with disbelief.

"Will you take a look at this list? Apply leeches, turpentine enema – whatever that is - catheterisation ditto, kaolin poultice, injections, padding splints, administration of oxygen. For sure, it'll be me needing the oxygen and a lot more beside if I'm ever going to master this lot."

Grinning cheerfully at her companion, she said, "I'm Jean, by the way; all the way from bonny Scotland, in case you hadn't guessed."

"You're rather far from home aren't you? Whatever made you come to Morford?"

"Quite simple really. Most of the family left the land of the haggis, bagpipes and heather at the end of the twenties and drifted down to the Midlands to find work in the mines. Consequently, I've got an assorted gaggle of my 'ain folk in the vicinity, so I'm a local girl now, I suppose, although it'll take more than a wee while to lose the accent."

"Oh, I do hope you won't because I think it's lovely," Cathy assured her. "By the way, if you're Cameron and I'm Chapman I think our rooms are next to one another as well."

"Aye, they are. I followed you down the stairs on our way here. Well, it looks as though we're likely to be joined at the hip for the next few years, so what say that we make the most of it and throw in our lot together?"

Nodding in happy assent the pair made their way towards the dining room to see what delights awaited them in the shape of supper.

"Mind you," said Jean, "whether I'll ever eat anything remains to be seen because this collar is absolutely killing me and I've only had it on for a short while."

"I couldn't agree more, but I think I may have the remedy. My godmother used to be a nurse and she gave me two helpful tips. To prevent your collar from making your neck sore, rub a bar of damp soap along the inside of it."

"And what's the other one?"

"If your feet are aching appallingly by the end of the day – as apparently they will do - rub them with methylated spirit, powder with talc and lay on the bed with them resting up the wall."

"What a happy prospect to look forward to," chortled Jean as the pair made their way down the corridor in a slightly more relaxed frame of mind.

Little could they have realised then that this would be the start of a friendship that would see them supporting each other through thick and thin with unswerving loyalty, sharing generously whatever they had, enjoying together the treasured moments of leisure and relaxation to the extent that both became fairly regular guests at each other's homes on days and nights off duty if they happened to coincide. Their backgrounds couldn't have been more different yet they both adapted with pleasure and ease to the glaringly converse lifestyles.

Almost overnight it seemed to Cathy that she had left behind the sheltered world of gym-slips, ankle socks and comparative innocence. She now found herself in a position which required her to grow up at a great pace, both mentally and emotionally. Yet she wasn't deterred. Life had become exciting, offering a journey into the unknown and presenting undreamed of situations to be faced up to. The weeks and months sped by at an amazing rate. The familiar daily hospital routine took place around the multi-faceted flotsam and jetsam of human beings who happened to find themselves washed up in the various

291

wards. Each day invariably brought fresh experiences and challenges and Cathy's confidence grew steadily as the tasks in her schedule were tested and approved.

Between them the nurses became philosophical about the highs and lows of their chosen profession. If one was going through a bad patch, the others were there to carry her along. All this was set off by the social life they somehow managed to cram into their lives. The gregarious Jean introduced her friend to the delights of Caledonian dancing and they snatched opportunities to go The Palais. Here Cathy discovered a natural talent for attracting partners with apparent ease.

"They're round her like the proverbial bees," her outspoken friend informed a slightly dubious Roger during the course of one of her visits to the Canonry.

"Dare we ask if there is anyone special?" her father ventured tentatively.

"Heavens no, I'm just enjoying myself. Anyway, I haven't got the time or energy for a serious relationship."

Any inward sigh of parental relief was dashed somewhat by the irrepressible Jean.

"I think Cathy likes tempting them into the honey pot where they flounder around in their size nines then sit licking their fingers after they've been kicked out."

"Don't credit a word she says, Dad. Madam here is all talk and she simply delights in being outrageous."

"I put it all down to my repressed Scottish upbringing at the hands of the elders of the kirk," she volunteered, casting a mischievous sideways glance at Roger. "My outlook's really broadened since I started coming here. All the pomp and ceremony and music and colour at your cathedral has gone straight to my poor, strictly brought up, head."

"And if you believe that you'll believe anything," Cathy exclaimed.

Not to be outdone her father decided to retaliate in kind.

"You must try to forgive our pagan practices Jean. Here in the south I'm afraid we're still trying to catch up with our enlightened brothers over the border."

292

Rising to his feet he started to help his wife in the task of clearing the meal table, only to be brought up sharply at his guest's vehement protests.

"Och, please Mr. C. I wish you'd come and convert my lot. Leastways, I wish they'd take a leaf out of your book where their womenfolk are concerned."

"Goodness! I think you'd better enlarge on that one, Jean," he retorted in mock horror.

"Well you certainly wouldn't get any of the men in my family lifting a finger to help out at home."

"It's nice to think I have at least one redeeming feature."

With the chores completed they made their way into the garden to relax in the cool of the evening.

***

The summer of 1938 had been exceptionally hot. Morford shimmered in a perpetual heat-haze, and soaring temperatures made working conditions particularly trying. The nurses coming off duty each evening, their uniforms clinging uncomfortably round sticky bodies, felt limp and drained.

"For sure, this must be the only unenlightened profession that expects its staff to wear the same clothes all the year round," Jean moaned. "I can't wait to strip off and have a long soak."

"Not yet you don't," said Cathy. "We've simply got to get all our belongings packed up and the rooms cleared ready for tomorrow. Remember, everything has to be in the entrance hall by eight o'clock, ready for the carrier."

Flinging the doors and windows wide in an attempt to create a breeze the two set about the task of sorting through the accumulated debris and acquisitions of almost three years. Other voices wafted along the corridor as each member of their set applied themselves to the business of transferring to one of the three convalescent homes administered by the Infirmary. The following morning the twelve nurses assembled together in the classroom for a final briefing from Sister Tutor with firm advice to use the three months ahead wisely.

"You will find the work far less demanding and there will be little or nothing in your surroundings to act as unnecessary distraction, which I fear some of you have succumbed to here in Morford," she said, casting a reproving eye on various figures in turn.

"Such an environment should prove more conducive to study and revision for the final examinations which await you shortly after your return. I will also remind you that, despite my earliest advice, one or two of you have still failed to complete your schedules. If this situation is not addressed there will be no question of you sitting the exam."

With a sigh of relief Jean muttered in an aside, "At least we haven't got that worry."

The remark was caught by the sharp ears of Miss James.

"To my surprise that is so, Nurse Cameron. Nevertheless, don't be too quick to pat yourself on the back. Your theoretical knowledge and subsequent written work still leaves something to be desired."

Returning her attention to the rest she indicated the piece of paper in her hand.

"This is the list of your forthcoming placements. When you know where you are going proceed to the car park and board the vehicle assigned to take you to your destination. And kindly remember you are not going on holiday."

Keen to learn their fate, it would have been possible to hear a pin drop.

"To Shepherdstone Convalescent Home - Nurses Cameron, Chapman, Dawson and Harris." With scarcely concealed beams of delight the eyes of the two friends met. They had not been separated.

Their transport crawled slowly out of the city and within a few miles they found themselves entering pleasant countryside. Evidence of a continuing urban sprawl could be seen but the houses were of higher quality, better spaced and more attractive. The village of Shepherdstone with its cluster of small cottages still nestled around the ancient church but there was ample evidence of more recent, private development of prestigious proportions as the professional businessmen working in Morford sought to remove themselves and their families to greener pastures. While the local amenities appeared rather limited it was clear that the place could provide for the necessities of daily living without any distractions.

Suddenly their driver swung the car left up a gravelled drive and came to a halt outside an impressive doorway which stood open. They had arrived. None of the girls really knew what to expect and their initial reaction was that they were being dumped in some old manor house. The ivy-covered entrance led into a large oak-panelled hall in which their luggage stood waiting. The Sister-in-Charge greeted them warmly enough, gave them their room numbers and indicated that they should claim their belongings and ascend the impressive staircase in order to unpack and get into uniform.

"Where on earth are the wards?" questioned Jean. "And it's so old."

Trudging along a corridor with uneven and slightly creaking floorboards they peered at the heavy doors until they lighted on one bearing both their numbers.

"We're sharing," said Cathy. "That'll be a laugh."

Wondering what next they would find they entered the room and stopped dead in amazement. It was lovely, spacious and light and totally unlike the rather institutional layout they were used to. Making for the window which looked out from the back of the building they quickly got their bearings. Three modern, single-storey wings had been built on to the original house so that the whole formed a square around a rather pleasant courtyard garden. A lawn edged with shrubs and small trees ran to meet the agricultural and grazing land which spread out beyond. It was so peaceful and on the clear air the birds could be both seen and heard, the unfamiliar scents of the countryside assailed their nostrils, while the occasional lowing of cattle reached their ears.

"Wow! This really is something, Cathy. Different, but I think we're going to like it."

And how could they not? Everything seemed that little bit more relaxed, the nursing care less acute, the patients more cheerful and less demanding. Far from having insufficient hours to devote to individuals, they were now actively encouraged to spend time gently probing those emotional problems and social needs which could so often hinder the road to recovery. They were seeing their charges from a quite different perspective. No longer were they desperately ill and highly dependent but simply in need of extra rehabilitation that would afford them the opportunity to take up the reins of family life and resume work again.

For many of them the time spent convalescing was the first holiday they had experienced away from the city. However, there were always the moaners - men who would never be happy away from the teeming streets within easy reach of a betting shop and corner pub. Then there were the women unhappy at the thought that their often demanding families could possibly cope without them, or who couldn't envisage a life without shops and the endless doorstep chatter. Although these folk often failed to be charmed by the country idyll, comparison between their state of well-being on arrival and departure bore more than adequate testimony to the benefits which accrued from their stay.

Initially, Cathy and Jean basked in this new-found freedom but once they too had plumbed the country lanes, fields, bridle paths and limited delights which Shepherdstone had to offer, they were sensible enough to appreciate Sister Tutor's advice that they were being presented with the perfect opportunity to prepare for their final hurdle to qualification. Having a short afternoon break, Cathy took herself off to the far end of the garden with text books and notepad. About to settle herself against the bole of a tree she heard voices and sounds of activity coming from the adjacent field. Venturing to a gap in the hedge she watched with interest the efforts underway to gather in the harvest of wheat, observed only that morning from her window, glowing golden in the early sun.

A young lad perched on a tractor towing a wooden trailer swung through an open gateway. At his shoulder swayed the alert figure of a black and white collie dog, while following after them loomed an impressive piece of farm machinery. A couple of men leapt out of the trailer and within minutes the drivers of both vehicles had commenced in tandem the slow circumference of the field.

Cathy was supposedly studying but her eyes flickered desultorily in the occasional wafts of welcome breeze. Even in the shade it was very warm and her eyelids seemed incapable of remaining open.

"You won't get much work done that way!" called a nearby voice which successfully roused her from her reverie.

Looking up she saw that the tractor had come to a standstill and the driver, stripped to the waist, his tanned skin burnished and sweating, was making short work of the contents of a bottle. He was a pleasant-looking young chap of about her own age as far as she could assess. His actions were swift and methodical and his muscles rippled as he checked round the vehicle, drawing some handfuls of vegetation from the dark interior of the huge wheels.

"You are making me feel positively guilty," she replied.

"Don't be. I bet they work you hard enough inside that place so you enjoy your rest in the fresh air. We don't charge for it and the view's free as well."

Putting his fingers to his mouth he let out a piercing whistle and the dog emerged from the depths of uncut wheat, "Come on boy, there's work to be done."

Indicating the panting animal, he said, "This is Rags by the way."

With that he remounted the tractor and with a cheery wave of his hand was off again.

In the ensuing days Cathy found herself following the steady progress taking place in the fields around Shepherdstone. Corn stooks stood sentinel where once the grain had waved freely. Hay was cut, tossed and turned eventually to be pitched up onto the lumbering wains and carted off. The activity was non-stop yet had an unhurried, comforting rhythm to it. Even the patients ventured forth to admire and exclaim at these pastoral scenes which were so alien to them.

On her evening off Cathy decided to go for a stroll along the lanes and once more came upon the young tractor driver wheeling a well-worn motorbike out of a gateway at the side of a rather pleasant mellow stone farmhouse.

"Hello again," she smiled. "How's the harvesting coming along?"

"On target, so I'm treating myself to an early break. Thought I'd drop in at the local before heading home". He eyed her for a moment before suggesting casually, "Would you care to join me for a jar?"

Momentarily taken aback, she was minded to refuse but, much to her surprise, found herself replying, "Why, that would be lovely, if you're sure."

"Great! Gather up your skirts and hop astride the pillion."

With a feeling of daring Cathy tentatively did as she was bid. Sensing her unfamiliarity with the procedure, her escort commanded her to hold him round the waist and, with a sudden zoom, they were off. However, the exhilaration afforded by this experience was of short duration. Parking expertly in the car park of the Shepherd's Arms in the village centre, he helped the girl to dismount.

"Would you prefer to sit inside or out?"

"Oh, I don't really mind."

"Right, you make for that table over there and I'll get the drinks. Cider okay for you? They do a rather good local brew here."

"Thank you, that will be fine," she managed somewhat breathlessly.

Within a surprisingly short time she watched him striding back across the grass bearing a foaming tankard of beer and a smaller glass of beautiful golden liquid which he set in front of her.

Taking a deep draught, after which he rubbed his lips together appreciatively, he turned to look at her. Jerking his head towards the pub he said, "They're a noisy lot in there. Wouldn't be able to make ourselves heard. After all, I don't even know your name yet. I'm Jim by the way - James Masterson in full and Jim to my friends."

"And I'm Catherine Mary Chapman, known to most people as Cathy."

"Do you live anywhere in the vicinity?"

"No. I've been in Morford at the Royal for three years but my family lives in Hertfordshire. You are clearly on your home territory."

"I don't live in Shepherdstone, if that's what you're thinking. I'm only over here to help my brother out."

"Your brother?"

"Yes. For my sins I'm the younger of twins by a small margin. Bob is being reckless enough to commit his head to the noose at the end of October. Far too soon in my opinion, the daft clot. Consequently, he's up to his eyes trying to make the house here fit for his bride while still keeping up with the everyday demands of the farm which are pretty heavy at this time of year. I help to work the main family farm with Dad, a few miles to the west. However, all this land around here also belongs to us and my brother is taking it over and settling into the place where we met this evening. I've been dispatched to give him a hand until the harvest is in and I'd just had a quick clean-up there before returning home."

Folding her arms on the table in front of her Cathy ventured, "You know, I always thought us poor nurses worked incredibly hard and long hours but watching you these last days, I think you come a close second."

"It's not a rest cure," he said, pulling a cigarette from a crumpled packet, "but I can't ever imagine doing anything else. It's in the blood I suppose. My family has farmed in this area for over one hundred years." Quickly collecting himself he pushed the cigarettes towards her. "Sorry, I didn't ask if you smoked."

"Not for me thanks. I tried once and didn't find it a particularly pleasurable experience," she said wrinkling her nose.

Refreshed with a further drink they continued chatting easily together until Cathy looked at her watch and with a start jumped up yelping, "Help, I must dash. I haven't got much time before I shall find myself locked out. Thank you for a lovely evening."

"Come on then, I'll run you back on the bike."

Seconds later she clambered down from the pillion and prepared to make a beeline for the front door, but not before her escort grabbed her arm. "Would you like to come to our annual harvest hoe-down next Friday evening?"

Eagerly she replied, "That would be great if I can get the evening off."

"Just push a note through my brother's letterbox if it's on and I'll pick you up here at seven o'clock. And bring a friend if you like – the more the merrier."

By dint of persuasion, juggling of the roster and a sympathetic Sister the necessary permission was granted.

"How on earth does one dress for a 'do' like this?" Cathy wailed.

"Clean, casual, crisp, cotton and colourful," Jean decided.

Standing at the drive entrance they presented an attractive picture – or so Jim thought as he drew up in a clearly much-used Morris saloon.

"Hop in," he bade them after introductions had been made. "I've given it a bit of a clean inside so you shouldn't get too dusty."

Suddenly they found themselves leaving the village and heading off in a completely unfamiliar direction.

"Where exactly is this dance?" Cathy queried. "I thought it was local."

"No, it's over at our place in Hollowdene and we use a couple of barns there for the event. It's actually something of a tradition locally. Nothing very grand, I'm afraid, but good fun all the same. I think you'll enjoy it."

"Och, I don't doubt we shall," Jean responded. "All-in wrestling would make a pleasant change after our usual boring routine."

Expertly swinging the car down a winding lane, Jim grinned.

"We may be thought of as country clodhoppers by you townies but I hope we can do a bit better than that for you."

And indeed they did.

Leaving the vehicle parked outside a rambling, large farmhouse which had clearly been added to by more than one generation, they headed in the direction of the numerous outbuildings to the south of the property. The place seemed a positive hive of activity with people of all ages coming and going between two large barns from one of which came the lively strains of dance music.

"Come and get a drink first," he said. "This one is set up as a bar and all the food is in here as well." So saying he led them into a lofty, pleasant space beautifully decorated with harvest produce. Garlands of apples threaded onto gaily coloured ribbons were wound round the posts. Barrels of cider and beer stood on a makeshift stand in one corner while long trestle tables groaning with an assortment of food ran the whole length of the centre.

"If you fancy anything, just help yourself then go and perch on one of those hay bales round the side. It's all very informal."

It certainly was very different to anything that Cathy had experienced before although her friend compared it favourably with the Scottish ceilidhs which she had once so enjoyed. Introduced to numerous of Jim's friends they soon found themselves swept up into lively rounds of country dancing interspersed with more up-to-date numbers.

"Are you ready for a bit of a break?" he suggested after a while, "because I rather think I'd better introduce you to my family."

Following him across the barn he came to a halt in front of a stocky, weathered man of average height, dressed in shirt and flannels topped by a Fair Isle pullover, his arm casually round the waist of a pleasant looking fair-haired woman in her late forties.

"Mum, Dad. I thought you'd like to meet Cathy and Jean from Shepherdstone Convalescent Home."

Once again they were made to feel most welcome and passed a few moments in easy conversation.

Suddenly his mother addressed her husband, "Ted, don't you think it would be a good idea if Jim introduced them to your aunt?"

"Splendid thought. It'll make her evening. Father too, for that matter."

Pointing towards an elderly couple, the lady seated in a wheelchair by a small table, their son dutifully took the girls in tow.

"Grandad, Aunt Sadie, I thought you'd be interested to have a chat with my two friends here, they're both nursing at the old Court."

A very upright gentleman rose to his feet and took Jean's hand while Cathy found herself looking into the pale, lined face of a clearly frail old lady. The eyes lacked sparkle but were alert and her breath rose and fell in a shallow rhythm.

"Oh, how wonderful," came the softly spoken but quite animated voice.

"Great Aunt Sadie can tell you all sorts of things about your place of work both here and in Morford," said Jim, arriving with two more chairs. "But don't keep them talking all night the pair of you - they've come to dance and I shall reclaim them very shortly."

Having seen the two girls settled the elderly man said, "Right, let's start again. I am John Masterson and this is my sister Sadie. Our parents started the farm here which I later took over and my son and grandsons now manage between them."

Sadie quickly chipped in, "Although we were both born here I spent

301

much of my young days in Shepherdstone. Painters Court, as it was then called, had been our mother's childhood home and I loved it. Eventually, when John took over the farm here, Mother was left the house but it was leased then eventually sold to the Infirmary."

"How fascinating," both girls murmured appreciatively.

"My sister trained at the Infirmary you know," John Masterson interposed proudly.

"Really! You must possess a positive mine of information," they pressed eagerly.

Time sped by as the old lady readily relived the past and clearly gained great pleasure from listening to their accounts of nursing at the present time.

"Which ward do you think you've enjoyed most?" she asked Cathy.

"Female medical," came the reply without hesitation. "To tell you the truth, I'm hoping to obtain a staff nurse position there when I qualify."

"I can remember the children's wards being built," Sadie confided. "That was quite a breakthrough in those days and how I loved the time spent there."

"And is that what you chose to do when you completed your training?" pressed Jean.

Almost dreamily, as though viewing the past through the mists of time, she looked beyond them before saying, "No. I always preferred dealing with people as individuals so I leapt at the opportunity to visit and care for them in their own homes. It was only a very modest enterprise here in Morford initially but look how it has grown nationally so that it is now a special branch of nursing in its own right."

"How long did you carry on in the profession?" Jean pursued.

The elderly lady's face clouded over momentarily and her brother quickly intervened.

"Unfortunately, my sister's health has never been robust."

Putting her hand on his arm she interrupted, "I'm afraid my heart isn't all that it might be and, as you will have discovered, nursing is physically demanding. When the house at Shepherdstone was leased to the Infirmary for convalescent purposes I suppose I did have fond hopes of becoming involved but it wasn't to be. I did volunteer during the war when it was used to rehabilitate injured troops."

Standing up abruptly John Masterson eyed her closely and said, "I think you've probably had enough for one night my dear and we mustn't keep these young ladies from their dancing, you know."

"Please don't fuss, John. This has been a rare treat for me."

Smoothing the soft blanket over her knees she continued as though the interruption had never occurred.

"Much as Mother and I loved the place it was clearly impractical to think that we could ever live there which is why the decision was taken to sell it. The hospital was keen to purchase it and the result is what you see today."

"What an amazing story," Cathy exclaimed. "And you should take great pride and comfort from the knowledge that so many people are benefitting from it, just as you had hoped."

Any further conversation was prevented by the appearance of Jim accompanied by a homely-looking soul who positioned herself behind Sadie's wheelchair and, bending forward to release the brake, remarked, "Goodness me, do you know what the time is? I think you've had more than enough excitement for one day so I'm going to take you home, although I doubt you'll sleep tonight."

"Mrs. P's right Great Aunt. Besides, I can't have you monopolising my partners any longer."

With that the girls took Sadie's hand in turn, thanked her profusely and watched as she made her exit to calls of farewell on all sides.

"What a remarkable character," said Jean, "although she really doesn't look too well."

"Don't be fooled," Ted Masterson commented having arrived with his wife in time to catch the remark. "She's been an invalid for the greater part of her life, requiring admission to the Royal in a parlous condition more times than I can remember, yet she always seems to bounce back."

"You know what they say about creaking gates," Maureen added. "Well, in Aunt Sadie's case I think it's true. For all her heart problems she'll outlive us all."

Sauntering back in the direction of the dancing Cathy proceeded to question her companion further.

"Does she live with you at the farm?"

"Good heavens, no! She likes her independence far too much for that and she's actually quite a private person. One of the advantages of a place like this is the fact that there is usually the odd cottage to be had, or ground on which to build something. Actually, Aunt Sadie used to own the farmhouse at Shepherdstone where Bob is living. It got too big for her so she exchanged it for something here, had it all done up and furnished with some of the nice pieces from her old home. She's close by so that the parents keep a good eye on her and one or two of the farm workers' wives take it in turns to help her out every night and morning. Believe me she's very well cared for."

"She never thought of marrying then?" asked Jean.

Jim looked at her with a grin. "Young lady, don't you know there are some things it doesn't do to pry into?"

"What on earth do you mean by that?"

"Well, I guess every family has their skeleton in the closet and as far as I can judge we are no exception. From what I can gather the old girl was married but he turned out to be a bit of a bad lot, or something. Anyway he took off for Australia, I believe, and she reverted to her maiden name. I can never recall anything other than the present set up. The past is certainly never referred to and why should it be if that's the way she wants it?"

Within seconds the trio found themselves swept up in sets for the Dashing White Sergeant and the rest of the evening was spent in high good spirits. Finally, exhausted but happy, they piled into the car and sank back into the seats while Jim sped, somewhat recklessly, along the dark lanes to Shepherdstone.

During the rest of their stay at the convalescent home Cathy and Jim developed an easy friendship and contrived to spend as much time as possible together. Having discovered a convenient hollow in the base of a tree bordering the rear garden they commandeered it as a postbox and it became the receptacle for their messages and any amusing little items which they came across and wanted to share. At the end of October she found herself being invited to Bob's wedding at which Jim was best man. The family just seemed to absorb her without question and she felt relaxed and contented in their company.

As they hovered outside the church while the happy couple had their photographs taken Aunt Sadie confided: "I really can't understand why they need to rush into marriage so early. He's far too young, don't you think?"

Overhearing this Jim rushed to defend his brother. "While I would agree with you in the normal event, this different. Those two have known each other since we were all in prams and as far as I know there has never been anyone else for either of them. As they have decided that there never will be I suppose it seems a bit daft to hang around."

"And what about you James?" she probed a little archly. "Are you going to follow your twin in your usual inimitable fashion?"

"Good Lord, no," he laughed. "You'll have to hang onto that rather fetching hat for a bit longer Great Aunt."

"And very wise too," commented his father. "Things seem to be getting a touch unsettled these days. What with the odd bits of disquieting news which keep reaching us from Europe and Churchill banging his war drum, I think we're all going to have more than enough to occupy us."

Before he could say any more the previously silent figure of John Masterson briskly interrupted. Glancing meaningfully in the direction of his sister he said, "Let's have no talk about troubles and war today Ted, if you please. It's probably nothing but a storm in a teacup so let's enjoy the day."

Anxious not to neglect her parents, who lived for the rare moments when she was able to return home to 'The Close', Cathy planned to spend a couple of days with them following her two weeks on night duty. With work on the farm slowing in pace as the autumn days glided towards winter, and shorter hours of daylight limiting what could be achieved, Jim offered to drive her to Hertfordshire. Somewhat to her astonishment she accepted the suggestion enthusiastically.

"Though I'd better warn you that it's nothing like you're used to," she ventured rather tentatively.

"That's okay. It'll be an interesting change."

Pam and Roger greeted their daughter with obvious love and eagerness and prepared to welcome Jim with the warmth they extended to all their visitors, albeit with a hint of curiosity. "After all, this is the first young man Catherine has ever brought home," Roger commented.

"Do you think there's something in it then?"

"I really couldn't guess. They seem happy enough in each other's company without any overt signs of anything deeper."

Delighting in every detail of Cathy's nursing exploits, and listening with interest to all that had happened during her most recent placement, it was an elated group who shared the evening meal in the old kitchen.

"We don't stand on ceremony Jim when it's just us." Roger half apologised.

"That's fine by me, it's just like home from home," said their guest.

After he had left to face the drive back to Hollowdene, Cathy slipped an arm companionably through her father's.

"What do you think of him, Dad?"

Without hesitation he replied, "He seems a very pleasant, straight-forward young man. Why, should we be attaching some importance to this relationship?"

Pam found herself waiting rather tensely for the response.

"Nothing like that at the moment, so you can put all thoughts of engagements, wedding bells etc. out of your minds," she grinned impishly. "He's great company, his folks are lovely but I'm simply enjoying life."

"Quite right, my darling. That's exactly as it should be and we're more than pleased for you."

Two days later they deposited Cathy at Shepherdstone once more, were suitably impressed with the location and seized the brief opportunity to meet the irrepressible Jean again. Driving home, talk was full of thankfulness for their daughter's obvious happiness and the satisfactory way in which her career was taking shape.

Chapter Two

A Tangled Web

Ate to soon the tranquil time at Shepherdstone came to an end. Once settled back in the old utility of the nurses' home and the regimented discipline of the daily routine those days quickly became just a pleasant memory. Gone were the opportunities for snatched meetings with Jim, although he could occasionally be found riding into Morford on his motorbike at the least chance of taking in a movie or a few hours of dancing at the Palais. With the final examinations only a matter of months away, causing Sister Tutor to hound and harass them relentlessly, coupled with the transfer to their final wards in order to master any skills still lacking, thoughts of pleasure weren't high on their list of priorities.

At that time radiotherapy treatment was still in its infancy. The Christie Hospital in Manchester, founded in 1892, was the only hospital in the provinces for the research and treatment of cancer by means of radiation. Although the Royal had been ministering to those stricken with this awful disease, it was but recently that they had begun using radium. This had necessitated the provision of two small wards specifically assigned for the purpose, and the very first consultant in radiotherapy was appointed with links to a major radium centre.

Cathy found herself grappling with the challenges presented in the care and treatment of this cruelly afflicted, but largely uncomplaining, group of people. Constantly surrounded by patients whose life expectancy was usually fairly limited did little to lighten the spirits and she found it extremely emotionally demanding. Coupled with the unsettling news filtering through from the world stage and the typically uninspiring November weather, it did nothing to relieve the general feeling of gloom that seemed to surround her.

Remembrance Sunday saw her marching through the streets of Morford to the Cathedral, one among the contingent of staff representing the hospital. The nurses, their red-lined cloaks and cross-straps redolent of the blood spilt on those awful battlefields, provided the only splash of colour to an otherwise grey scene. Was it everyone's imagination or had more folk than usual left their normal Sunday morning activities to swell the crowds lining the streets?

Earlier that morning the hospital had paid tribute to previous members of staff who had lost their lives in the Great War. A wreath of poppies was laid at the foot of the memorial plaque in the chapel and she found herself listening acutely as the names were read out.

"Lucy Dane, Queen Alexandra's Royal Army Nursing Service," intoned the voice of the senior consultant sonorously.

It came as no surprise to Cathy who, from her earliest days at the Royal, had seen the inscription and recognised that this had to be the full name of the woman who had actually given birth to her.

A slight shiver went through her as she listened once more to the famous words:

'They shall not grow old as we that are left grow old.
Age shall not weary them, nor the years condemn.
At the going down of the sun and in the morning,
We will remember them.'

Raising a finger to disperse the tear running unbidden down her face she was aware of Jean's sideways glance. "It's terribly moving, isn't it?" her friend whispered, and she simply nodded in agreement.

The mood lifted momentarily as everyone prepared to celebrate the festive season. Wards vied with each other to win the trophy for the best decorations and there was much hilarity as rehearsals got underway for the annual 'Christmas Revue.' Roger and Pam made a brief visit bearing gaily wrapped gifts and tasty offerings plus a small but beautiful nativity tableau for display on Cathy's ward. This was much admired and their daughter proudly escorted them round the hospital so that they too could share in the experience.

On Christmas Eve she and Jean donned their red-lined capes once more and joined the scratch choir of carol singers making the rounds of

308

the wards by lantern light, to the evident appreciation of the patients. The following day Sister distributed a small gift from the tree to everyone, the Mayor of Morford processed solemnly from bed to bed and one of the consultants duly arrived to ceremoniously carve the turkey. Visitors in high spirits were recipients of the unusual treat of tea and cake and, by the end of the day, the night staff arrived to find their charges tired but happy and more than ready for sleep following all the excitement.

Presented with quite an unexpected evening off on Boxing Day, Cathy was thrilled when Jim arrived to whisk her off to Hollowdene to share in the family celebrations.

Rather to her surprise there was no sign of Aunt Sadie.

"She really isn't very special at the moment," said his mother in response to the girl's queries. "She joined us for lunch yesterday but was more than ready to return to the haven of her own home."

"The colder weather never suits her," admitted Ted. "She gets very breathless and that tends to make her a bit agitated."

"Is there anything I can do to help while I'm here?" Cathy offered tentatively.

"Bless you for the thought, my dear," replied John Masterson. "All her needs have been attended to and we each take it in turn keeping an eye on her. You just concentrate on having some fun while you can."

Swiftly grabbing her round the waist Jim whisked her off in the direction of the hall from where a huge bunch of mistletoe swung from an oak beam. Quite unashamedly, and to hoots and calls from one and all, he soundly kissed the startled Cathy.

"How's that for starters?" he said impudently.

And the blushing recipient had to admit that it was rather good.

As Morford struggled in the grip of the particularly bitter winter of 1938, the Infirmary staff worked unceasingly to fulfil the demands being made on over-stretched resources. Chronic chest and heart cases seemed to beat a never-ending path to the door of the casualty department, with the elderly succumbing steadily to the adverse conditions. Charitable organisations and benefit clubs dug deep to find the extra money with which to provide fuel for the needy but it appeared to do little to stem the tide of admissions to the Royal. Here many of them reached the end of their pilgrimage through life and the nurses began to lose count of the number of last offices they were obliged to perform. Like most of her colleagues, Cathy experienced her first introduction to death very early in her training and was now more than competent to deal with the practicalities involved. Nevertheless, this in no way rendered her immune from the general feeling of sadness and loss.

The inhospitable weather showed no signs of abating. Snow fell intermittently throughout the first two months, blocking roads, bringing factories to a halt and causing a positive glut of fractured limbs. Almost too tired to concentrate Cathy and her friends found the days of their final examinations drawing steadily closer.

"I'll be that relieved when it's all over," Jean wailed despairingly. "My poor addled brain refuses to absorb one more fact. I knew it would be hard but this really is an ordeal."

"Well we can't do any more now," replied a rather philosophical Cathy. "We've done our best and we must simply hope that's enough." With which they trooped into the examination hall, full of nervous tension, to be put through their paces both theoretically and practically by the Central Examining Board.

A mere couple of weeks later twelve excited but apprehensive girls gathered in the corridor outside Matron's office to learn the outcome of their three years and three months of endeavour. Not particularly renowned for displaying her feelings Matron Giles emerged with the Sister Tutor at her heels. Surveying the anxious brood with a kindly and sympathetic smile she forebore to keep them in suspense any further and promptly distributed the batch of long brown envelopes she was holding. Trembling hands wrenched at the contents and white faces scanned the information contained in them. One by one delight and realisation spread across the faces of each of them. They had all made it. After giving them a few minutes to indulge in the screams and shrieks of delight, the relieved embraces and the non-stop chatter, Matron clapped her hands briskly.

"Needless to say, Sister Tutor and I are delighted at your success, although it is no more than we have come to expect from our trainees. Well done."

Turning to reach for a piece of paper from a nearby table she continued. "All that remains now is for you to learn where you have been assigned as Staff Nurses."

Twelve pairs of eyes gazed unswervingly in her direction.

"We have taken into consideration your stated preferences, discussed them with the Sister concerned and reached conclusions which we hope will reflect your particular attributes."

Looking down at the list she said, "When you all know your destinations you will first go to the sewing room to obtain your new uniforms, change into them and present yourself to your respective ward sisters after lunch ready to commence duty.

"Nurse Cameron to Jameson Ward, male accident and orthopaedic.

"Nurse Chapman to Priestman Ward, female medical.

"Nurse Dawson to... "

Quietly they remained listening until that good lady finished, but a jubilant Cathy was already rejoicing inwardly at her good fortune. She had achieved what she hoped for.

The formalities over, she rushed to the nearest telephone box and, with fumbling fingers, inserted the coins which would connect her to her parents. With tears, laughter and exclamations of delight they savoured her success together.

"Oh Catherine, my darling girl, just you wait! We are going to have such a celebration as never was."

True to their word, Roger and Pam arranged a party in Hertfordshire at the earliest opportunity. Circumstances and general pressures had prevented the official marking of their daughter's coming of age in November, so an event was devised to do justice to both occasions.

Privileged to be able to use an ancient beamed, but well appointed, refectory in the Cathedral grounds, her father arranged for caterers to provide a spit roast in the old tradition, accompanied by wine, music and dancing. Former friends from school mingled with new ones from Morford, while relatives, including her godparents, looked on with affection and pleasure. It was well after midnight when the last guests

311

departed and those staying at The Close could relax in comfort and relive the evening.

At last Roger and Pam managed to get their daughter to themselves.

"Happy, darling? Have you enjoyed yourself?"

Still flushed and sparkling from the exhilaration the auburn-haired girl in her striking, deep turquoise dress adorned with a double string pearl necklace, a gift from her parents, hugged them both in turn.

"It was the most wonderful occasion. I never dreamed anything could be so perfect. Thank you both so very much."

Reaching up to the mantelpiece in the lounge, Roger brought down the familiar blue leather case. Turning to Cathy with a smile full of love and pride he said, "Here is something to complete the day. Take your silver buckle my dearest girl, for you have truly earned it."

"And may the future be kind to you and bring you all that you hope for," added Pam.

Gazing with renewed fascination at the elegant tracery, the words came from her on a deep sigh of contentment, "I don't think I have ever been happier."

Within a week of her return to the Royal the last winds of March struck with unusual force and bitterness, once again bringing the odd snowfall and inducing further episodes of ill health among the population. Returning to Priestman Ward from her afternoon break ready for the evening shift she found herself being greeted with obvious relief.

"Oh, it is good to have you back Staff Nurse. Things have been really frantic for the last two hours. We've admitted three new patients and the nurses are just finishing getting things in order. One has still to be given a full assessment and prescribed for by the house physician but he has been called away on another emergency."

Removing her starched cuffs Cathy began to roll up her sleeves and fumbled in the pocket beneath her apron for the pair of elasticated white frills which were used to neaten the effect.

"Where would you like me to start?" she asked.

"One of the latest intake is, in fact, decidedly poorly and has been placed in the side ward. However, that is not the only reason. This lady

312

was originally on the nursing staff here and her family has a long, and indeed historic, connection with the Royal. Matron has already been down and the Consultant himself has just left with instructions that he wishes her to be 'specialled' for the first twenty-four hours."

"That will effectually leave us with a pair of hands short," sighed Cathy.

"Indeed it will, and I'd like yours to be the pair of hands employed in this singular situation."

Removing an extremely thick set of records from the desk in front of her she said, "The patient's name is Miss Masterson."

"Do you mean Sadie Masterson who used to own the convalescent home at Shepherdstone?"

Regarding her Staff Nurse with some surprise she nodded her head. Feeling that some further explanation was called for Cathy volunteered: "I met her several times last year when I was doing my three months there and I got to know some of the family quite well."

"Well, there's a happy coincidence. How much do you know of her medical history?"

"I was told that she has long been a chronic invalid due to heart problems and that her admissions to the Infirmary are almost legendary."

"Very true, as this thick wad of notes testifies, and I think I've been around to see most of them," commented the older woman ruefully. "The basic problem stems from a severe attack of scarlet fever, sustained during her training here, which sadly resulted in rheumatic complications which caused carditis and permanently damaged her heart. Over the years each episode has compromised the organ that little bit more and left her that much weaker. To be quite frank, had she come from the usual working class background it is unlikely that she would have survived this long."

Cathy interrupted to say, "She is completely surrounded and lovingly cared for by the family and various helpers and they all seem to hold her in high regard."

"Indeed, her brother and his son are sitting with her now although, when you have introduced yourself, I think it would be a good idea if

313

you suggested they return home and we will contact them should it be necessary."

"How bad is she, Sister Moore?"

"Her condition is serious. She has congestive cardiac failure with considerable difficulty in breathing. Oxygen is being administered and you will need to take and record accurate observations every fifteen minutes. She has been written up for different medications including morphine which was given about an hour ago."

Handing Cathy the folder of notes she indicated that it was time for her to commence her vigil.

"Ring the bell if you need anything and someone will come immediately."

Quietly Cathy entered the small, sparsely furnished room and, having relieved the frightened-looking student nurse, turned to meet the eyes of the two men seated either side of the austere hospital bed.

"Cathy," Ted exclaimed, swiftly rising to his feet, "by all that's wonderful."

Smiling gently at both of them in turn she softly murmured her sadness at the recent development and explained that she had been assigned exclusively to care for Sadie.

Her gaze then came to rest on the enfeebled figure propped up against a pile of pillows. An oxygen mask tied across her nose and mouth failed to hide the extreme pallor of the barely recognisable face and the bluish tinge around her lips. Placing her fingers on the wrist she could scarcely detect the thready, irregular pulse under the coolness of the skin. Positioning her face close to Sadie's she gently spoke her name but there was absolutely no response. Taking a clipboard bearing a chart she proceeded to record her observations meticulously.

Without looking up she said, "Jim told me she hasn't been so well lately but I never dreamed I'd see such a marked change in her."

"The winter months are always difficult times for my sister and this year has been particularly harsh, I'm afraid."

As Cathy finished writing she motioned both men to accompany her to the door. "I am going to have to speak very quietly because, although Miss Masterson seems to be unaware, it is never possible to be sure how much patients in her position can hear. Do you understand?"

Both men nodded. "How bad is she Cathy?"

"I'm sure the doctor has told you that her condition is grave and nothing has occurred since her admission to alter that. However, in these situations it is vital that the patient isn't allowed to become agitated, excited or distressed but remains relaxed and peaceful in order to give the heart a chance to recover. To help achieve that she has been given morphine and this will be repeated when necessary. It is extremely unlikely, therefore, that she will rouse sufficiently to be able to communicate in any way. May I suggest that it would be sensible for you both to go home and get some rest? You can telephone later on and I promise that we will inform you if there is any significant change."

"Will you be staying with her?" John Masterson pressed.

"Of course, until I go off duty and then I shall be replaced by one of the night staff. Don't worry, she won't be left."

"Come on Dad. We can't do anything useful here and she's in good hands." The older man approached the bed and gazed long at the occupant then, covering her hand on the counterpane with his, whispered, "Goodnight old thing." With a final farewell they set off back to Hollowdene.

The following morning Cathy, anxious to know what had transpired in the night, arrived on the ward a little earlier than usual to find absolutely no difference in the situation. 'Specialling' a patient is a lonely task and a somewhat weary colleague greeted her arrival with relief. Having satisfied herself that all the observations were up-to-date she set about blanket-bathing Sadie, changing her nightdress, attending to her pressure areas and particularly her mouth toilet, in order to alleviate the dryness cause by the prolonged oxygen intake. Ringing the bell she summoned a nurse to help her change the sheets, remake the bed and re-position the patient.

Despite constantly trying to engage her in conversation there had been no signs of any response up to this point. Suddenly, a hand fluttered up towards the face mask and grabbing the tubing attempted to pull it away. Gently, Cathy captured the waving, shaky limb and rested it back on the sheet.

"All right Miss Masterson, let's have a little rest from this for a while and see what happens shall we?" So saying she disconnected the oxygen and prepared to watch carefully. After a short while the paper thin lips started to move against each other and the tongue emerged in a weak attempt to moisten them. The offer of a sip of water was barely acknowledged but as Cathy, skillfully supporting the grey head, raised a feeding cup to her mouth Sadie swallowed with obvious gratitude.

"Well done. You'll be enjoying a nice cup of tea in no time. Just have a pause and we'll try again in a moment."

Due to take her three-hour break at eleven o'clock, Cathy was delighted to witness the very first indications of a marginal improvement in Sadie's condition before her replacement arrived. Hurrying to the telephone she called Hollowdene with the slightly better news then, after changing into mufti, she sped into the city in search of a gift for her father's approaching birthday.

Sister greeted her return to duty with a smile.

"You will be delighted that your patient's condition appears to be stabilising, Staff Nurse. The consultant has expressed himself surprised but satisfied. Her respirations are quite shallow but she is managing without oxygen. Her family arrived a short while ago and are with her now. Once you have recorded the next observations we can extend the interval to every half hour, especially while they are with her."

On entering the side ward Cathy was surprised to see Jim who had accompanied his parents and great uncle. Greeting her warmly, Ted gestured towards the considerably more alert figure of Sadie resting comfortably against her pile of pillows.

"A bit different to yesterday wouldn't you say?"

"Indeed it is. It's amazing what can happen within the space of twenty four hours."

Going to stand by the bed she smiled down into the tired eyes.

"I'm just going to check you over Miss Masterson and then I'll leave you in peace to enjoy the company of your family."

"It's James' Cathy isn't it?" she said weakly peering up at her. "How nice dear."

"Cathy has been your special guardian angel ever since you came

316

here," her brother informed her. "It's not everyone who gets such preferential treatment."

"Thank you my dear, thank you so much," she whispered.

Reaching for her patient's wrist in order to check her pulse Cathy became aware of a tensing of the arm and a gasping intake of breath from Sadie. Looking up she saw an expression of bewilderment in her face and became aware of a gaze fixed on her waistline as an unsteady hand waved to try to touch the silver buckle which fastened the belt encircling it. Desperately trying to raise herself forward her voice came in a ragged breath.

"Where did you get that buckle from? Where did you get it? John, make her tell me."

Clearly startled, Ted, Maureen and Jim stared at Cathy as Sadie evinced every sign of increasing agitation.

"Steady on old thing," her brother responded soothingly. "Don't get yourself worked up."

There was no damming the flow, however.

"Where did you get it from? Where did you get it?"

Clasping the trembling hands firmly in hers Cathy replied quietly, "It was given to me by my parents when I qualified as a nurse shortly after my twenty-first birthday. Jim was there for the party, weren't you?"

"Too right I was. It was a super do."

Before he could say any more Sadie's voice rose even further.

"It isn't hers John, it isn't. It was Mother's, and mine and Lucy's."

Thoroughly alarmed at the state into which her patient was working herself Cathy sought to reassure her.

"Miss Masterson, please try to keep calm. Most of the trained staff wear these buckles and they can sometimes seem very similar."

Undoing it, she held the buckle so that Sadie could see it more clearly. This had quite the reverse effect than that for which she was hoping. Roused beyond belief the frail lady wrestled to sit up all the while agitatedly gesticulating at the buckle.

"I'm so sorry," John said. "My sister seems to be confused. She did indeed have one like it and I... "

His words were abruptly cut short.

Clutching at Cathy's apron Sadie's voice moaned in anguish. "You're my Lucy's Mary aren't you? You're my Lucy's Mary."

The young nurse trying to cope with a fraught situation later had no clear recollection of her actions. Almost rooted to the spot by Sadie's words she stared in shock and disbelief. Her head was in a whirl as she strove to maintain the demands of professionalism above the emotions which threatened to engulf her. Extending a hand towards the bell push above the bed-head she pressed on it long and hard whilst, with the other, she reached for the oxygen mask. Almost immediately the door opened. Rapidly assessing the situation Sister came to her assistance.

"I'll take over here, Staff Nurse, while you take the drug cupboard keys and draw up an injection of morphine. And please get someone to ring for the house physician."

Grateful for the opportunity to escape and a need for focused action Cathy sped to the task almost like an automaton. Within minutes she was back with the kidney dish bearing the charged syringe and the stock bottle which Sister carefully checked before nodding to her to administer the dose.

Vaguely aware of the family hovering against the wall in bemusement, she entered and signed the details on the chart, retrieved her belt from the floor where it had fallen and, anxious to avoid any questioning, left the room just as the doctor arrived.

In a trance she went through the motions of replacing the morphine and locking the drug cupboard then set about cleaning the syringe and replacing it in a tray of methylated spirit.

"You're my Lucy's Mary. You're my Lucy's Mary."

The words throbbed like a relentless tattoo in her head. Whatever was she supposed to do now, she speculated wildly? She was aware of feeling uncomfortably warm and there didn't seem sufficient air to breathe. With beads of perspiration forming on her brow, head spinning and concentration fading, Cathy crumpled to the floor in a faint.

After being allowed to recover briefly she found herself accompanied to the sick bay in the nurses' home by one of her colleagues. Home Sister clucking round her like a mother hen, eventually succeeded in tucking her into bed and bidding her rest for a while, drew the curtains and departed leaving the door ajar. As she lay there the words returned unbidden.

"You're my Lucy's Mary. You're my Lucy's Mary."

Finally the tears coursed down her cheeks and her shoulders heaved with sobs.

It was in this state that Jean found her having been summoned by Sister to collect the necessary toiletry items from her friend's room. "Cathy, what's the matter? Whatever's happened, for heaven's sake?"

Chokingly she replied, "I just can't tell you."

Grabbing Jean's arm hard she managed to get out, "Please telephone my Dad and ask him to come immediately. It really is urgent."

The next minute Sister was back bearing a warm drink, clicking her tongue and shooing the bewildered Jean away with a flap of her hands. In the end emotional exhaustion overtook her and she sunk into a merciful sleep which effectively precluded any further thought.

Thoroughly alarmed by Jean's unexpected and slightly incoherent phone call, it was with considerable haste and concern that Roger and Pam drove to Morford.

Presenting themselves at the nurses' home it seemed to take an interminable time before they gained access to their daughter. Home Sister was none too pleased at this unbidden intrusion into her domain.

"I cannot imagine why you have been troubled. Staff Nurse simply fainted on duty. It does happen occasionally, especially if they neglect themselves. Probably went without a meal if the truth were known," she pontificated.

"Still, as you're here you'd better come through, although she's been sleeping these last couple of hours."

Cathy, however, had been roused by the sound of her father's voice in the corridor. As they entered the room she raised herself up on her elbow, let out a heartfelt cry of relief and found herself being gathered into a pair of loving arms.

Finally, seated one on either side of her, they listened with growing horror as the tale unfolded. Never in their wildest fantasies had they expected anything like this.

"What am I going to do, Dad? Whatever am I going to say to everyone? Whatever are they all going to think? I just can't face anybody."

"You won't have to my darling. That's what we're here for and I will deal with it. You try to rest here quietly with Mum while I go and sort things out. You've had a nasty shock but it will be all right, you'll see."

Roger's approach to Home Sister with the news that he needed to see the Matron as a matter of some urgency coincided with a telephone call from the general office requesting that Miss Giles be informed as soon as Staff Nurse Chapman was in a fit state to talk to her. As a result he soon found himself in the familiar entrance hall of the hospital and was duly ushered into Matron's office. She listened gravely as the facts emerged and the picture formulated.

Eventually she was compelled to respond. "I really don't know what to say, it is so extraordinary."

The phone on her desk began to ring. Excusing herself she listened intently then, replacing the receiver, she looked her visitor squarely in the face. "I'm afraid that was Priestman Ward to tell me that Miss Masterson has just died."

Following Sadie's death, Jim agreed to drive his mother back to the farm leaving his father and uncle to sort out the details and try to make sense of all that had happened. Having been summoned to Matron's office she introduced the three men, saw them settled and discreetly withdrew.

Now Roger once more found himself embarking upon the electrifying catalogue of events that had led to this moment. As the details slowly emerged the listeners became increasingly stupefied and incredulous. Finally John exclaimed, "You'll have to forgive me but I simply can't take it in."

"How on earth is Cathy feeling?" Ted asked anxiously.

"Shocked, bewildered, horrified and upset, in fact she's experiencing a whole range of reactions which is only to be expected."

"And she really had no idea about any of this?"

"Oh, she was completely aware of her adoption and knew that her natural mother's name was Lucy Dane who had once trained at this hospital. She had even traced her name on the plaque in the chapel."

"Of course, the name Masterson would have meant nothing to her," John offered.

"Precisely," said Roger.

"I think I had better explain," the older man sighed. "What with one thing and another, my poor sister's life wasn't easy. Not only was her health indifferent but she managed to contract what I can only describe as a most unfortunate marriage. In no way could I abide Herbert Dane and never understood how she allowed herself to become involved with him, let alone marry him."

He appeared to reflect for a moment before carrying on.

"Part of the problem was that Sadie had a genuine concern for the working classes and a real social conscience but her nature wasn't robust enough to prevent her being taken advantage of or becoming something of a doormat I'm afraid."

"Not a bit like her mother," added Ted.

"No. Sadie admired her enormously but she didn't have the same spark."

"But her daughter Lucy inherited it," Ted leapt in. "Goodness, I can recall my cousin as a real feisty character and great fun."

"Yes, Lucy was the high point of my sister's existence. She adored her and was so proud of her. Her death in the war was an absolutely devastating blow but it also resulted in the end of the marriage. I don't know all the details for she declined to confide in me, nor would she accept any help. Although we were quite close, in many respects Sadie was quite a secretive and private person and dealt with matters herself through her solicitor. However, from what I could gather Herbert cleared off to Australia with another woman and Sadie positively refused to speak about it, except to say that she never wanted to hear his name mentioned again. As a result, and having neither husband nor child to consider, she reverted to her maiden name."

"Even so Dad, I find it extraordinary that you had absolutely no knowledge of the fact that Lucy had given birth to a baby."

Passing his hand across his forehead John snapped in annoyance. "Why on earth didn't she come to me and confide in me? I know she

321

couldn't have coped with a little one on her own, but Ted and Maureen would have been more than ready to take her on, wouldn't you? You always wanted a little girl," he sighed.

Looking somewhat ruefully at the older man Roger suggested that he had already furnished the reason.

"You have the answer in two words, Herbert Dane. He was quite objectionable when my friends called to appraise him and his wife of the facts pertaining to Cathy's birth. He categorically refused to even acknowledge her existence, have anything to do with the matter, or allow his wife to. They later became Cathy's godparents and found the whole episode most upsetting. They were utterly distressed on behalf of your sister."

"My God, I could swing for that blighter. He didn't like me and I can assure you the feeling was entirely mutual. I certainly never visited Shepherdstone when I knew he would be around. The wisdom of hindsight is a wonderful thing but, looking back, I can't help wondering whether Lucy had discovered her father's other life. It would certainly account for the hostility she showed towards him."

"Yes, that could be it, Dad," said Ted. "Don't you remember that when Lucy came over from France for Gran's funeral they had the most awful go at each other and he stormed off? And didn't she take you to one side and ask you to keep an eye on Aunt Sadie because she was worried for her?"

"You're right, Ted. Perhaps I should have made it my business to try to press her harder but she always played things close to her chest. Clearly I had no real inkling what my sister must have suffered emotionally at the hands of that man."

"Never mind, Dad, at least she was comfortable and cared for once she moved to Hollowdene. Look how well she and Mum got on and how lost she was when she died. After that I think she rather enjoyed being something of a matriarchal figure, you know. Let's at least be thankful for all that."

Finding that conversation had dwindled to a halt and anxious to get back to his daughter, Roger stood up to make a move.

"Thank you for agreeing to meet me and listen to my explanations at what is clearly a difficult time. One thing I hope you won't do is to hold Cathy responsible for Sadie's death because that is undoubtedly how she will react when she learns of it."

Both men hastened to speak as one.

"There's absolutely no question of that."

"That poor girl has been the unwitting pawn in this whole situation," Ted protested. "We've grown very fond of her and all we want is to see her come through this ordeal as swiftly as possible."

"What happens now?" Ted addressed Roger.

"In what way do you mean?" he countered, rather surprised.

"Well, we will be able to see Cathy, I hope. I mean, do you think she will come to the funeral? Jim's going to be quizzing me on all these things when I get home, to be sure. Come to think of it, I don't know what his reaction is going to be when he finds out that they're cousins."

"Oh, what a tangled web we weave," muttered John.

As Roger opened the door and walked into the entrance hall, the others followed closely on his heels. Stopping to shake hands he saw the older man looking earnestly at the striking portrait of a lady.

"That is Kate Oliphant, founder of this hospital, Sadie's and my mother, Lucy's grandmother and Cathy's great-grandmother. I wonder what she'd make of all this," he pondered sadly shaking his head.

On Matron's advice Cathy was granted compassionate leave until after the funeral.

She was frankly dreading the ordeal but knew that she owed it to her grandmother and the family at Hollowdene to be there. They had been so kind and Jim, in particular, had become very special. She couldn't help wondering how they would react when they met. All she could feel at the moment was a great numbness.

In the event it was an amazingly serene occasion and her parents marvelled with pride at her composure. Jim made things easy when he gave her a kiss and a big hug saying, "Well, well cousin. No wonder we hit it off from the start. Obviously it's pretty powerful stuff we've got flowing through our veins."

Cathy smiled at him gratefully as he squeezed her hand and everyone relaxed.

John Masterson bade her come and sit by him as he had something to show her. In his hand was a large envelope and she looked on curiously as he drew from it a few photographs.

"We found these when we were going through my sister's effects," he said. "There is just the name 'Mary' on the back but I'm guessing they are of you as a small child."

Cathy gazed at them in surprise then looked towards her parents.

"That's right," Roger replied. "For a while we sent a photo to Sadie's solicitor every year on your birthday. We addressed them to Mrs. Dane which he acknowledged on her behalf with gratitude but, quite properly, never told us that she had changed her name. However, we didn't think it appropriate to continue after the age of seven."

"We just wanted to give her something to remember her daughter by," said Pam. "Although we were so blessed I have always felt sad for her."

"And I can only imagine what bitter sweet pleasure they afforded her," John replied. "Thank you and bless you for that."

Taking another sealed envelope he handed it to her. "This is to be opened when you get home Cathy. We have put together a collection of photographs of Lucy and Sadie which you might like to keep."

Turning to her parents he said, "I do hope you won't mind."

"It's a wonderful thought." Roger replied. "Isn't it my darling?"

"I can never thank you enough," Cathy answered gratefully.

Following a very simple service they returned to the farm and, once they had refreshed themselves with the wonderful spread provided by his daughter-in-law, John drew Cathy, Roger and Pam to one side saying, "I wonder if you would be good enough to spare me a few moments?"

Ushering then into another room he gestured them to chairs.

"I just wanted to explain the situation regarding my sister's will. Sadie wasn't, strictly speaking, a hugely wealthy woman, although she enjoyed a comfortable existence thanks to a previous legacy from her parents. Fortunately, they had the good sense to deed it solely to her and to her heirs which they could do by then, thanks to the Married Woman's Property Act. I do know that they were never completely

324

happy with Sadie's choice of husband and I imagine they wanted to protect her in some way. Under the circumstances, how right they were."

Seating himself at the table he produced an official-looking envelope and pushed it forward.

"That," he said, "is a copy of Sadie's will which the solicitor left with me to give you knowing that you would be coming here today. In it you will see that, after various bequests to her great-nephews, people who helped to care for her and a donation to Morford Infirmary, the remainder of her estate passes to you, Cathy."

An expression of stunned bewilderment came over her face. "Oh no, please no," she cried out in consternation. "I can't possibly accept it. I don't want it."

Turning towards her parents she asked in almost accusatory tones, "Did you know anything about this?"

Roger moved to place an arm round her shoulders. "I can see how this has come as yet another shock to you at a difficult time Cathy and, yes, we knew it might be a possibility."

As the young woman opened her mouth to launch forth a tirade, he held up his hand with a finger to his lips and continued. "When we adopted you, the solicitor intimated that your grandmother was not without means and that instructions had been left for some provision to be made for you in the event of her death. Over twenty years have since passed and for all we knew her financial circumstances could have changed. She might even have altered her will. Therefore, there was no point in telling you about something that might never happen. We were confident that the solicitor would contact you in due course if it became necessary as, indeed, he has done."

"Don't be angry, darling," her mother intervened. "Simply be grateful and see it as a measure of her love and concern. Remember, it was she who wanted to make sure that you would also receive the silver buckle."

John Masterson smiled at her. "You know Cathy, love takes many forms and you have been truly blessed because you have it in double measure. If neither my beloved niece nor her mother could raise you,

Sadie cared sufficiently to ensure some provision for you. I am just profoundly thankful that you had such wonderful parents and an upbringing that has made you the special person you are. She would be so, so proud of you."

With tears trickling down her cheeks she got up to kiss the elderly man. "There, there, my dear. Just know that there will always be a welcome for you at Hollowdene."

"I don't know what to say," she said in a voice quivering with emotion.

"Then don't say anything, for words aren't necessary. Although there is one thing I would ask you to bear in mind if you will. When you come to study the details you will discover that part of Sadie's estate is the little stone cottage in which she lived, which she purchased from me after selling me the farmhouse at Shepherdstone. Obviously we shall be thrilled if you want to keep it and use it for yourself. If, however, you ever decide to sell it, I would be most grateful if you would allow me or Ted to purchase it so that it can revert back to the estate."

"Oh. I simply can't take all this in at the moment," Cathy replied, "but of course I'll remember what you've said."

Returning to the lounge they all exchanged the fondest of farewells before returning to Hertfordshire.

As the car proceeded rhythmically towards her home Cathy sat quietly in the back deep in thought. A difficult hurdle had been surmounted yet she felt empty inside. Not for the first time since Sadie's death she pondered the way forward.

Chapter Three

A Dark World

Although it was only the end of August the day had been cool, thundery and overcast. Wafts of mist were swirling in from the direction of the river as Cathy made her way through the warren of streets eager to reach the familiar comfort of her modest room. The uncanny half-light between dusk and night was accentuated thanks to the blackout restrictions which only heightened the eerie silence which brooded over the capital. Office workers had long since scuttled in droves to the various stations where the trains, with lights obscured, snaked their way towards the dubious safety of suburbia.

Suddenly the air was pierced by the all too familiar rise and fall of an air-raid siren and she quickened her steps determined to get to her destination at all costs. The strains of the siren faded only to give way to the throbbing sound of an aircraft engine. Fingers of light sprang from nowhere as searchlight beams criss-crossed the sky seeking out the intruder and, almost on cue, the ack-ack battery camouflaged in a nearby park clattered into life. Shrill whistles sounded as wardens patrolled their beats urging folk to take cover but Cathy pressed on doggedly. She was cold and tired and felt sorely in need of a wash at the very least, for it was unlikely that there would be sufficient hot water for a bath. For a moment she thought wistfully of those days when such things had been taken for granted but now fell within the category of luxuries. Her reverie was broken as she heard footsteps approaching and the figure of an air-raid warden confronted her.

"Come on miss, this is no place to be. Get yourself down into a shelter," said a gruff but kindly voice. "There's one round the corner in Grange Gardens." As if to lend speed to his words the air was rent by the most tremendous bang and a juddering thud which shook the ground. "Bloody hell luv', run for it. C'mon for God's sake." Grabbing her by the arm her would-be saviour propelled her along until they both collapsed down some steps into a primitive dug-out reinforced with concrete, corrugated iron and sandbags.

There were only a handful of people perched uncomfortably on the wooden slatted bench that ran round the sides. A hurricane lamp stood on a shelf and someone had lit a primus stove and set out enamel mugs on a tin tray in the hope of providing a cheering cuppa. Her companions, raising languid eyes to acknowledge the new arrival, caught sight of her uniform which caused one bright spark to say, "We'll be OK tonight lads, we've got us our own Florence Nightingale sent from heaven. Welcome to the Ritz, Nurse."

Smiling at them she gratefully accepted the indifferent brew thrust into her hand. "Get that down you my duck. Afraid it 'aint that strong but we're a bit short on tea." Cupping her hands lovingly round the chipped enamel she leaned back against the cold wall and was soon lost in deep thought.

Following her grandmother's death Cathy had reluctantly allowed herself to be persuaded back to her post at the Royal. Despite her misgivings the whole episode had proved to be only a nine-day wonder. Matron and Sister were both unexpectedly understanding and supportive while Jean, in her forthright Scottish way, did much to deflect any unwanted curiosity from other sources. Nevertheless, she couldn't seem to settle and was unable to recapture the earlier delight and pleasure which her role afforded.

She still received an enthusiastic welcome each time she visited the farm but things between her and Jim were not the same. The spark had gone and would not be rekindled.

With the help of her father she had negotiated all the legal details and emerged in quite a comfortable financial situation in addition to the cottage, which she had opted to retain for use as a holiday retreat for herself, her family and friends. John was delighted at the idea and an accommodating farm worker's wife was engaged to keep an eye on the place and make sure it was cleaned and aired regularly.

On the surface things couldn't possibly have been better. However, the outlook nationally appeared to be increasingly grim and coincided with the completion of her year's post-registration period at the Infirmary. This proved to be the catalyst that provoked her into action.

Quite often thoughts of her grandmother would creep up on her and she listened with fresh interest to all that John Masterson could relate regarding his sister's years of nursing. She learned of the social conviction which had driven her to devote all her energy to care for the sick in their own homes, certain that therein lay the greatest need.

In those days it had been a somewhat fragmented service though that changed with the pioneering efforts of Liverpool philanthropist, William Rathbone. Then, in 1887 a national fund to commemorate Queen Victoria's Jubilee was used to found the Queen's Institute of District Nursing. Over the years this professional organisation grew and prospered. The nurses came under the jurisdiction of local authorities but from its headquarters in London the Institute set the standards nationwide and trained the staff. Comparatively poor financial rewards proved a deterrent to some and there were constant drives to raise money and recruit staff. The public were encouraged to join their local district nursing association in order to obtain care when needed.

Subscribers paid little over one penny a week in order to receive the free service, while those who did not were charged one shilling and sixpence for each visit made by a nurse. There was no charge for the very poor and the aged. This scheme was well advertised on the wireless and in cinemas nationally and, coupled with increased voluntary fundraising efforts, bore considerable fruit.

Thanks to Sadie's generosity a low salary wasn't a problem and Cathy felt increasingly drawn to the idea of carrying on where her grandmother had left off. In some way it would be a kind of tribute to her memory and she felt challenged by the prospect. Her application to train was duly accepted and, to the consternation of her parents, she settled into a large old house in the London borough of Southwark which did service as a home, local clinic and place of instruction. This was like another world and poles apart from anything which she had so far experienced.

In the nineteenth and early twentieth centuries the Borough was one of the most densely populated areas in the country. Lying to the south of the River Thames and the City of London, and in the shadow of an ancient cathedral, it comprised a mix of small pockets of limited prosperity alongside larger slum areas of extreme deprivation. The residents followed a variety of occupations but, due to its proximity to the river, many were seafarers, lightermen or warehousemen, or employed in the allied trades of shipbuilding and repair, or at the commercial docks which ran alongside the city's flowing main artery.

The hub of the place was the old Borough Market which owed its position to a location by London Bridge which, until the eighteenth century, was the sole crossing over the Thames and thus the only link between London and southern England. The original market was held on the bridge itself, but later moved into the grounds of St. Thomas's Hospital, where it continued for several hundred years. Then a new one sprang up in Borough High Street which became something of a 'red light district'. When it was closed in 1775, another area was purchased called The Triangle and in 1801 the whole market area was covered with a Crystal Palace style glass and iron roof which finally came to nestle under the shadow of the South Eastern railway viaduct, sandwiched between two arches.

This then was the background and environment within which a handful of nurses, under the watchful eye of the Superintendent, strove to carry out their duties and hone their skills in humble homes and tenement buildings situated in a positive maze of streets.

The first weeks had been bewildering as Cathy struggled to cope with a completely alien environment inhabited by people very different to the residents of Morford.

By and large their homes weren't palaces and most of the residents weren't exactly blessed with an abundance of this world's goods, yet she had never met a more cheery and good-humoured lot. They were invariably welcoming and ribbed her mercilessly for her rather more refined accent which contrasted strongly with the local Cockney strains.

Her companions in this venture were equally friendly, ready to help and quick to share their knowledge and experience. The Home possessed a large treatment room in which some clinics were held and where Cathy rapidly came to grips with the intricacies involved in maintaining the black leather nursing bag with which she had been issued. The white cotton liners had to be changed, washed, starched and ironed at the end of each day and the contents replenished or re-sterilised. She learned that when removing one's coat in a patient's house it must be folded into a parcel with the lining innermost and placed on a chair on a sheet of newspaper to ensure that the wearer did not transfer any 'unwanted little visitors' onto her person if at all possible. She also had to come to grips with the mastery of an assortment of unwieldy bicycles kept in the back yard. Their sedate 'sit-up-and-beg' style was hardly prepossessing and bore little resemblance to the lighter and definitely more fashionable model which her parents had bought for her but were decidedly better than nothing on occasion.

Cathy revelled in her new surroundings and took every opportunity to familiarise herself with the landmarks, exploring the old historic buildings, the abundance of shops and the many attractions which the city had to offer. She would frequently pause on Southwark Bridge which afforded a glimpse of the Tower of London to the north and the dome of St. Paul's Cathedral on the opposite bank. Below, the sinuous Thames snaked a fluid path bearing a constant flow of traffic. Lighters, barges, cargo ships and other assorted craft went about their business and the whole place hummed with activity.

She scarcely had time to acquaint herself with the varied demands of District Nursing before the long-feared announcement came. In a wireless broadcast on September 3rd 1939 the Prime Minister solemnly announced: "Britain is at war with Germany". The wail of the siren was heard immediately, rumours of imminent invasions and air-raids were rife and talk was of nothing else.

Straightaway, steel hats and respirators were issued to all Queen's Nurses and they found themselves drawn into helping with the plans to evacuate the capital's children to places of safety.

Cathy found the sight of youngsters suddenly being separated from their parents quite harrowing, as was the effect on the family members left behind, some of whom were her patients. This was compounded by those who, with the typical grit of Londoners, refused to let their children go, preferring to take their chances together.

On a weekend visit home, when the Battle of Britain was being waged in the skies over southern England, Roger and Pam tried to persuade their daughter to take a post nearer home in the interests of her safety.

"There is absolutely no way that I will leave London now," she said. "Anyway, nothing's happening apart from the odd air-raid siren going off, presumably to keep us on our toes."

Hunched within the confines of the shelter, as the raid played out overhead, she reflected ruefully on that phoney period of inaction, at least as far as England was concerned. However, events were indeed moving fast on the Continent and she would never forget the sight of weary but thankful soldiers passing through London following the evacuation of Dunkirk in May.

Now, here she was caught up in the sporadic bombing which had commenced at the end of June but, even on that late August night, it didn't seem of any great significance.

"Probably just a stray chancing his luck," the warden commented after a long period of silence had elapsed.

"Does that mean we can go?" asked Cathy.

"Better not risk it 'til the All Clear, luv."

As if on cue, the sustained sound heralding the end of danger echoed across the City. Gathering her nursing bag, tin helmet and gas-mask she thankfully set off to complete her journey little knowing that this had simply been a dress rehearsal for what was to come.

On September 7th the nurses gathered in the treatment room after the evening meal to finish their tasks and prepare for the next day. They weren't unduly concerned when the alert sounded but within a short space of time it became clear that this was different. The air was rent with noises. The hum of planes, the whistling and crashing of bombs, retaliatory gunfire and the sound of falling masonry presented an alarming sound. Huddled together in a large cupboard under the stairs they waited, and waited, and waited. Finally, as the clamour abated and fingers of dawn began to show in the east, they tentatively emerged.

Debris and shards of glass littered the hallway. Their ears were assailed by the terrible crackling of flames and their nostrils beset by the smell of smoke, dense clouds of which filled the atmosphere. Gingerly moving out into the street they saw in the distance and down by the river, massive flames leaping up into the sky and it was possible to make out a warehouse ablaze with the outline of a gasometer silhouetted against the glow. Bells from fire engines and ambulances rang out and the streets became alive with scurrying people.

After assessing the damage to the Home and clearing up as best they could the nurses were dispatched on their rounds and to render what aid was needed. Mercifully, casualties among their regulars were non-existent. "It's them poor devils further down the river wot's copped it Nurse. Well, let's hope Hitler's satisfied," said one old man.

Only Hitler was far from appeased. The next two days and nights were one continuous barrage of bombs, fires, and the homeless, injured and bereaved. The night bell of the Home pealed as patients whose houses had fallen round them sought sanctuary. The hospitals coped with the severely injured but the sheer volume of homeless fast became a distressing problem. Clutching pitiful bundles of belongings and rescued treasures from the ruins they spilled into any available space. In the duty room, minor wounds were treated and babies bathed and fed.

"They can't possibly stay here," the Superintendent protested to a warden. "There simply aren't the facilities and we don't possess a shelter."

Preparing for just such a situation as this work had begun, in the first half of the year, at Borough tube station to seal off the section of the line that ran underneath the Thames. Six new staircases were built down to the tunnels allowing access for three hundred people per minute to a maximum capacity of fourteen thousand. Now it came into its own as night after night the population of London scurried down like rabbits to their burrows. Altogether, use was made of eighty underground stations to house about one hundred and seventy thousand people. Even so, survival wasn't assured. The worst civilian disaster of the war occurred at Bethnal Green where one hundred and seventy three men, women and children died descending to so-called safety. One drawback was that the quality of the air on the platforms frequently left much to be desired. As a result many preferred to take their chance in the various street shelters and those erected in back gardens but they were often ineffective and costly in terms of injuries and fatalities.

The fires which resulted from that first raid on the docks left the way well-lit for the heavy German bombers which came relentlessly, night after night, to give the place a terrible battering. Almost on the dot of seven-thirty in the evening the sirens would sound and the guns start up their chatter, while barrage balloons hovered in the sky over London like great silver elephants on wire cables. Sited one to two miles apart they were raised whenever there was risk of a raid.

Then came the onslaught as the bombs rained down. The sky became one huge red glow, visible for many miles around, as the dockland areas with their stockpiles of timber, paint, foodstuffs, oil, wine and spirits burnt and continued to burn for days. MacDougall's flour mills with their tall silos was an outstanding landmark.

Cathy and her colleagues struggled on for another two nights until they were finally completely blasted out of the Home. The nearby explosion had been deafening, then there was silence and the lights failed. With the next detonation the front of the house collapsed. "Are you alright in there?" called a warden as the beam from his torch picked them out in their hidey-hole under the stairs. "The structure at the back doesn't seem too bad and you can get out that way if you go gingerly but whatever you do don't use any naked lights, there's a gas main gone outside."

Salvaging what they could of their personal belongings they set off for the schools and church halls, hastily designated as rest centers where many still sheltered, to see what help they could give. When Cathy returned to the Home some hours later the rescue squads were still digging the bodies out further down the street.

Life in London became pretty grim. Buildings had been strengthened with sand-bags and windows bricked up. Trams and buses still ran wherever possible and people tried to work as normal but education was severely disrupted as the majority of the schools closed. The sound of 'Wailing Winnie' punctuated everyday activities and was invariably the signal for the gun batteries on Clapham and Dulwich Commons, in Hyde Park and many other sites, to open up adding their reassuring clatter to the general cacophony. "Hold tight – here comes another one," became a repeated watchword.

Many civilians, who were either unable or unwilling to join the military, became members of the Home Guard, Auxiliary Fire Service, Air Raid Precaution Wardens or Fire Watchers. Boy Scouts guided fire engines and ambulances to where they were most needed and became known as Blitz Scouts. The Women's Voluntary Service sprang into action and became a lifeline for thousands by amassing and distributing an endless supply of clothing. On top of this they also made emergency washing facilities available and, by establishing a network of canteens, they somehow contrived to feed ever-increasing numbers. Women were trained to provide school meals for those children still at school and learned to cater for and manage large quantities.

In Southwark they set up a child welfare centre, organising crèches for the under-fives whose mothers were needed to work for the war effort. The Ministry of Health arranged to pay the health and welfare costs of all 'transferred workers' – those who had been drafted to work in munitions factories. This involved the District Nurses who were paid at the rate of ninepence for each nursing visit made. Everyone was trying to 'do their bit' and to keep spirits high.

For Cathy and her colleagues the most pressing problems were to find accommodation and establish bases from which they could operate. The first was temporarily solved by moving into the nurses' home at nearby Guy's Hospital. Nevertheless, the Superintendent wasted no time in her search and late the following day Cathy found herself dispatched to view a possible new residence.

In the centre of the Borough stood a large Georgian parish church. Possessing a spectacular ceiling, a fine organ and stained glass, it also boasted an enormous crypt which it was felt could be more effectively used in the present crisis.

Casting a somewhat jaundiced eye over the imposing edifice, Cathy mounted the steps and found herself being greeted warmly by the waiting vicar, an amiable man who she judged to be nearing retirement.

Taking her by the arm he ushered her inside and led her towards the back of the building whilst submitting her to a potted history en route. Approaching a hefty pair of doors in a vestibule he informed her that this was the west end of the church giving access onto Mercer's Street. Off to the right was another smaller door which now stood open. A dim light showed a flight of broad, stone steps leading into the bowels of the building. Following him apprehensively she became aware of cheerful voices engaged in seeming good-humoured banter. Slowly adjusting her eyes to the relative gloom an involuntary gasp escaped her as she surveyed the scene confronting her. A vast cavernous area containing numerous tombs and marble wall plaques of all shapes and sizes stretched out in front of her. Three women on hands and knees were scrubbing the stone flags as if their lives depended on it. One hastily extinguished a cigarette while the others looked at her with interest.

"Now ladies, this is Nurse Chapman who will soon be well known to all of us."

Cathy smiled at them dutifully.

"And these," he continued, "are some of the little band who are trying to bring some order and comfort to the place."

"Well, if we've gotta kip down 'ere of a night and you've gotta live and work out of 'ere, somat's got to be done aint it?" one of them chirped up. Whilst inwardly agreeing Cathy couldn't help feeling that they'd got an uphill task on their hands and her heart sank.

Seeing her face the vicar cheerfully informed her, "We've had quite a little crowd gathering here the last few nights and it's good to feel that the place can be put to better use in these extraordinary circumstances." Regarding her anxiously he queried tentatively whether she thought it would be manageable.

Feeling that something positive was expected of her she replied, "It certainly isn't as dank and musty as I thought it would be."

"Well, the old coke boiler stands in the far corner and these doors have been wide open all the time recently."

Laughing wryly she said, "If anyone had told me I'd be living and nursing amongst the dead I wouldn't have believed them but I guess anything's possible."

"This lot won't be givin' you no trouble duck, that's for sure," came a quick retort.

"Nah, you wait 'til we've done and this place'll be like a palace," another prophesied.

Feeling that this was a rather optimistic statement Cathy joined in the general mirth.

Her mood was hardly more sanguine when she phoned her parents after supper. More than relieved to hear her voice they were clearly aghast at the turn of events although Roger at least could see the funny side of her current situation. Mindful of the poster dominating the kiosk reminding everyone that 'Dangerous Talk Costs Lives', she was unable to furnish them with any great details for fear of having her call abruptly terminated by the ever-alert operators manning the nation's switchboards.

It wasn't until late afternoon on the following day that Cathy arrived at her new home complete with her meagre belongings. Nothing could have prepared her for the transformation that awaited her. The already overstretched utility services had somehow managed to erect a standpipe for water in the street outside and augment the inadequate electricity supply, while the Superintendent had procured a small steriliser and arranged the delivery of essential supplies. Standing on the broad stone ledge which ran the length of one wall stood four large urns for boiling water, while trestle tables held two large washing up bowls and a miscellaneous collection of crockery and teapots. Two zinc tubs were positioned underneath and scattered about were an assortment of chairs and mattresses, while hurricane lamps had been strategically placed in case of emergency.

Three burly dockers had man-handled a large Victorian wardrobe from the vicarage and were struggling to set it into place beside another sizeable cupboard brought down from the vestry, both to be used for lockable storage.

The main drawback was undoubtedly the extremely basic toilet facilities which consisted of a couple of buckets and disinfectant hidden behind screens in the farthest recesses, but needs must when the devil drives.

Catching sight of one of her earlier acquaintances she was quick to offer praise. "I never imagined you'd ever achieve anything like this and in such a short space of time."

"Never say die, my duck," she chuckled. "By the way, I'm Florrie and this is Daisy," indicating her companion. "Ethel," she called raucously, "our Nurse is here."

Hurrying over, the other member of the trio grabbed hold of Cathy's arm anxious to show her the final piece de resistance. Leading her towards the far end of the crypt her eyes were drawn to a faded brown velvet curtain suspended from a pole running between two tall tombs, affixed to which was a notice bearing the words: 'Strictly Private. Nurse Only'. Pulling it to one side with a flourish the redoubtable Ethel revealed an army camp bed with mattress, blankets and pillows, a wooden chair, a small table and a rickety cupboard.

"Wotcher think then?"

"I'm just dumbstruck, and thank you all so much. It may not be the Savoy but it's more than adequate and definitely cheaper."

"You aint 'eard 'ow much we're charging yet," Florrie chortled.

"Can't put a price on safety," Daisy cut in, "and this lot 'ave rested 'ere undisturbed and out of 'arms way for long enough. So I reckon it's good enough for us."

"At any rate, we're better off 'ere than down that bloody underground," Ethel added. "Tried it for a couple of nights but I couldn't stand it."

"Anyway, you get sorted luv and we'll see you when the balloon goes up."

As if on cue, the faint strains of the siren filtered down to the underground chamber.

"Bill," yelled the irrepressible Florrie, "leave 'orf that job and go and fetch the old lady, and don't forget the budgie or she'll 'ave your guts for garters."

Within minutes a visitor arrived to make sure everything was

There is no evidence that this large Georgian church in the parish of Borough was ever home to a nursing clinic in the Second World War, or that it provided refuge for Londoners during bombardments.

satisfactory. "It's better than that," Cathy assured the vicar. "They've all been truly marvellous."

"They're a good crowd," he said fondly. "Artful, stubborn, not always truthful maybe, nor averse to getting into the odd scrap, but they've got hearts of gold. If anyone has the mentality to withstand this frightful Blitz it will be them. Anyway, make yourself at home and I'll go and greet our guests."

So the motley crowd assembled and got themselves organised. Children were settled to sleep, the urns hissed and steamed to churn out endless cups of tea but gradually the conversation became more muted. Some formed groups to play cards whilst others knitted, read or simply sat lost in thought. Occasionally someone would venture down to keep them informed on the scenes unfolding outside.

Very quickly Cathy established a pattern to the day which started with a clinic in the crypt for the 'walking wounded' – those fit and able enough to attend for routine procedures. Then it was out into the streets to visit the elderly housebound and those whose condition made it inadvisable to come out. The list was always varied ranging from surgical cases needing dressings and rehabilitation, people suffering from burns and scalds who were often young children, diabetics, asthmatics, stroke victims, chronic respiratory conditions and cardiac problems. Lunch would usually be a sandwich eaten 'on the hoof' although she was often invited by her patients to share whatever they had prepared. Supplies had to be restocked, case notes written up and her nursing bag replenished before she could turn her thoughts to attending to her personal needs. The vicar had kindly put the bathroom at the vicarage at her disposal and the laundering of her uniform was being undertaken at the hospital so she counted herself fortunate.

Each evening she joined the little group of regulars which usually swelled in number as the night progressed. She also learned to sleep quite well in her makeshift bedroom safe in the knowledge that someone would wake her if her services were needed.

A few nights later a particularly ferocious bombardment brought a steady flow of homeless, frightened people who kept arriving from out of the darkness to relate tales of an ever-worsening situation. Towards dawn Cathy saw a group of rescue workers trudging wearily down the stairs to stand in front of the table where Florrie was wielding the teapot. In answer to any questions they had little in the way of good news to offer.

She saw the vicar approach one of them and drawing him to one side requested to be furnished with details.

"The Wells' house had a direct hit and we haven't been able to locate any of them. Pat Green and her children were pulled from the rubble of theirs but are in hospital."

"What about Big Pete?"

"He's on night shift down at the docks so he doesn't know what's happened."

"Dear God, what a homecoming for him."

"That's if he makes it. The Pool of London surely can't withstand much more of this. There are fires everywhere and buildings simply collapsing into piles of rubble."

Brushing a hand across his eyes he merely managed to spread the grime further.

Looking up the vicar beckoned her to come over. "Cathy, I'd like you to meet David Murray who is the curate here when he isn't involved in numerous other tasks."

Covered in dust and cement powder from head to foot it was impossible to determine either his age or the colour of his hair. He gazed at her from red-rimmed eyes and giving a wry grin said, "I take it you must be the resident ministering angel. You'll have to excuse the mess I'm afraid but it's been quite a night."

"It's a silly question, but are you alright or can I do anything?"

Sighing deeply he replied, "Not unless you're a miracle worker and can stop this absolute carnage. Sorry, I'm being facetious. Actually, I think I am going to require your intervention before long because I reckon I've got more debris in my ears than there is lying in the streets. I certainly can't hear as well."

Smiling she replied, "It's probably nothing that a good old ear syringe won't cure. When you feel up to it just say and I'll take a look."

"Many thanks but I think my most pressing need is to get some sleep. Some extra pairs of hands have arrived from the suburbs so I'm going to take advantage of a break." Getting to his feet he took her hand in a firm grip saying, "It's nice to meet you, I just wish it was under different circumstances."

Turning back to the vicar he added as an afterthought: "Oh, by the way, most of the windows on the south side of the church have gone, which seems pretty trivial in the scheme of things I suppose."

Gathering up his tin helmet and a pair of heavy industrial gloves he took his leave while the vicar, with a heavy heart, moved off to begin his round of visiting the injured and bereaved and to organise a clean-up of the damage.

Only two days later Buckingham Palace was bombed and within hours the King and Queen visited the hard-hit East End on the first of their spontaneous tours of the ravaged city. This evoked great excitement amongst the crypt contingent.

"Do you think they'll come 'ere?" was the question on everyone's lips. Determined not to be caught out Florrie immediately set aside a tray with their 'best' china just in case.

On the same day His Majesty called for a National Day of Prayer. It was strongly felt that in circumstances such as those being faced it was time to bring the nation down on its knees and back to God.

The Superintendent decreed that the nurses should attend as a group. Filing into the rather dusty pews Cathy spotted many of her patients and Florrie had rounded up most of the crypt regulars. Some members of the emergency services also appeared taking time off from their arduous tasks. She let her gaze wander round the ornate interior and cast an eye towards the organ seat where an extremely competent exponent of the instrument was quietly playing.

The congregation rose as choir and clergy processed down the centre aisle and she looked with interest at the now neat figure of the curate. Aged about thirty or so he was slightly taller than she had thought, his hair turned out to be quite dark and his voice proved to be pleasing to the ear.

As the service drew to the finale, lusty voices joined to sing Isaac Watts' setting of Psalm 90 – 'O God our help in ages past, our hope for years to come'. Never was a plea more heartfelt and called for. With suitably patriotic fervour they responded to the music of the National Anthem before leaving the building to the rousing strains of Elgar's Pomp and Circumstance March. Would their cherished land of hope and glory be able to withstand the onslaught and remain free? Re-inspired and with morale high the residents of the Borough determined that it would.

Almost as if in defiance the very next day a German plane, with Buckingham Palace clearly in its sights, was rammed by an RAF pilot out of ammunition and Westminster Abbey sustained damage.

As the vicar remarked on one of his visits to the crypt, "The enemy are striking at the heart of all that we hold most sacred and dear."

Unfortunately one of the halls serving as an emergency treatment and rest centre also received a direct hit. The Superintendent arrived at the crypt shortly after tea to inform Cathy of the news.

"Is Nurse Parker alright?" she enquired anxiously.

"Thankfully she was out on her rounds at the time but it does mean that she is now without a home or base. Things seem to be working very well here Nurse Chapman so I want her to move in with you, at least for the time being." Cathy was delighted for she liked Connie Parker and would appreciate her company and the mutual support which they could give each other.

Her arrival shortly after coincided with frantic activity on the stairs as four men of assorted strength and know-how were struggling to manoeuvre an upright piano down some wooden planks and into the crypt. David, positioned at the top, caught sight of Cathy's bemused face and called out, "Don't blame me, this is Florrie's doing."

Never far from the action, her familiar voice informed the onlookers that it would now be possible to cheer everyone up with regular sing-songs. "Nothin' like it for raisin' the old spirits Nurse, you'll see."

"The thing is Florrie, which spirits are you hoping to raise," she retorted, "the long-term residents or just the newcomers?"

Letting out a belly laugh she shrieked, "You're a proper card you are, Nurse."

"Welcome to the madhouse, Connie. You can see I'm badly in need of some back-up."

Swiftly setting about reorganising space and arranging a rota for taking clinics, undertaking the visits and being on call at night they both felt well pleased with the way things had turned out.

The early part of the night was relatively peaceful except for the sounds emanating from the new piano which was being played with energy and enthusiasm rather than accuracy and skill.

The vicar was introducing himself to Connie when David approached Cathy saying, "Would this be a good moment to get to know each other properly or does this put you off?" he queried fingering the strip of white round his neck.

"Heavens no, quite the reverse," she laughed. "I was brought up surrounded by 'dog-collars' so I find it rather homely."

"I'm intrigued already, tell me more. Let's grab a mug of tea and see if we can find a slightly quieter spot," he said, above the rising strains of 'Don't sit under the apple tree'.

Tucking a couple of cushions under one arm he strode off, finally sinking to the floor with his back resting against a large, ornate tomb. Motioning for Cathy to join him they settled themselves comfortably. After taking a few sips of the scalding tea, he set it to one side, wrapped his arms round his knees and said, "Right, explain yourself."

Having listened to her he exhaled slowly. "Phew! Residentiary cathedral canons are a bit out of my league, I'm afraid."

"Dad's not a bit like that," she protested, "you'd like him."

After a pause he said, "Can you answer me a question?"

"I'll try."

"I'm intrigued by the buckle you're wearing. Does it signify something special, only Connie doesn't have one. Is it something like winning the gold medal for excellence?"

"Good gracious no, I'm not in that category. However, I suppose it is my most prized and treasured possession."

"May I ask why, or am I being too nosey?"

Gazing ahead, she remained silent as though trying to martial her thoughts and choose her words. Suddenly, almost unbidden, the whole story came tumbling out. It was as though a dam had been released and she withheld nothing. David had the good sense to remain completely silent until she had finished.

Looking at him aghast she apologised. "I'm so sorry. I don't know what came over me. I've never fully spoken about it to anyone before, let alone a stranger."

"How do you feel now that you have?" he enquired gently.

"I don't really know. A bit shocked because it isn't like me at all. In another sense I suppose there's a feeling of release."

"Well, it's an incredible story and thank you for sharing it with me."

"Thank you for being such a good listener."

"It simply goes with the territory." Looking up at the recumbent figure on the tomb, he went on: "Just remember, Josiah Grimwade, gentleman of this parish, you have been privy to the equivalent of the confessional, so no chatting to the others when we've gone."

At this Cathy shrieked with laughter. "You are an idiot."

"Thank you for the vote of confidence," he replied solemnly.

After another few sips of tea he ventured another question.

"You have managed to discover an incredible amount about your family history for someone in your position. I'm just curious whether you've ever been tempted to try to trace your natural father?"

"Not for a moment. I absolutely adore my dad and it would seem a disloyalty to him. After all, I didn't set out to unearth anything at all – it never even crossed my mind to. It just seemed to happen."

"Do you know anything about him other than that he was blinded in the last war and went to St. Dunstan's?"

She thought for a moment before saying, "I certainly can't recall ever being told his surname although I seem to remember my godparents referring to him as Marcus. I think he'd been a schoolmaster originally."

As David showed no sign of responding she said, "Why are you asking?"

"I suppose I'm secretly wondering how you would react if he ever were to emerge as your grandmother did."

"I hardly think that's likely, do you?"

David remained quiet, gazing into space. Looking at him questioningly, Cathy found herself saying: "I'm beginning to get some very funny vibes. Why don't you say something?"

"OK, I'll be honest with you. From the little you've said, there's a germ of a thought niggling in my mind that makes me think I may perhaps have some idea who your father is."

Cathy regarded him with near horror. "You can't possibly have," she gasped. "Don't be ridiculous."

Patting her knee with a reassuring hand he said: "Of course you're right. I have absolutely no proof but you've given me quite a lot of circumstantial evidence."

Positively aghast she said: "Do you mean it's somebody I know. Have I already met him?"

"Not to my knowledge, no."

"Aren't you going to tell me?" she pressed.

"Not until I've got proof, rather than just a hunch."

"So what are you going to do?" she asked diffidently.

"Absolutely nothing unless I have your say-so and you tell me that you want to pursue matters further. After all I could be wrong. Teasing as it may be for you can I suggest we leave the matter for the time being, and try not to lose any sleep over it? When all's said and done it's not the past that is important but the present and future. At the moment the present looks pretty grim and the future is an unknown quantity that we must wait to unfold, which is just what I suggest you do."

"You can't just leave me up in the air like this," Cathy protested.

The piano playing had ceased and people were getting ready to settle down for the night. True to form the wail of the siren sounded and David bade her a hasty goodnight as he went to collect his gear.

"Try to sleep tight, Cathy. Nothing has really changed and tomorrow's another day."

"There's a fat chance of nodding off peacefully now," she said accusingly. However, somewhat to her surprise she found that she actually slept amazingly well.

Chapter Four

Further Revelations

Following a shared Sunday lunch at the vicarage with Connie and David they each prepared to go their separate ways. Catching up with Cathy at the end of the path David said, "Have you got any pressing things that need doing or do you fancy a walk?"

"Bar emergencies, the rest of the day's my own for a change."

Strolling onto Southwark Bridge her companion threw wide his arms and gesturing around said enthusiastically, "I absolutely love this place. Do you know anything about its history?"

"Not really but I feel sure you're going to enlighten me," Cathy groaned.

Leaning with their arms on the parapet they stood silently contemplating the river and taking in the evidence of the recent destruction that had taken place. Pointing towards Bankside he said, "That was the disreputable theatre district where Shakespeare once lived and his plays were performed there at the Old Globe and Rose Theatres and the Hope Playhouse."

"I'm afraid I'm not a great fan of the Bard," she confessed.

"Shame on you! Perhaps Dickens is more your style. He lived in the Borough as a young teenager working in a blacking factory while his father was in the Marshalsea Debtors Prison. Every time I walk through the churchyard I see its surviving wall."

"Guilty again, I'm afraid I've never noticed."

"Actually, quite a few of the inmates who died whilst incarcerated are buried there. It's also the area in which *Little Dorrit* is set."

"I found that such a sad story," Cathy sighed.

"Maybe, but it was true to the time."

Warming to his subject, he continued with the literary thread saying, "If you look at the High Street and close your eyes, can you envisage the Tabard Inn featured in Chaucer's *Canterbury Tales* and imagine the pilgrims congregating there? That went up in flames in just the same way some of our heritage is falling victim to circumstances beyond our control. For instance, not far away is the Anchor Inn from where Samuel Pepys watched the Great Fire of London unfold."

"Goodness, you are a mine of information. I had no idea so much happened here."

"That's the trouble," David enthused. "If only folk stopped to think about the past occasionally, they would see that what is occurring now is little different. Although the firepower is more violent the end results are very similar, yet the city continues to survive. I have to tell myself that each morning when I look across the river in order to confirm that St. Paul's is still standing. It's the only way I can remain optimistic."

"Oh, I do that too. Just to get a glimpse of that huge dome on the skyline gives you heart somehow," Cathy exclaimed.

"Throughout history this great city has seen tragedies and triumphs. Take our church for instance. Various ecclesiastical buildings have stood there before but due to different factors they fell and were rebuilt. At the steps of the previous one Henry V was received with acclaim following his victory at Agincourt. That battle was the first where the standard bearing a red cross for St. George of England was raised."

"You really are passionate about history, aren't you?" his companion teased.

Turning towards here he replied with a chuckle, "I suppose I should apologise for boring you. I do tend to get carried away and forget that the subject isn't everyone's cup of tea."

"Please don't bother because I'm finding it absolutely fascinating when seen through your eyes," she smiled. "By comparison, the lessons at school were rather dull."

"Thanks," he grinned. "You see, I happen to think that the past can teach us so much. For instance, in spite of the good and the bad, London has endured through countless ages, and it will now. We've got to cling on to that."

Slowly retracing their steps, David paused to indicate an untidy plot of waste ground. "Do you know what that used to be?"

"Haven't the foggiest," Cathy laughed. "It looks a bit of a tip."

"Well, it's known as Cross Bones graveyard which for centuries was a piece of unconsecrated ground for the burial of 'single women', or prostitutes to you. This whole area was teeming with the dregs of humanity. It was the receptacle of all the vice and immorality of London and the abode of thieves and undesirables of every kind."

His companion gave a shudder. "If you're trying to cheer me up it's not a very pretty picture to paint."

"They weren't particularly pleasant times, any more than they are now albeit for very different reasons."

Cathy gazed at the derelict site. "It seems so unfair that there are all those tombs in our crypt, yet these poor souls are consigned to obscurity due to circumstances beyond their control. What with poverty and the diseases of their 'trade', I should imagine their lives were pretty short."

"If they're remembered," David added, "it's as the Winchester Geese."

"Whatever for?"

"Because they were actually licensed by the Bishop of Winchester to work within the Liberty of the Clink as this area was known. It was under his jurisdiction and he had a palace somewhere nearby. The City of London itself didn't allow brothels."

"Yet they weren't allowed a Christian burial," Cathy almost spat with disgust, "so much for the church."

David grinned ruefully. "I'm afraid the church has done some pretty questionable things in its time. Actually, this spot also became a cemetery for paupers, stillbirths and new-born infants and there are said to be literally thousands of unfortunates buried here, one on top of each other."

"What a sad little place," she sighed. "Nobody would ever guess what it was. It ought to be properly marked. I shall never be able to pass it again without remembering, and future generations should as well."

Casually taking her hand in his, the couple sauntered on in easy companionship. As they neared their destination, David ventured to ask whether she had any further thoughts regarding her natural father.

"I suppose I am curious," she admitted.

"What woman wouldn't be?" he laughed lightly.

Ignoring that remark, she continued. "I guess I'm just apprehensive about what I may discover and any future implications which may result."

Choosing his words carefully, he said, "Cathy, you have to remember that there will always be a chance that Marcus won't want any involvement."

The girl stopped in her tracks. "Gosh! I've been so wrapped up with myself that I have to confess I never gave that possibility a thought."

"Don't forget," David continued, "that there is also the likelihood that I might be completely mistaken, although I think it improbable."

Kicking aimlessly at some fallen leaves she muttered, "Oh, I just can't decide, so don't do anything for the time being."

For over a week their paths never seemed to cross. From the vicar she learned that David's days had been one long round of taking funerals and visiting the bereaved and the hospitalised. At some point each evening or night he had been out with the rescue teams.

"I don't know where he gets his energy and stamina from," the older man said enviously. "And to think the Forces turned him down on medical grounds. Well, their loss was our gain."

Cathy had often wondered why he had never enlisted for active service but never liked to ask. Now she had the answer.

Preparing to set off on their visits Connie said, "Don't forget it's Florrie's big sing-a-long tonight whatever you do."

The habitués of the crypt had been talking of nothing else having been promised something 'a bit better than usual.' In the event she was late having been delayed tending to a patient as he finally succumbed to pneumonia. Tired and dispirited, as she stood at the top of the flight of steps leading to her makeshift home, she was aware of raucous voices singing 'Roll out the barrel'. Without a break the pianist launched into 'Bless 'em all' and everyone joined in with gusto.

Making her way towards the cupboards she smiled ruefully in Connie's direction, dropped her black bag on the table, struggled out of her coat and removed her hat. Ethel who was manfully wielding the urns set a mug of tea before her as the assembled company broke into 'This is the army Mr. Jones.' Suddenly she was aware of David at her side with a chair.

"Take the weight off your feet and sit and relax and enjoy. They're in good form tonight."

"Who's that at the piano?" she asked.

"That's our organist who has done a superb job of tuning a rather worn-out instrument to obvious good effect."

Gazing across the intervening space, in the somewhat dim light Cathy observed the upright figure of a distinguished-looking man with grey hair. His hands flowed rhythmically across the keys and she noted that there appeared to be no sign of any written music.

The song came to an end and Florrie bustled forward importantly to invite everyone to give a very big hand to "our very own Vera Lynn." A neat-looking woman in her fifties took her place alongside the piano and the tempo changed. A pleasing voice broke into the haunting song 'A Nightingale sang in Berkeley Square' and the audience sat spell-bound only to break into rapturous applause as it came to an end.

"Encore, encore!" went up the cry until the poignant tune of 'The White Cliffs of Dover' echoed forth, to be followed in turn by 'We'll Meet Again.' They cheered enthusiastically until Florrie announced an interval for refreshments.

"Who's the vocalist?" said Cathy.

"That's Joan, his wife. Why don't I introduce you?"

So saying, he took her hand and drew her towards the piano. Putting a hand on the man's shoulder he said cheerfully, "Well done maestro, you've both got them eating out of your hands."

A head turned in response and she found herself looking at a sensitive face from which stared a pair of sightless eyes. Well that explained the lack of music was her immediate thought.

Suddenly she went rigid as she heard David say, "Marcus, I'd like you to meet our District Nurse, Cathy Chapman. Cathy, this is Marcus Appleton and his wife Joan."

As if on auto pilot, she stooped to place her hand into the one stretched out towards her. Before she could find any words Joan said, "Actually, we've heard quite a lot about you from our neighbours. The Slaters are always singing your praises."

With relief the shocked girl responded, "They're a lovely old couple but I do worry for them. Their mobility and general health is so poor that I wish they could be persuaded to move to a place of safety until this is all over."

"I'm afraid you'll have an uphill fight on your hands, Nurse," Marcus replied in a quietly cultured voice.

"Please, do call me Cathy. I'm not on duty now. Having said that, I really must go and sort out my things in readiness for tomorrow. Thank you for making this evening such an outstanding success. It means so much to them all."

So saying she set off in the direction of Josiah's tomb and flopped to the floor. David lowered himself beside her to be met with a face seething with anger.

"How dare you. How could you?" Cathy raged. "You promised me that you would do nothing without consulting me."

"Contrary to what you think I haven't broken my word," he assured her. "Marcus and Joan are completely unaware of who you are."

Only partially mollified she went on, "You do believe in shock tactics don't you?"

"Quite frankly it seemed the simplest thing to do. This way your curiosity has been satisfied, the final piece of the jigsaw is in place and if you want to walk away without further involvement Marcus will be none the wiser."

Continuing to mull things over in her mind she was forced to ask, "Are you absolutely sure that he is my father?"

"Well, I have to admit that every 't' isn't crossed nor every 'i' dotted but how many men by the name of Marcus, who were schoolmasters, fought as a Lieutenant in the First World War and were blinded in action, do you think there are in the country?"

Reluctantly she had to agree with him.

"Have I handled things so badly?" he begged. "I thought it might just help to complete the picture for you."

351

"I suppose not. I think I must be immune to shocks by now, but for goodness sake don't go producing any more skeletons from the closet. The only one left that I can think of is my ghastly grandfather who decamped to Australia."

He laughed with relief. "There's no chance, besides which he's probably dead."

All the while her glance kept returning to the figure at the piano. Getting to his feet David turned to pull her up. "Just sleep on the matter for a while, there's no rush. Things may seem clearer in a day or two."

Unfortunately they didn't, nor was there much time to think about it.

During the period since that first September raid London was to be subjected to relentless bombardment for fifty seven consecutive days and nights. However, between November and February the Luftwaffe switched tactics by also transferring their attention to Britain's industrial ports and cities. However, Coventry was among the first to undergo the terror much earlier on September 15. A fortnight later Cathy was given the luxury of a forty-eight-hour pass to visit home.

Scarcely had she arrived when the phone rang. Roger answered it only to call for her to take it. She was thrilled to recognise Jean's voice who was equally delighted at the unexpected contact.

"I didn't know how to get in touch with you quickly so I was hoping your Dad would be able to help," she said, the words falling over each other in her haste.

"Slow down Jean, where's the fire?"

"That's just the point. You will have heard what's been happening up here these past weeks. We've got several families of homeless from Coventry that we're trying to accommodate but places are drying up. Uncle John and I wondered whether you would be prepared to allow us to use your cottage?"

"Of course, you didn't need to ask. I'm only too glad to be able to help because I know just what it's like."

For a few minutes they exchanged guarded chitchat before Jean said, "There is one other thing. I was going to write but I'm not exactly certain where you are at the moment. I don't really know how to put this, but I think Jim and I have got something going between us and I'm not too sure how you feel about that?"

"You daft thing," Cathy hooted. "Jim isn't my property and if it works out I'll be thrilled for you. I'll even come and dance at your wedding."

With fond farewells they rang off and Cathy hastened to update her parents. Conversation was of little else but the war and they were both anxious to hear her first-hand accounts. They laughed as she amusingly described the goings on and the characters in the crypt, while knowing that there was nothing at all funny about the situation. They listened with horror as she recounted the scenes of devastation, the appalling injuries and loss of lives and homes.

"We've been so fortunate here by comparison but we are coping with a huge raft of evacuees, and local people and organisations are doing what they can to support the war effort."

"Do you know what I'm most looking forward to? An undisturbed night between sheets in my own bed," Cathy declared. "That's one of the awful things, just seeing how tired everyone looks. The constant lack of sleep, the patriotic pressure to keep working hard, the night-time fire-watching or warden duties, the black-out and the constant stress and worry of what is happening to loved ones elsewhere. Black mourning arm-bands are becoming commonplace and it's all bound to take its toll."

Whilst revelling in the unaccustomed peace and comfort of the Canonry, and a blessed normality to life which she hadn't experienced for months, one thing gnawed away at her. She found it completely impossible to raise the matter of Marcus or to seek their advice as how best to proceed. Returning to London laden with goodies she reported her failure to David.

Placing an arm round her shoulder, he said, "Cathy, no matter how much advice you seek or how many people you consult, you and only you, can possibly make a decision."

After pausing for a moment she sighed, "You're quite right, of course. Go ahead and we'll see what happens."

"Well done," he murmured and lightly brushed her forehead with his lips.

Within a matter of days David met her as she returned from work with the news that he had spoken to Marcus who confirmed what he had suspected.

"How on earth did he take it?" she asked worriedly.

"Stunned, of course but also delighted, you'll be pleased to hear."

"What about his wife?"

"Apparently Joan has always known of the existence of a child somewhere and it was she who suggested that I take you round to have tea with them on Sunday, if you can manage it."

In the event her day had been hectic, with no time to change out of uniform before the appointed hour. It was not without some trepidation that the pair of them arrived at the neat Victorian semi, with its token narrow strip of front garden, situated in a quiet street lined with the familiar plane trees, close by the cathedral. David gave her hand a reassuring squeeze as the door opened and they were welcomed by a smiling Joan.

"Cathy, come in, come in. You can't imagine how excited and thrilled we both are."

After taking their coats she led them into a comfortable sitting room which was dominated by a baby grand piano. Standing with one hand resting on it was Marcus gazing anxiously in their direction.

Reaching his side she gently placed a hand on his arm saying, "Thank you so much for agreeing to see me."

Quickly covering her hand with his he responded, as if with relief. "Cathy, any gratitude is mine, believe me. I humbly salute your courage."

"You don't know how much my legs are trembling," she laughed nervously, "so much for courage."

"Well, please sit down before you fall down," he responded in similar vein. "Make yourself comfortable."

Never did time pass with such ease, both learning as much as possible about the intervening years. Finally Marcus said, "A lot has happened for both of us since that Christmas Day when I met you for the one and only time and you sat on my lap playing with the cords of my dressing gown."

354

Taking the hand of his wife who was sitting beside him, he continued. "From the moment I encountered Joan at St. Dunstan's she will tell you that I've always had this worry in the back of my mind as to how life had treated you. If I were never to see you again, I can now at least die happy and at peace knowing all is well and that you haven't suffered too much as a result of the selfishness of your natural parents. In a few short hours you have brought me that, and I thank you."

Joan, seeing the tears beginning to slide down the girl's face, pressed a hanky into her hand and announced her intention of refreshing the teapot. With amazing perception Marcus said, "Don't upset yourself Cathy, and for goodness sake don't allow this to tear you apart emotionally. You clearly have two wonderful parents who mean the world to you. For that I shall be eternally grateful. The one thing I particularly don't want is for you to feel that you now have another emotional commitment. You owe me nothing my dear, so please don't feel that you have to maintain this contact."

"Would you rather I didn't?" she asked shakily.

"Never fear, Joan and I will always welcome you with open arms if, or when, you feel so inclined."

David became aware of Cathy fumbling at her waist and watched as she removed the belt from her uniform. Walking over to Marcus she placed it in his hand.

"Do you recognise this?"

As his fingers discovered and caressed the metal tracery he smiled. "It's Lucy's silver buckle. She was so proud of it and she would have been so proud of you Cathy, believe me."

Joan took it from him and looking at it said, "To think that it was actually this which brought you together again."

"If Cathy hadn't confided her story to me in the crypt that night when I asked about the buckle, then we certainly wouldn't be sitting here this afternoon," David replied.

"Well, at least it's one good thing to come out of this ghastly war," Marcus concluded.

Walking home, David asked, "So how do you feel now?"

"I don't really know. It's still all a bit surreal but I'm pleased I went."

"And am I forgiven for stirring all this up?"

"I suppose so but you're not off the hook yet. Somehow I've got to confront my parents with this latest development and the least you can do is come with me for moral support."

"Right, but just let's get tonight over first," he replied as the wailing of the siren sounded through the streets.

Taking to their heels they ran back to the crypt in time to throw themselves down the stairs as the first bombs fell. Grabbing his gear together David went out into the night just as the noise of a huge explosion shook the ground even in their dungeon. Within an hour he reappeared calling urgently for Cathy and Connie to grab their tin hats and nursing bags.

Outside, it was almost like daylight as flames from a nearby factory shot into the air and the sound of falling masonry added to the nightmare.

"There's a family trapped in an air-raid shelter in one of the back gardens in Tannery Street including a young baby," he shouted above the din, "and an ambulance hasn't reached us as yet so we may need some help."

For what seemed like an eternity the two girls stood by helplessly as the rescue squad worked away systematically removing debris. Occasionally a voice would ask for silence while the names of the victims were called out. Eventually, a baby's muffled crying reached their ears. The team redoubled their efforts and the cries became clearer.

"Nurse!" called one of the men. "You're smaller than the rest of us. Come and see if you can feel anything through this hole. We don't want to shift any more until we've got something certain to go on."

Dropping her bag, Cathy inched across the rubble and, kneeling uncomfortably, pushed as far as possible into the cavity. Groping round with her hand she came across something soft which she made out to be an arm. Discovering a wrist-watch, she felt in vain for a pulse. The crying came persistently and indignantly from under the arm. Retreating carefully she outlined the location and situation whilst the workers directed their efforts towards enlarging the spot.

"Try again, Nurse."

Taking off her heavy coat she lay flat on her stomach and, with both arms extended in front, squirmed partway into the space. It was sufficient. Her hands came into contact with the edge of what she thought to be a carrycot. Tentatively she gave a tug and it slid a fraction nearer until, straining with every sinew, she felt two kicking feet. By raising her hand she could just touch the rim of the hood and above that she determined the collapsed metal sheet of an Anderson shelter acting as a canopy. Nothing seemed to be falling as she gingerly coaxed the cot forward. She pulled once more and it came a little further as she retreated. Extricating herself from the aperture she lugged it the final foot until her arms were in a position to reach inside and, gripping firmly the bundle of blankets enveloping a writhing and highly indignant form, wrestled it into the open air. Dashing forward Connie scooped the infant up and with cheers from everyone made for the crypt. Cathy was assisted to her feet and David placed her coat round her shoulders.

"You've done fantastically. Go and get yourself cleaned up."

"What about the others?" she implored.

"We'll go on trying but, sadly, I think we know what the result will be. Now off you go."

Towards the end of October the Superintendent's suggestion that Cathy take some time off was music to her ears. That evening she approached David and asked if he would be prepared to come home with her.

"Sure," he agreed, "if you think it will help, although I can't be away for more than a night, I'm afraid."

Her parents were thrilled at the news but also a little intrigued. Was romance blossoming for their daughter amidst the ravages of war?

They welcomed David with their usual warmth but it wasn't until they were gathered round the table for the evening meal that the opportunity arose for real conversation. Talk inevitably centred round the war, especially the events in London.

"What happened to that poor baby?" Pam asked, after hearing the story of the dramatic rescue.

"The grandmother arrived and has taken him to live with the family, thank goodness." Cathy was fulsome in her praise of David's unflagging rescue work.

"The stupid thing about it all is the fact that when I tried to enlist for active service, I was rejected," said David. "Well, I think I've probably seen as much action, if not more, than many troops."

"Can I ask why they turned you down," said Cathy, "or would you rather not say?"

"It's no great mystery. I'm afraid I have suffered from asthma since childhood. Oh, then they threw in flat feet for good measure," he added as an afterthought. "Not very romantic I'm afraid."

Cathy was quick to interrupt. "David, you are working in the very worst environment for an asthmatic. Every day you're exposed to tons of debris and dust, not to mention the river mists, and we really don't have much in the way of medication to help, yet I would never have suspected for one moment."

"Ah, that's down to my devoted, country-loving mother who sets great store by nature's remedies. You medicos don't have all the answers," he teased Cathy.

"So, what's the secret?"

"A formula using herbs and spices combined with honey. Mum lives in a village in Kent and keeps me supplied with honey from her neighbour's hives which I take daily with ginger in milk and water. Sometimes I use garlic cloves boiled in milk and I chew fennel regularly and also eat a few figs, although those are becoming increasingly difficult to get hold of now. Anyhow, this little witch's brew seems to do the trick but you can imagine how arcane that lot sounded to an army recruitment officer!"

They all laughed especially when Cathy added: "Well, I think you've more than earned your spurs."

"Praise indeed. Thank you gracious lady," he murmured and offered a mock bow in her direction.

Never was there a more relaxed gathering yet, despite casting meaningful and questioning glances in Cathy's direction, she evinced no sign of broaching the reason for his presence. In the end, he decided to take the bull by the horns.

"I'm sure you are wondering why I am here," he said, addressing Roger and Pam. "The fact is that her ladyship here seemed to think she needed some moral support in a certain matter which she is finding difficult to convey to you. Seeing as how she is showing no indication of disclosing it, and as she thinks it's all my fault anyway, I rather sense that it's down to me to do the batting."

Noting the slightly alarmed look appearing on Pam and Roger's faces he hastened to reassure them. "Perhaps I didn't express that very well," he grinned. "Rest assured, your daughter isn't 'great with child' as the Good Book phrases it."

Ignoring Cathy's blushes, without further ado he launched into a straightforward account of the events that had brought them to this moment. When he had finished, Roger, whose gaze had frequently been directed towards his daughter, inhaled deeply before remarking: "I thought I would never be more surprised than I was when circumstances revealed your grandmother, but this is utterly incredible."

Pam simply looked at Cathy before quietly saying: "Are we such ogres, or so possessive, that you felt you couldn't come to us with this news?"

"No, no, no!" she groaned. "Don't you understand? I don't want another father and I didn't go out of my way to resurrect all this, neither did I want either of you to feel hurt because I'd followed it up."

"You are a silly goose," Roger grinned. "I find corners far too uncomfortable to go off and skulk in one! Besides, this is rather exciting, or are you intimating that you wish the discovery hadn't been made?"

"Can you tell us about him?" Pam asked gently.

"Actually, he's just the sort of person you would both like very much under ordinary circumstances," Cathy said. "He's tall and quite distinguished-looking despite his sightless eyes. He has a quiet, pleasant voice – in fact he's a very gentle man."

"As you will have gathered, he is a talented musician," David added, "and that is how he earns a living. Not only is he our organist but he tunes pianos and gives piano lessons both privately at his home but also to the boys at the Cathedral school."

"He's also something of a linguist," Cathy continued. "Apparently he was once a schoolmaster and taught languages and he now does a bit of translating with the help of his wife."

"I'm just so thrilled to hear that Marcus married," said Pam. "I never could bear the thought of his loneliness, poor man."

"You'd get on like a house on fire with Joan," her daughter volunteered. "She's a lovely person and very like you in some ways."

"Well I, for one, can't wait to meet them, if they would agree to it," Roger declared.

"I think you'll find they'd be only too pleased," David assured him. "When we get back, Cathy and I will see what we can fix up."

It was on a happy and contented note that the four of them retired to bed that night.

The following morning, much to David's delight, Roger offered to take him round the Cathedral.

"I'd better warn you that he's addicted to history," Cathy commented.

David smiled apologetically. "I'm afraid it comes from having a father who taught history at the local grammar school and I think some of it rubbed off on me. I don't think your daughter fully appreciates my ramblings."

"Don't forget to tell Dad about the Bishop of Winchester's geese," she called mischievously after their retreating figures.

"So then," Pam said when David had finally left to catch the train back to London, "is this going to be Mr Right?"

"Believe it or not, my match-making Mama, we are simply good friends – to use a hackneyed phrase."

Roger laughed before saying, with just a hint of seriousness: "Just remember, often the best relationships, the ones that last, are frequently those rooted in friendship. And one day, the person who was just a friend is suddenly the only person you can ever imagine yourself with."

"I also happen to think you may find that David is viewing things rather differently," her mother persisted shrewdly.

"Well, I've absolutely no intentions of embarking on a wartime romance," their daughter declared firmly, "so you can forget it. I've

360

seen enough of that with a couple of the nurses who both got swept off their feet by two dashing airmen who begged them to pledge undying love. I think that, in view of the constant dangers and uncertainty facing them, they desperately wanted something to hold onto. Anyway, it's all academic because they were both shot down and killed. Quite frankly, I don't want to risk the heartbreak of that kind of loving."

Roger paused for a moment before saying: "My dear, love is always risky. A simple car accident or fatal illness would have the same effect. It simply isn't possible to take out an insurance policy that will guarantee against such events."

Cathy returned to work with much to occupy her mind. Time to devote to her thoughts, however, was subsumed by the enthusiasm and excitement which the locals were directing towards the rapidly approaching Christmas season. Despite rationing and the still parlous general situation that prevailed there was a growing determination on their part to make this one something special.

"I'm blessed if we'll let that there Adolf put a mockers on it, even if we've got to spend it down here," Florrie announced one evening as they once more assembled for the nightly routine.

From that chance comment sprang the idea of holding a community party on the evening of Christmas Day with everyone making a contribution to the catering. The bit firmly between their teeth the contingent of regulars went into overdrive. As a result, when Pam and Roger paid a flying visit to London only days before, they were amazed to see the crypt garlanded with a motley assortment of paperchains, while a somewhat over-decorated Christmas tree stood proudly in front of Josiah's tomb. David had escorted them there following a highly successful and happy time spent with Marcus and Joan. Much to Cathy's disappointment the sheer volume of nursing visits had prevented her from being there so she was anxious to hear the outcome.

"We all got on so well that we have invited them to spend New Year with us at the Canonry," Roger informed her. "They really could do with a break, poor things."

"We're also going to suggest that Donald and Alice join us," Pam added. "It will be quite a reunion."

361

"If only you and David could make it, that would be the icing on the cake," her father urged.

"That's wonderful but I'm afraid I can't promise anything at the moment," Cathy replied.

Overhearing this, David assured him that, by hook, crook or on a broomstick they would be there on New Year's Eve.

"And how do you think you can guarantee that?" Cathy asked somewhat tartly.

"I'll simply go and work my charms on your Lady Superintendent and all will be accomplished," he replied confidently.

In the event his charms weren't necessary.

The only respite from the bombing actually occurred on Christmas Day. Cathy and Connie set out early in the hope of completing the bulk of their visits by lunchtime. Despite the events of the past year they found the spirit of their patients undaunted. Everyone was determined to celebrate the season, come what may.

The outbreak of the war had changed the lives of many women worldwide, with large numbers entering the workforce for the first time. Resolved to inject a sense of normality into life they doggedly set about catering for the needs of their families in an attempt to dispel any sense of gloom and foreboding.

Even larger numbers than usual made their way to church services and it wasn't until mid-afternoon that the two nurses could join up at the Vicarage to share a traditional turkey dinner, courtesy of Roger and Pam, who had presented them with the necessary ingredients on their recent visit.

It was with a pleasant feeling of satisfaction that they made their way to the crypt to prepare for the party. Marcus was already seated at the piano quietly playing the old familiar carols as the families gradually assembled in party mood. A few youngsters tore around the crypt in boisterous fashion weaving in and out between the tombs, whilst others excitedly showed off their treasured presents which had often been acquired with difficulty.

As the evening progressed so the merrymaking rose. They sang lustily and even managed some dancing. David, his arm firmly round

Cathy's waist, entered wholeheartedly into the Lambeth Walk and a straggly line of revellers lurched between the tombs to the strains of the Conga. A surprising selection of food never showed any sign of running out but as the time wore on some of the men settled down to play cards and the youngsters were persuaded into sleeping suits. Secretly, however, everyone was waiting for the all too familiar sound that had punctuated life for so long, but the night was clear and the skies devoid of any menacing threat.

" 'Appen 'itler's so chocker with food and drink 'e's forgotten the time," someone suggested.

"I hope the old bugger's got chronic indigestion and drunk 'imself into a blinder wot 'e never wakes up from," said Florrie with feeling.

Cathy, enjoying a smoochy dance number with David, found her head resting comfortably against the front of his jacket. The music stopped and, before she could break away, one hand lifted her chin and he kissed her gently but firmly on the lips.

"David... " she started to say only to be interrupted by the irrepressible Florrie.

"Blow me down, are you allowed to do that in your job, Reverend?"

"Merely demonstrating artificial respiration," he replied nonchalantly. "Anyway, you're only jealous." With that he strode across the floor, swept her in his arms and kissed her soundly to the delight of all present. For once that good lady was lost for words although her husband was heard to comment: "Blimey, I 'ope he knows what 'es taking on."

The festive season was no sooner over than the bombing of London resumed with the most devastating raid of the Blitz. On the evening of December 29th 1940 German aircraft attacked the City of London itself with incendiaries and high explosives causing a firestorm known as the Second Great Fire of London. The medieval Great Hall of the City's Guildhall was destroyed along with those of many old livery companies. St. Paul's Cathedral was only saved by the dedication and determined efforts of the firemen and the devotion of a band of volunteer firewatchers high up on the roof. An iconic photograph appeared on the front page of *The Daily Mail* on New Year's Eve showing St. Paul's, still standing tall and proud amidst a pall of thick black smoke.

Fire tenders from all the outlying areas rushed to the aid of the stricken capital. Fire floats on the Thames directed their powerful jets onto the inferno of blazing homes and warehouses, and men armed only with stirrup pumps fought desperately against almost impossible odds to bring things under control as buildings collapsed around them. Only once before in the history of the City had there been such a conflagration.

The heat was unbearable. Those huddled in the crypt could only watch as exhausted rescue workers appeared from time to time to snatch a hasty breather from the smoke and flames and gulp down a mug of tea. Cathy eyed David with concern as he sunk into a chair wheezing and coughing.

"You really must rest. If you persist in carrying on like this you'll have a full-blown asthma attack and then you'll be no use to anyone."

"It's the sulphurous smoke," he gasped. "I've never known anything like it."

"Let me make you up an inhalation then please, please go and lie down. You can use my bed if you like."

"Are you going to be in it?" he asked impishly.

"David, for goodness sake, keep your voice down," she hissed. "Nobody would think you're a clergyman."

Nonetheless, the incident was sufficient to render him temporarily unfit for action.

Coming face to face with the Nursing Superintendent next day he pleaded his case. "I've been offered the chance to recuperate in the country with Nurse Chapman's parents but I can hardly go and leave her here, can I?" he stated artlessly.

"Well, as she worked over Christmas perhaps two days' leave is due," she twinkled, "but no longer. After all, there is a war on, in case you'd forgotten."

It was a happy group of people gathered in the Canonry on New Year's Eve and Cathy rejoiced at the good fortune which had contrived to bring together all the people who meant the most to her. After joining in the Watchnight Service in the Cathedral the party made their way back across the precincts with hope in their hearts that the year ahead would indeed be better.

David took Cathy's hand in his and drew her aside into the shadow of the former Abbey ruins.

"Happy New Year, my love," he murmured as he took her firmly in his arms and kissed her, holding her as if he would never let her go.

Cathy initially submitted passively but after a second or two her hand crept up to caress the back of his neck and she found herself running a finger through his hair.

Finally releasing his grip he held her slightly away from him and looking into her eyes said: "I love you so very much, my darling. Will you agree to marry me?"

Looking at him aghast she tried in vain to find her voice. "David, don't be ridiculous. You can't possibly be serious."

"Come on my Cathy, don't play coy. I think I fell in love with you on the night of the silver buckle, as I shall always remember it. For heaven's sake, you must have had some inkling as to how I felt about you?"

"Not really, no," she replied. "I hadn't been thinking in those terms."

"Does that mean that you don't feel anything for me at all?" David asked quietly.

"Of course I do," she answered without hesitation. "I'm fond of you, admire and respect you, and I'm happy when I'm with you."

"Well, at least that's something." Looking at her seriously he said: "Respect and admiration you know, is simply love in plain clothes."

"Love is also commitment," she replied, "and I don't know that I want to make that at this point in time. Look at all the grief and pain that so many folk have gone through, and are still experiencing, as a result of losing those they hold most dear in this wretched war. I can't bear the thought of going through that."

"So, if I go out in an air-raid tonight and get killed, you won't feel anything simply because we aren't married?"

As she opened her mouth to protest, he went on. "To love, whether it is in war or peace, is to lay oneself open to the possibility of pain. My darling, what you are implying is that in order to avoid suffering one must not love, and that is sad."

"I simply don't want to put myself in the position of being vulnerable to hurt," Cathy cried in despair.

"Do you really want to go through life without experiencing all the joy and happiness which love can bring? There will always be a chance that ghastly things will occur in the best of times but love is being vulnerable to being hurt. You never lose by loving Cathy - you only lose by holding back."

Taking her by the shoulders and looking her squarely in the face David spoke earnestly.

"Cathy, do you think for one moment that Marcus ever regretted the love he experienced with Lucy despite everything that happened?"

"I suppose not."

"Although he lost not only the woman he loved so desperately but also the chance to bring up the child who would be a constant reminder of her, he also found himself in the position to find happiness again. You have seen how much he and Joan mean to one another, and thank God for that, but it doesn't mean that his feelings for Lucy ever completely left him. I don't know, and I can't begin to imagine, what thoughts went through his mind that afternoon when he was reunited with you, but he has survived everything that has come to him, which has made him the wonderful person that he is."

"David, you really have sprung this on me in your usual headlong fashion, but what is the rush? After all, you've only known me for a few months. Can't we just go on as we are for a bit longer?"

"I'm afraid that isn't an option, my dear."

"Why ever not?"

"Well, quite apart from the fact that underneath this 'dog-collar' there courses the blood of any normal man," he said with a grin, "there is another matter."

"Which is?"

"Just before Christmas, the Bishop asked to see me and suggested that it is time I move on to a living of my own."

In dismay Cathy croaked: "Move. Where to?"

"Still in the diocese of Southwark, but out in the suburbs of Surrey. His Lordship seems to think that I should gain some experience in quite a different type of parish."

"Have you agreed?"

"Well, it is promotion and I've been to visit the place and like what I see so… "

"When do you have to go?"

"Certainly by Easter."

Shaking her head as if in bewilderment Cathy sank down onto the remains of an ancient wall and a shiver ran through her body.

"Are you cold?" asked David in concern. Sitting down beside her he gently took her in his arms and she involuntarily snuggled closer.

"I think I'm suffering from shock," she responded.

"Perhaps the kiss-of-life would be appropriate," he suggested, expertly rising to the occasion.

Cathy found herself clinging to him with an intensity of feeling she didn't know she possessed. How could she possibly let him go? Without realising it he had insinuated himself into her life to become the very cornerstone of it.

"David, please don't leave me," she mumbled into his overcoat. "I can't bear the thought of Southwark without you there."

"Steady on my dear; you'll actually be telling me you love me next."

"That's just the trouble, I rather think I must do."

Holding her at arm's length he gazed unwaveringly into her eyes before saying chokily, "Do you really mean that Cathy?"

"Yes, you wretch. Your shock tactics have worked as usual."

"And you promise to marry me as soon as humanly possible?" he persisted.

"Yes. Yes. Yes," she replied in a daze.

Kissing her passionately he broke off to say: "You have made me the happiest man alive, Cathy."

"And you have swept me completely off my feet. My head is in an utter whirl."

Pulling her to her feet he enfolded her in his arms once more. "Well my darling, here we are on the threshold of a new year. We don't know what it will hold for any of us. We can only look forward with hope. Tonight you have given me the greatest incentive possible to do just that."

Pushing her away slightly he said anxiously: "I trust you're not going to regret this in the morning and have second thoughts."

"No chance. You're stuck with me for good so let's go and break the news to the family. In the interests of propriety, I suppose you ought to ask Dad for my hand in marriage first," she suggested.

"Don't worry on that score because I've already forewarned him of my intentions."

"You've what? Were you so sure of my response?"

"Far from it but I lived in hope."

"Whatever did he say?"

"He expressed himself as being unsurprised, ecstatically thrilled at the opportunity to get shot of you, and wished me all the best," he replied with relish, only just managing to duck in time to avoid a well-aimed blow from his 'intended'.

Grabbing her by the hand they headed for the Canonry in high spirits, anxious to share their news before everyone disappeared off to bed.

***

The following three months passed in a whirl as Cathy worked her notice whilst trying to collect together enough basic furnishings to help David move into what was to be their new home. Simultaneously, plans had to be made for the wedding which, from necessity, would have to be an austerity affair, much to her parents' disappointment.

Nevertheless, the occasion lacked nothing as friends past and present gathered in the Cathedral to watch a radiant bride walk down the aisle on Roger's arm whilst Marcus proudly played the organ and her godfather conducted the ceremony. The whole event provided a bright moment of relief and promise for the future in the midst of gloom and uncertainty.

The last major attack on London occurred on May 10th 1941 which was a spectacular fire bombing. The sky over London was scarlet from the light of the fires in which many important buildings were either damaged or destroyed, among them the British Museum, St. James's Palace, Lambeth Palace and Big Ben. After this the raids gradually became less frequent bringing a welcome respite to the beleaguered citizens. The cost had been high. Forty three thousand civilians lost their lives, eighty seven thousand were injured and a million homes had been destroyed.

The crypt had served its purpose well and the facility was closed, leaving the regular occupants to rest in peace once more. This time, however, neither Cathy nor David were there to witness any of it. Returning from an extremely brief honeymoon, spent at the cottage in Hollowdene, they cast an eye round their first home together.

"What a few months this has been," David said, as he drew Cathy to him in a loving embrace. Sighing contentedly she replied: "I could never, ever have imagined that it would end like this, but I wouldn't have it any other way."

Any thoughts Cathy might have harboured regarding her future nursing employment were very quickly terminated. Within a couple of months the early signs of a pregnancy were confirmed. As she continued to bloom so David was driven to remark teasingly that she looked just like a galleon in full sail. In the event his comment was fully justified.

On a late winter morning in 1942 she was admitted to the local hospital and, with commendable speed, a lusty baby girl made her appearance into the world followed, a short while later, by an uncomplaining but healthy little boy.

At that time diagnosing a twin pregnancy was extremely hit and miss. X-rays were discouraged unless absolutely essential. Detection of multiple births relied heavily on the skill of the doctor or midwife to abdominally palpate more than one foetus during ante-natal examination, or the chance discovery of two different heartbeats when using a foetal stethoscope.

The waiting father and grandparents greeted the news with a mixture of shock, relief and delight. Cathy's reaction was far more practical as she considered the problem of acquiring all the extra

369

equipment needed to meet this contingency at a time when little in the way of prams, cots and other nursery accoutrements was available in the shops. Clothes and material were only obtainable on coupons and many ingenious ways were found to get round the problem. 'Make-do-and-mend' became the household watchword. Car rugs were not subject to coupons and a skilled needlewoman could transform them into a coat or jacket. Similarly, from time to time, parachute silk would appear on market stalls and was snapped up to be dyed and transformed into underwear or blouses. If the war had taught folk anything it was resourcefulness. 'Waste not, want not' could be heard coming from the lips of someone who would otherwise never have given the object or meal in question a second thought.

David was quick to utilise his boyhood skill at growing vegetables and speedily transformed part of the vicarage garden into an allotment, in response to the call to 'Dig For Victory'. Cathy organised regular parish collections of silver paper, milk bottle tops, bottles, jamjars and newspapers, which all went towards the war effort. She became a familiar figure in the locality as she pushed the twins, in the hard-come-by second-hand pram, out and about on some mission or other.

"Are you missing your nursing, darling?" David asked her anxiously one evening after the usual marathon of getting the children bathed and settled – hopefully for the night.

"Not one little bit, you may be surprised to know," she replied without hesitation. "I am more than happy with my lot. Anyhow, there's no way I could fit it in with being a vicar's wife and mother of twins. The days are more than full as it is and I think I'm discovering the real me that had been hiding behind a uniform, if that makes sense."

"It's music to my ears," her husband said with relief, settling back in his armchair.

Not until the start of 1944 did the Germans attempt another mass attack on the City. Although it continued for three months it lacked the proportions and effectiveness of the Blitz but the suburban areas were equally affected.

On June 13, only days following the activity of D-Day, the siren sounded shortly after midnight. An unusual aircraft sound was heard

370

and looking up a plane could be seen caught in the searchlights and moving very fast. It made a loud noise a bit like a motorbike and a bright flame erupted from the tail end of it. After a few seconds the engine stopped and the searchlights lost contact as it glided downwards. There was a total silence for about ten seconds then a loud explosion as it landed. This was one of Hitler's vengeance weapons and the sound of an approaching 'Doodlebug' would freeze the blood and force the concentration. "Keep going, keep going," folk would plead under their breath. When the engine finally cut out and it dived to the ground, the silence was deafening as people coped with their fear, praying that this wouldn't be the one to get them. Five days later one landed on the Guards Chapel in Westminster as men were gathered for the morning service, killing 119 personnel, including the military band, and over one hundred and fifty were injured.

A Morrison table top shelter had been erected in the dining room of the vicarage and they started the habit of settling the fast-growing twins into sleeping bags at bedtime, joining them later. It was a bit cramped but afforded some sense of protection. David found himself once more involved in air-raid warden duties and local rescue work.

Nevertheless, the news was not all gloom. Along with all members of the medical professions, Cathy rejoiced at the revelation that 'a wonder drug' had been found that would successfully treat bacterial infections. Although Alexander Fleming had originally made the discovery in 1928, it wasn't until 1944 that it was capable of being produced in quantity. Named Penicillin, it marked the start of the antibiotic era.

However, revelation of the ground-breaking invention was momentarily eclipsed.

Just as people thought things couldn't get any worse the next joker in the Führer's arsenal fell on Chiswick at the end of the first week in September. The V2 rocket was deadly and frightful because it would arrive without any warning and there was absolutely no defence against it. Completely out of the blue there came a massive, massive explosion, a blue flash and a rumbling sound, resulting in a huge crater as it detonated just above ground level thus maximising the blast effect.

The impact on morale was devastating so when, even despite this latest show of force, it was felt to be safe enough to replace the total blackout with a partial dim-out, the public mood lifted. Coupled with the better news from the Continent, people dared to hope that the end was in sight.

Enjoying an afternoon making cardboard eggs for the twins, in readiness for Easter, the little family was interrupted by the ringing of the telephone. David returned faced with the heart-rending task of breaking the news of the deaths of both Marcus and Joan as the result of a rocket falling on a street of shops, one of the last such attacks of the war. Catherine's body became wracked with uncontrollable sobs. She could not believe that the loss of this man, who had so lately appeared in her life, would have such an effect.

Within hours her parents arrived to support her and they relived the happy occasions in which they had all shared as a true family, and the wonderful memories that would remain of a loving couple and a remarkable man. Fingering a snapshot taken at the baptism of the twins, which showed Cathy leaning over the back of a sofa as Marcus held the two babies, she wiped away a tear and angrily commented on the complete injustice of it all.

"Hadn't he suffered enough as a result of war?" she railed. "He only narrowly survived the last one, although not unscathed, and now, just as it seems that the end could be in sight he has become a victim again. It's all so unfair."

David held her close and voiced what they were all feeling. "Thank God that at least it was instantaneous and they were taken together. Marcus could never have survived the loss of Joan."

It was a subdued group who returned to Southwark that April to clear the couple's house, make arrangements for its sale and to dispose of the contents. The only thing Cathy was determined to claim was Marcus's piano.

"You don't play," David remarked.

"I know, but it is a beautiful piece of furniture and the one thing that will always remind me of him," she replied firmly.

The funeral service was held in the war-ravaged church conducted by the vicar, who appeared to have aged even further, and assisted by Donald. In the once familiar surroundings they paid their last respects accompanied by some old familiar faces from those unforgettable days of the Blitz. Cathy's eyes were inevitably drawn to the organ seat, where the organist from the cathedral was now playing, and reflected how wrong it all seemed. That was Marcus's place and always would be in her eyes.

Making their various ways home the couple found themselves on Waterloo Station with time to spare. Tucked away in a corner above the concourse was a small cinema dedicated to showing Pathé newsreels. It was by far the best way to reliably keep abreast of events, both nationally and worldwide, so they decided to kill time in this fashion. Settling down into the seats David draped an arm lightly across his wife's shoulders whilst the images flashed onto the screen.

Suddenly, the next clip appeared starkly headed in capital letters 'BELSEN'. The audience sat in stunned silence as skeletal figures moved inside the infamous concentration camp like wraiths amidst stockpiles of emaciated dead bodies. Fifty thousand sick and starving people waited for treatment while a bulldozer pushed their less fortunate companions into trenches for mass burial. The shock and enormity of the outrage took people's breath away. This couldn't possibly be happening – it was evil beyond comprehension. They stumbled out into the daylight in total silence and disbelief. No-one spoke a word.

Only weeks later on May 8th 1945, Winston Churchill announced Victory in Europe and declared it a public holiday. The streets were packed with thousands of civilians and service personnel. Every face was smiling, some with tears of sheer joy and relief, overlaid with the unrestrained sounds of laughing and singing. Spontaneous street parties sprang up everywhere; church bells were ringing, musicians played, people got drunk, kissed and danced with anyone who took their fancy; some climbed lamp posts or paddled in street fountains. No traffic moved. It was as if the world had gone mad with happiness and jubilation. It was actually OVER.

The celebrations knew no bounds but just went on and on. Hundreds of thousands flocked to the churches to pray and give thanks to God for deliverance. But there were many who stayed at home and cried quietly, with their memories, their photographs, or their War Office telegram. They had little to celebrate, it was a hollow victory.

After conducting the local civic service of thanksgiving to mark the end of the hostilities, David and Cathy sank back on the sofa. With the twins peacefully asleep in their beds, the couple reflected on the events of the past five years and the impact made on them personally. It had revealed reserves of strength and endurance and uncovered an ability to cope with hardship, austerity and deprivation, injuries, tragedies, death and bereavement beyond anything they could have envisaged. They had also witnessed an amazing stoicism and selflessness among the ordinary people and a comradeship and remarkable outpouring of community spirit.

They had experienced much, suffered much, loved much and lost much but, above all, it had resulted in the flowering of their marriage and the creation of new life. Now they were on the threshold of a new tomorrow and they offered up a prayer of thanks and hope for the future.

Part Five
The Demise of the Buckle

Chapter One

An Age of Change

❦❦ Cathy, Have you read this?" David called to her. "It's actually here in black and white."

Coming into the kitchen she went to stand beside him and stared at the headlines in the newspaper: '*A Momentous Day. July 5th 1948. The National Health Service is born.*'

"I can't fully take it in, or see how on earth it can possibly work," she commented.

"It's certainly a brave undertaking and one that will make a considerable difference for young and old alike in the community. I guess we'll just have to wait and see whether it can possibly deliver all that is proposed," David replied.

"Just imagine not having to pay for a surgery visit or doctor's house call, and all prescription medicines only costing a shilling," Cathy reflected. "It sounds almost too good to be true."

Aneurin Bevan's hugely ambitious plan to bring good health care to all, free at the point of delivery, had been a national talking point for some time. Financed entirely from taxation, it meant that people paid for it according to their means, each person contributing something, with everyone entitled to receive the same treatment.

"It will be interesting to see whether it actually operates in practice," Cathy mused.

Putting some washed-up crockery away in a cupboard, she turned back and paused before saying, "Would this be a good moment to float a proposition to you?"

"Now what wicked scheme are you plotting?" he smiled at her indulgently.

Sinking onto a chair Cathy, who had turned 30 the previous year, started to explain something which she had been mulling over in her mind for the past week. Very aware of her husband perched casually on the corner of the table, she took a deep breath and launched forth.

"I know I've always maintained that I don't miss nursing, and that has been absolutely true. However, since the twins started school last year I do seem to find myself with time on my hands. I reckon that I'm a fairly well-organised person."

"Indeed you are, my love," her spouse interrupted.

Casting a somewhat reproachful look at him, she continued. "If I'm really honest, there's only so much satisfaction I can gain from cooking, housework and parish life, and I have absolutely no intention of becoming your unpaid curate," she said impishly.

Eying her carefully, he paused for a moment before asking: "What are you suggesting?"

"I know I can't return to hospital or district duties because everything on offer is virtually a full-time commitment. However, I chanced to see an advert in last month's Diocesan Magazine for someone to work, purely in a voluntary capacity, assisting the social case worker in the Moral Welfare Office. It's only part-time - two days a week - so it should be doable. I know it isn't a paid post, but that isn't a great issue for us. Or is it?" she asked hesitantly.

"Not at the moment," David reflected. "However, your financial legacy is beginning to dwindle a bit and certainly won't last forever."

"I do know that," she replied, irritated. "But, as I'm not in a position to earn anything at the moment, at least I could still make use of my caring skills and contribute something worthwhile."

"What exactly does the role entail?" he queried.

"From the very limited information given, I think it involves working with unmarried mothers."

"It's all very laudable, and something which our parish supports financially, so if that's what you want, give it a try and see what happens," he said with a rueful grin. "I did wonder how long it would be before you were itching to take up the cudgels again."

"Well, mercifully, Lucy didn't need recourse to such a service when she found herself pregnant with me all those years ago. If she had, I imagine the outcome for me could well have been very different. Although things turned out so superbly as far as I was concerned, I'm sure that isn't the case for many illegitimate children. The recent war has also thrown up its casualties in that area, not least the problems resulting from misjudged relationships, especially those resulting from the influx of black American troops. Those children are particularly hard to place for adoption, so part of me feels that I would be repaying, in some small measure, the good fortune which I enjoyed. I know I'm not expressing this very well," she sighed.

"Actually, your reasoning does you credit, darling. By all means follow it up, find out a bit more and see what happens," he encouraged. "I'm a firm believer that if a thing is meant to be, then it will be."

On a rather grey day, Cathy alighted from the bus which had taken her to the largish town which housed the Moral Welfare Office situated in the centre of the diocese. The address proved to be an anonymous semi-detached, Edwardian house in an equally unexceptional road, the front door of which was discretely situated at the side of the building. An unobtrusive plate, attached to the adjacent brickwork, was the only means of assuring the caller that they had come to the right place.

Not knowing quite what to expect, she rang the bell and found herself greeted warmly by a smartly dressed woman of about forty five years, who ushered her into a small, modestly furnished sitting room.

"My name is Dorothy Ashby and I'm the senior social worker for the diocese," she introduced herself. "Sit down and make yourself comfortable while I rustle up some coffee, or would you prefer tea?"

"No, coffee's fine, thank you," Cathy assured her.

Once settled, her interviewer said. "We were particularly drawn to your application because of your previous nursing background and experience. You are clearly used to dealing with a wide range of people, in varied situations and you will have an added awareness. Furthermore, and most importantly, you will understand the need for strict confidentiality, which is vital in this particular role. Also, as a mother yourself, I imagine you must feel some empathy with those who come to us for help," she stated.

Cathy nodded her head in agreement.

"How much do you know about our organisation and the work we do?" Dorothy questioned.

"Well, only what I've read in material provided by the diocese to the parishes, and I attended a talk given by one of your team who addressed our Young Wives group," she replied.

"That's a good opening but, at the risk of repeating what you may already be aware of, I propose to start at the beginning. Do feel free to interpose with any queries you may have."

"Thank you," Cathy responded gratefully.

"The Moral Welfare Workers Association is a professional body for social workers which was established in 1938, primarily to deal with the unfortunate outcomes of extra marital sexual relationships and prostitution. Of all the groups of lone mothers, the unmarried have fared worst historically and sometimes found themselves ending up in the workhouse or asylums."

Cathy gave a shudder. "It's so inhumane that it doesn't bear thinking about," she commented.

Dorothy smiled in agreement. "Fortunately, things are slightly more enlightened now. In the postwar period, changing ideas about sexual morality have begun to erode the rigid boundary erected between the married and unmarried. However, there has recently been a notable increase in the number of babies coming up for adoption."

"And is that solely what you are involved with?" Cathy asked.

"Not entirely. Moral Welfare Social Workers and Case Workers are employed across the country, in the main by voluntary agencies. The Church of England is one such body and probably the largest. Mainly due to past events, one of its principal contributions to social welfare is the provision of a service which operates mainly for the benefit of unmarried mothers and their children. It is a useful piece of work and an area which the local authorities haven't yet shown themselves eager to occupy themselves with. After the war they set about arranging the provision of residential care homes and subsequent adoptions, plus the management of the problems associated with irregular sex relationships."

"I suppose you not only have to address the situation with the girl herself but the wider family too, which must have considerable implications?" Cathy probed.

"Absolutely right. The unmarried mother often feels that she is being judged, and perhaps condemned, by her family, local community and by society in general. It is not unusual for a parent to reject her, and this is especially true where the fathers are concerned, who simply want to get her away from the area and save the family any disgrace. If the baby is the outcome of a liaison with a married man that presents another difficulty because, where possible, we do try to get some financial support from the putative father, which is seldom easy."

"And that's when they come knocking on your door," Cathy reflected.

"Yes. Sometimes a girl will appear on her own but more often than not she will be brought by her mother on the first visit. After this she can then find herself alone. Occasionally she is referred by her doctor or by a parish priest."

"So, where exactly would a voluntary assistant fit into this scenario?" Cathy asked.

Smiling broadly, Dorothy said, "My word, you are eager."

"It's just that I can't see what use an untrained person could possibly be," she replied.

"The problem is that, due to an increased demand for our services, we are becoming rather swamped. In the first instant each new applicant is seen by a social case worker. There is one based in each of our offices, and she remains with the girl from beginning to end. Each one is answerable to me and I am their recourse when required. However, they are the first point of contact and the initial interview is conducted by them. Of necessity it is detailed and time-consuming. Once accepted, the girls return here for regular, ongoing appraisal and support."

"So you don't actually get to meet the clients yourself?" Cathy probed.

"Not unless something occurs that requires my intervention," she replied. "Each case worker does submit a monthly report to me, so I'm very au fait with what is going on," she smiled.

"Now, let's get to the point of this meeting," Dorothy said. "In order to try to ease the pressure, we think the right volunteer worker could be invaluable here in the office. It is envisaged that, when a newcomer arrives, this person would be the 'meeter and greeter', fill in all the initial details on the case notes, including taking a case history. She would then introduce her to the case worker, who will conduct a formal interview. If the girl attends with someone else, usually her mother, the case worker will first see them both together. However, it is also important that she has the chance to spend time with the girl on her own, who may wish to voice ideas that are often very different to those in the minds of her parents. At this point the mother would be asked to sit outside - usually reluctantly I might add. This is when the assistant comes in again and where people skills are so vital. Over a cup of tea the volunteer can present a less threatening face and, by simply chatting sympathetically, may well elicit information regarding the general background, relationships and attitudes currently pertaining at home. All of which could prove very useful to the case worker."

"A sort of friend in the back room," Cathy grinned.

"Exactly," Dorothy replied. "It is also unhelpful, when interviewing someone, to be constantly interrupted by the telephone ringing, so answering calls would also be part of the role. Similarly, many of the check-up visits could possibly be dealt with by an assistant."

"It sounds rather like the outpatients department," Cathy opined.

"A very good analogy, only referral on to the consultant wouldn't always be necessary if things were progressing without problem. At each visit the girls also bring with them the record card of their ante-natal clinic details, which the volunteer would be expected to enter into the case notes. This does ensure that they are compliant in their attendance. Defaulters also have to be chased up which is something else the assistant could usefully do. When the time comes for the mother to be admitted to one of our residential homes prior to delivery, all the requisite information accompanies her."

"Can you explain a little about these homes?" Cathy requested.

"We have two in this diocese," Dorothy explained. "Each can take twenty five mothers and their babies. They're not isolated but well away from urban areas, which may seem rather hard. The regime is organised, but is neither draconian nor harsh, as is the general perception and sometimes the case I'm afraid. However, most girls come from largish towns or cities and there is always the temptation to escape from what they perceive to be, quite wrongly I might add, a form of punishment. We don't get many 'fliers' but inevitably there will be the odd one who can't cope with the discipline, or being away from their normal environment. Fortunately they tend to make their way back here, simply because, at the end of the day, they have nowhere else to go."

"It is difficult enough having to contend with the emotions of any normal pregnancy, without all that extra baggage," Cathy sighed.

"Unless you are particularly hard and brazen, as some of them can be, it is a testing time when decisions have to be made. Although a girl may have firmly stated her intention of placing the baby for adoption, will she actually decide to do so when the moment comes? If not, we have to do some pretty nifty footwork in order to find another solution, which is often neither easy, desirable nor possible."

"Presumably that is why they have to spend six weeks before and after the birth at the home?"

"I know there are those who think it cruel that these girls have to care for their babies during that time. However, it is necessary in order to ensure that they realise precisely what they are doing and what giving them up will actually mean. It is an attempt to avoid, at all costs, the trauma occasioned to adoptive parents when a mother demands to take the baby back. Such an event is extremely difficult and time-consuming for the case worker. Sadly, despite the best-laid plans, nothing is ever certain until the girl actually signs on the dotted line," Dorothy sighed.

"When the time comes for their admission to a home, how is that managed?" Cathy asked.

"Until now they have always been taken and fetched by their case worker who will also visit at least twice during their period in residence, or if requested by the matron. Obviously this is also extremely time-consuming and it is hoped that the new assistant will be able to undertake some of this aspect. I suppose I should have enquired earlier, but do you drive?" said Dorothy.

"Actually, I do," Cathy responded eagerly. "My husband taught me immediately after the war and I passed my test in 1947."

"Well, that's something else in your favour." Dorothy eyed her steadily. "I can tell you now that we haven't exactly been inundated with suitable applicants for this post, and the few I have already interviewed weren't particularly inspiring. To be honest, most were simply good, well-meaning, Christian souls, but more than that is required as I hope I have managed to impart."

"Indeed you have," Cathy replied with feeling. "Though, one thing you haven't gone into is the process of adoption."

Dorothy paused for a moment before saying, "Of course that is a very rigorous and complex business, and rightly so. However, that aspect of the work isn't something which would come within the remit of the volunteer," she hastened to add.

Noticing Cathy's slightly dejected, non-verbal, response she felt drawn to ask whether this news disappointed her.

She thought for a moment before saying, "Not really. You see, the thing is that I myself was adopted and I suppose I was just curious to see how it all comes together."

"My dear, what an amazing coincidence," Dorothy was drawn to comment.

"It was actually one of my reasons for applying in the first place. I was so incredibly fortunate in my adoptive parents and I just wanted to give something back."

Relaxing in her chair, the Senior Social Worker emitted a sigh of satisfaction.

"Well Cathy, as this appointment is to be left to my discretion, I think I can truthfully say that, if you are still interested, we will be happy to have you on board," Dorothy declared.

"Oh, that's amazing," Cathy exclaimed with delight. "I wasn't expecting an immediate decision but I truly am keen to give it a try. Thank you so much."

"Naturally, all this is subject to two satisfactory references, which I don't envisage will be a problem. Also, there is a three-month trial period on both sides. Although it is a voluntary post, any expenses incurred on behalf of the department will be reimbursed."

"When do I start?"

"Ideally, as soon as possible, although I am aware that your children's school holidays are coming up which may present a problem."

"Not at all. They spend time with each of their grandparents at some stage and we are fortunate to have a holiday cottage, which affords the opportunity to be flexible regarding our breaks."

"In that case, all that remains is for me to confirm this in writing and I will contact you to arrange a date for you to commence. Thank you for coming and for your undoubted enthusiasm," Dorothy said in parting.

Cathy flew homeward on wings and burst into the vicarage, eager to inform her amused husband that at last she felt useful again!

Feeling that it called for some sort of celebration, David's suggestion that they seize the opportunity to have a long weekend away at Hollowdene was met with ecstatic approval.

Jim and Jean greeted their arrival with their customary delight. The two families had maintained a strong friendship and their respective offspring enjoyed the visits no less than their parents. Once unloaded and settled into the cottage, they sat in the garden sharing drinks in the still hot evening sun.

Cathy couldn't wait to acquaint Jean with the details of her latest venture.

"How exciting," her friend commented. "However, I've got news for you too, and you'll never guess what."

"You're expecting another baby," David hazarded.

"Please, do me a favour," Jim groaned. "The two boys we've got are quite enough. thank you."

Jean interrupted impatiently saying, "Nothing like that. You see, I've actually landed a job as well."

"I thought the work of a farmer's wife was never done and kept you occupied from dawn to dusk," David joked.

"It's not exactly people centered, or cerebrally demanding," Jean responded tartly. "It certainly doesn't make any use of my hard-earned skills."

"Just what I felt," Cathy interposed.

"Apparently, my dear wife has had enough of cows, muck, tractors and all things agricultural, especially a husband with straw behind the ears," Jim said gloomily.

"Oh, don't be so ridiculous," his spouse protested.

David interrupted, "Jim, you have my sympathy. I know the feeling only too well."

"Do be quiet the pair of you," Cathy demanded.

"So what are you going to be doing?" she asked impatiently.

"Actually, I'm going to be the relief Night Sister at Shepherdstone Convalescent Home," her friend announced triumphantly.

"Goodness, how ever did you wangle that?" Cathy questioned.

'Well, virtually nothing has changed since our day. Night duty still consists of working twenty four nights on the trot before getting the princely reward of six nights off."

"Don't remind me," Cathy groaned. "I felt like a zombie by the eighteenth night."

Ignoring the interruption, Jean continued. "You will remember that a Sister used to be sent out from the Royal to provide cover for old Sister Saunders' nights off, and they were never the same people two months running. Well, she has since retired and the decision was made to appoint a regular part-time relief, purely to undertake those six nights. I applied and, chiefly due to my proximity to the home I suspect, I've got the post."

"You jammy devil," Cathy exploded.

"I know. Working just one week a month suits me fine. Just imagine it," she enthused.

"I don't know what you think Jim, but since the war ended these women have got ideas above their station," David said wickedly.

"Tell me something," Jim responded. "Just because they held down an assortment of jobs during the war, they think they're indispensable. Simple domesticity is far too mundane for them now."

Cowering under the physical assault from both women, who had been joined with glee by four excited children, the two men finally sank to the ground in surrender.

The first half of the twentieth century saw the development of technologies that created labour-saving devices, such as electric stoves, refrigerators, steam irons, vacuum cleaners, washing machines, tumble driers and dishwashers. Initially, many were beyond the reach of the average family. By the second half, advances in electronics yielded microwave ovens, slow cookers, and appliances that could be set on a timer and programmed and these goods gradually became more financially viable. This considerably reduced the domestic workload even further. They operated without the presence of the human launderer, cook or housewife, thereby allowing women greater freedom and choice than ever before, thus permitting them to pursue their own course in life.

Cathy took to her role at the Moral Welfare Office as to the manor born. She formed an immediate rapport with Claire Wright, the case worker, and developed a friendship which soon extended socially.

As the evidence of her capabilities and skill at handling difficult situations surfaced, so she began to take on more complex tasks, relishing the challenge. By the end of the three-month trial period she had become a valued and much appreciated member of the team.

Arriving at the office one morning she found herself greeted by a plainly irritated Claire.

"Whatever's the matter?" she asked.

"Just sit down and let's have a cup of coffee," her colleague replied. "I am so angry that I think I may well need a brandy as well."

Furnished with the appropriate refreshment, Claire proceeded to explain her outrage.

"You'd think that, by now, I should be immune to the antics of some of our clients but this one really does take the biscuit."

Producing a case file, which was considerably bulkier than normal, she tossed it into Cathy's lap. Sensing her bewilderment, Claire continued. "You do all you can to help these girls and this is how they repay you," she said crossly.

"In approximately one hour's time, you are going to have the doubtful pleasure of meeting another new applicant for help, only this one happens to be far from new. In fact her appearance will be for the third time of asking, no less."

"Surely, there must be a mistake?" was Cathy's immediate response.

"Oh, there's no mistake, I assure you," Claire responded bitterly. "I only wish there were." Sinking back into her chair she set about familiarising her colleague with the facts.

"Shortly, you will make the acquaintance of Shirley Long, or 'Our Shirl', as her mother calls her, who will undoubtedly be accompanying her wayward daughter. What I would like is for you to read these notes first and then sit in on the interview. I will explain to them that you are there simply to record the details. If nothing else, your presence should stop me from strangling her," she grimaced.

When the doorbell rang, Cathy answered it and found herself face to face with a tallish, blowsy-looking girl of nineteen and a dowdily dressed, older woman who didn't exactly give the impression of being the brightest star in the firmament.

"Come in," she said with her customary warm smile. "Mrs. Wright is expecting you, so I'll take you straight through."

Claire rose from behind her desk and extended a hand to mother and daughter in turn.

"Well," she said, "we meet yet again. Although I have to confess that I had hoped the previous encounter would be the last."

Dumping a well-worn shopping bag on the floor, the older woman shuffled onto a chair saying: "So did I Mrs. Wright, so did I."

Shirley merely grinned and, taking a seat, made an effort to tug an exceptionally short, cheap-looking, black taffeta skirt somewhere approaching the direction of her knees.

"When is this baby due?" Claire queried.

A clearly relaxed and unconcerned Shirley informed her that it wasn't for another six months.

"You see, we came early in the hope that you'd be able to do something about it," the mother wailed appealingly.

Eying her reproachfully, Claire replied, "Now, you know very well, that particular avenue is quite out of the question."

"But we can't keep going on like this, can we, Mrs. Wright?" the woman protested, as though the whole business was somehow the fault of the social worker.

Claire turned towards the plainly unrepentant Shirley, who was assiduously picking at her teeth with long, bright scarlet finger nails.

"At our very last session, I seem to recall advising you that, if you had plans to continue to indulge in sexual activity, you must ensure that some kind of protection is used."

Without looking up, the girl truculently informed her, "There's only them damned rubbers, and my bloke won't use them 'cos he says it's like doing the job with socks on!"

Cathy stared at her with some degree of fascination.

"That's as may be, but he's not the one who has got to sort this sorry mess out, is he?"

"Suppose not," Shirley mumbled.

"Which brings me to my next question. Your last two babies were the result of liaisons with black American airmen," she reminded the girl. "Dare I ask what colour this one is going to be?"

Bringing her head up with a jerk the girl reacted immediately, saying quite unashamedly, "Why, black of course."

Putting down the pencil she had been fiddling with, Claire looked her square in the face before saying: "As I told you last time, these babies are incredibly hard to place for adoption. In fact, it may interest you to know that the two you have already produced are still in a County Council Home. I might also add that this is at no small expense to taxpayers like myself and Mrs. Murray here. If you are going to persist in this activity, may I suggest that you act with some responsibility and at least confine your attentions to your own countrymen? What is so special about the others, for goodness sake?"

In a flash the miscreant informed her. "Once you've had it with a black, you wouldn't want no others!"

Completely stunned by Shirley's honesty and sheer brazenness, Cathy cast a glance at her friend, who was plainly struggling to keep a tight rein on her feelings.

The situation was further compounded when the girl's patently inadequate mother, leaned forward in her chair and said: "The trouble is, Mrs. Wright, that 'our Shirl' does enjoy it so!"

Following their departure, Claire and Cathy sat in the little lounge scarcely knowing whether to laugh or weep.

"For heaven's sake, I like dark chocolate, but it is possible to have too much of a good thing," the frustrated social worker was driven to say.

Meeting with Mrs. Ashby two days later, three heads were put together in an earnest, but likely insurmountable, attempt to find a solution for Shirley's ongoing problem.

"The trouble is that we don't have anything, other than sheaths, to offer these girls," Dorothy said. "It is well known that the types of men that Shirley consorts with are usually very 'anti-sheath.'"

"I wish that the rules pertaining to the provision of Birth Control weren't so rigidly proscriptive," Claire sighed.

"What we could do with is a friend, who is sympathetic to our cause, to work in a Family Planning Clinic, prepared to be our eyes and ears, and discover if, when, and where, there is any possible way round this dilemma," Claire concluded.

"What you are really after is a participating mole," Cathy said. "Quite frankly, if they are to be of any possible use, that person would need to be actively engaged in clinic work." Two pairs of eyes regarded her keenly.

"Therefore, may I suggest that ideally we need a tame doctor or nurse. As neither of you fit that category, I suppose it's up to me," she twinkled. "How would it be if I went on a course and trained as a Family Planning Clinic Sister?"

Gazing at her in disbelief, Dorothy said: "You mean you're actually prepared to do that for us?"

"Quite prepared. Anything which might help to prevent any more Shirleys."

"What must you do and what will you need?" Claire enquired, eager to help the process along, if at all possible.

"Simply apply in writing and wait and hope, I guess. Let me go and get a notepad and pen."

Although the first birth control clinic in the UK had been set up in 1921 in London by Marie Stopes, under the slogan 'Children by Choice not Chance', it took another decade before the Family Planning Association was formed. From 1930, the Minister of Health permitted local authorities to provide contraceptive advice but only to 'married women, for whom a further pregnancy would be detrimental to health'.

Almost inevitably, steps were taken in an attempt to broaden this remit to include others. However, it wasn't until 1946 that a formal training in contraceptive techniques was established in recognised clinics.

To Cathy's delight her application was accepted and, once more, the silver buckle was retrieved from its case and placed around the waist of a white, button-through dress.

Diaphragm caps and cervical caps known as 'womb veils', spermicidal cream, the ubiquitous sheaths and the unreliable rhythm method and coitus interruptus, were virtually all that pertained at the time, with the former still only available to those who were married. The other methods were notoriously unreliable.

In 1952 clinics started to give advice to 'those about to be married', which was often a somewhat loose interpretation, and unofficially widened the window.

Although the contraceptive pill arrived in 1961, it would not be until 1967 that the NHS agreed to give birth control advice regardless of marital status, and longer still before it was provided free of charge.

Cathy duly gained the required certificate and took a post in the clinic in the town, working two evenings a week, whilst still maintaining her commitment at the Moral Welfare Office.

Having built up a good relationship with most of the clients, at their final discharge visit they would be referred to Cathy for future contraceptive management, as best she could.

The clinic had probably never before been confronted with so many young women 'about to be married'!

"You know what we ought to do,' David announced at breakfast one morning.

"And what's that may I ask?" said Cathy with an affectionate smile.

"Pay a visit to the Festival of Britain," he responded with his customary enthusiasm.

"Yippee!" came the unanimous and eager response from the jubilant twins. They each had their own memories of standing on a bridge spanning the Thames the previous year, and looking down onto a scene of devastation and seeming chaos. Their parents had assured them that it wouldn't be long before they would be able to return to see something very different.

Flicking through the pages of the newspaper he was reading, David commented: "It seems ridiculous to have this attraction literally on our doorstep yet fail to experience it."

"Rather like living in Wimbledon but never seeing the tennis," his wife said dryly. For some time she had been trying to interest her reluctant spouse in that particular direction, which was even closer to their home, but without success.

Ignoring the dig being aimed at him, he continued. "According to an account in this paper, although the whole thing was criticised initially as a huge waste of public money in these straightened times, the event has attracted ten million visitors in the first five months, which seems quite incredible."

The Festival of Britain, originally organised to mark the centenary of the Great Exhibition of 1851, took place in the summer of 1951. Its primary aim was to demonstrate Britain's contribution to civilisation, past, present and future, encompassing the arts, science and technology, and industrial design. However, after the destruction of the war years, with the resulting austerity, ration books and make-do-and-mend mentality, the Festival also aimed to raise the nation's spirits whilst showcasing the very best of Britain.

Although it was a national event, London was at its heart. Various buildings sprung up on the south bank of the Thames, much of which was an area of bomb sites, war-damaged or derelict Victorian industrial buildings, and railway sidings.

Despite the fact that the Festival took pride in Britain's past, most of the exhibits looked to the future. In one of the pavilions, many Londoners glimpsed their first ever television pictures, little imagining how this innovation would come to dominate lives in the years to come.

By the end of the war, much of London was still in ruins. Reconstruction and redevelopment were seen as high priorities, especially housing, and the Festival project was not without its detractors and critics, who viewed the whole thing as a total waste of resources. The great British public, who were solely dependent on what they were fed by the press and radio, could only 'suck-it-and-see'. And taste it they did!

Alighting from a train at Waterloo Station, David and Cathy shepherded two children, agog with excitement, through the concourse and out into the street. Turning left they made their way towards the river. Standing on Waterloo Bridge, the two adults leant on the balustrade and gasped in disbelief at the transformation of an area once so familiar to them both. Therefore, they were somewhat surprised when Peter, tugging at his father's sleeve, demanded to know 'what that very tall chimney is'. Grinning broadly, David informed him that it was actually very old and called a Shot Tower.

"What! A place where people go to get shot?" the lad asked in awe.

Giving a laugh, his father assured him that its only purpose was to provide little pellets, known as shot, for use in guns.

"Wow!" Peter was clearly impressed.

Dawn wasn't in the slightest bit interested in such irrelevances.

"What's that huge building?" she asked Cathy.

By following her pointing finger, and consulting a guide map, she was able to inform the girl that it was the Festival Hall.

"What happens there?"

"Well, it's a theatre for performances and concerts," her mother replied.

"With a stage and everything?"

"That's right."

"How wonderful," Dawn breathed. "Can we go inside?'

Catching the tailend of the conversation, her father shattered her hopes. "Not today I'm afraid, because you have to book seats. Don't worry, you'll get the chance to attend something one day," he promised her. Little could he imagine how true this would prove to be.

"Come on," he enthused. "Let's get down there onto the river bank."

This sufficed to open up another vista. They duly admired the Skylon, a futuristic-looking, slender, vertical, cigar-shaped structure that appeared to float above the ground. A popular joke at the time was that, like the British economy, "It had no visible means of support."

Adjacent to the Skylon was a temporary, prefabricated exhibition centre. Known as the Dome of Discovery, at that time it was the largest dome in the world. A number of galleries on various levels transported visitors on a journey destined to take them to The Living World, Polar Regions, The Sea, The Earth, The Land, The Sky and on to Outer Space.

"Outer Space," the young Peter said bemusedly. "What's that?"

Excitedly the twins darted from one exhibit to another, sampling whatever captured their fancy, exchanging experiences in passing.

After finishing their picnic lunch, eaten in the Festival Garden, and having satisfied the twins' demand for ice creams, which were still something of a post-war treat, they sauntered leisurely along beside the river.

"Come on," David said to his wife. "Let's go and experience a bit of nostalgia, shall we?"

Calling to the children to 'keep up', hand-in-hand they made their way toward Southwark Bridge. Once standing on it they surveyed the scene in silence, each lost in their memories.

"What's so special about this?" asked a clearly bored Dawn.

Peter, however, was absorbed in watching the variety of river traffic travelling in both directions.

Turning their attention to the children, Cathy said: "I wonder which of you will be the first to spot the dome of St. Paul's Cathedral?"

"Me," Dawn claimed excitedly, pointing to the familiar landmark.

"Let's cross the road," their father suggested.

Rushing to the other side they gazed upstream.

"Who can see the Tower of London? he asked.

"I can, I can," his son proclaimed. "It's over there on the right, and there's the bridge that opens up to let the tall ships through."

"Well done," David replied. "One day we'll have a trip along the river on one of those boats," he promised.

Leaving the twins pointing things out and chattering happily to each other, he took his wife's hand again.

"Was it only ten years ago?" he sighed.

Laughing, Cathy was driven to say: "You mean the day I received my history lesson, I presume?" She proceeded to parrot: "That was the old disreputable red-light district where Shakespeare's plays were performed at the Globe and Hope playhouses."

Grinning broadly, David voiced his satisfaction. "I'm impressed."

"So you should be," she said. "I'm not just a pretty face you know!"

Putting his arm round her, he drew her close.

"Any regrets my love?" he murmured.

"Absolutely none," she responded unhesitatingly.

However, there could be no doubt that the high spot of the day for the children was a visit to Battersea Pleasure Gardens.

Originally known as Battersea Fields, the site occupied marshland reclaimed from the Thames and land formerly used for market gardening. The northern parts of the park had been transformed into pleasure gardens lit with coloured lights and featuring a new water garden and fountains, a Tree Walk, which involved navigating a path along raised wooden walkways suspended between the trees, the Guinness Clock and The Far Tottering and Oyster Creek Branch Railway. This was a narrow-gauge railway displaying many of the Heath-Robinson type features found in some Punch cartoons. Another part of the transformation was the Battersea Fun Fair complete with rollercoasters, the most spectacular being the Big Dipper. Alongside were the usual variety of swings, slides, roundabouts, dodgem cars, a ghost-train and other fairground attractions.

The whole day had provided them with a positive cornucopia of experiences and delights. Arriving home exhausted yet exhilarated, the twins were asleep almost before their heads had touched the pillows. Resting with their feet up in the comfort of the lounge, the couple happily reflected on the success of the day. Little could they know the effect it had on Dawn. Years after the event had passed from her parents' minds, their daughter was to pen a verse which would win her an award in a poetry competition.

THE FESTIVAL of BRITAIN

Out of the dirt and grime of London town
Came sounds of hammered metal, steel on steel.
Spread along the river bank was seen
The growth of giant buildings gaunt and bare.
Unfinished yet, they raised their girdered heads,
Whilst midgets, working through the night and day,
Continued in the frantic rush of time
To finish gardens, concert halls and towers.
All this in preparation for that glorious day
When pomp and show would take the place of cranes,
And foreigners would pay the tribute due
To English work and style and craftsmanship.
On a memorable day we watched with eager eyes,
Gazing upon the transformed scene in wonderment.
Tantalising glimpses into the future emerged
Hinting at unbelievable things as yet to come
Alive with unimaginable possibilities.
And at the end we rendered thankful praise
To those who worked that others could enjoy
The Festival of Nineteen-Fifty-One.

Only a few months after their memorable outing, David approached Cathy with the suggestion that they ought to be contemplating a move.

"I've been in this parish for ten years now, which is more than I had expected. It's been a happy time," he reflected. "However, the time is coming for the twins to change to secondary education. I imagine we'd both like to think that we could find somewhere that will afford them the very best opportunity, don't you?"

"I know you're right," Cathy sighed. "Although, I must confess to a feeling of horror at the prospect. Just think, ten years of accumulated junk to sort out," she groaned.

So it was that, on a day at the end of July 1953, the little family embarked upon another adventure.

It was with a heavy heart that Cathy said goodbye to her friends at the Moral Welfare Office and Family Planning Clinic. She had found unimagined fulfillment in both positions and couldn't help wondering whatever she was going to do now.

Chapter Two

Finding Their Feet

The move to Richmond, on the banks of the Thames, proved to be fortuitous. Not least was the chance for the twins to attend the respective boys' and girls' grammar schools. Close at hand were an impressive range of shops and an excellent repertory theatre. The riverside walks were a constant delight and Peter was soon in his element when he joined the local rowing club.

Once again they found themselves to be truly blessed.

The nineteen fifties not only marked a significant turning point for David and Cathy, but was also a pivotal moment in modern medicine, heralding the beginning of a new age of discovery and rethinking. Although developments and innovations were to be expected, they came in positive leaps and bounds. These included the introduction of mouth-to-mouth and cardiopulmonary resuscitation (CPR), which would prove so effective in saving lives previously regarded as irredeemable. The structure of DNA was revealed. It disclosed the very substance that makes life; a human cell that contains genes, which are made up of chromosomes and the very basis of living tissue. This in turn allowed the study of diseases caused by defective genes, such as cystic fibrosis and Down's syndrome. Tests were developed to detect defects in babies, such as an amniocentesis procedure for spina bifida and Down's syndrome.

Ultrasound and Magnetic Resonance Imaging (MRI) began to make it possible to detect diseases without the use of radiation. The link between smoking and lung cancer was established, although it would be many years before the information had any impact on a population where both men and women puffed away with steady enthusiasm.

Programmes such as the drive to immunise against polio, diphtheria and rubella, came into being, thereby emphasising that the primary aim of the NHS was to provide good health, not simply the treatment of illness. Some of the rather draconian rules which had hitherto held sway were relaxed. Daily visits to children in hospital were now allowed, as opposed to half-an-hour on Wednesdays, Saturdays and Sundays.

Thanks to a burgeoning pharmaceutical industry, new medicines began to abound. The synthesis of Penicillin sparked the golden age of antibiotics. With the discovery of Streptomycin, TB was considered to be well on the way to extinction. A tremendous boon to the treatment of those suffering from arthritis was the advent of the steroid drugs such as Cortisone. Monoamine Oxidase (MAO) inhibitors were introduced to treat psychosis, and tranquilisers appeared. Unfortunately, this would also serve to set the stage for the 'drug scene' of the swinging sixties.

The decade also saw the first open heart surgery, pacemaker device and heart-lung machine. Therefore, it was not surprising that spending on the NHS started to exceed what had been expected. Despite this, improvements and innovations continued to be implemented.

"Where, oh where, am I possibly going to fit into this fast-moving world?" Cathy wailed to her amused husband. It had taken time to settle into their new home and surroundings, and to get to grips with the demands of a very different parish. Nevertheless, it wasn't too long before she began to get itchy feet. What to do next was the big question.

Following the inception of the NHS, it had rapidly become clear that there were some glaring and pressing problems and deficits which needed to be addressed urgently. An ever-increasing number of people were presenting themselves at doctors' surgeries, seeking treatment for non-life-threatening conditions which they had borne stoically, often for years, due to an inability to pay. This soon imposed an immense strain on hospital facilities. GPs began referring seemingly endless numbers of patients, with hernias, varicose veins, prolapsed wombs, bunions and ophthalmic problems such as squints, cataracts and glaucoma, to the respective consultants. It didn't take very long before the realisation dawned that most Outpatient Departments were woefully inadequate and severely understaffed to meet the need.

It was entirely due to this shortfall that Cathy literally fell into a post as a Sister in Outpatients at a nearby hospital. With the twins happily settled in their new environment, steadily growing up and becoming that little bit more independent, she threw herself wholeheartedly into this new role, which she pursued contentedly for some years.

Pedalling furiously up the vicarage drive, Cathy was just in time to hear the last of Petula Clarke's appeal to her 'Baby Lover' blasting forth from a bedroom window. Before she had even propped the bike up against the wall to enter the house, Perry Como was launching into 'Magic Moments' accompanied by the voice of a clearly appreciative Dawn._Entering by the back door she struggled in with a bag of shopping, hung her coat up in the cloakroom, and made her way towards the kitchen, just as David emerged from his study to meet her. Scarcely acknowledging his greeting she sighed loudly. "This is all I need after the day I've had. Outpatients was like a war zone. What with demanding consultants, missing notes, disgruntled patients and running late, we were constantly playing 'catch up' but never seemed to." Looking at him despairingly she implored: "Can't you get her to turn that thing down? I should think half of Richmond can hear it."

The song had come to an end but before her amused husband had time to react Connie Francis began belting out 'Who's Sorry Now'.

"I know someone who's going to be very sorry in a moment," said Cathy. "Where's Peter?"

"In the dining room doing his homework," David replied.

"Well, I only hope he's got a good set of earplugs," she retorted.

Going to the bottom of the stairs her spouse let forth a stentorian bellow. "Dawn, Mum's home so make your way down."

"Can I do anything?" he asked on returning to the kitchen. "If it's any help there's a fruit crumble on the worktop. Old Mrs. Dobson kindly brought it to the Mother's Union meeting for us. I've put the oven on in readiness and I've peeled some potatoes."

"You truly are a gem and a life saver," Cathy hugged him appreciatively. "Actually I had already prepared a shepherd's pie last night while you were out, so I'll just do some veg. It won't take long and we can have your potatoes tomorrow."

"Hi Mum," said Dawn, sauntering into the kitchen. Without turning round from the sink where she was scraping carrots her mother commented, "How you can possibly give any attention to your homework with that racket going on defeats me. Neither can your brother be expected to. You are not the only person living in this house you know."

Before the girl could reply her father took one look at her and raised his eyebrows, remarking casually, "Are you by any chance thinking of going off somewhere this evening?"

Cathy spun round and gazed at her daughter in disbelief. "For goodness sake! You look like a trollop with all that make-up plastered on, and you're certainly not going anywhere dressed like that."

"Oh Mum, please," Dawn wheedled. "I won't be late, I promise."

David promptly intervened. "Quite apart from the matter of your appearance, you know the rules - no outside activities on a school night."

"You're such a pair of spoilsports," she sulked. "All the others will be there."

"Really," her father grinned. "So if I ring up the homes of the rest of your classmates, will I learn that every one of them is sallying forth to sample whatever delights you have in mind? Shall I give it a try?"

This suggestion served to bring forth a loud groan and the opinion that they were 'so unfair'. David reflected for a moment before saying. "Actually, you have more freedom than many of your contemporaries but it's never enough, is it? You are forever trying to push the boundaries." His daughter pouted mutinously.

"Instead of cavorting round looking like a second-rate chorus girl or film star, it would be more to your credit if you gave some serious thought as to what you are going to do when you leave school. There's less than a year now, you know," her mother said, "and we don't seem to be any the wiser."

The reply when it came was so vehement that it took both parents by surprise.

"Well, I'll tell you one thing for sure - there's no way I'm going into nursing. You can keep your precious silver buckle."

"I can't tell you how relieved I am to hear you say that," Cathy replied quietly.

"As will the hapless British public feel who might have found themselves in your care," said her father with a grin.

Regarding them with a belligerent glare she informed them dismissively: "Oh, I could do it if I wanted to."

"I rather think that nursing does require certain attributes which you haven't demonstrated as yet," David smiled.

"Anyway, it's all academic because I intend to do something quite different," she said, tossing her head airily.

"Anything specific in mind?" he persisted.

"I'm not saying any more at the moment, so don't push me."

"Well, while you're pondering your future, do you think I could push you into laying the table for our meal?" Cathy asked as she turned her attention to the cooker. "We'll eat in here tonight as Peter's commandeered the dining room."

As if on cue her lanky son wandered into the kitchen. "I'm starving, is dinner ready? Oh, by the way, I'm afraid my rugby kit's in a bit of a state. The ground was like an absolute quagmire today but I have put it all in a bucket to soak," he offered.

"Welcome home Mum, nice to see you," Cathy replied with a trace of sarcasm.

"Did you win?" his sister interrupted.

"Of course," he replied smugly. "By the way, Neil got well and truly clobbered and has gone to hospital with a possible broken arm, so he won't be able to go out with you this evening."

An awkward silence descended before David responded. "So much for 'everyone will be there' young lady." Turning to Peter he said, "As it happens your sister wasn't going anyway, so there's no problem."

Exchanging glances, the pair took their places at the table.

"Thanks a bunch," Dawn hissed at her brother.

"How did I know you hadn't told them," he muttered aggrievedly.

Cathy and David exchanged surreptitious smiles. Although the twins were as different as chalk and cheese, both in looks and temperament, there was an unspoken rapport and loyalty between them. Many were the times when Cathy wondered how on earth two children from the same pod could be so completely unalike. Except, as David often reminded her, the womb may have been shared but their pods were individual. They weren't identical, for which their parents never ceased to give thanks. Peter had been such an easy and contented baby and changed little as he entered his teens. Although he loved sport, he was equally committed to his studies and was quite content to spend time with his books and homework. Almost fanatically devoted to his rowing and rugby, he was quite prepared to join in the activities at the Youth Club, which included regular dances, but hadn't evinced the slightest interest in the opposite sex, as yet.

Dawn, however, would have tried the patience of Job. Noisy, outspoken, stubborn and nonconformist, her temperament was mercurial and she was certainly no shrinking violet. Boys, the latest magazines, pop music, dancing, the theatre, cinema and singing she loved with equal enthusiasm. Attempts to be an ardent follower of the current fashion trends, if she got the chance, were only matched by the rate at which she tried changing her hair style and experimenting with make-up. Although there was no doubting her intelligence or abilities, as far as academic work was concerned she did the bare minimum to keep her head above water.

Cathy often secretly wondered what would become of them both. Placing the plates of food on the table and having seated herself, Peter said, "Has she let you in on her latest news?"

"What news?" the other three chorused as one.

"You know the boys' and girls' schools combine each year to produce a play. Well, our Dawn has only landed the lead role this time."

Over the years they had watched with amusement as their daughter progressed from a very bossy Angel Gabriel in the nativity play, danced and sang her way through numerous other roles and won prizes at various poetry and speaking competitions. This had culminated in an unforgettably maniacal performance as Lady Macbeth the previous year. Both parents had become quite accustomed to chauffeuring her to endless dancing classes, rehearsals and events.

402

"Are you going to tell us?" David enquired, "or is this to be yet another of your little secrets?"

"Actually, I'm going to play Joan of Arc in George Bernard Shaw's 'St. Joan'," she announced triumphantly.

"Phew, that's going to be a bit of a challenge, isn't it?" her father commented.

"Are you taking part, Peter?" Cathy asked.

"No way! You know I don't like that sort of thing. Although I did offer to be the person who lights the touch paper when she gets burned at the stake," he grinned impudently.

Eying his daughter affectionately, David suggested that this was a cause for celebration. "Congratulations my love, and we look forward to the performance."

"I've got absolutely loads of lines to learn," Dawn sighed. "You will both help me, won't you?" she implored.

"Please tell me we're not going to be treated to endless versifying as she trails round the house for weeks doing a Sarah Bernhardt?" her brother groaned.

"I think you'll find this house is more than big enough to accommodate everyone's needs without any problem," Cathy announced dryly. "You can squirrel yourself away somewhere while we help Dawn. Actually, I'm quite looking forward to it. It will certainly make a change from Outpatients."

"Thanks Mum, you're a star," a jubilant Dawn squealed with delight.

"Perhaps your grandparents would like to come as well," David suggested.

"Oh, that would be lovely. We haven't seen them for ages."

"I only hope they get to appreciate the full volume from the record player they gave you at Christmas," her mother grimaced. "It might make them think twice before choosing your next present."

Over the ensuing weeks, peace reigned in the vicarage as Dawn threw herself into preparations for what she hoped would be her moment of glory. With the news that the costumes were being hired and the make-up done professionally, her cup of happiness was overflowing.

The evening of the final performance duly arrived. David and Cathy, accompanied by a thrilled Pam and Roger, made a slow progress to their seats as they stopped to acknowledge the greetings of numerous people for, due to their respective roles in the parish and hospital, both were well known in the area. Despite good reports of the previous three evenings they were clearly anxious that Dawn should give of her best and sat, somewhat tensely in the seats, only too aware of the gnawing pit in their stomachs. The curtain rose and, as the play progressed, so they began to relax. By the interval it was clear that, barring accidents, the production would exceed everyone's expectations. When it eventually came time for Dawn to deliver her monologue, the spotlight and all attention was on her. A hush descended as her voice, full of pathos and despair, echoed round the hall.

"Yes, they told me you were fools and that I was not to listen to your fine words nor trust your charity. You promised me life but you lied."

Cathy squeezed David's hand and, feeling a tear begin to trickle down her cheek, was thankful for the darkness. When the curtain finally came down the applause was unstinting. One by one the cast came forward and when Dawn appeared it was to receive a standing ovation.

"She really was incredible," Roger commented. "We had no idea she had such talent."

"I certainly wouldn't have missed it for worlds," Pam enthused. "You must both be so proud."

Graciously accepting the plaudits bestowed from friends, they made their way out. Standing at the door was Miss Jarman, the English and Drama mistress, who was a familiar figure as a result of their encounters at numerous parents' evenings and events.

"I do hope you were impressed," she greeted the couple. "Dawn has tried so hard and I think you will agree that she really managed to pull it off."

After they had both duly expressed their delight and offered thanks for her part in it, she said, "I wonder whether I could ask you to come and see me next week because there is a matter I would like to discuss with you both privately."

With a date set for Monday they left for home somewhat bemused and apprehensive. "Goodness knows what she's been up to now," Cathy voiced dubiously. "She really is a law unto herself and so unpredictable."

"Whereas you were always such sweetness and light," David mocked.

"Believe me, she had her moments," Pam smiled indulgently.

"Yet you turned out all right," Roger added. "Just wait and see because Dawn will surprise you, mark my words."

Following a pleasant family weekend it was with curiosity, tinged with some misgivings, that the couple seated themselves in front of Miss Jarman. After exchanging pleasantries regarding the recent performance she said, "I expect you are wondering what all this is about?"

"I must confess to some concern," David replied.

"Don't worry. Your daughter isn't in any kind of trouble," she said kindly. "The thing is that, as you know, this term all our pupils are having to focus on their futures so that we can work with them in order to help them to achieve their goals where possible." She paused momentarily before continuing. "However, what you don't know is that Dawn has expressed her aspirations to pursue a career in acting."

A stunned silence descended. Eventually finding his voice David exclaimed: "Good heavens, we had no idea. She's never even hinted as much."

"That wasn't because she didn't want to tell you, but more out of worry as to how you would react to such an idea, I gather."

"Not the sort of path people expect the vicar's daughter to go down, is that it?" David commented ruefully. "You know, having to go round carrying that label can be quite a burden. I don't think folk have any idea how hard it is for the children of clergy, who can feel somewhat stigmatised and handicapped by this dog collar. Ridiculously, everyone seems to have perceived ideas and expectations of them, especially regarding how they should behave and what they should do."

"Exactly so," Miss Jarman smiled sympathetically. "Which is why I have offered to prepare the ground, as it were. After her recent success this seemed as good a time as any."

"Frankly speaking, what are her chances?" Roger asked, leaning forward in his chair.

Clasping her hands together on the desk she surveyed them calmly before saying, "They are potentially very good. What neither you nor Dawn know is that in the audience on the final night was a teacher from RADA, who has been a friend for many years. In fact, we were at school together. She is of the opinion that there is just, and I stress the word just, a possibility that Dawn could be in a position to be awarded a scholarship to study there."

"Phew!" David almost whistled. "This needs a bit of taking in." Turning to his wife he asked for her thoughts on the matter.

Cathy leant forward on her seat and said, "This has come as a bit of a shock. I mean, we know how much she has enjoyed the elocution and drama lessons and performances that she has taken part in, but we simply didn't envisage the possibility of her taking it further. We thought it was simply a pleasant hobby."

Hesitating for a moment, she continued, "Well, if Dawn has set her mind on this, and if Miss Jarman thinks she has a chance, we must do what we can to support her. Although I can't help hearing that song reverberating in my head: 'Don't put your daughter on the stage, Mrs. Worthington'."

At this they all laughed.

"So, what's the next step?" David asked.

"First of all she will have to apply officially in writing, including a portfolio of all that she has done so far. Hopefully she will then be called for an interview and audition. At this, she will be required to perform something chosen for her at random, plus a piece of her own choice. I am firmly of the opinion that the monologue from 'St. Joan' would be as good as any. Then we sit and wait. Obviously I will prepare her as best I can but she also has to realise that she can't afford to let up on her schoolwork, especially English Literature in which the Academy will be looking for a good grade. She really will have to concentrate on reading as many of the appropriate literary works and recognised plays as she can, in order to be able to discuss them intelligently if asked."

"Well, if this doesn't motivate her to get her head down, nothing will," Cathy said firmly. "Of course, we'll do all that we can but it's really up to her."

"And we'll certainly make sure she understands that," David affirmed.

Thanking the mistress for her time and the efforts she had made on behalf of their daughter, a slightly shell-shocked couple left the school and tried to digest the news.

On her arrival home Dawn was ecstatic. Throwing her arms round each of them in turn, she wept tears of joy. "I was so sure you wouldn't approve that I just can't believe it. I'm actually going to RADA."

"Steady on sweetheart," her father counselled. "Don't set your heart on it completely because you haven't been accepted yet."

"You will have to put in some hard work and commitment in your remaining time at school if you are to attain this dream," said Cathy.

"I know. Miss Jarman's been through it with me and I will, I will." Pirouetting round the kitchen table she grabbed her startled brother and attempted to propel him into an impromptu dance.

"For goodness sake, sis, calm down. I hope we won't have to endure this fever-pitch for the rest of the year," he said goodnaturedly.

"Well, it isn't every day we get to welcome a budding actress into the family," his father smiled. "I think the artistic juices are beginning to surface."

"Although, where they've come from I can't imagine," Cathy remarked. "The theatre certainly hasn't featured in my family, so far as I'm aware. She must get it from your side, David."

Before he could reply, Peter flung himself onto a chair saying: "Of course it's in the family. She has inherited it from both of you."

"I don't know how you make that out," his mother protested.

"Just think about it," he sighed. "There's Mum attending to a sick patient who suddenly throws up all over her. What does she do? Cradles him comfortingly and calmly says, "Don't worry, it really doesn't matter." Like hell it doesn't! She's simply putting on a very good act."

"Don't be ridiculous, Peter," she exclaimed.

"It's true," he persisted. "I reckon that inside every nurse is a frustrated actress trying to get out."

Turning to his father he, continued with his theory. "As for you, Dad, every time you dress up in your gear each Sunday and climb into the pulpit, you are taking centre stage to deliver an oration. You are both actors."

"I don't think I'd put it quite like that," David said wryly.

"Well, I would," his son replied, "and I herewith rest my case."

"And there speaks the wannabe legal waller," Dawn chortled. "Poor Mum and Dad don't stand a chance."

For some time Peter had made no secret of his intention of trying to get into university to read Law, to which end he was diligently applying himself, and the staff at his school saw no reason why he shouldn't achieve this. There was no doubt that these two post-war children were entering a world offering far greater freedom and choice: a world that was very different from the one previously inhabited by their parents.

Chapter Three

Upwards and Beyond

P eter and Dawn both realised their aspirations for advancing future career hopes and, in 1960, one set off to RADA in London, on a scholarship, the other to Oxford.

Although undeniably proud of their achievements, Cathy and David had been secretly dreading the expense that such undertakings would incur. Fortuitously, the late fifties and early sixties brought in the growth of the local education grant system. This not only offered unheard-of opportunities for those who were previously prevented due to the financial cost involved, it also ushered in a totally new and wider range of students, both to the stage and universities.

Alongside this, the period of growth in the NHS continued. New drugs kept on appearing at an amazing rate. Amongst these were the cytotoxic drugs for use in chemotherapy, which were to have a profound effect on the treatment of many cancers. However, there could be no doubt that the miracle of the decade was the pioneering achievement of Dr. Christian Barnard in performing the first human heart transplant. This set the stage for dramatic and wide-reaching advances in cardiac surgery.

One of the most significant advances of the 20th century was the introduction of the contraceptive pill. Inextricably linked to the swinging sixties, free love and women's liberation it became available in 1961 but only for those who were married - a regulation which persisted until 1967. Around the same time, intrauterine devices made their appearance. Popularly known as 'the coil', this mechanism was inserted into the uterus, thereby providing long-acting, reversible birth control. Such innovations were to revolutionise the choices open to women.

They were now becoming empowered in an area of life that had previously been denied to them.

Only days after the departure of Peter and Dawn from home, the couple felt the need to get away. Much as Cathy might have moaned about the twins at times, the house was now very quiet.

"Right! Enough of this empty nest syndrome," David announced. "Let's go down to the cottage for a few days and dust the cobwebs off."

Over the past three years, it had become an increasing rarity for the twins to accompany their parents to Hollowdene anymore, and they had to accept that the simple, old-style, family holidays were a thing of the past, as were so many things.

People were beginning to appreciate the delights of foreign travel, which was now coming within the reach of folk who had previously been content with the British seaside or holiday camps.

They found themselves voicing their thoughts to Jean.

"I agree. It simply doesn't seem the same," she said "We're in a similar boat. Although Simon is aiming to take over from Jim at some stage, he's just about to go off to agricultural college."

"No such dang-fangled thing in my day," Jim grumbled, coming into the room at that point. "Once upon a time you learned on the job, but all that is changing."

"Duncan's already left home to study engineering, so I know how you feel," Jean mourned.

"Never mind," David added. "Think what you will save on repairs to all your farm equipment, once he's qualified." Shaking with laughter Jim responded, "You obviously don't realise that he's doing an apprenticeship with the British Aircraft Corporation. Somehow, I don't think my tractors are likely to get much of a look in."

Getting to his feet he suggested that they both clear off to the Shepherd's Arms for a drink and leave the women to their own devices.

"Good," Jean retorted, "then Cathy and I can have a real natter, so scoot off the both of you!"

Settling themselves comfortably in the well-lived-in lounge, Cathy cast her eye over the room. "Do you know that this always brings back memories of Uncle John for me?' she sighed.

"Yes, he certainly was something of a figurehead and, although it is so long since he died, his presence does seem to permeate the fabric," her friend commented.

"Anyway, back to the present. How is life in Outpatients?"

"If I'm completely honest, I'd rather like a change," Cathy confessed. "However, I'm hanging on to the job for the moment because, now the twins have left home, I strongly suspect that David will shortly be moving on to pastures new."

"I don't know how you cope with the constant requirement to change location," Jean remarked.

"What about you?" her friend inquired.

"You may well ask," Jean replied. "I think I told you that the Royal closed down the convalescent home because of a perceived lack of need for that kind of care today. Added to which, in view of all the developments that are happening, it was an expense that management could ill afford. Consequently the hospital have sold it. The rumour is that it will become a private nursing home. To be honest, I have to say the job was a bit of a doddle and didn't exactly stretch me. I almost felt guilty for taking the money."

Cathy nodded her head sadly.

"Consequently, I was put out to grass and, after almost two years of domesticity, I rather gave up on the idea of working again. Then, completely out of the blue, two months ago, I received a phone call from the Assistant Matron at the Royal, asking whether I would be interested in taking on another post."

"They must be desperate," Cathy said. "Oh, I don't mean it like that," she apologised ruefully. "Staff shortages are becoming common almost everywhere these days."

Ignoring the remark, Jean continued. "The long and short of it is that I was offered three choices; full time Ward Sister; part-time in theatres, or full time Night Sister."

"And, what did you settle for?"

"Full time nights. You know I never could abide theatre work."

Sitting bolt upright in her chair, Cathy positively shrieked at her friend.

411

"You must be nuts. Twenty-four night stints would positively finish me."

Smirking with delight, Jean proceeded to enlighten her bemused friend that things were very different.

"Full time night duty now consists of working for ten nights and then having six off."

"I don't believe it. It's certainly not before time. Gosh! It's almost like working every other week."

"Exactly," Jean agreed with satisfaction.

"I almost wish I could join you," Cathy sighed enviously.

"Why don't you persuade David to move here for his next parish?" she suggested.

"No chance. His whole life has been spent 'south of Watford Gap' and he is very much rooted in the Southwark Diocese, I'm afraid. Added to which, I must own I like it there too," Cathy assured her. "Everything in life, seems to be changing at a rate of knots at the moment. It's difficult enough to keep abreast, without adding to the problem."

"You can say that again," Jean responded with feeling. "However, I can provide you with a good laugh on the subject of change."

'Go on," Cathy grinned.

'Initially, I found it so hard to get my head around the fact that everything seemed to be disposable. Except the patient, of course!" she added wryly.

Cathy roared with mirth.

"I kept on asking what to do with various items that you and I would once have re-used, only to be told to throw them away. I must say that it didn't sit easily, especially given my Scottish background," she said, self-mockingly. "Not to mention thinking back to the pre-NHS frugality, when everything had to be accounted for down to the last teaspoon in the ward kitchen."

"Don't remind me. The number of times I staggered off duty late because something had gone missing, and we couldn't leave until it had been found," her friend shuddered.

"However, my absolute debacle came on the second night. I was doing the early morning round of the wards allocated to me. Priestman, your old stomping ground, was in chaos, which was hardly surprising considering the exceptional number of emergency admissions they had received. The junior nurse was way behind with her tasks so, being the kind, loving and helpful soul that I am, I offered to go and do the pre-breakfast diabetic urine tests, while she retired to clean up the sluice. There's only so much goodness in my soul," she grinned.

"You're all heart," Cathy interposed sarcastically.

"Quite! So off I went to the treatment room. There were about six specimens lined up but, where oh where was the testing equipment? Having searched the cupboards, to no avail, I made my way to the sluice. 'Nurse, I wonder if you can tell me where I can find the bunsen burner and Benedict's Solution?' I enquired in all innocence. This simple request was met with a totally blank expression. 'What's that,' the girl asked. 'Well, it's what we use to test urine for sugar,' I replied patiently. Totally bemused, she regarded this, clearly antediluvian, character with pity, informing me that: 'I must have had a job to cart that lot out to the Crimea' with me'."

"What cheek!" Cathy exploded. "Can you imagine addressing old Sister Moore like that?"

"Precisely," Jean said. "Quite apart from her effrontery, how was I supposed to know that we now have neat little bottles of uristix, which only have to be dipped into the specimen to give an instant result? Very different to the time we expended holding a test tube in a flame, only to see the contents spurt up the wall."

"It's all handed to them on a plate, these days," Cathy declared. "When you think of the hours we spent cutting and making gauze swabs, rolling cotton wool into balls and packing then into stainless steel drums for sterilisation in the autoclave. Now it's all pre-packed and done for them in the Central Sterile Supplies Department, and they simply throw the surplus away."

Warming to the subject, she pressed on.

"Do you remember having to boil instruments, enamel bowls and gallipots, glass hypodermic syringes, stainless steel needles and rubber catheters in the ward steriliser?"

'Not to mention patching rubber gloves with a puncture kit and powdering them with French chalk. I can smell it now," Jean professed.

"And what about the cotton face masks we had to boil and wash on night duty, then dry them on the radiators, and get them ironed, rolled up and put back in the mask jars by the time the day staff arrived?" Cathy chimed in. "Now there are convenient boxes of disposable paper ones."

"What's more, all of this had to be fitted in around the medical and bodily needs of the patients," Jean declaimed.

Clearly enjoying their trip down memory lane and subsequent rant, both women leaned back in their chairs in a positive glow of self-satisfaction.

"They reckon they're overworked," Cathy was finally drawn to declare, "whereas they've actually never had it so good, if they did but realise it."

With the self-righteous opinion of now-outdated experience, the pair of old hands firmly decided that the present-day nurses 'didn't know they were born'!

The nineteen sixties proved to be an awesome decade, not only for the family but for the whole world. David, having responded to a summons to meet the Bishop, returned with the news Cathy had been dreading. It was time to move on again.

"It will be like going back to where we both started," he told her with enthusiasm. "An inner-city district of south-east London, in a part of the boroughs of Lewisham, Bromley and Southwark, no less."

"What's the vicarage like?" was his wife's immediate reaction.

"Haven't a clue, love. We go on a recce later this week," he replied, with all the eagerness of an explorer setting out for uncharted climes.

The parish proved to be pretty run down, with areas of deprivation and a considerable ethnic population. The vicarage was nothing special but, spurred on by the promise of some help in the shape of a curate, they agreed to take the plunge and moved in.

Cathy and David were thrilled when Dawn completed her course at RADA and emerged with the award for most-promising student and the promise of a place working in repertory theatre.

Not to be outdone, nine months later, Peter was selected to row in the annual University boat race. The entire family congregated on the riverside at Mortlake, shouting and cheering uproariously as the Oxford crew emerged victorious. Their pride and joy eventually knew no bounds when he gained his university degree in the following year and joined a prestigious law firm in London. The family had truly come of age in an even more remarkable age.

One of the greatest success stories of the twentieth century began with the opening of the world's first purpose-built hospice. In founding St. Christopher's Hospice, Sydenham in 1967, Dame Cicely Saunders made an extraordinary contribution to the alleviation of human suffering. The changing social trends of the nineteen fifties saw most people dying in hospitals, rather than in their own homes. This change reflected the growing number of treatments which were becoming available. The medical professions were increasingly coming to view death as failure. Cancer was the most feared diagnosis. The accompanying physical pain afflicted at least 75% of cancer sufferers, and appropriate painkillers were rarely used. Morphine was considered addictive, too dangerous and was only administered by injection.

Cicely Saunders set out to discover practical solutions and to disseminate them widely. The combination of science and dedicated nursing care marked the beginning of the medical specialty known as Palliative Care. Such care involves a holistic approach, caring not only for a patient's physical needs, but also the spiritual. psychological, social and emotional components. This philosophy of total wellbeing marked a new beginning, not only for the care of the dying but for the practice of medicine as a whole. Doctor Cicely Saunder's research into the study of pain control showed the value of giving regular doses of oral diamorphine. It not only prevented pain breakthrough but allowed the patient to remain mentally alert.

The inspired concept of 'total pain' or 'total suffering' having physical, emotional, social and spiritual components, gave a wider approach, or framework, for the understanding and care for patients at end-of-life. This was something which Cicely Saunders learned from the patients themselves as she sat beside them, listening to their concerns and feelings on life's last journey. She realised the value of spending time with, and listening to, both patients and their families, encouraging them to talk, ask questions and express their feelings, and by giving sensitive but truthful answers, it was possible to alleviate their emotional pain.

Similarly, elements of spiritual pain often resulted from guilt about the past or fear of what happens after death. Thus emerged the concept of a multi-disciplinary approach to end-life care. This involved the roles of doctors as assessors and prescribers: nurses as the main care-givers; chaplains to address the spiritual issues; social workers to embrace any social problems and various therapists to offer a comforting range of treatments to soothe, relieve tension, and promote a general feeling of wellbeing. Little could David guess the profound effect this particular innovation would have on his life.

***

The sound of the telephone woke David and Cathy from the sleep into which they had but recently descended. Groping for the bedside light switch, the resulting glow disclosed the fact that it was gone midnight. Lifting the receiver David was greeted by Dawn's bright and breezy voice.

"Hi, Dad."

In the years since leaving drama school, contact with their daughter had been extremely sporadic. They rarely knew where she was, as she toured the country with a repertory company, and had learned to make do with her infrequent calls, assuming that 'no news was good news'. Occasionally they would get the chance to watch her perform, if she happened to be appearing at a theatre within reasonable distance, or Peter would update them on the equally rare occasions when the mood stirred his twin to get in touch. She remained as mercurial and free-spirited as ever and was clearly in her element. With that her family had to be satisfied.

"Whatever's the matter?" David asked anxiously. "Are you alright?"

"Relax Dad, I'm fine," she responded breezily.

However, no such polite enquiry as to the state of her parents' well-being was forthcoming. Dawn had become rather selfish and totally self-centered. "You'll never guess what?" she carried on excitably.

"I'm sure I won't," her father sighed in resignation.

"Tell Mum that her beloved daughter is actually going to be a nurse! Unbelievable isn't it?"

"I presume, and sincerely hope, you're joking," he responded, with a degree of irritation.

"Oh, for goodness sake, hand me over to Mum."

It eventually transpired that Dawn was to play the role of Florence Nightingale in Richard Berkley's play 'The Lady with a Lamp'.

"Amazing, isn't it?" Dawn chortled happily.

"Indeed it is," her mother was driven to reply, scarcely able to keep her tongue in her cheek.

"The thing is, I wondered if I could borrow your buckle? It would be just perfect," her daughter rattled on.

"I'm not sure about that," Cathy said hesitatingly. "Knowing you, you'd probably lose it."

"I won't, I won't," Dawn protested.

"Besides which, such objects didn't feature in the Crimea," her mother informed her.

Quick as a flash came the response. "There is such a thing as poetic license, you know. Anyway, it doesn't all take place in the Crimea."

Only weeks later, the entire family retraced their steps to Richmond. Comfortably seated in the theatre, they watched with fascination and pride as the silver buckle made its debut stage appearance, to great acclaim.

One year on, the seemingly impossible happened when a man actually landed on the moon in 1969. Achievements like this dictated that change was inevitable and occurring at a pace that was difficult to keep up with.

"Do you remember when we visited the Festival of Britain?" David asked his wife.

Deep in thought, she nodded absentmindedly.

"We went round the Dome of Discovery and were invited to explore the possibilities of space, which was something beyond the realms of our comprehension. Yet, here we are, only eighteen years later, standing on its very threshold."

With a troubled look, Cathy simply said: "Where and how will it all end? That's what worries me."

"Come on," her husband said briskly. "This is no time for speculation or maudlin introspection. Let's escape to the cottage."

Once more the start of a new decade saw them ensconced in the place which had been such a wonderful bolthole and refuge throughout their life. Chewing over the latest developments with her friend, Cathy found herself confessing to some misgivings.

"It's all this sexual freedom that bothers me," Cathy moaned to Jean. "The moral landscape seems to be changing completely. Dawn's racketing around, getting up to God knows what I wouldn't wonder."

"Well, don't even think about it. What the eye doesn't see, the heart can't grieve over, as the saying goes." Quite frankly, with the amount of testosterone emanating from my two sons, I think I'd rather not know!"

The advent of the contraceptive pill not only empowered women with control over reproduction. It also ushered in an age of greater sexual license, which was to result in promiscuity, falling standards of moral behavior and the gradual fracturing of marriages with ever-increasing family instability. Although no one wished to see a return to the old stigmatisation of unmarried mothers, such a state was soon to become the accepted norm. Far from being a source of disgrace and disapproval, it seemed to develop into something to be worn almost as a badge of honour.

In the past, young, single mothers had little hope of being able to raise babies on their own. A generation of social reforms, state support in the shape of finance and housing, and an increasing tolerance of different kinds of family structure completely changed the landscape. By the end of the century people would not turn a hair and the pendulum steadily began to creep too far in the opposite direction. Self-respect, respect for others and the old mores that had provided some stability and order in the community were largely becoming eroded. Approaching rapidly was the anything goes, me-me-me society, where what the young wanted they had to have, and furthermore they had to have it now, regardless. Sadly, such profligacy would only serve to impinge adversely on subsequent generations.

Gazing round the cottage, David was drawn to say, "The poor old place is looking a bit tired now, isn't it?"

"It certainly could do with some TLC," Cathy agreed.

Sinking onto the sofa, she gave a long drawn-out sigh.

"Penny for them," her husband grinned.

"To be quite honest dear, I think the time has come to part company with it. Over the years it has served us, our family and friends, well. Now, if we are truthful, it is more important that we realise some capital. We will soon have to think of purchasing a home for our retirement."

David stared at her in surprise. "Are you sure, love?"

"Quite sure," she responded firmly.

Jim and Jean were devastated when they heard of their plans.

"It won't be the same without your visits," Jean wailed.

"On a more practical level," Jim said, "I'm afraid I won't be able to buy it back from you. I know that was something Uncle John expressed a desire to happen, in the event of you no longer wanting it. Times have changed considerably since then," he grimaced ruefully. "Not only can I not afford to do so," he informed them, "I also have no use for it."

Cathy stared at the floor, seemingly downcast.

"You'd do far better to put it on the open market, you know. The recent upward surge in the housing market will undoubtedly ensure that you get a good price for it. Added to which, old stone cottages like this are greatly in demand as people seek to distance themselves from the city."

So another page of history was turned.

Any sadness occasioned by the closure of this chapter in their lives, was eclipsed by a ray of light. Peter's legal career was progressing by leaps and bounds and he had moved into a pleasant flat in London. Both parents were intrigued and delighted when he phoned to inform them that he now had a girlfriend who he would like them to meet. Bustling round, making preparations for an evening meal, his mother awaited their arrival with a mixture of pleasure and apprehension.

"I wonder what she'll be like," Cathy mused anxiously.

"She'll be fine," David reassured her. "Just trust your son because at least he's got his head screwed on."

The back door opened and Peter entered the kitchen with his arm round the waist of an attractive, dark-haired girl, casually but smartly dressed and discreetly made up. Pushing a bottle of wine into his father's hands he said, "Mum, Dad, meet Sally."

"It's good to see you both and a lovely surprise," Cathy assured him.

Accepting a proffered bunch of freesias from the slightly diffident girl, she smiled at her kindly saying, "I don't know why you have been treated to the tradesman's entrance, my dear, but that's men for you!"

Once seated and furnished with a drink, Peter said triumphantly, "Mum, I think you are going to be very pleased and impressed when I tell you that Sally is a nurse. Now, isn't that a coincidence?"

Grinning at his son, David commented mischievously, "I do hope you didn't choose her simply because of her profession."

"For goodness sake, do be quiet," Cathy interposed

Turning to her guest she continued. "That is amazing, Sally. Where are you nursing?"

In a soft, pleasing voice, she replied, "Actually, I'm a midwife."

"Oh, I do admire you," Cathy said. "It was one branch of nursing that never really appealed to me, although I have sometimes regretted not doing the training."

Pausing for a moment, she went on to ask, "Did you do your general as well?"

"Yes. I trained at Kings College in London, then went on to Queen Charlotte's Maternity Hospital, which is where I'm currently employed."

"Hence the fact that we are here on a Tuesday evening because everything has to be arranged around her rather unsocial off-duty," Peter added.

"There's no need to make excuses to me," his mother assured him. "I remember the problems only too well."

"As do I," her spouse responded with feeling. "At least you aren't having to fit your dates around air-raids as well."

The conversation was non-stop. Sally immediately felt at ease with them both and, by the end of the evening, Cathy and David were unanimous in their opinion that their son had struck gold, which was just as well. Enjoying a final drink, Peter dropped his bombshell.

'I know that this will come as a bit of a bolt from the blue but I have to tell you that I have asked Sally to marry me and we will be celebrating our engagement this weekend."

"By Jove lad, you don't waste time, do you?" his father quipped.

"I saw the whole picture and quickly reached my verdict. It was an open and shut case," Peter replied, taking Sally's hand and squeezing it.

"We are well used to shocks where your sister is concerned - not all of them agreeable, I might add," Cathy said. "However, this is quite a pleasant shock."

"If you are brave enough to take him on, you have our profound thanks and every blessing," his father assured her.

Only two months later, a very proud David conducted their marriage service while Cathy unashamedly allowed a tear or two to trickle down her cheeks. Dawn duly allowed herself to be manipulated into a bridesmaid's dress, which certainly wouldn't have been of her choosing, and managed to conduct herself with a commendable degree of restraint. It was a happy day.

Dawn's aspirations advanced steadily and she departed from the theatre to try her hand in television. Her family watched some of her roles with barely disguised astonished amusement, and occasional horror. Very occasionally she would, unexpectedly and briefly, fetch up at the homes of her parents or Peter and Sally, often with a new man in tow. To their surprise, and not a little consternation, she suddenly took off for America to try her luck in the film business. This resulted in even less contact, if such a thing were possible. News occasionally surfaced by way of the odd review or press snippet.

"We've entered the space age and our Dawn might just as well be resident on another planet," her twin commented wryly.

Any qualms which Cathy and David may have secretly harboured, with regard to their daughter were totally eclipsed when, twelve months later, Peter and Sally presented them with a grandson. This gave rise to another proud moment for David when he baptised a clearly reluctant and noisy Michael.

Thoughts of work couldn't have been further from Cathy's mind as she embraced her role as grandmother-in-charge whenever her daughter-in-law requested.

"Do you think you could bear to cope with him for a weekend?" Peter asked.

"Of course, dear, we'd be thrilled," Cathy exclaimed with delight.

"Any particular reason?" David probed.

Peter and Sally glanced at each other before replying. "The thing is that, convenient as my flat once was, with the arrival of 'his lordship' we are rapidly running out of space. Added to which, neither of us is enamoured by the thought of bringing up a child in London. Therefore, we want to spend a weekend house-hunting, which will be better accomplished without Michael in tow."

"Have you anywhere specific in mind? Cathy quizzed.

"No, we're keeping all options open," their son declared. "It will be quite an adventure."

Neither parent was prepared for the news on their return.

"We've found just the place," they exclaimed in excitement. "It's an old manor house but rather run down. It needs a lot doing to it and will present us with something of a challenge."

"We are absolutely determined to restore it to its former glory," Peter enthused.

"Of course, it's going to take time and a lot of hard work," Sally said.

"Naturally, it needs quite a bit of money spent on it, so none of this is going to happen overnight," her husband interposed. "However, I'm earning well, and we got it for an absolute snip," he finished.

"It truly will make the most wonderful family home," Sally said dreamily.

"May we ask where this desirable residence is located?" David enquired.

Once again the couple looked at each other.

"It's called Moat Court and is situated in a village near Canterbury in Kent," Peter said, almost defiantly.

His parents carefully assimilated the news before David said, "Hardly convenient for your work, son. You'll have to commute."

"Actually, the firm have got a pretty sizable office in Canterbury and I hope to get a transfer there. It's a very busy branch so I don't envisage a problem," Peter replied confidently.

"Well, we can't wait to see it," Cathy affirmed stoutly, while secretly dreading the thought of a move further away from them. She hugged her grandson tight, determined to make the most of every precious moment.

Come the day, she didn't have much time to miss them for, almost immediately, she received the news that her mother appeared to have serious health issues and was undergoing tests. As both Pam and Roger always seemed to enjoy excellent health, Cathy had managed to put the thought of any possible impending problems to the back of her mind. During the journey to her former home, she spent the time considering the practicalities of ensuring future care for both of them. On her arrival, she found that her mother had been admitted to hospital that morning with a diagnosis of pancreatic cancer.

With David's complete agreement, and despite her father's protests, she moved into the small house in the Cathedral Close, where the couple had set up home on their retirement. Six weeks later, Pam was dead. Cathy was devastated. Not only was she struggling with her own grief, but the anguish of seeing the pain of loss it engendered in her father was almost unbearable. David was her tower of strength and comfort as she wrestled with the depth of her emotions.

Only nine months after this event, she arrived home from an overnight stay with Peter and Sally in Kent, to find her husband anxiously awaiting her return. Sitting her down, he took her in his ams and broke the news that Roger had sustained a massive heart attack whilst at the wheel of his car. Mercifully neither he, nor anyone else, was injured in this incident but he was pronounced dead at the scene. Wracked with pain and distress, Cathy could only cling to her husband and sob uncontrollably. It truly was a double whammy which inevitably took its toll.

The ensuing few months passed in a blur of activity which such events occasion. House clearance, legal matters, personal details and a welter of bureaucracy consumes those that are left to sort it all out, leaving little time in which to grieve. All the while there was something to do, Cathy's days were filled with purpose and action. By the end of the year, when nearly everything that needed to be done had been accomplished, Cathy sank into a kind of lethargy from which she found it difficult to rise. Christmas came and she went through the motions like an automaton. However, the New Year brought the couple news that would lift their spirits, and serve to end their 'annus horribilis', when Peter and Sally announced the impending arrival of another addition to the family.

"Sometimes, life does have a way of compensating for loss by providing another focus," David reflected.

Thus the couple prepared to look forward again. Cathy had long since relinquished any desire to return to nursing and the silver buckle was consigned to its case in a drawer.

For David it wasn't so simple. His present post had proved to be no sinecure and he felt himself to be lacklustre and running out of steam. However, seven years remained before he could contemplate retirement. What he needed was a change of direction. Ever since settling into his present parish, he had become a regular visitor at St. Christopher's Hospice which was only a few miles distant. In the first instance, it had been for the purpose of following up a parishioner who had been admitted. He had found the whole atmosphere and ethos of the place compelling. As a result, he started to attend some of the lectures and seminars on various aspects of the care given. The Hospice movement was drawing people from all over the country, and the world, who were anxious to discover more about palliative care.

After months of careful thought and contemplation, David reached a decision. This was the work to which he now wanted to devote himself. The Hospice was where he felt he belonged and was needed. On a beautiful summer evening in 1975, in a simple, moving service held in the hospice chapel, David took up a post as Chaplain there.

Chaplains working in a hospice face the spiritual challenges which often confront patients at the end of life. They can be called upon to adopt the role of comforter, mediator, ethicist, educator or counsellor. They must establish relationships of trust and acceptance with patients of different faiths and those with none, who often have a wide range of non-religious requirements. These may include simply wanting someone to listen and 'be there for them'. There is often the need to address their concerns for the future well-being of family and friends, especially in cases where there is dysfunctionality and long-festering rifts, plus a requirement to help in overcoming fear, or assisting patients to find peace of mind and some element of hope. Such help and support is extended not only to the patient, but to the families and members of staff who, while finding such work rewarding, may also find it stressful. Constant confrontation and exposure to the death of others, can result in caregivers needing to re-evaluate their own mortality and the very meaning of life. As such, the Chaplain was a vital member of the multi-disciplinary team offering unconditional acceptance, reassurance, non-judgmental support and help with developing coping strategies.

In all his various ministries, never had David felt such satisfaction and fulfillment. He found himself facing each day with enthusiasm, energy and with a smile on his face.

This change of direction also necessitated the provision of a new home. With absolutely no regrets the couple vacated the uninspiring vicarage. For the first time in their married life, they were able to choose and purchase their own residence. Purely for convenience, they opted for a modern flat close by the hospice. On occasion, Cathy would accompany David, as she had offered to be a volunteer, helping out wherever needed. The hospice was a registered charity and, as such, heavily dependent on public donations and free pairs of hands.

It was during this exciting time that they had another happy experience, when they welcomed their second grandchild into the family. Holly was a perfectly delicious little bundle. "I can't think why your mummy and daddy want to name you after a prickle," David murmured softly to the baby in his arms.

For David and Cathy, this final stage in their professional lives was one of joy and contentment. Therefore, it was with mixed feelings that they took the decision to retire as the seventh decade drew to a close.

Chapter Four

The Wheel Comes Full Circle

"What are you going to do now that you've retired then?" Peter asked his father.

Casting a glance in Cathy's direction he replied, "We haven't given it any real thought. To be quite frank, it all seems a bit unreal at the moment. I guess it will take a bit of getting used to."

"Are you going to stay in the area?" Sally persisted.

"Probably not," Cathy said. "After all, having moved so many times there's nothing to tie us to any particular place. We're certainly not rushing into anything."

"Absolutely not," David interposed. "Any move we make will likely be our last so we've got to plan for our requirements into old age, ghastly as the prospect of that sounds."

Coming to put an arm round her husband's shoulders, Cathy continued. "We may have given up work but hopefully there's still a lot of life left in us. Ideally, I suppose it would be sensible to consider a bungalow. To be honest, I've had my fill of large, inconvenient vicarages and endless flights of stairs. Neither do I want to stay in our flat, convenient though it is. Being on one level would be bliss."

"Rubbish! That's what's kept you young and fit," David joked.

Getting to his feet, Peter's enquiry as to whether anyone fancied a drink was greeted with enthusiasm.

"But definitely not sherry," his father stressed. "I reckon I've drunk enough Bristol Cream and Amontillado in my time to launch the Queen Mary. Why people seem to think that it is the appropriate tipple for the clergy I'll never know. It's either that or tea! Just think, never again will I have to hear the dreaded question, 'More tea, vicar?'"

Amid hoots of laughter Peter suggested that a nice brandy might

426

prove more acceptable. "Now you're talking, although you mustn't get me into bad habits," he grinned, "because I certainly shan't be able to afford them."

Once having catered to their various needs, Peter relaxed back into an armchair and stretched his legs out in front of him.

"Can we return to the matter of your future plans," he probed.

"Why all this interest?" Cathy asked suspiciously.

"Simply because, if you are thinking of relocating at some stage, Sally and I wondered whether you would consider moving down here to be nearer to us?"

Husband and wife once more exchanged glances. There was a momentary pause before David said, "May we enquire into the rationale behind this idea?"

"Well, not only would we love for you to be closer but, if you think about it, it makes sound sense. Thankfully, as you rightly say, you are both fighting fit at the present and long may it continue. However, should the occasion arise that you need some help, at least we would be on hand. After all, goodness knows where Dawn will eventually settle. She's like the proverbial butterfly, flitting here and there."

"It's a very kind and generous thought on your part but the last thing we want or expect is for either of you to be responsible for us in any way," David asserted.

Regarding his father questioningly, he said, "So what are you going to do if the time comes that you can't cope?"

David shrugged his shoulders. "Goodness only knows. Probably go into a home for aged clergy, I expect,"

Cathy smiled at him fondly. "I have only one thing to say to that - God help the other aged clergy!"

At this they all joined in the general mirth at the prospect.

"Seriously though, give it some consideration," Sally suggested, "because we really would be thrilled if you did come down to Kent."

"That's very sweet of you," her mother-in-law replied. "I don't suppose this would have anything to do with the prospect of convenient babysitters and child-minders by any chance?"

"What a nasty, suspicious mind you've got," her son retorted.

"Although now you've mentioned it... "

"I rather think you have probably sold the idea," David grinned. "Your mother can't wait for the chance to be a hands-on grandmother, can you my love? She really missed it when you moved down here."

"And there are some very nice locations round about," Sally added. "I know it's a little different to what you've been used to but I'm sure you'd enjoy it. It's transformed our lives since we left London behind."

"I'll have you remember that you are talking to a Man of Kent," her father-in-law boasted. "I was born and bred in the county. It's her ladyship here that you've got to convert. After all, she's never really lived anywhere other than in cities and pretty sizable towns, whereas I can already feel the straw beginning to sprout behind my ears again," he pronounced with an air of satisfaction.

Cathy sighed and rolled her eyes heavenwards before saying, "I think you can safely say that it is a real and exciting possibility and one to which we will definitely give some serious thought."

So ended a delightful weekend at Moat Court, which was to mark the beginning of the end, as it were.

A hectic round of visits to estate agents and hours spent pouring over brochures of desirable residences, followed by numerous viewings, finally resulted in the purchase of a bungalow overlooking orchards in a delightful village close by the cathedral city of Canterbury.

"I really think we've found a little piece of heaven," Cathy remarked. With this, she sank exhausted into an armchair and surveyed the packing cases which still remained to be emptied, with appropriate homes to be found for their contents.

"I have no doubts at all that we are going to be very happy," David replied. "However, I think our most pressing need at the moment is a hot bath and bed."

"And tomorrow will be the start of our new future together," Cathy sighed contentedly.

And, indeed it was. They willingly engrossed themselves in the life of the village and David was always in demand to take church services locally, especially when there was an interregnum. So life continued to be pleasantly fulfilling. When Sally decided to return to midwifery,

Cathy readily took her part in doing the school run and child care, secretly elated at the opportunity. She remembered, only too well, how she had tried to juggle the self-same demands at a time when part-time nursing roles were few and far between and there were no such things as playgroups, day nurseries or nursery schools.

Of necessity nursing was having to become far more flexible in order to meet the ever-growing demands for more staff. Gone were the days when ward sisters remained unmarried, being wedded to the job instead. If the tranche of highly trained nurses, who had left to taste conjugal bliss and motherhood, were to be attracted back, management recognised that there would have to be a readiness on their part to change and compromise. Consequently 'Back to Nursing Refresher' courses were now being run in the hope of boosting the demand for staff.

Cathy positively relished her role in 'locum-parentis' to Michael and Holly, as and when the occasions arose. On fine days she and David would meet them from school and whisk them off to one of the nearby beaches in order to pursue their pleasures, fortified with a picnic.

"You are sure it's not too much for you?" Sally quizzed on occasion.

"Absolutely not," they protested in unison. "We're loving it and it's keeping us fit."

"You really would win the prize for the best in-laws a girl could have," she smiled appreciatively.

Her own parents had undergone an extremely acrimonious divorce and were resident at opposite ends of the country. Of her father she saw nothing and her mother was an infrequent, and sometimes petulant, complaining visitor. Marriage to Peter had provided her with a taste of the family love and stability she had missed out on and for which she was so grateful. David and Cathy had welcomed her warmly, profoundly grateful that their son had clearly found happiness, in marked contrast to his sister's seemingly turbulent love life and subsequent childlessness.

Dawn's occasional visits were, perforce, sporadic and, although she attempted to engage with her young niece and nephew, she was clearly out of her depth and not particularly interested. Snotty noses, dribble and sticky fingers on her haute couture attire was not her idea of a good time.

It had almost become a regular event for the grandparents to share Sunday at Moat Court with the little family there. Peter and Sally had lavished time, money and care on restoring, improving and extending their old property, which now boasted a beautiful garden and thatched summerhouse. Peacefully savouring a cup of coffee after a pleasant meal, Peter regarded his father thoughtfully.

"Do you ever miss your old life, Dad?" he questioned.

Looking up in surprise, David responded immediately. "Not one little bit. You see I still take part in the enjoyable parts of church life, without having any of the worries. If the roof falls in while I'm taking a service, or some unscrupulous rogue steals the lead from it, it's not my responsibility to put it back on! In other words, all the pleasure but none of the pain and sweat."

He paused briefly. "Having said that, I have to confess that my last assignment was an oasis. After years of hectic, and sometimes frustrating, parish life, those precious final years were in complete contrast. The chance to spend unhurried time alongside very special people, in an air of calm and peace, was a great privilege."

"So you don't miss having a voice in things, or a project to tackle?" Peter persisted.

David eyed his son suspiciously before saying, "Look, if you want something, just come out with it instead of all this pussy-footing around."

His son grinned. "Well, you know how involved I have become with the local hospice project since it started two years ago, and I act in a legal capacity for them. Although progress has inevitably been rather slow, we are now gaining considerable momentum and are looking for one or two more trustees. I just wondered whether it might appeal to you?"

Sally looked at him winningly saying: "Honestly, you'd be so useful in view of your previous experience as a hospice chaplain, not to mention your counselling skills. And at least you have some real knowledge of the subject. Therefore you would be invaluable as someone who could talk with authority, publicise and fundraise for the cause."

"That's exactly right," her husband enthused. "We are becoming inundated with requests for speakers to address various groups. However, we have very few who can do so with any sense of real knowledge and experience."

"And how many nights have you two spent discussing this, I wonder? It's a pity you haven't got anything better to do, isn't it Cathy?" he said wickedly.

"Actually, I happen to think that Sally's got a point," his wife replied. "Furthermore, I know you'd enjoy it, and it would give you an added interest."

"Talk about no rest for the wicked and less for the sinful," David moaned. "If it will please you and keep you quiet, I'm prepared to meet the Chairman and discuss it further. More than that I'm not saying."

Settling back in his deck chair he closed his eyes and announced his intention of having an afternoon siesta.

The opening of St. Christopher's Hospice in London had marked the beginning of attempts to develop palliative care across the country. Kent was particularly disadvantaged by distance from any such facility. In 1978 a small but enthusiastic group had formed with the intention of building a hospice in the south-east of the county. A hard-working Council of Management, consisting of dedicated people, drawn from all walks of life, many still with full-time work commitments, were labouring long and hard to bring this dream to fruition. It took very little for David to be persuaded to accept the role as a trustee in a project which was very dear to his heart. He also enjoyed the company of a completely new set of friends. The move had the added advantage of providing an unexpected opportunity for Cathy.

At that time, District Nursing was unable to provide an evening or night service in many areas. Only too aware of the plight of patients suffering with end stage illnesses, and the anguish of their families struggling to cope with them at home, the project committee was desperate to offer some sort of interim measure that would enable them to make available some useful, practical facility, even before the doors of the hospice could officially open. As a result a scheme was instigated whereby volunteers would be trained, in order to equip them with sufficient knowledge and expertise to allow them to sit with patients during the night hours, thereby enabling hard-pressed relatives to obtain some sleep. They weren't expected to perform tasks requiring skilled nursing, simply those undertaken by any caring family member.

Unsurprisingly, some volunteers who had responded to the appeal were retired nurses. Cathy was once more in her element and David sometimes found himself alone at night, occupying one half of a double bed.

Meanwhile, the nineteen eighties also saw the management structure of the NHS changing as modern processes were introduced. Unfortunately, it was not an unmitigated success. Managers were appointed, often with little or no background or knowledge in health-related matters.

"A hospital is not a production line at a car plant, and patients are not simply vehicles to be transported through the system," Cathy commented, somewhat pithily.

Over-inflated salaries caused resentment among the workers at the coalface, who had to bear the day-to-day pressures of actually delivering the goods. Nor did such a move necessarily result in improved services or inter-staff relationships. Nursing was no longer seen as a vocation, merely the first rung on a career ladder, to be climbed as quickly as possible. Ambition is commendable but not when it comes at the expense of the patient. If the ascent of that ladder couldn't be achieved by the delivery of direct patient care and contact, then so be it - there was always management. The NHS gradually became riddled with people obsessed with titles, desperate to underline their perceived importance, or ensure that they were accorded their correct status by displaying the appropriate handle. Executives, Directors, Officers, Consultants, Administrators, Controllers, Commissioners, Specialists, Managers and Supervisors all proliferated in order to confuse, impress and clearly stamp their position and authority in the hierarchical pecking order.

"I don't even know what half of them mean, let alone what they actually do," Cathy complained to her daughter-in-law.

There were undoubted gains for both nursing and the NHS. Sadly, it was also to lose much that had been good in an era that was swiftly passing into the history books.

Since the mid-nineteen eighties, the computer and internet came to have a revolutionary impact on culture and commerce, including the rise of near-instant communication by means of electronic mail, instant messaging and two-way interactive video cells. A generation brought up on IT, computers and mobile phones, only seemed happy when either glued to a VDU, or pressing buttons to text and email, rather than spending time in meaningful conversation. In this technological world, the art of real communication was being lost. As Cathy watched Michael and Holly engaged in just such activities, clearly avidly enjoying themselves, she was drawn to say: "Neither of you will ever be capable of interacting socially, face-to-face. Furthermore, you'll both probably suffer from repetitive strain injury to your thumbs as a result of all this constant button pushing!"

Turning to her grandson, she continued, saying, "Given the volume of sound at which you insist on playing your music, there is also every possibility that you will be stone deaf by the time you're forty. Not to mention the damage those ear phones are occasioning."

It was inevitable that this technology would also impinge on nursing. In the race to meet targets and avoid costly litigation, staff were to become so busy covering their backs, sitting at terminals, inputting data and watching computer screens, that the patient ceased to be the main focus of their attention. Their eye was being taken off the ball and concentrated instead on outcomes and end-results.

Yet, despite all of this so-called labour-saving gadgetry, people would find themselves with less time to interact on a personal level, instead becoming the victims of the very thing supposedly designed to help them. That, at least, was how Cathy and many of her generation viewed it. David became used to her tuts and rants. "I don't know that I would even want to nurse in this current climate," she declared.

The fifth decade of the NHS saw nursing develop even faster than before. It began with one of the most controversial changes ever made to the profession - the introduction of clinical grading. The system moved all nurses on to grades such as D, E and F and worked on the basic idea that pay should be dictated by tasks performed rather than rigid job titles. It became an extremely divisive issue as some people doing the same job were being put on differing grades to their colleagues. Trade union intervention resulted and the unthinkable happened when a wave of strikes and protests came from nurses who feared the NHS would collapse because of low pay, staff shortages and lack of investment. Morale reached an all-time low.

"If I were to return to nursing today, I know exactly where I'd come in the new pecking order," Cathy asserted to her daughter-in-law. "Grade A, that would be me."

"I don't think there is a Grade A," Sally replied.

"My dear girl, there's bound to be. It's the lowest of the low and probably denotes the cleaner!" she said sarcastically.

Pausing for a moment, she was finally drawn to say: "Come to think of it, I can imagine no better place to be. Ward Sisters always treasured the domestics above the nurses. They did everything in their power to keep them sweet, claiming they were far more useful and valuable!"

Accompanying this debacle came a revolution in nurse training with the implementation of Project 2000. Although a few universities began offering degree courses in nursing in the late seventies, the numbers applying were quite low. The new training, which commenced in 1990, took it away from hospitals and based nurse education firmly in universities and colleges, where the focus was heavily on theoretical knowledge and academic preparation. It created a common foundation for all nursing students, followed by specialisation in one of four branches of nursing - adult, children, mental health and learning disabilities. A newly qualified nurse became a Registered General Nurse (RGN) in place of the former State Registered Nurse (SRN). Nursing students became supernumerary when working on clinical placements and were not allowed to be used as an extra pair of hands, unlike their former counterparts who literally gained their proficiency and skills at the bedside, augmented with release from duties for blocks of lectures, theoretical in-put and study. The move also heralded the end of the

State Enrolled Nurse (SEN) training. It was felt that this invaluable grade of nurses were being exploited so no more would be trained. Those already in post were encouraged to undertake to do a conversion course in order to become an RGN. This, along with a wider restructuring within the NHS itself, had a real impact on nursing and redundancies became common.

Under the NHS and Community Care Act, NHS Trusts were created and these became independent bodies encouraged to compete in order to raise standards. There was a steady privatisation of NHS services with certain areas, such as cleaning and catering, going out to commercial tender. When Trust status came in, it led to financial problems. This resulted in hospital closures, more redundancies, job freezes and short-term contracts, partly due to the fact that the NHS was not receiving sufficient funding from the government.

At the same time, another branch of the profession sprung into being as Practice Nursing boomed during this decade. There were comparatively few practice nurses at that time but the GP contract of 1990 began to pay GPs for carrying out health promotion, screening and preventive work. This necessitated doctors employing the requisite staff to undertake such a task. These nurses suddenly found themselves allowed to do things they would never have been able to in the hospital, such as vaccinations, ear syringing, smear tests and the immunisation of babies. There was much greater autonomy. Nurses were running their own clinics, admitting and discharging patients, prescribing, and ordering investigations like X-rays and blood tests. Many left District Nursing and hospitals to pursue this new role, further diluting the pool. This was the decade when a lot of 'sacred ground', previously thought of as the domain of doctors, was claimed and trodden on by nurses.

All these changes inevitably altered the face of nursing. Although there were some positive gains, there were those who felt much that was good had been lost. Cathy came to the conclusion that nursing bore little resemblance to the job she had known and loved. The profession was changing and becoming very driven. Life, in all its strands, was careering forward in a headlong rush towards an unknown destination and uncertain future.

Chapter Five

All's Well That Ends Well

Tranquil in their comparative backwater, Cathy and David were content to relax with the knowledge that their life together had been blessed as one of happiness and fulfillment. In 1992, they were joined by their beloved family and a host of friends to celebrate the occasion of their Golden Wedding, which they did with pride and thanksgiving. Three years later, the pair had just returned home, after attending the parish harvest supper and auction of produce, as the telephone rang. Dumping two beautiful cauliflowers on the table, David lifted the receiver.

"Goodness Jean, talk about a blast from the past!" he exclaimed. "I hope this call doesn't mean that something's wrong? Oh, you want Cathy. Well, there's a surprise. I didn't think you were pining for the sound of my dulcet tones. Here she is," he said.

Cathy literally snatched the phone from his hand in her eagerness. "Jean! How lovely to hear you. I hope nothing's the matter?"

She listened intently for a few minutes before David heard her say: "I don't know about that Jean. It's quite a way to come and not exactly at the best time of year. Also, it's been so long and I don't really know how I feel about it."

She paused again before saying, "Look, let me discuss this with David and I'll ring you back. Bye."

"Problem?" he asked.

Shrugging herself out of her coat, she hung it up and made for the kitchen. "I'll get us a hot drink and tell you about it."

Sitting round the old, well-loved table that had witnessed so many family pow-wows, Cathy regarded her husband with troubled eyes.

Always tuned to every nuance of her emotions, David put a hand over hers. "What's up my love?"

"Apparently, some of the nurses, in the set I trained with at the Royal, have contacted Jean with the suggestion that we have a reunion while we're all still young and fit enough."

"That's a fantastic idea," he enthused. "Why the hesitancy?"

Almost unbidden the words came tumbling out.

"Well, it's been such a long time, and so much happened at the end, and I've never been back to the Royal, and I don't know whether I want to resurrect it all. Apart from which I shan't recognise any of them except Jean, and it's a long way to go. I know Jean has invited us both to stay with them but I'm not really sure," she sighed.

"You are a goose," David said fondly. "Of course you must go and if there are remnants of any ghosts still lurking about, you can put them firmly to bed. Go and ring Jean and tell her that we'd love to come."

Wending their way along the once familiar lanes to Hollowdene, the memories came flooding back. How happy and carefree it had all been, Cathy mused. She had been content to accept the little she knew of her early days and had settled into the comfortable persona of Catherine Chapman. Then came a series of bombshells, and it was all down to the silver buckle. She had arrived in Morford as one person and seemingly left as another. Opening her handbag she found herself fingering again the familiar filigree tracery for, on some unbidden impulse, she had felt obliged to bring the buckle with her.

"You're very quiet," David said. "Are you OK?"

'Yes, I'm fine but I shall be more than a little pleased to get into the warm."

"Your wish is my command," he replied as he swung the car into the farmyard.

Even before the sound of the engine had faded, Jim appeared and Jean was seen framed in the light of the open doorway, eager to greet them. During the homely meal that followed, Jean outlined the planned programme.

"Janet Dawson still lives in Morford, although she's Janet Sykes now, and we're all congregating at her house for coffee. The time until a

437

buffet lunch will be spent catching up, and what a lot of that there's going to be," she exclaimed excitedly. "You're not going to believe it but all twelve have responded and are coming. Sarah's over from Canada and is staying with Janet, and Moira was due to arrive from Australia yesterday."

"My word, that's some reunion," David remarked.

Jim stood up to refill the empty wine glasses and gave heartfelt thanks that the spouses weren't included in this junket.

"Can you imagine it? It'll be worse than all the geese and hens in the yard put together once that lot get going."

"Now don't let's spoil their moment of rekindled youth," smiled David. "You and I can indulge ourselves in more suitable pursuits."

"Well, I was wondering whether you fancy a spot of shooting," his host replied.

Cathy looked aghast. "He's never fired a gun in his life," she spluttered.

"As it happens, madam, I'll have you know that, even after fifty three years of marriage, you still don't know everything about me," he announced with satisfaction. "I used to shoot regularly as a boy," he said smugly. "Hopefully the art will resurface as easily as the proverbial bike ride. I shall look forward to it."

"To return to the itinerary," Jean continued impatiently. "After lunch we are to make our way to the Royal for an escorted tour, followed by tea. We then return to Janet's to freshen up before departing for the Shepherd's Arms in Shepherdstone for an evening meal," she finished triumphantly.

"Except, of course, that you have omitted to mention that the Shepherd's Arms is now some sort of bistro pub going by the name of 'The Shepherd's Crook', presumably because it's highly over-priced," Jim commented cynically.

Jean glared at him. "Don't you dare say another word."

Determined that nothing was going to spoil their day, they contentedly made their way to bed.

The day dawned overcast but mercifully dry. As Jean drove the car towards the city she became acutely aware of her friend's silence.

"What's up?" she enquired. "You're unusually quiet."

Cathy gave a sigh. "Do you know, I can scarcely recognise anything. It's all so different."

"Well, it's bound to be after all this time, you chump. Though, surely you must have been to Morford when you used to stay at the cottage?"

"Somehow, I never had any desire to," she replied. "If shopping was needed, we tended to go to one of the little market towns in the opposite direction."

"I never realised that, in which case I'm afraid you are going to be in for a bit of a shock, so you'd better brace yourself," Jean said.

An ugly network of new roadways had virtually ensnared the once familiar countryside that was now part of Morford's sprawl.

Jean confidently negotiated the heavy traffic as Cathy gaped with jaw wide open.

"I might as well be in a foreign country," she was driven to say. "Look at the faces and the shops and the dresses," she shrieked. "And what in heaven's name is that?" she demanded, as they crawled along in a traffic jam.

"That, my dear, is one of the largest mosques in the country," Jean grinned. "The Morford Asian community is the largest group. Now, the celebrations of Diwali, Eid and Vaisaki have virtually superceded our traditional Christmas, Easter and Harvest Festivals."

In shocked fascination, Cathy steadily drank it in.

"Someone or other has said that Britain can now be described as a nation of immigrants," Jean grimaced. "For heaven's sake woman, surely this can't come as a surprise to you after London?"

"Oh, I know all about Bradford, London and other big cities. Our old parish was a prime example but the immigrants there were chiefly Afro-Caribbean. By and large, they were a happy crowd and integrated really well into the community. For some totally inexplicable reason, I failed to make a similar connection with Morford. How naive or ignorant is that?" she admitted.

Over the last half of the century, migration had made Morford one of Britain's top ethnic cities. Given the postwar demand for workers, there was a considerable incentive for many people to emigrate from all corners of the Commonwealth, and beyond, as part of the resettlement boom. They had tended to congregate in the areas of the city where affordable housing was available. The evidence was there in the vast array of different faces and distinctive cultures which they had brought with them. This was only too apparent in the colourful clothes; the huge variety of different, but often delicious, food; the unique religious buildings; the countless shops selling gold jewellery and saris and, of course, the multitude of different languages and dialects.

"If you go to the old street market that we used to frequent, it's like visiting the Tower of Babel," Jean informed her.

"And we all know the outcome of that," Cathy pronounced. "Total chaos and confusion."

Once safely ensconced in the comfort of Janet's home, tongues were soon wagging. It was almost as though the intervening years had never existed as they picked up exactly where they left off. Lunch consumed, they made their way to the Royal and parked in a multi-storey car park which had been built opposite the old main entrance, where modest old houses had once stood. Several faces dropped in bewilderment, much to the amusement of the few who were familiar with the latest developments.

"As a result of our love affair with the motor car, parking generally, and hospital parking in particular, has become a nightmare, hence this monstrosity," Janet said.

Following her, the little group progressed towards a totally new, and very different main entrance, which was miles away from the old one, or so it seemed.

Unimpressed, they stood in front of it, while trying to take in the actual position of it and the positive explosion of modern buildings which had mushroomed around the former hospital. Entering through the automatic glass doors they passed into the entrance hall and mouths again fell open in disbelief.

"It's like a flipping airport complex," Moira pronounced in her undeniable Australian twang.

A flower shop displayed its colourful blooms, whilst another provided anything from books and cards to bottles of drink and confectionery. Seated at tables in a cafeteria, a miscellaneous gathering refreshed themselves amid a babble of multi-tongued conversation, while babies reposed in their buggies and children ran around.

Flopping onto a convenient chair, Sarah voiced the sentiments of most of them. "Holy Jehosophat," she exclaimed irreverently.

"Come on you lot, keep up," Janet ordered as she marshalled her chicks along the warren of wide, and seemingly interminable, synthetic-floored corridors. Signs proliferated everywhere, directing the uninitiated hither and thither, while a steady flotsam of humanity made unremarkable progress to unknown destinations, all bent on accomplishing unspecified tasks. A motley assortment of unfamiliar, and often unprepossessing, style of uniforms, emerged from here and there. Mufti-clad figures displayed their identity tags, usually at waist level, disclosing their name and details to anyone of appropriate height with keen enough eyesight to assimilate the information. The little procession was brought to an abrupt halt and gazed around uncomprehendingly.

"This, my old fruits, believe it or not, is the original main entrance," Janet declaimed, in the manner of one pulling a rabbit out of a hat.

In silence the 'old contemptibles' contemplated the scene.

"Well, you could have fooled me," one remarked.

"Where are the old portraits and the bust of Victoria?" Cathy asked.

"You'll soon see," their guide informed her with a wicked grin.

Emerging from out of this strange and uncharacteristic ether, an equally strange-looking woman appeared and greeted Janet warmly. Aged somewhere in the thirties spectrum, her average height and looks were unremarkable. The same could not be said of her appearance. Flowing, shoulder-length brown hair encircled a bespectacled face which sat atop a rather dumpy body This was clad in a peasant-type, long-sleeved blouse below which billowed an ethnic-style skirt of multi colours. Brown 'Jesus sandals' adorned her feet, the whole effect finished off with a pashmina wrap.

"So," she proclaimed to the goggle-eyed group, "you are some of the Royal's illustrious forebears, and it is a huge privilege and pleasure to welcome you back here today."

441

Smiling genially at them, she went on to announce, "My name is Jo, and I am one of the student nurse lecturers and tutors."

Trying to withhold their gasps of disbelief, they were forced to suspend breathing for a moment. Loitering at the back and muttering soco voce, Moira was heard to say: "Come back Sister James, all is forgiven."

Patently unaware of the impact she was making, Jo continued.

"As you know, Morford Royal Infirmary is now part of the University here, and it has expanded and developed over the years to become one of the leading hospitals in the country. All of this has resulted in great changes having to be made, in order to embrace the brave new world of nursing and medicine. If you like to follow me I'll try to highlight some of those changes."

Coming to the end of a fascinating whistle-stop tour of the facilities, they found themselves back in the old entrance hall. Smiling broadly at the intrepid band, she bade them to come with her on one final voyage of discovery. Descending a once familiar staircase, which used to lead to the equipment and store rooms in the basement, they emerged into a vast, brightly illuminated area, aesthetically laid out with large, glass showcases, pictorial display boards, and long tables groaning with artefacts.

Confronting them for the last time, their guide informed them that this was the Royal Infirmary Museum of which they were very proud. "I am going to leave you to spend the remainder of your visit here. Please feel free to take your time," she stressed. "It has been an absolute delight and honour to welcome you back here. Do have a safe journey home," she said.

It wasn't long before astonished remarks and gales and shrieks of laughter filled the underground cavern.

"Do come and look," Sarah implored. "There's a model wearing our old uniform, cloak and pleated cap. Gee," she reflected, "I never thought I'd actually find myself an exhibit in a museum in my lifetime."

"And here's our old schedules we were given the day we started," said another.

Familiar ancient enamel and stainless steel bedpans and urinals leered at them mockingly. Excitedly, they moved from one exhibit to another, exclaiming all the while.

As though by some magnetic force, Cathy had been drawn to the far end of the long room. On the wall two oil paintings hung either side of the marble bust of Queen Victoria, just as they had done for so many years. She stared hard at the likeness of Kate Oliphant until her gaze focused on the sliver buckle, clasped at the waist of a Victorian blouse of pintucked silk, atop a severe, straight, long black skirt. Coming to join her Jean, sensitive to the possible emotions being stirred in her friend, asked quietly, "Are you OK?"

Taking the silver buckle from her bag, she held it up against the portrait. It was almost as if the earliest depiction glared back in proud defiance.

"I wonder what they would make of all this," Jean mused.

Cathy took one last look. Turning away she said. "One thing's for sure. My dear great grandmother had absolutely no idea what she was setting in train."

It was a somewhat subdued group who returned to Janet's home to prepare for their evening out. However, the mood soon lifted as they sped towards Shepherdstone in convoy. Perhaps mercifully, it was too dark for them to appreciate the transformation that had modernised the former convalescent home. By the time they had settled themselves into the ambience of the Shepherd's Crook, and once fortified with the requisite liquid refreshment, tongues were soon back in animated conversation, interspersed with unladylike roars of laughter, as they fondly reminisced. Towards the end of the evening, Sarah felt drawn to say, "It's been great but I shall never return to the Royal, you know. That simply wasn't my well-loved alma mater."

A silence descended upon the group again, eventually to be broken by Janet. "Do you remember when we all went to see the musical 'Salad Days' at the old Empire?" she asked.

"Of course we do," the others chorused.

"Yes, but do you also remember this song?"

Turning to her tape recorder, she pressed a button and the haunting strains filled the room.

Whatever our memories are
We mustn't say those were our happiest days
But our happiest days so far.
So if I start looking behind me and begin retracing my tracks
I'll remind you to remind me we said we wouldn't look back.
And if you should happen to find me with an outlook dreary and black
I'll remind you to remind me we said we wouldn't look back.

The music faded away and the group of twelve old friends sat as though lost in thought. In the end, one of them broke the silence.

"I suspect that today has been a mixed, but nonetheless lovely, experience for each one of us, and a bit of a nostalgia trip that I wouldn't have missed for the world. Now, the time has come for us to part once more and I guess the message we must take with us is this. Much as we will always treasure those memories, they lie firmly in the past. We now have to live in the present, however unpalatable some of us may find it, and focus on the future with whatever it holds in store. The dear old Royal that we once knew and loved doesn't exist anymore."

Eleven pairs of eyes regarded her and eleven heads nodded in mute agreement.

Unsurprisingly, the moment of quiet reflection was broken by Jean's still broad Scottish accent.

"Come on, cheer up," she said. "I propose we drink a toast."

"And the toast is what exactly?" Cathy asked.

"To us, and to the future," she replied firmly.

During the leisurely drive back to Kent, David reached across to pat his wife on the hand and said: "Despite your misgivings, have you enjoyed the weekend?"

"Very, very much," she responded unhesitatingly.

"So, no regrets?"

"None whatsoever."

"And are all the ghosts laid to rest?"

"Absolutely. In fact, beyond resurrection," she said, while secretly fingering the silver buckle in her bag. "Let's just get home and concentrate on the rest of our lives."

Sadly, within a week of their return, that resolve was shattered. Invited to attend a pre-Christmas fund-raising gala in aid of the hospice, Cathy went into the bedroom to change. Searching for her handbag, she checked the contents and came across the buckle. Taking it out, she placed it on a cut-glass tray on the dressing table. Time being short, she resolved to put it away in its case before she went to bed.

After a most enjoyable evening, they drove home from Canterbury along the dark lanes, now and then glimpsing unseasonally early lights twinkling on a few Christmas trees in cottage windows, eagerly anticipating the forthcoming festival.

Pulling into the driveway, David silenced the engine, got out of the car and made his way to the the front door, fumbling in his pocket for the keys. However, keys weren't necessary. The door was standing open. Groping for the light switch he flicked it on, only for it to reveal a state of some disorder. Turning to his wife he said, "Cathy, touch absolutely nothing on your way in because we've been burgled."

Standing in the lounge she surveyed the scene aghast while her husband phoned the police, who responded to the call with commendable promptness. Casting their eyes over the scene, they enquired as to whether the couple could immediately detect if anything was missing, especially cash.

"We don't keep any in the house," David replied. "Also, our credit cards, cheque book etc. are in my wallet and my wife's handbag which we had with us."

Looking around him he continued. "There are a pair of silver candlesticks gone from the mantlepiece above the fireplace and a silver flagon from the trolley over there."

Suddenly, a pitiful cry came from the bedroom.

"No, please no," Cathy wailed. "David, they've taken my precious silver buckle."

She flung herself into his arms and gripped him tightly, sobbing as though her heart would break.

Competently, but sympathetically, the police took charge and continued their examination of the property. Returning to the bedroom the sergeant said:

"My initial assessment leads me to believe that this was not a professional job. I strongly suspect that it is the work of youngsters, probably looking for money to fuel their need for drink or drugs. If that is the case, I'm afraid it is very unlikely that we shall be able to track them down."

Cathy moaned in distress.

"However, if we are lucky, they may have left some fingerprints which could perhaps be identified."

Addressing David, he enquired whether there was anywhere that they could stay for the night.

"Well, we could go to our son's, but is that really necessary?"

"I really would prefer that nothing was disturbed until our forensic team have had a chance to go over the bungalow thoroughly," he stated.

Once more, David made his way to the phone.

Peter and Sally both arrived and regarded the scene with horror and anger. Seated on the bed in order to cradle her mother-in-law comfortingly, Sally could scarce bear the older woman's anguish.

"Why, Sally? Of all the things here, why did they have to take my buckle?"

There was to be no consoling her.

Less than two weeks after this traumatic incident, David suffered a coronary heart attack. He had been clearing up the autumn leaves in the garden. Cathy was in the kitchen preparing lunch. Glancing across at him as he came into the room, she stopped what she was doing to take a closer look.

"Are you all right dear, because you don't seem that special?" she said. Clearing the newspapers from the ancient armchair, she instructed him to come and sit down.

"I told you not to attempt all that today. You're trying to do too much," she fussed.

Breathlessly, David walked slowly across the room and, clearly exhausted, flopped heavily into the chair.

There was a pallor to his face and beads of sweat stood out on his forehead.

"Are you in any pain?" Cathy asked him sharply.

"Not really," he said wearily. "It's more like indigestion."

Without waiting to hear more, she flew into the hall and with shaking hands rang 999. By the time the ambulance arrived, David was unconscious. Calmly and efficiently, the crew set about the task of resuscitation, whilst Cathy floated helplessly in the background. Without taking his eyes from what he was doing, the older of the two men informed her that they would be taking her husband to hospital in Canterbury.

'Perhaps there is someone you'd like to contact," he suggested.

With leaden feet and uncooperative legs, Cathy again made her way to the phone. With a tremor in her voice she spoke to Peter at his office.

"It's OK Mum. I'll be with you immediately," he assured her.

"There's no point," she cried. "They are taking him to the hospital and I will accompany him in the ambulance, so it is much more sensible if you meet us there."

With commendable speed, David was transited into the resuscitation unit. Seated on a bench outside, mother and son each wrestled with their thoughts. Eventually, Cathy gave a huge sigh.

"In all my years of nursing, this is one aspect that was always a bit peripheral. Of course, we tried to show consideration and understanding for the relatives but were inevitably focused on treating the patient. I never envisaged that, one day, I would find myself in that position, nor did I fully appreciate how hard and lonely it is. Your ears are tuned to every sound, with eyes fixed on that door, waiting for it to open in the hope that someone will come and give you some news."

Squeezing her hand, Peter said, "The waiting is interminable, isn't it? The trouble is that one feels so damned useless."

A few more minutes elapsed before he asked her, "Will you be all right if I just try to contact Sally to let her know what's happened? I promise I won't be long."

"Of course dear. You go," she said absently, her mind clearly on the only thing that had any significance.

Almost instantly, he was back with the news that his wife was just about to start her lunch break and would be down directly. Sally's presence had a calming effect on both of them. With her arm around her mother-in-law she quietly assured her that David was in the best possible hands and would be receiving superb treatment. As if on cue, the door swung open and a casually dressed doctor appeared with a stethoscope draped, almost nonchalantly, round his neck.

"Mrs. Murray?" he queried.

"Yes," Cathy whispered, inwardly dreading what was coming next.

Gently smiling at her, he proceeded to inform her that her husband's condition had been stabilised. The sighs of relief from the three people sitting tensely in the corridor were palpable.

"Of course, he isn't completely out of the woods yet and the next twenty four hours will be crucial," he added. "Nevertheless, the situation is looking positive at the moment. He is breathing unaided but is on oxygen and intra-venous fluids. His vital signs and responses are satisfactory and the heart trace is within acceptable limits at this stage."

"What happens now?" Peter asked.

"Well, he will be closely monitored and, if all goes well, we hope to transfer him to a bed in the Coronary Care Unit by this evening."

"Can I see him, please? "Cathy pleaded.

"Of course," he smiled, "but only for a few minutes. He has been sedated, therefore is rather drowsy and unlikely to communicate. Tough as it may seem, I suggest that you go home, and visit again later on. Naturally, we will contact you in the event of any deterioration in his condition."

Looking at Sally in her uniform, he enquired where she worked.

"I'm on the maternity unit," she replied, "so you can reach me there, if necessary, and I'll be straight down."

As David continued to make a steady recovery, and Cathy's initial anxiety started to lift, so began a tendency to question and criticise. Remembering the intensive bedside nursing given to such patients in former years, she was horrified at the speed with which her beloved husband was mobilised and encouraged to become self-caring.

"It's far too soon and too quick," she protested to Sally, who was driving her back to Moat Court, following a hospital visit. "And the nurses haven't been paying regular attention to his oral hygiene, you know. The general care certainly isn't what it was in my day, that's for sure. They're even talking about discharging him home in a few days but I'm sure it's far too early."

Her daughter-in-law pulled of the road and parked the car by a farm gate. Taking Cathy's hand in hers, she turned to face her. Very gently she said, "Mum, I know what an anxious and frightening time these past few days have been for you. Mercifully, thanks to the skillful action on the part of a whole team of different people, Dad has come through this ordeal. If you stop to think, years ago it would have been highly unlikely for a man in his condition to even reach the hospital, let alone survive. It has also been found that, rather than languishing for days in bed, patients make better progress, and avoid the risks of complications such as thrombosis occurring, with early mobilisation. Similarly, it is well recognised that people make speedier recoveries in their own environment, whenever possible. I also know that is where Dad would prefer to be. I accept how difficult it is for you to take all of this in but, although you may neither approve of nor agree with things as they are, just try to be thankful, and a little grateful, for the outcome."

Cathy remained silent for the rest of the journey home.

Christmas at Moat House was a quiet, and rather sombre, affair that year. Much to their son's consternation, and despite his implored protestations, the couple insisted on returning to their bungalow immediately after New Year's Day.

'You've both been so kind," Cathy said, "but we really do need to be on one level and I can look after Dad now."

Even before Sally had settled them in safely, Peter was ensconced in the offices of the hospice architect, discussing the possibilities of building a self-contained granny annex onto the side of their property. There was ample space but Peter was adamant that it must marry in with the age of the existing house, and the appropriate materials used. He was assured that such a sentiment would undoubtedly be a requirement of the planning authorities. However, no insurmountable difficulties were envisaged.

"How long will this take?" Peter enquired anxiously. "By the way, the cost is not the main issue, I want it done quickly, if not quicker."

"With plain sailing, a favourable wind, and if all the factors involved fall neatly into place, it might just be ready by Easter, which happens to occur at the latest date possible this year. I'll do my very best, stress the urgency, call in a few favours and we'll hope for the best."

True to his word the work was completed on target and a delighted husband and wife surveyed the recent investment in their property with satisfaction.

"All that remains now is to persuade your parents of the wisdom in such a move," Sally sighed. "I don't think Mum will pose a problem. She hasn't fully recovered from the burglary and is still quite nervous. Dad is another matter. Underneath that benign exterior he can be quite determined."

"I don't think the poor old chap has got much fight left in him," Peter said. Kicking at the ground irritably, he reflected. "This growing old lark isn't much fun, is it? Not for those living through it, nor for those who love them and can only watch."

Since their return to the bungalow Cathy and David had stayed firmly put. With his diminished mobility and loss of confidence, he found the mere effort of getting to, and into, a car a tedious struggle. Neither would his wife leave him, except to pop to the village shops. Consequently, they were blissfully unaware of all the activity that had taken place at Moat Court. On Easter Sunday, Cathy and David were persuaded to make the effort and come for lunch. As Peter's comfortable car transporting the couple drew up at the rear entrance, Cathy's eyes alighted on the latest construction.

"Good gracious," she exclaimed. "Isn't your place big enough already? What on earth is that for?" she remarked. "You haven't splashed out on an indoor pool, have you?"

"All in good time, Mum, and everything will be revealed," he grinned. "You might even get the chance to sample it."

After lunch, David and Cathy were taken to view the latest addition to the property. Passing through a new door in the breakfast room they entered a small, but functional kitchen/diner which led into a delightful sitting room, with French windows looking out onto a small patio area. Another door led into a bedroom complete with ensuite bath/shower.

"What do you think?" their son demanded.

"It's all very nice," his father commented, "but, for the life of me, I can't see why you need any more facilities."

Grinning wickedly at him, Peter said, "That's because you're a man, Dad. You're not thinking like a woman."

"What on earth do you mean?" Cathy interrupted.

"Well, truth to tell, this place is getting a bit too much for Sally to run, so we thought a live-in housekeeper would be the answer."

There was a stunned silence. Finally, Cathy looked at her daughter-in-law, saying, "I can't imagine you agreeing to that for one minute. It simply isn't your style, dear."

"Let's go back to our lounge and relax with a drink," Sally said.

Taking his father by the arm, Peter followed the pair. Once settled comfortably, the couple revealed their plan and waited with bated breath for an explosion of protest, which never came. Within a week David and Cathy were happily installed in their new residence and Sally, inadvertently, gained a willing home help. Thus began their twilight years or, as David remarked with his typical humour: "Our time in God's departure lounge!"

***

Although Michael had left home some time before to go to university, once having obtained his degree in computer studies he returned to take up a post locally at a college of higher education. However, after experiencing freedom, he had no intention of settling under the parental roof again and acquired a flat near his work.

Nevertheless, he was something of a regular visitor, if only for the benefit of enjoying regular home-cooked food and the money it saved. It wasn't long before he acquired a girlfriend and, having ducked the issue for as long as possible, finally decided to present her for inspection. Katie proved to be a delight and won the hearts of them all. Quietly spoken but articulate, polite, warm-hearted and sometimes amusing, she appeared to melt into her surroundings quite naturally. Eying his grandmother with glee, he proceeded to inform them that Katie was undertaking the Bachelor of Nursing degree course.

"That's wonderful," Sally enthused warmly. "Us old hands will look forward to learning much more about it."

"A lot of new-fangled nonsense," Cathy was heard to mutter.

Within a matter of weeks she had something else to moan about when Michael announced that Katie was moving into the flat with him, as they were now officially 'an item'.

"Which doesn't mean anything at all," his irritated grandmother commented to her daughter-on-law. "They might just as well say they're 'shacked up together', which is another expression I loathe."

"Mum, they're going to do it whether any of us approve or not," Peter said. "Of course it doesn't sit comfortably with your generation, and we're not exactly over the moon, but I'm afraid that's the way things are today."

During the course of the next two years, there were to be numerous occasions when Cathy and Katie had some rather lively exchanges regarding the merits of the old training versus the new. Sally had warned the girl to just ignore her. However, Katie seemed to enjoy the arguments and was always endlessly respectful, patient and courteous in her dealings with the old lady.

"I don't know how you put up with it," Michael said to his paramour.

"Oh, it's all perfectly harmless," Katie protested. "Anyway, I quite like hearing about what it used to be like."'

"Katie and I don't argue," Cathy informed him. "We just have meaningful discussions."

"And I act as referee," David said, amid much laughter. "I can assure you it's all good-humoured and I'm sure both parties are learning a lot."

Nevertheless, tensions became heightened as media reports began to appear, almost daily, reporting cases of poor nursing care, failing hospitals, patient neglect and a raft of complaints.

"I couldn't believe my ears, when I heard about the girl who refused to clean up the bed of a patient who had vomited, claiming that she was a degree nurse and didn't do sick."

"I do have to agree with you, Mum," Sally sighed despairingly. "That sort of publicity doesn't do the profession any good at all. What

I'd like to know is, where was the Ward Sister?"

"Precisely," Cathy declaimed. "A ward and its staff will only be as good as the Sister in charge of it. Of course I put it down to a lack of discipline. You can't run an army without discipline and the same goes for a hospital."

There was a long pause before she continued with her tirade.

"You know when it all started, don't you?" Clearly having no intention of waiting for a response, she pressed on. "The day staff started calling everyone by their Christian names, for one. You can't be all Bill, Bob and Ben and pally with people, then expect them to respond appropriately when you attempt to discipline them. It's all about respect, as well, but that seems to have gone out with the ark, along with everything else. Then, of course, they abolished caps and brought in a range of ghastly uniforms which no one takes any pride in any more. What with all of that and this new training, it was a disaster waiting to happen. I said no good would come of it, and it hasn't. All that has happened is that a once proud profession has gone and shot itself in the foot. Too posh to wash indeed!"

"Phew!" her son cringed in mock terror, remarking, "I wouldn't like to come up against you in court, Mum."

"Gran for Prime Minister," Holly whooped.

Towards the end of her training, Katie was sitting in the garden with Cathy when she said: "You know, in many ways I envy you."

"Good gracious, I can't think why."

"Well, there's no denying that you worked hard and the hours and the off duty were appalling. Yet you clearly found more time to interact with the patients than we seem to manage today."

Cathy thought for a moment before saying, "It's not your fault, my dear, and I know that where you are at the moment, in Intensive Care, everyone receives the very best care imaginable. We didn't even have such a facility and those patients had to be nursed on the wards, with the result that many of them died," she said quietly. "Because of your knowledge and ability to cope with the latest technology, many more people are surviving to tell the tale."

The pair fell silent again.

'The trouble is," Katie resumed, "Our patients are, increasingly often, in today and out tomorrow, which doesn't give us a chance to know them. It's a case of two entirely different worlds."

"It is indeed, it is indeed," Cathy acknowledged.

Looking straight at her, Katie said. "At the end of the day, I guess nursing is still the same job that you did, but I am having to do it with very different tools and in a very different climate. Nevertheless, the focus for both of us will always be the delivery of the best quality care possible. I think we can agree on that, can't we?"

Cathy smiled gently at her and said, "You'll do all right Katie, you'll do all right."

"Not unless I actually manage to qualify, I won't."

At which they both laughed.

***

So time rolled on.

"Hi Dawn," Peter's voice reverberated down the telephone. The recipient screwed up her eyes, blinked mistily at the bedside clock and tried to ignore the man lying next to her, who was sleepily pulling a pillow over his head.

"Peter you are an absolute... " she cried.

"Sorry it's such an early call," her twin apologised in unrepentant tones. "I know how much you need your beauty sleep these days but, quite frankly, you're such a difficult person to get hold of."

Ignoring his platitudes Dawn, by now thoroughly awake, almost shrieked at him.

"What's happened? What's wrong? Is it the parents?"

"Calm down," he soothed, "There's nothing the matter and no need for stage hysterics."

"You can be an absolute beast sometimes," she moaned. "So, why the call at this ungodly hour?"

"Well, I don't know whether it's escaped your attention but, in a mere two weeks, Mum is going to be celebrating her eightieth birthday. I wondered if you had given any thought as to how we should mark the occasion?"

"Oh Lord! What day of the week does it fall on?"

"It's on a Sunday."

"Thank heaven for small mercies," she said breathing a sigh of relief. "Things are absolutely frantic darling, but I can at least do Sundays."

"I thought you weren't appearing in anything at the moment? he said wryly.

"I'm not. Nonetheless, there is something in the pipeline so, people to see, things to do and all that," she breezed airily. "I'm busy, busy, busy. The theatre never sleeps, you know!"

Grinning to himself, Peter pressed on. "Returning to the matter in hand, what do you suggest we do?"

"Darling, I'm quite content to leave it all in your and Sally's capable hands. Just let me know when and where, and what you want me to contribute, and we'll turn up," she cooed disarmingly.

"We?" The question hovered in the air. "Do I gather that there is a new, significant other?"

There was the briefest of pauses before the reply came. "Well, I really do hope so this time," she said, gazing at the object in question with a smile.

"Good heavens, Dawn. Don't you think it might be an idea to warn the parents beforehand. You can't simply turn up with a complete stranger in tow. Dad will have another heart attack."

"Stop fussing so. I suspect they are both immune to my goings on by now," she commented, "and it will be a nice surprise for them."

"I wouldn't bet on it, and I'm not risking having Mum's day spoiled in any way, so get it sorted beforehand. A simple phone call would do the trick. I imagine you've heard of Alexander Graham Bell," he muttered sarcastically.

"Oh Peter, for goodness sake lighten up. You're coming over all heavy on me."

A short pause ensued before Dawn asked, "By the way, what does she want for her birthday?"

"I haven't the faintest idea," her long-suffering brother almost exploded in exasperation. "You're a woman - use your imagination and just get on with it. When all the details have been finalised I'll send them in the post, so there's no room for any excuses."

His wife tried hard to conceal her amusement as he replaced the receiver. "I gather your sister is running true to form," she sympathised. "She may like to give the impression that she is a helpless airhead on occasion, but she's as tough as old boots. I sometimes wonder what flows through her veins? A mixture of water, milk, syrup and vinegar, I shouldn't wonder," he muttered in frustration.

Getting up off the bed, she said. "I gather that it's all being left to us as usual and, quite frankly, that's just how I prefer it."

So saying, she made her way downstairs to the kitchen, gathered a pad of paper and pen and sat down to plan.

Arriving for breakfast, Peter was keen to hear about her deliberations.

"I honestly think it would be better if we held a lunch party here," Sally said. "Generally speaking, November isn't the best month for the elderly to be ferried around. Your father is now eighty seven, not very mobile or in the best of health, and isn't really happy outside of his own comfort zone."

"Very true," Peter sighed. "He is certainly showing his age, poor old chap. And Mum has never really been the same since the burglary. So what do you suggest?"

"Well, it's not going to be a big gathering. Most of her remaining old friends live miles away and are of a similar vintage, therefore, unlikely to come. With the possible exception of Jean and Jim, of course, who we can happily accommodate for the weekend. Obviously there will be us four and Katie, Dawn and this new chap, and maybe a few of the friends she has made locally, especially from the hospice. I don't envisage many more than twenty or so, which we can easily fit in here, and I'll provide a suitable menu. I've already made her cake which only has to be iced."

Peter eyed her lovingly. "You truly are a star and I never cease to appreciate your capabilities, organisational skills, creativity and everything else. Nevertheless, I don't often play the heavy husband but, for once, I'm putting my foot down. I think your ideas are good, but no way are you going to do all the work. Therefore, I insist that we hire caterers, who will also wait at table and clear up afterwards. After all, it isn't as if we can't afford it and I want my wife to be uninterruptedly 'front of house' for a change."

Throwing her arms round his neck, Sally simply smiled saying, "What luxury and, for once, I'm not going to argue with you. I graciously accept your kind offer, my Lord!"

Ambling into the kitchen at that moment, Holly demanded to know the reason for the 'impromptu love-in', as she put it. "Absolutely fabulous idea," she endorsed. "We'll give Gran a fantastic celebration."

However, none of them could possibly foresee just how fantastic it was going to be.

When the day arrived it was unseasonably bright and pleasant which was, perhaps, a good omen.

"What's the betting our dear Dawn will arrive late in order to make an entrance?" Sally mused as she put the finishing touches to the already impressive table settings.

Peter, busily engaged in organising the wines and spirits, merely grinned. "You can bet your life she'll be late, but whenever she comes and whatever she wears, there's no way that she can possibly upstage you or Mum," he declared firmly. "You are positively stunning and, as for Ma, just look at her."

Glancing into the lounge, they smiled fondly at the sight of Cathy, regal in a beautiful new dress of lilac, sitting on the settee beside David, both engaged in animated conversation with Jean and Jim.

'We had no idea just how amazing your accommodation is," her friend pronounced. 'Your letters definitely didn't do it justice."

"It certainly is the most lovely country house and garden, yet so warm and homely," Jim confessed, toasting himself beside the log fire in the old inglenook. "We're green with envy."

David looked around him and gave a deep sigh of satisfaction. "We are indeed blessed. Not only has our son done very well for himself in his career, but we have a daughter-in-law who is one-in-a-million. It is largely down to their love and generosity that we find ourselves so comfortably placed at this stage of our existence."

Cathy smiled contentedly. "Life has been very good to us and, make no mistake, we are hugely grateful."

The sound of a car making its way up the drive heralded the first arrival and, to Peter and Sally's utter amazement, Dawn appeared. They viewed her undeniably smart but understated outfit with scarcely veiled surprise. Where was the usual flamboyant apparel and artistic make-up to which they were accustomed? Hugging her brother with enthusiasm, she murmured greetings and air-brushed an ineffectual kiss in the direction of her sister-in-law before handing her a bunch of flowers.

"Lovely, lovely to see you both. It's been so long, and you both look splendid," she remarked in rather less affected tones than her generally effusive salutations.

Turning, she took the hand of the man standing hesitantly behind her. "I would like you to meet Greg," she said, quite simply.

The couple found themselves shaking hands with a gentleman of about sixty, boasting a full head of snow white hair. Of average height and build, he had a friendly looking, well lived-in face with piercing blue eyes and was smartly dressed.

"It's extremely good of you to include me in your family celebrations," he said, in a cultured, well-modulated and agreeably mellow voice.

"We're delighted that you could come," Peter assured him. "Did you have an easy run down?"

"Very smooth and trouble free, I'm relieved to say," came the ready reply. "I insisted that we leave early because you never know, what with the roads and traffic these days, and I can't abide being late."

As this was a sentiment that had never seemed to worry Dawn one jot, the couple exchanged surreptitious glances.

"Anyway, give me your coats, go through into the lounge and I'll get you a drink," Peter said.

"Oh, that will be bliss," Dawn replied. "If it's not too much trouble Sally, I wonder if I could have a cup of coffee?"

To date, her sister-in-law's experience of that lady's liquid requirements had been the desire for something considerably stronger than coffee. Once again masking her surprise, she assured her that it would be no trouble whatsoever.

Dawn duly greeted her parents with hugs and kisses and there was no hiding the pleasure her presence gave to them.

"So, you've managed to winkle us out again, my girl, and may I say what a treat it is to see you," her father announced gruffly. "I might also add that you are looking particularly lovely."

"You're not doing so badly yourself," she responded. "You may have given us some scares at times but you always manage to bounce back just the same as ever, thank goodness."

Cathy, who had been regarding her daughter in some disbelief, was drawn to say, "Somehow you seem to look different darling, but so well. Come and sit beside me and tell me all your news."

"Of course I will," said the amazingly compliant Dawn. "However, first things first. Mum and Dad, I'd like to introduce you to Greg."

Both parents gazed with interest, tinged with apprehension, at the man now bending down to take their hands in turn.

"I have been looking forward to meeting Dawn's family for some time and I can't tell you what a pleasure it is," he said with obvious sincerity. "I only hope you don't think I'm gatecrashing a private celebration?"

"Gracious me, no. Our children's friends have always been welcome," David assured him, with some economy of truth. When he considered his daughter's assorted gaggle of acquaintances over the years, who had largely been there one day and gone the next, he had to confess to a certain lack of enthusiasm.

"Anyway, enough of that nonsense," Dawn interposed, with just a trace of her normal bossiness. "Happy, happy birthday, Mum and here's a little gift from both of us."

The smartly wrapped parcel bore all the trademarks of her daughter's usual extravagance. Aging hands tore excitedly at the wrappings to reveal a large white box. Lifting the lid, the clearly intrigued lady discovered three superb, pure cashmere shawls, in exquisite colours, nestling on a bed of crisp tissue paper. Lifting one out and gently caressing the soft fabric against the side of her face, Cathy couldn't disguise her delight.

"Dawn, they are absolutely gorgeous. Thank you both so much," she said, grabbing at each of their hands. "It's very extravagant but you couldn't have chosen anything better."

"It's no more than you deserve, Mum and we hope that you'll enjoy wearing them," a clearly elated Dawn replied. "Now, hotch up and tell me all that's been going on," she suggested cosily.

Retiring briefly to the dining room, Sally faced her husband, "Unbelievable. Stark raving unbelievable," she burst forth. "Please tell me I'm not dreaming. I can hardly credit my eyes and ears. Is this a genuine transformation, or is your sister merely acting out another stage role?"

"Search me," her equally puzzled spouse replied. "Anyhow, don't knock it while it lasts. The main thing is that Mum's clearly over the moon."

"Do you think it's got anything to do with this Greg character?" Sally pondered. "You have to admit he's a bit different from the usual run of Dawn's conquests."

"From the brief conversation I've had with him, I gather he's some sort of producer. Actually, if first impressions are anything to go by, I quite like him. At least he's not a 'toy-boy' and, if he manages to tame my beloved sister, I shall be eternally grateful," he said with undoubted feeling. "Come on my love, back to the fray before we're missed."

One by one, the guests assembled and the room hummed to the sound of animated conversation. Sally and Peter, circulating between the groups, effected introductions where necessary and decided that never had there been a more relaxed conviviality, which continued effortlessly throughout the meal.

Eventually they all retired to the lounge for coffee and the numerous presents were admired. Cathy, radiant with the glow of joy and contentment, knew that she hadn't been quite so happy for a long time. Standing in pride of place was the birthday cake, lovingly iced and skillfully decorated by Sally. Waiters appeared unobtrusively ensuring that the glasses of champagne were distributed.

Peter rose to his feet and appealed for a moment of hush. In a short speech, expertly delivered, and laced with affectionate humour, he paid fulsome tribute to a remarkable wife, mother, grandmother, nurse and friend to so many over the years. The toast was proposed and duly drunk. Clearly deeply moved, Cathy could manage little but heartfelt thanks by way of reply. As folk prepared to resume their almost non-stop exchanges, Michael brought a deeply reluctant Katie into the centre of the room and asked if he could crave their indulgence for a few more minutes.

"As some of you here will know, Katie and I have 'been an item' for three years now."

If Cathy winced at the terminology, few noticed.

"During that time she has been training for a Bachelor of Nursing degree. I have no intention of usurping Gran's big day. However, I would be grateful if you would all join me in another toast. Last week, Katie received the news that she has gained her degree and is now a fully qualified nurse."

A ripple of approval and applause went round the room before Michael continued. "I can't help feeling that the coincidence of this occurring at a time when a very fine former nurse is celebrating another milestone achievement, must bode well for Katie's future. I ask you, therefore, to raise a glass to Katie."

"To Katie," they echoed, and the plainly embarrassed recipient quickly prepared to make her escape.

"Not so fast," Michael said, catching hold of her hand. "Before she flees the scene," he grinned, "I have one more duty."

Fumbling in his pocket he brought out an unremarkable looking cardboard gift box.

"What most of you don't know is that my beloved grandmother has voiced some pretty outspoken views at times regarding this 'new-fangled idea of nurse training' as she puts it. As you can imagine, there have been some quite sparky exchanges between her and Katie on occasion. All perfectly amicable I assure you," he added with a grin, to the sound of amused laughter.

"However," he continued, "I too have been on the receiving end of Gran's perceived wisdom for some weeks," at which he pulled an impish face at Cathy.

"According to her, no self-respecting, trained nurse is complete

461

without a silver buckle. Goodness knows why, or what possible benefits it actually bestows on the wearer, except to hold her waist in," he said, to sounds of further laughter.

"Well, my Gran can be jolly persistent and I have lately received some regular 'ear-bashings' on the subject. The simple information that they are going out of vogue because they can't be worn with many of the modern uniform designs, cut absolutely no ice with her at all."

Turning to a bemused Katie he handed her the box saying, "As instructed, and at no little inconvenience and expense, I have great pleasure in presenting you with your silver buckle."

The room erupted with the sounds of laughter, cheers and clapping as a blushing Katie unsuccessfully tried to hide her discomfort at this unwanted publicity. When the noise had subsided Michael said: "Well, you might at least open it after all the trouble I've been to."

A silence descended as the young girl removed the lid. A tremulous moment hung suspended before they heard her say, "Oh Mike, it's absolutely beautiful. Thank you so much."

Throwing any embarrassment to the wind she flung her arms around his neck and, to more cheers, kissed him soundly.

"Right, that's the floor show over. Normal service will now be resumed." With which the young man flopped gratefully into a chair and proceeded to demolish the remains of his drink.

Peter sauntered over to him and commented in a quiet voice: "Well done, that was masterly."

Meanwhile Dawn, who was seated once more beside her mother, called across to Katie to bring the box over to show Cathy. Smiling happily the girl willingly complied, and mother and daughter regarded the object with interest.

"It certainly is a fascinating piece," Dawn commented.

Holly, peering at it from behind the sofa voiced the opinion that it was 'really cool'! Looking up at Katie, Cathy enquired whether she was allowed to remove it from the container.

"Of course you can. Please do," the young girl urged her.

Carefully the older woman's fingers lifted the buckle out and moved gently over the tracery. Sally, who had been observing her carefully, noticed the wistful look on her face and the slight tremor of her lips. Moving across to her husband she quietly expressed her concern.

"I'm not so sure that this was a good idea. I think it is simply stirring painful memories, which will merely serve to make Mum emotional."

Glancing across to the sofa they saw her exchanging words with her husband who was seated by her side. Taking the buckle from her clearly shaking hands, he was seen to study it carefully before undoing the clasp which joined the two halves. Reaching for his glasses he scrutinised it again, turning the object from front to back.

Suddenly his voice was heard calling across to his grandson. "Michael, if it isn't impertinent, may I ask where you purchased this?"

Somewhat surprised, the young man came to stand alongside him. A pregnant silence now engulfed the room.

"Actually, if I'm completely honest, I didn't set out with any intention of buying one," he confessed ruefully. "I simply happened to be browsing in some of the little old secondhand shops in a back street in Canterbury during my lunch hour and noticed it on a tray in a window, along with some other bits and pieces of jewellery."

"I'm not going to insult you by asking how much you paid for it," the old man said.

"No, please don't," Michael implored him, "because I'm afraid it wasn't that expensive after all," he replied, casting an apologetic look at Katie.

Cathy, who was once more caressing the buckle, looked at her husband and suggested with a serene smile: "I think you'd better tell him don't you?"

You could have heard a pin drop as David calmly announced to his bewildered grandson: "Do you know that, quite inadvertently, you have given your grandmother the very best eightieth birthday present she could ever wish for? Incredible as it may seem, this is my dear wife's precious silver buckle. The very thing that brought us both together in the first place, over fifty years ago."

"Steady on Dad," Peter expostulated. "It's highly unlikely. After all, it's about eight years since it was stolen."

The atmosphere was electric.

"I can assure you that I am one hundred and fifty per cent certain, and I'll tell you why."

"Please, do," Sally whispered.

"Well, quite apart from the fact that we both recognised the design, there is a clinching detail that none of you are aware of. When Cathy was working in her last nursing post, one of the metal loops, through which you slip the petersham belt, became thin and broke at the base. I took it to a shop and had it soldered back in place."

Triumphantly, as if delivering irrefutable evidence in a courtroom, he declared: "If you care to examine the reverse side of the buckle you will see signs of that repair, faint it is true but nevertheless visible to those who know what they're looking for."

Leaning back on the settee as though exhausted, he firmly proclaimed: "I hereby rest my case, as my son would say!"

Taking the buckle from him, Peter and Sally inspected it. Almost disbelievingly, Peter informed the onlookers that it seemed as though his father was right.

"Well done, Dad. Well done. Everyone here is delighted and so happy for you both, especially Mum.'

Cathy, however was scarcely listening. Turning to her daughter she took her arm saying: "Would you be kind enough to do something for me?"

"Of course," Dawn replied "What is it?"

"If you go into my bedroom in the annex, you will see a bedside chest of drawers. In the second one down are my scarves. Underneath them you should find a blue leather jeweller's case which I would like you to bring to me, please."

"I'll come with you," Sally said excitedly, and the pair scuttled out.

An excited buzz had started to break out when Greg asked if somebody could possibly inform those not in the know, the significance which this particular buckle holds.

"I rather think that Dad's the best person to answer that question,' Peter said, smiling towards his father.

David once again leant forward in his seat to hold centre stage.

"Encapsulated in that buckle are almost one hundred and fifty years of nursing, social and family history. It has been handed down through the generations from the end of the Crimean War, and the era of Florence Nightingale, through two world wars, to the present day. It has witnessed more changes, toil, heartbreak, joy and tears than any of you here can possibly imagine. Now it will be up to Katie to carry on the proud tradition."

"What a saga," Greg breathed appreciatively. "What an incredible saga."

Before any more could be said, Dawn and Sally burst in bearing the blue leather case. Taking it from them Cathy carefully opened it and lovingly placed the buckle in its niche on the now fading white satin.

"Somehow, I could never bring myself to throw it away," she confessed, almost apologetically. "And what a good job I didn't."

Smiling, she beckoned Katie to come to her. Placing the case in her hands she looked straight into her eyes and said, "It cheers my heart to know that, once again, it will be in excellent nursing hands. The first owner of this buckle was actually called Kate, so it seems appropriate that it should end up with Katie."

Completely overcome, the poor girl could barely get the words out.

"No really, I can't possibly take it. Michael," she cried imploringly, "please help me."

Putting an arm protectively around her shoulders, he stared long and hard at Cathy. "Are you quite sure, Gran?"

"Quite sure," she replied unwaveringly.

Impulsively, Katie bent to kiss the old lady. Straightening up, she smiled at her lovingly.

"Thank you. Thank you so much for your trust and, I assure you, I'll do my very best to live up to it."

Turning to Michael, she said: "Without doubt, this will be my most treasured possession and one day I might even be able to wear it," she sighed wistfully.

"Well, that would be wonderful," Cathy responded. "In the meantime, it would be rather nice if you two could stop play-acting and actually get round to marrying one another," she commented archly to her grandson. "I think you've had quite a long enough dress rehearsal.

Quite apart from which, I would like to ensure that the buckle does remain in the family," she concluded pointedly. Once more the cheers of approval rang out.

"I don't know about anyone else but I think this calls for another drink," Peter remarked and, with a spring in their steps, he and Sally set out with a will to furnish folk with more champagne.

Coming up to Dawn, Greg perched himself beside her on the arm of the settee. "Phew! This is some family you come from," he exclaimed. "I've never regarded you as one to hide her light under a bushel," he grimaced, "but you and I have got to get down to some serious work, because this would make a terrific TV series," he enthused.

Dawn evinced all the signs of a cat that has swallowed a gallon of cream. Addressing her family she calmly informed them that they would probably be seeing rather a lot of both her and Greg in the future.

"That will make a change,' her brother muttered under his breath.

"I might even move in while I attempt to do the necessary research, garner all the facts, compose my thoughts and write," she said, with just a trace of her former theatrical air.

At this news her twin emitted a loud groan. "Please don't tell me I've got to build another granny annex," he pleaded.

"Just you be careful who you are referring to as a granny," Dawn retorted. "Although, on reflection, don't you think a garden room might be more appropriate? Such an ambience would undoubtedly encourage my creative juices to flow more freely," she reflected dreamily.

"Lord give me strength," Peter was driven to pray. Clapping a hand to his head he said again, "Please. Someone just give me strength!"

Quickly scanning round the room to ensure that everyone had a glass in hand, he asked them all to stand.

"I think you will agree that this has been a pretty incredible and momentous day all round. It only remains for me to propose one last toast." With that he raised his glass to deliver the final words.

"Family and friends, I give you The Silver Buckle."

Enthusiastically the response echoed back:

"The Silver Buckle!"

The History of Silver Buckles

The buckle is a clasp with two symmetrical sides and was traditionally used for fastening cloaks, capes and belts. They were made from silver, silver-plate or brass and ranged from a solid piece of simple, plain designs, to elaborate filigree.

Thought to have originated early in the Victorian era, they were attached to belts as a decorative ornament to emphasise the slimness of a woman's waist and to maintain the neatness of a skirt and blouse.

Due to their composition and the method of production, the cost would have been beyond the means of many.

The decoration was originally achieved using a hand-craft technique called saw piercing, which is highly skilled and labour-intensive. A similar effect was later made possible by a mass production technique known as punch piercing. This method is cheaper and the result is usually simpler and more standardised.

Towards the end of the nineteenth century, following the formal establishment of nurse training, this type of buckle came to be known as a nurse's buckle. It became a recognised part of the uniform of a State Registered Nurse.

A few hospitals designed their own and presented them to their nurses on attaining the qualification. Whilst some were given by parents as a reward for success, many nurses purchased their own.

They were a source of great professional pride, always fondly treasured and are now quite collectable.

Bibliography

Part 1

The Times newspaper, various
The Illustrated London News
Life of Florence Nightingale, Sir Edward Tyas Cook, Macmillan, 1914
Notes on Hospitals, Florence Nightingale, Longman, 1863
Notes on Nursing 1859, Florence Nightingale, Harrison of Pall Mall, 1859
Biography of Florence Nightingale, Colin Matthew, ODNB
Florence Nightingale 1820-1910, Cecil Woodham Smith, Constable & Co, 1950
Eminent Victorians, Lytton Strachey, G.P. Putnam's & Son, 1918
Leicester Royal Infirmary 1771-1971, Frizelle and Martin, Hospital Management Committee, 1971
The Rose of Sebastapol, Katharine McMahon, Orion, 2008
The Crimean War, Andrew Lambert, Manchester University Press, 1990
Band of Angels, Julia Gregson, Touchstone Books, 2010
Blood on their Petticoats, Geraldine Humphries, Olympia Publishers, 2009
No Place for Ladies, Helen Rappaport, Aarum Press, 2007

Part 2

The Northampton Shoe, Arthur Adcock, Northampton, 1931
Built to Last?, Kathryn Morrison, Royal Commission on Historical Monuments, 2004
Northampton 1835-1985: Shoe Town, New Town, Cynthia Brown, Phillimore, 1990
Health, Medicine and Society in Victorian England, Mary Wilson Carpenter, ABC-CLIO, 2010
William Rathbone and the Early History of District Nursing, Gwen Hardy, G.W.&A. Hesketh, 1981
A History of the Queen's Nursing Institute, Monica Baly, Croom Helm, 1987

Part 3

Eighteen Months in the War Zone, Kate John Finzi, Patala Press, 2016
Experiences at a Base Hospital in France 1914-15, an account by A.L. Walker
British Railways and the Great War, Edwin A. Pratt, Franklin Classics, 2018

A War Nurse's Diary, anon., Diggory Press, 2005

Muddling Through: BEF Ambulance Trains 1914, Peter Palmer, Western Front Association, 2010

The Roses of No Man's Land, Lyn MacDonald, Michael Joseph, 1985

QA Royal Army Nursing Corps, Juliet Piggott, Leo Cooper Ltd, 1975

Wartime Nurse: 100 years from the Crimea to Korea, Eric Taylor, Robert Hale, 2001

Grey and Scarlet, letters from war areas by army sisters on active service, ed. Ada Harrison, Hodder & Stoughton, 1944

Forearmed: a history of the Intelligence Corps, Anthony Clayton, Brassey's (UK) Ltd, 1996

British Military Intelligence, Jock Haswell, Littlehampton Book Services, 1973

Sub Cruce Candida: A celebration of one hundred years of army nursing, Eric Gruber von Arni and Gary Searle, Qaranc Association, 2002

The Women's Suffrage Movement, Elizabeth Crawford, Routledge, 1999

One Hand Tied Behind Us, Jill Liddington, Jill Norris, Rivers Oram Press, 2000

Part 4

Nursing Schedule from Leicester Royal Infirmary

A History of the Queen's Nursing Institute, Monica Baly, Croom Helm, 1987

The Southwark Mysteries, John Constable, Oberon Books, 1999

The Bishop's Brothels, E.J. Burford, Robert Hale, 2015

The Longest Night, Gavin Mortimer, Orion, 2005

Walking the London Blitz, Clive Harris, Pen & Sword, 2003

Blackout, Connie Willis, Spectra Books, 2010

Acknowledgements

I wish to record my heartfelt thanks to Anna Foster of YouByYou Books for her patience and professional expertise in bringing this book to publication. Also to Alison Renno for the creation of a beautiful and inspirational cover design. Finally to my daughters, Suzanne and Debbie, for their loving support and encouragement in helping me to keep going and surmount the hurdles.